Praise for *The Starling Inn*

"An enchanting novel that seamlessly weaves humor, romance, and profound emotional depth within the eerie and beautiful confines of an old hotel, The Starling Inn is an absolute must-read for anyone who loves a perfect blend of dark, haunting tales and playful, flirty romance. What truly sets this novel apart is the author's exquisite, nuanced portrayal of loss. Therese masterfully intertwines Millie's grief into the narrative, creating a profound connection that deeply resonated with me. The setting of The Starling Inn is the most standout feature for me. The Inn is a character in its own right, with its spooky ambiance and many mysteries. Therese's vivid descriptions bring it to life, making it easy to visualize the old, creaky floors and the hauntingly beautiful surroundings. And, of course, we have the absolutely charming and electric chemistry of Millie and Ethan. If you like playful, flirty dialogue, this is definitely the story for you. The romance is an absolute blast to read from the moment of (re)meet-cute to Happily Ever After."

Kaycee Racer, goodreads

"The spooky, cozy, gothic fall read you've been craving. Impeccable writing, well thought out and lovable characters. I was on the edge of my seat, desperately putting the pieces together alongside Millie and rooting for her from the start. And who doesn't love a lumberjack, cinnamon roll of an mmc? This book has everything, both recommend for your fall TBR!

Kate Kimbrell, goodreads

"THE BANTER. THE TENSION. THE HISTORY. Every single time Millie and Ethan were even in the same room I had tingles and the world stopped. This book gave me life. The element of a spooky inherited inn that may be haunted and cursed hooked me into reading. What is a ghost? What is it that haunts us? But it was the journey of Millie and Ethan learning from and about their pasts that kept me almost literally glued. Besides this being one of the best banter and rekindling relationships I will probably ever read, I love the personal history of the inn and the neighbors that unfolds in this book. I love that there were so many layers to this book to be obsessed with. Like Millie using her researching genius to discover truths about the past. Like Ethan learning to share more about himself. Like an interesting looking cat Frank. I HIGHLY recommend this book to those looking for well written tension between two characters, and looking for a story about discovering the past to learn from it."

Mari_thecraftyreader, goodreads

THE STARLING INN

CLAIRE THERESE

GIRL PUBLISHING

This book is dedicated to my husband

CONTENT NOTE

This story explores life and love, as well as loss and grief. There are discussions of death in different forms—including parental death, substance abuse, and death by suicide. Please read with care.

CHAPTER ONE

Are ghosts real?

Tacky TV ghost hunters with their electromagnetic nonsense and patchouli-scented tarot card readers will tell you, unequivocally, yes. "Look," they'll say, "here's our proof."

But it's all nonsense. They can't know. Not really. It's up for each of us to decide on our own.

I believe in being haunted by people that you've lost. I believe in wanting to see someone you love so badly that you wish them into existence. The beautiful, devastating longing that is grief following a death. Tears summon your ghost to you, and they are impossible to banish—memories follow you everywhere. In those moments, the ghost is as real to you as the ground beneath your feet, as the sky above your head.

I believe in scary stories with old morals hidden in the middle. Stay out of the forest because there are spirits and witches hidden within. The realities of the woods—getting lost, starvation, predators—aren't as compelling a tale.

I believe old houses can play tricks on your mind. Imagine all the feet that have tread there before yours when you look down at a worn wooden step. Wonder if someone has died in the room you are standing in as you step through thresholds.

I believe ghosts haunt us in ways that bring us joy amidst our mourning—like old family recipes written in my grandmother's tidy cursive handwriting. When I go to the library, I still see my dad in the stacks, patiently hunting for one of those boring, old guy spy novels while my eight-year-old self runs toward him, holding as many books as I can carry.

I see ghosts in the dark circles I find under my eyes today, as I peek at myself in my rearview mirror.

Turquoise water and vibrant red, orange, and yellow trees line the road as my companions. The shade from their towering heights casts dappling shadows across my dashboard as I drive up, up, up, the twisting road to confront my home and a ghost that's been haunting me.

Maria Russo sizes me up as I step out of my car onto Uncle Rowan's pine-lined driveway, brisk air whipping against my hand-knit scarf. She's standing on the porch like a guard dog with her arms crossed and her nose scrunched up against the cold. Or maybe it's scrunched up at me.

Is she the one who found him on the beach?

From the information provided by the hospital, all we know is that Rowan was found just outside the house at the foot of the cliff.

He liked to go for morning walks. Every day, for as long as I can remember, he would get up with the sun and go for a walk. I remember kicking up gravel, trying to keep up, three running strides to match each one of his, while the day spread out ahead of us with the sunrise, full of possibility.

Did he fall? Perhaps. A slip on a dew-slick rock, followed by an uncontrollable tumble down the craggy hill.

Or did he...

I put my arm around myself protectively as I turn to face the inn.

It perches on a rocky cliff like a scene in a melancholy painting. The last of daylight is now fading as I examine the sun bleached blue-gray clapboard siding, frosted with decorative white mill-work. My gaze rests on the turret where my bedroom was, then falls to the wrap-around porch. Century-old trees encroach on its high-pitched roof like they are reaching toward it with gnarled fingers. Sleepy, once-grand lilac bushes line the path to the door. Just like Maria, it's all a little more worn than I'd remembered. A two-story Victorian on the shore of Lake Superior, built as a boutique summer retreat for socialites a hundred or more years ago. It's grand and shabby, terrifying and beautiful, all at the same time.

And now, in a cruel twist of fate, it's mine.

I don't finish the thought; my throat thickens with unshed tears as I approach Maria.

"Millie." She nods her head at me in a curt greeting.

"It's nice to see you again, Maria." It has been ten years or more since I crossed paths with my uncle's neighbor. As a child, I was terrified of her and her booming voice calling for her four boys to come home for dinner as night crept in.

"Here's my spare key," she says. I'm surprised to learn that I tower over her now. "And a lasagna to hold you over until you can go shopping."

"Thank you. That was kind," I reply, taking the key and aluminum tray full of oven-baked pasta. She doesn't return my smile, and instead stares at the house behind me, eyes wary.

"That's my number, in case you need anything," she tells me, gesturing at a note on the tray. "And Ethan's number. My stepson, you remember. He knows how to fix things, and the house needs a lot of work. You didn't inherit a mansion, you know."

"I thought Ethan lived in the city." I tuck my hair behind my ears self-consciously. I will *not* be calling him.

"He did for a while but moved back to town a few years ago." She smiles at the thought of her adopted son. "It's been so nice to have him back."

"How is he doing?" I ask, trying to sound more casual than I feel.

"You know Ethan. I don't think he'll let us see how much he's hurting. He's still trying to make everyone laugh."

That's one reason why I liked him so much.

"Would you like to come inside?" I ask Maria politely, while silently hoping she declines.

"Best be going." She makes the sign of the cross, murmuring prayers under her breath, with wide eyes fixed on the house. "And you'll need to feed Frank. The food is in the sunroom."

I'm ashamed that it's been so long since I've visited, that I didn't even know Rowan had a pet.

Then she leaves, chin tucked down against the wind. I watch as she disappears through trees down the trail to her adjoining property, the fog from her prayers floating on the cold air after she is gone.

Strange.

I remember her being the sort who would steamroll you with talking. My mother would avoid her if we saw her, because a quick run-in with Maria at the grocery store would turn into a *multi-hour* conversation with us unwilling victims. You go to the store for a gallon of milk, then suddenly you are paralyzed by propriety in the refrigerator section, listening to her drone on about her hairstylist's second cousin's affair.

Just as a flock of birds soars overhead, heading south for the winter, I grab my black duffel bag out of my car. I snap a picture of the inn and text it to Ben, Sarah, and my mom.

"Glad you arrived safely," my mother replies. She's too wrapped up with my stepfather and her charity obligations to do anything about this place with her own hands.

"Wow!!! Millie, that's Gorgeous!!!" Sarah exclaims. The house *is* three-exclamation-points-capital-G-gorgeous, but Sarah is also a three-exclamation-points-about-everything sort of person.

No answer from Ben. I might get a messy response text at 3 a.m. when he gets home. Or a late morning text when he finally wakes up from a drunken slumber, hours after I start my day. We couldn't be more opposite, my brother and I. Irish twins, born only a year apart. While we are both students at the University of Illinois, this year I've been busy finishing my master's in history. Benjamin, on the other hand, has been busy with year six of a four-year degree in business—and sleeping his way through a sorority.

The wooden porch could use a fresh coat of paint. The boards creak beneath my faux leather boots. Sunlight is quickly fading, and next to the heavy wooden door is a placard emblazoned with *The Starling Inn*—a patinated clue to the house's story. I cup my hands and peek inside through the leaded glass sidelight windows, but it's too dark to make anything out within.

A stiff wind pushes at my back as I use my spare key on the engraved doorknob, icy beneath my fingertips.

Nothing happens. The key sticks in the lock and won't turn.

I take it out and try again. Jiggle furiously. It doesn't budge.

Fuck.

I take a deep breath and rest my forehead against the wood.

My mother isn't wrong—I know that this is probably a bad idea. But I'm doing it anyway. I didn't have other commitments grounding me to Chicago. Unlike Ben, I've only got one class left, and it's online, so I could spend a few weeks here planning the memorial, packing up the house, and meeting with a realtor while also finishing my last semester.

And to be honest, I am aching to confront Rowan's ghost. To learn more about his last moments and shake off some of the grief and guilt I'm carrying. I'm hoping to come out of this with some kind of peace, a revisiting of our shared memories.

I try the lock again, squinting in the dark, as the sun has fully set. My eyes dart to the surrounding forest with its impenetrable shadows creeping up closer and closer, barely kept at bay by the weak, flickering light spilling from the porch lights and painting the tree trunks. I look down at my phone and notice that my signal bars have dropped the closer I got to the house. I am truly alone out here. The hairs on the back of my neck stand up.

"Please," I beg, and try the key in the lock again. It works this time.

With a complaining groan, the door swings open into a pitch-black room.

***

It smells unmistakably like every old place. The bouquet of decomposition—warm old wood, vanilla, faintly musty. Ashy fireplaces, smoky leather, and cobwebs hidden in the walls.

I try to flip on the light in the lobby, but nothing happens. Most of the multistory room stays shadowed, semi-familiar shapes obscuring my view, the grand stairway switchbacking up into darkness. After the old door groans shut behind me, the only noise is the creaking floorboards where my footsteps fall.

I have that feeling. You know the one—that painful awareness of being in someone else's house, something nagging me that I shouldn't be here.

Unwelcome.

At night.

All alone.

I can't see the details right now as I stand in the lobby, but I know they are there. To my right, an archway opens into the living room, with couches arranged in front of a grand fireplace. To my left, another archway frames the dining room, its candelabra topped tables beneath a coffered ceiling. If I walked through the living room and into the parlor, I would find a pianoforte sitting silently. The stained-glass windows, the lacy millwork, the opulently framed fireplaces in every room—it usually strikes me with awe. But today it's all shadowed, making me shiver. I feel torn between a dichotomy of feelings; nostalgia and longing, outweighed by unsettling fear.

I have so many beautiful memories in this place. But there's something about being alone in the dark, some uncontrollable terror. One part of your brain that just doesn't want to listen to reason.

When the lobby lights refuse to turn on, I use my phone as a flashlight, illuminating the brass skeleton keys hanging in tidy rows behind the gleaming, wooden check-in counter. I snatch key No. 2 and take a steadying breath before tucking it into my pocket.

I leave my luggage at the foot of the grand staircase then make my way downstairs to the kitchen. My phone just barely brightens my path down the narrow hallway that leads to the back porch and servant staircase. An icy wind chases me, tickling my neck, sending goosebumps down my spine.

Drafty old house.

The light doesn't turn on in the kitchen either.

Is fear of the dark something anyone truly grows out of? Or do we all get the willies when one of our senses is stripped away? Perhaps it's an ancient fear baked into our bones. The ones who were afraid of the dark survived, after all.

The beam of my flashlight falls on the kitchen cabinets. They have crooked doors, like a set of bad teeth. There's scuffed, busy linoleum underfoot. The sliding glass doors should open onto a patio and kitchen garden, but they've been stuck with the blinds drawn closed for as long as I can remember. A small table with Windsor chairs takes up one corner. Nothing in the room looks remotely like it matches the vintage opulence of the rest of the place.

There are crumbs on the counter and a few dishes in the sink. I swallow the heavy feeling in the back of my throat, walk through the kitchen, and place the lasagna in the powerless avocado-green fridge, hoping for the best.

When I was young, I would sometimes find myself retreating to the kitchen for its unremarkable normalcy. I remember being seven years old, sitting on the counter eating toast while Rowan made coffee and let me chatter endlessly.

Somewhere in the house, I hear a sound. I jerk my head toward the noise. It's coming from upstairs.

Giving in to my fear, I bolt up the stairs, only slowing long enough to grab my duffel on the way to my bedroom. My flashlight glances off the delicate spindles on the staircase, the busy wallpaper, and the artful window that I know will depict a bird in the daylight.

No signs of whatever made the noise.

I breathe a sigh of relief when I flip on the bedroom light of Room 2, and it actually works. Thankfully, the electrical problem seems to be limited to the lower levels.

My bedroom differs from what I remember, but it is similar enough that it brings me comfort to see it. Someone had recently painted it with a fresh coat of modern dusty plum, but on the nightstand is a rectangle frame holding a piece of the busy floral wallpaper that used to adorn the walls. I trace my fingertips over the pattern. The wainscoting, once sticky with layers of paint, has been stripped and refinished to its original dark wooden gleam.

A pink, velvet-tufted chaise stands along one wall, and a familiar antique, mirror-topped dresser stands along the other. The same brass metal frame bed I remember takes up most of the cozy room, adorned with a fresh white comforter. It was all staged and fluffed, ready for a guest. I feel a bit like Belle walking into her enchanted palace, with the furniture rearranging itself for her arrival. That's the whimsical explanation. The real explanation—the heartbreaking one—is that after all this time, my uncle kept the room ready for me, waiting for me to come back.

Through the windows, I can see the absolute blackness of the lake, tiny pinpricks of light at random intervals along the shore reminding me that Maria's house, and a few others, are very far away.

After dropping my duffel on the bed, I call my best friend. It takes a few tries because of my intermittent signal, but finally, the call connects. I add *fix the Wi-Fi* to my mental to-do list.

"Don't get murdered, OK?" she chirps through the screen. "You are in the perfect setting for a *grisly* murder scene. You are literally all alone in a cabin. In the woods. In the middle of nowhere."

"OK, firstly, Sarah, I know, that's why I called you. Secondly, stop listening to so many true crime podcasts. Thirdly, it's not a cabin, it's an old inn. Fourthly, I'm not that alone. The neighbors are within walking distance and know that I'm here."

"Fourthly is not an actual word, but you know I love my murder podcasts," Sarah whispers, the rhythmic *swish, click* of knitting needles just barely passing through her microphone. "You love them, too."

She isn't wrong. But I wish I hadn't been listening on my ride here because now I am jumping out of my skin at every turn.

"Why are you whispering?" I ask her, and for some reason, I am also whispering.

"I don't know. I feel like I should. I'm on my first personal tour of a haunted house."

"There's no such thing as a haunted house," I assure her and myself. "But I did hear a sound, and I don't want to find out what it is by myself."

I flip the video app so it's forward facing. Having Sarah on video feels like a safety blanket, and even though she is thousands of miles away, back in the apartment we share with Ben in Chicago, I have the courage to explore a little.

Slowly, I peek my head into the bathroom that connects to my room. I jump when I see movement out of the corner of my eye, but it's only my reflection staring back at me from a simple oval mirror hanging above a new pedestal sink. A gorgeous clawfoot bathtub takes up most of the room. Marble hexagon tiles decorate the floor beneath it, and a sparkling gilded chandelier hangs above it like a crown.

It's *gorgeous.*

"Ooh, how lovely," Sarah breathes reverently.

"It is," I agree. "My mom said Rowan was restoring the place, but I'm not sure how much progress he made."

As I step out into the hallway, old maple floorboards creak under my feet. Eight wooden doors line the hall in a neat row, a glinting number bolted to each. Sconces glow on the cream-colored walls in between. I know that behind most doors are rooms with identical layouts to my own, each with an ensuite bathroom and picture windows overlooking the lake.

I freeze. At the end of the hall, there's a second, narrow staircase leading up to a doorway into the ceiling. The door is flung open, and I can see nothing but darkness in the attic above. A void.

My skin prickles.

"Uh... what's that, Millie?" Sarah asks.

"I think I'll save attic exploration for tomorrow in the daylight."

"Smart." Sarah's needles click faster with nervous energy.

Which door should I choose next?

My hand falls on the door of Room 3. I'm not surprised that it's tightly locked. "I've never been inside this one. I'm not even sure what's in it," I tell Sarah.

Moving on, I open the room next to mine. It's a mirror image of my room, except for the more masculine colors and furniture—Ben's room. It's also been beautifully updated.

"And this one used to be Rowan's office," I say, stepping through an open door into the library.

It is the same as I remember it—built-in bookshelves line two walls, and mossy green paint adorns the others, matching the forest just outside. My uncle would spend hours here working on his latest project; until the light faded from the wood-trimmed windows, and there were more ideas on the paper covering his drafting table than in his head. I'd spend hours here with him, too—reading every one of the spooky books he'd pass me. We'd spend entire afternoons in companionable silence, my nose in a book, his in his sketches. The room looks strange and forlorn without him in it. Too big and too small at the same time.

I can almost see his tall, slender form bent over the drawing table, concentrating. I brush my fingers against the charcoal-colored wool sweater, still draped across his chair like he would be back for it at any moment.

"Hey, are you OK?" The clicking of needles stops.

"I'll be fine." The tears I'm holding back are obvious in my broken voice. I take a shaky breath. "I want to be here. I should have come a long time ago."

"OK, OK. I get it. But I don't like you being there alone, and I can't get away from school until Thanksgiving break. How long are you planning to stay?"

"I don't know. Two weeks, maybe—only long enough to plan the memorial. And sort through Rowan's things, then list the house. We'll probably let a buyer have everything else. Or maybe I'll have an estate sale?"

"Do you think it will sell fast? It seems like such an amazing place."

"I don't know. It's pretty unique. I'm not sure if that's good or bad when trying to sell around here."

Suddenly, I hear a thud behind me, and fast, heavy footfalls echoing down the hallway. It is unmistakably the sound of something dropping from the attic and running toward me.

I'm not sure who screams louder, me or Sarah. I drop my phone, grab a heavy glass bookend off the shelf, and spin around, heart racing, ready to defend myself.

A speckled cat saunters through the doorway and sits just a few feet from me. Oversized eyes catch the light from my phone and reflect it back at me. He has a flat, grotesque face. He's so many different muddied colors that I'm not sure what color to call him.

"You must be Frank." I slowly let out the breath I was holding and set the bookend down. I hear Sarah frantically calling my name, so I pick up my phone from the floor and point it toward the doorway and its occupant.

"Millie! What's happening? Wait... is that a cat? Millie! Is that a cat? That is the ugliest fucking cat I have *ever seen*. He's staring at me. Make him stop staring at me!"

"He's not staring at *you*. His eyes are pointing in opposite directions. Who knows what he's looking at?"

"Why doesn't he have ears? Why does he look so surprised?" she whines.

"Shoo," I say, waving in his general direction while standing as far away from him as I can. I'm melting into the bookshelf.

But Frank doesn't move. The logical part of me knows he is just curious about me. Another part of me sees his strange face and thinks he hates the intruder in his space. I see the same judgment I felt from Maria. They think I'm a stranger who shouldn't be here because I didn't visit my uncle often enough.

They're right.

"Shoo," I say again.

Frank stares.

"You're trapped, Millie. You're probably going to die there. He's going to, like, eat your soul."

"You're not helping. And hold on, I'm going to make a run for it," I warn Sarah.

"Wait, he needs a distraction. Toss something for him to chase, then run past him."

"If this cat kills me, I want you to have Noreen, not Ben. He doesn't deserve her." Noreen is my 2003 Toyota Corolla that will outlast all of us. "Oh, and I need you to delete my browsing history."

"I swear. But let's not pretend you have anything scandalous or interesting in your browsing history."

She is correct. I don't have time for mischief, with the exception of all the Instagram stalking I've done on my ex-boyfriend.

Frank finishes his judging and decides to go on with his evening. I watch as he stands up, shakes like a dog, then walks away. As soon as I hear his heavy footfalls on the stairs again, I bolt across the hallway into the safety of my bedroom, slamming the door shut behind me.

"OK, I survived," I say, heart still beating a frenzied staccato beat. "That's enough adventure for today. I'll call you tomorrow." I blow Sarah a kiss goodnight then lock my bedroom door, keeping out ghosts, shadows, and cats.

***

My fingertips skim the walls, feeling the ridges and bumps of the velvety floral fabric wallpaper.

I pause at the foot of the stairs and look out over the living room, my loosely braided hair a heavy weight on my shoulder. The house is grand, clean, and shimmering in its newness. I take a deep breath and smell the wood smoke from the fire in the hearth, blazing bright and warm. Cigarettes, perfume, and leather armchairs.

I pull at my gown, its eyelet-laced throat cinched, seams scratchy at the wrists.

My eyes dart to the windows and meet impenetrable darkness. I wonder if there's anything out there, watching my pale face in the glass, searching. I feel like a ballet dancer in a music box, with monsters looking in.

From the drawing room floats the sound of someone playing the piano—a slow, sad melody. It's a macabre soundtrack as I glide up the staircase, one bare foot in front of the other, hand sliding up the fresh and glossy railing, the train of my nightgown trailing behind.

I reach the hallway at the top of the stairs. The gilded numbers on the doors are glowing, gently lit with warm light from the sconces. Inviting beds lie within—beckoning—but I look past them. I halt my nighttime stroll. My eyes dart upward, ever upward.

The attic is cavernous, a black hole stretching endlessly above me. It stares at me with fiendish malevolence, and I stare back, my pulse quickening, sweat beading on my brow. I feel goosebumps on the back of my neck, some small voice telling me I should not be here.

I tear my eyes from the attic.

By slow degrees, I turn to face the door of Room 3.

I can feel the attic watching. I do not turn my back on it, not entirely.

I try to open the door of Room 3, but it's locked.

What's inside?

What's inside?

I must know what's inside.

I pull at my gown, hot and tight. The piano picks up its tune again, a little erratic now.

I must know what's inside.

I reach my hand out and press my palm to the door. It's warm to the touch. I hear something through it, but it's muffled.

What's inside?

It's so hot, this gown. The long sleeves and high collar, laced up to my chin—suffocating. I claw at my throat, more and more, until nails are biting into my skin, drawing blood, trying to get it unlaced.

But what is that sound coming from the other side of the door?

I must know what's inside.

The piano stops playing.

I press my ear to the door and listen.

***

I wake up in a panic, tangled in the blankets and flailing like I am drowning in a lake. My heart is pounding, and blood is roaring in my ears. I'm hot, so unbearably hot. I win my battle against the blankets and fall out of bed onto the floor with a thud, sweat soaking into my thermal PJs.

It takes me a moment to remember where I am.

Rowan's house.

My purple bedroom.

I press my hands to my throat, scratched raw by my fingernails.

It was a dream. Just a dream. *Why is it so hot in here?* The melody from the dream is stuck in my head as I open my bedroom door, peeking out into the hallway beyond.

My eyes dart up to the attic door. Still open and black, flooding me with that sick feeling that someone or something is watching me.

I shift my eyes across the hallway to Room 3. It's still closed.

It was a dream, I assure myself.

But it *is* sweltering. Why? I was freezing when I fell asleep, my nose, fingertips, and toes little icicles under my blankets.

I follow a golden light spilling up the staircase into the hallway. I pause at the top of the stairs and listen, but the house is still and silent. Step by step, I walk down the stairs, the opposite trek of my dream. I drag my fingertips along the fabric wallpaper, sparse in spots, the fibers coming loose.

As I reach the bottom of the stairs, my chest tightens. A vast roaring fire is in the hearth. Crackling and violent, like someone had fed it moments before.

I'm not alone in this house.

My eyes dart around the living room, but I don't see anyone.

I turn on my heel and run back upstairs to my bedroom as fast as possible. I slam the door behind me, lock it quickly, and throw my back against it. My pulse is racing, and my breath is coming in gasps.

What should I do?

I want to hide under the covers. So, I do just that, bringing my phone to dial 911 with trembling hands.

CHAPTER TWO

"You mean to tell me there was no fire in your fireplace? You went to your room at around 8 p.m., and then you woke up around 2 a.m., and there was a fire in your fireplace at that time?" Officer Thickneck—I can't remember his actual name—repeats my words at me across one of the three tables crowding the opulent dining room. The dusty crystal chandelier above us barely illuminates his notepad, protuberant eyebrows, and the impatiently drumming fingers of his partner while the rest of the room disappears into darkness.

"Yes, that's what I said."

"This isn't the first time we've been called out here for nothing." He gives a *'Can you believe this nonsense?'* glance at his partner, Jones, before continuing. "Now, I told Rowan and I'll tell you the same thing—old houses make noises. Rattling pipes. Or maybe there's a critter. Call animal control and a plumber."

"I realize that old houses make noises," I snap back, my voice icy. I look over his shoulder at the windows—inky black, casting my sharply shadowed reflection back at me. I look gaunt and pale, desperate.

He's making it abundantly clear that he doesn't believe me. He is also making it clear—with a lingering gaze—that he noticed how the top few buttons on my pajama top had come partially undone with all the flailing around I'd done in my sleep, then running through the house in a panic.

I cross my arms across my chest self-consciously.

"I'm not talking about rattling pipes. There was a *fire*."

Officer Thickneck blinks at my icy tone. "Well, my partner and I did a walk-through."

"We didn't see any signs of forced entry, ma'am," Jones confirms, pausing his drumming fingers.

"Maybe someone was already in the house when I got here," I suggest.

"We didn't see signs of anyone here but yourself. I even checked the attic. Door wont close though, something you might want to get fixed."

"Thank you. But they probably left after they made the fire. Did you look outside for footprints?" I ask, agitated.

Thickneck sighs deeply at me, like all his patience is gone.

"Ma'am. For what? Why would someone hide in your house, build you a fire, then leave? I will not waste my time or my partner's time searching for footprints out there in the dark because you had a nightmare. Did you see someone flee your house? Is anything missing? Did someone commit some sort of crime?"

"No. I don't know. I don't think so," I admit, biting my lip. If someone did steal something, I'm not sure I would notice—there's too much stuff in here.

Thickneck closes his notepad with finality.

"You had a bad dream. Maybe you sleepwalked. Now, I suggest you go back to bed. Get some rest, and if you have anything tangible that you'd like to report, like vandalism or missing items, give the station a call tomorrow."

As I walk them to the door, Officer Jones pauses in the lobby for a moment and turns to me with kind eyes.

"I was sorry to hear about your uncle's passing. Nice guy," he says, his hands resting on his hips.

"Thank you," I reply, my voice going soft at the unexpected mention of Rowan. "He the one who called you out here last time?"

"Yes, ma'am. Happened quite a few times." Jones' gaze darts around the darkened lobby. "Not sure I'd be able to sleep here alone, either."

My teeth clench in frustration and my grip on the front door tightens. "What are you implying? That we made it up out of loneliness? Because the house is scary? To get attention? I'm not afraid of my shadow and I'm sure Rowan wasn't either."

"No, ma'am. Of course not. I meant no disrespect. People just aren't meant to be alone, is all. We see it a lot with old folks, calling us for every little thing. They just don't have anyone else left. You got any friends in town?"

"Sort of," I think of Maria and the lasagna in my fridge.

"Glad to hear it. You keep them close. And don't mind him," he says, tilting his head in the direction of the patrol car where Thickneck sits. "Call us again if you need."

I'm not sure that I will.

"Take care," he says, ending the conversation with a polite farewell nod.

***

Behind the tightly locked door of my bedroom, I toss and turn for unsettled hours until the sun rises, peeking in through the picture window on my wall. My brain keeps tumbling with the dream, the fireplace, and the indifferent police officer.

I don't sleepwalk. I don't even know how to build a fire. Well, I'm sure I could figure it out if I really tried, but it's not something I've done before—not a practiced thing I could do in my sleep.

I don't remember seeing logs by the hearth when I went to bed. Did someone bring them in?

I give up on sleep and pull myself out of bed. I shake away the dream and the police officers, focusing instead on the familiar and remembering the reason I'm here.

I scrub my hands over my face and get dressed for the day. I pull off my pajamas and root around in my bag until I find my pair of get-stuff-done sweatpants. They've seen better days. I pair them with a matching sweatshirt because the heat of the fire is gone, and the house is again frigid with the morning chill.

Then I notice a copy of *Jane Eyre* on the lower shelf of my nightstand. Rowan had kept it here for me with my bookmark still in its pages. I could pick up where I'd left off ten years ago.

If only I could do the same with him.

He had taught me that books were a little magical, and sacred, and he fueled my love of reading by sending me books every chance he got. A love for books is the greatest gift you can give someone. Reading is freedom. It's an escape. It's education. It's empathy. It allows you to see the world through someone else's eyes. I was raised by books, shaped by books—all because of my uncle. I caught his love of literature, and I'm so grateful.

And that's why I'm here. I'm here for Rowan, and nothing can scare me away.

With a deep, steadying breath, I focus on the task at hand: no fires, no attic, no locked doors, nor nonsense.

I'm here for Rowan, and I'm here for the freedom he's gifted me through his passing. When the inn sells, I'll inherit a third of the money.

If my mom's rough estimates are correct, it's enough to pay off my student loans or buy a house. I can graduate and not worry about what's next. I can take my time finding the right position or the right grad school. My mom and Roger will not have to support me.

I unlock my door and tiptoe down the steps, peeking around corners on the main floor.

The house looks different in the morning, in the soft, clean light. Not nearly as ominous as last night.

The silence is like a weight. It's tangible, thick, and still. You don't realize your expectations of so many noises in a house—fans, the hum of a refrigerator, electronic clicks, the cacophony of roommates, and the creaks on the floor—until you enter a home without any.

I swallow my unease. Push it deep down inside. Replace it with memories from my childhood summers spent here.

The living room is what I would call maximalist and my mother would call cluttered. Like many of the rooms in this house, an ornate chandelier hangs in the center of the room. There are so many things to look at that my eyes don't know where to rest first. Burgundy velvet drapes block most of the light from the old windows. Pleated lampshades sit atop antique ceramic lamps on elaborately carved, heavy end tables.

There is one item that is unmistakably Rowan—an out of place, mid-century modern emerald green sofa. It is flanked by two upholstered, uncomfortable looking chairs, which are all are arranged to showcase the marble surrounded fireplace dominating one wall. The seating area is pulled together with a Persian style burgundy rug, but it is hardly visible with tufted footstools and a heavy coffee table overtop it. A drink cart takes up one corner—complete with cut crystal glasses and a decanter with amber liquid inside.

Candlesticks and a row of mismatched pictures adorn the carved wood mantel above the fireplace. I step closer and cringe—it is painfully awkward to look at my school portrait. I'm all eyebrows, smiling shyly with braces, and it's evident that my mother styled my hair. It's my awkward adolescent stage.

Ben is smiling with bright confidence in his. The eyebrows have always looked way better on him than on me. He didn't have an awkward adolescent stage. Everyone should, though—it builds character. He has handsomely swaggered his way through life so far, and it's made him insufferable.

There's also a small picture of Rowan and my mom, eating ice cream on a bench, blue sky above them when they were kids. It's faded to sepia and looks like a hazy sweet dream.

Then there are pictures of people I don't immediately know—a chiseled blonde guy in a suit, holding up a diploma. Ethan, I think? It's been years since I've seen him, but those are his eyes. Rowan has one arm around him, and they are beaming at the camera. I touch the picture, my fingerprint leaving a trail in the dust over my uncle's rust-colored hair and square jaw. Rowan looks older than I remember. His eyes look a little more sunken.

There's another picture, this one of Maria and her family, with her husband and all of her handsome sons in a row, standing up straight and proud at what is undoubtedly a wedding.

Next is a large abstract one-line artwork of a woman's silhouette, dwarfing the surrounding pictures. And another illustration, this one of Frank, the cat. Rowan had drawn both pieces, and I'd recognize the style anywhere.

The last picture is me again, but instead of a school portrait, I'm sitting in a red Adirondack chair on Rowan's back porch. I'm probably sixteen, and it must be the last summer I came to stay with him. My gaze was fixed on the lake as the golden sun warmed my skin. I can't remember the last time I felt that warm and peaceful.

When I was a kid, we spent nearly every summer here. We would come as a family and enjoy Rowan and the sunshine. After my father died, my mother would leave Ben and I here—our summer visits lasting a little longer each time. I would wonder if she would ever come back to get us. Sometimes I wished she wouldn't.

After my mom remarried, our lives changed again. We moved to Chicago to follow my stepfather Roger's investment banking career. Rowan and my mom had a falling out because he didn't want my mom to marry him and take us away. I couldn't blame him. Rowan was saying what we were all thinking, that Roger was awful.

Then I started high school and got a driver's license. I spent my summers working and with friends, and the trip to Rowan's house seemed less and less appealing. When I went off to college, and even the perfunctory phone calls to him on birthdays and holidays dropped off because I was too busy for *anything* but school.

My mom kept in touch with her brother, passing along news about our lives, but they were never as close after her marriage to Roger drove a wedge in their relationship.

I remember the last time I talked to Rowan. It was a quick and shallow conversation almost a year ago, in thanks for a birthday card he'd sent to me. Like every year, he had made the card himself, with a cartoon he'd drawn on the front. This one had a doodle of a flower blowing out candles on a birthday cake. He'd always called me his little wallflower, which made me feel seen.

I should have tried harder to move past the small-talk and asked him how he was truly doing.

Was he lonely? The pictures on his mantel make me hope that he wasn't.

I tiptoe to his room.

The bed is unmade. A dusting of cat hair makes me wonder if this is where Frank has been sleeping. There's a stack of books on the nightstand next to a half-empty glass of water. It smells like Rowan: cigars and spicy cologne. I wonder how long it takes for the smell of someone to fade. My eyes brim with tears, and I push them down deeper.

I am in a house without a heart.

He's not here—not anywhere in this house where he died. He is not in his room reading. I won't find him in his office working, rubbing his temples from a headache. I won't hear him turning on his record player. I won't see him making breakfast in the kitchen or sitting outside on the deck in one of those red chairs, ready for a long talk about how I'm doing.

I should have called him more often.

I should have visited.

I will live with this guilt for the rest of my life, and at this moment, it feels too heavy to bear. But no matter how hard this is, I want to do this for him. Plan his memorial, get his affairs in order.

After all he's done for me, it's the least I can do.

*****

People process grief in different ways. My mother, she's a wallower. When my father died, she wept for years. She talked about her feelings to everyone at length. There were many phone calls, a lot of crying, and plenty of visitors. She wore her weeping heart on her sleeve for everyone else to deal with.

I was only ten when it happened, and I wasn't sure how to handle her broken heart. My world was collapsing. So, while my mother was crying, I started *doing*. I had to take that awful energy and use it for something good, or I felt like I would suffocate under it.

It is hard to get yourself moving when you are grieving—when your sadness is tugging you down like an undercurrent in a lake—but I learned to take it one task at a time. I don't think about everything I must do because that would be too much to handle. I focus on the small step in front of me.

I'm exhausted. I'm on edge. I'm grieving. I'm scared. So, it's time to get to work.

I pull the sheets off Rowan's bed and carry them in an awkward bundle down wooden stairs into the dugout basement. Frank follows, pouncing on something in a dark corner.

The basement has a packed dirt floor and sweating stone walls, and I am met with a thick and musty smell. A pendant light hangs from the wooden beams above, hardly casting a sickly yellow glow on the industrial-sized laundry appliances, not quite reaching the dark corners.

I load the laundry as fast as I can, then run back up the stairs, switching on my Kick-Ass playlist. Music blares out of my phone speakers, rattling the cobwebs. I pull my hair out of my eyes and into a bun.

I can do this.

I'm ready.

I jump up and down a few times and try to shake some heaviness away, then go down the servant's staircase to the kitchen, a later addition to the house.

I find trash bags under the sink and head back to the main level.

As I pass by the lobby, a bowl of apples on the check-in counter stops me in my tracks. They aren't red, shiny, or glossy like in a fairy tale. They are dull and dappled with pink, gold, and green. Each one is unique, some have leaves still attached. They're arranged in a bowl, like a bouquet. I don't remember them being there the night before when I'd reached over the lobby counter for my room key.

They were probably there, and I didn't notice them. It was dark, and I was tired, I assure myself, even though I'm not entirely certain I believe it.

I pick a wall in the dining room and hang sticky notes I find in the junk drawer for eventual piles of stuff—Donate, Trash, Stay, Keep.

Before I start, I need fuel. I jog down to the kitchen again, eyes lingering on shadowed corners as I go.

I fill the coffee pot with grounds—Rowan always splurged for the good stuff—and press start.

Nothing happens.

I grind to a halt—no coffee puns intended—pausing my playlist.

Great. I forgot that some of the power wasn't working last night.

When I open the avocado green fridge, its light doesn't turn on. Still, I find the phone number Maria taped to the top of the casserole dish and use the matching avocado green phone on the wall to dial the number written in her tidy handwriting. I don't bother searching Google for an electrician first because we're in the middle of nowhere and it's 7 a.m.

"This is Ethan," a deep voice answers after one ring and at the sound of it, I can feel my cheeks heating in a blush.

"Um, hi, Ethan," I say, clearing my throat. My voice is slightly scraggly from the nightmares and the lack of coffee. "This is Millie Atwater, Rowan's niece. I'm not sure if you remember me. The power is out at the inn, and I was hoping for your help."

"Millie. Hi. Of course I remember you." There's a weighted pause, like he wants to say something more. But then he continues, "I was planning to come by today, anyway. I'll be there in 20."

"Thanks. See you soon." I hang up the phone on the receiver with a satisfying clack. I find myself freeing my hair from its messy bun, and nervously comb my fingers through it.

CHAPTER THREE

Exactly twenty minutes later, a sharp knock echoes through the hallway. Opening the heavy wooden door, I see a familiar figure standing on the porch, his hands casually tucked into his front pockets.

He's wearing a black puff coat, a gray knit cap, an easy smile, and a scruffy beard. After a stressful twelve hours, he's such a refreshing dose of normality that I slightly relax my grip on the door.

"It's nice to see you again, Millie. What's it been, a decade?"

"It's nice to see you too. I wish it was under different circumstances."

"Yeah," he sighs. "How are you holding up?" he asks.

"As best as can be expected, I guess. Thank you for coming on such short notice," I say, stepping aside to let him in. He's a giant, his broad shoulders filling the doorway as he steps through it. I'd forgotten how tall he was. Part bear, straight out of the Michigan woods.

He takes off his coat, and I can see then that the coat wasn't adding much bulk. He is still stacked like the friend you call when you need to move a couch out of your sixth-floor apartment. The years look good on him. The crinkles in the corners of his eyes from when he smiles have multiplied. His beard is new, and it makes him look more masculine and wilder. But more approachable. It covers up the strong-jawed handsomeness.

I like it.

I wonder what he thinks of the changes in me.

"It's no problem. I'm here anytime you need me, right next door," he replies, slipping his brown leather hiking boots off. He lines them up on a mat near the door, next to my own shoes and a pair of what must be Rowan's.

"I'm sorry for your loss, Millie," he adds, turning to me, and I can hear the sincerity in his voice. When his weary blue eyes meet mine, they linger. In that moment I can see that his soul is just as heavy as mine.

"Thank you, Ethan. I'm sorry for your loss, too. I know you and Rowan spent a lot of time together."

He doesn't say anything for a moment, and I watch his chest rise and fall, like he is doing a breathing exercise, or maybe trying not to cry.

"Let's get some light in here, eh?" He clears his throat and changes the subject, then uses the brass window lift to open the transom above the front door.

"It's cold outside," I protest, pulling my sweater tightly around myself.

"It's not *that* cold," he retorts.

I follow as he walks from room to room in wool socks with the confidence of someone who owns the place, opening blinds and cracking windows. Bit by bit, daylight floods the claustrophobic corners, banishing the shadows and replacing them with the crisp air blowing in off the lake. I squint at it all like a confused vampire.

"What have you been doing to keep busy the last few years?" he calls out. "Rowan said you were away at college."

"Studying history," I call after him.

"What are you going to do with a history degree?" he asks, one eyebrow raised. "Teach?"

"Maybe." It could be curiosity in his tone, but at the moment, it sounds like judgment or ridicule. Everyone asks this question, and I *hate* the implication that my degree is worthless, or that there's anything wrong with teaching.

I follow him into the dining room, where he pauses at the sticky notes I hung on the wall—Donate, Trash, Stay, Keep. His gaze meets mine, fierce and hurt.

"Are you planning to sell it, or stay awhile?" he asks carefully, like he's scared to hear the answer.

"Definitely selling. I want to get it on the market as soon as I can."

"He's only been dead a *few days.*" Ethan's blue eyes are cutting.

"Well, someone has to do it," I say, crossing my arms over my chest.

"We haven't even had a memorial yet." His voice is laced with disappointment as he pushes past me into the next room.

"You can't just walk into someone's house and start opening windows," I sputter at him, as he throws open the drapes in the parlor.

"You'd rather sit alone in the dark?" he asks, and I can hear the derision in his tone.

"No, but I called you for help with the electricity, not..." I gesture to the windows. "Whatever it is you're doing."

"It's most likely a tripped breaker. I'll go check out the electrical panel and be right back."

He leaves me standing there, frustrated and chilly in a soft white shaft of sunlight.

***

"I've been telling him to get an electrician out here to look at this kitchen for ages, but he wanted to start renovations upstairs first."

After only a few minutes of poking around the electrical panel, Ethan is upstairs, and the coffee pot is now working. The smell of fresh coffee fills the air, making my mouth water.

"Thank you, again. You'll have to show me how to do that, so I don't have to call you if it happens again."

"No. Just call me. Don't do it yourself."

I frown at him. "Don't tell me what to do. I'm capable of flipping a tripped breaker switch."

Ethan closes his eyes and pinches the bridge of his nose.

Who am I? Why am I being such a stubborn asshole? It must be lack of sleep. I'm overwhelmed, full of negativity, and he's just annoying enough for me to regurgitate it all over him.

"What do I owe you?" I continue.

"I'll take a cup of coffee and put the rest on your tab. Get a real electrician over here when you can. And don't plug too many things in at once 'til then."

"My tab?" I ask, opening and closing cabinets, looking for the coffee mugs. I can't remember where Rowan left them.

He doesn't respond. With annoying confidence, he opens the exact right cabinet and pulls out *my* mug. Of all the mugs, he picked the one I made for Rowan in art class in the third grade. The lumpy, probably doesn't even sit flat, Rowan's-favorite-color-green mug. I didn't even know he had saved it. It definitely wasn't because it was beautiful.

I feel that tightening in my chest, and thickness in my throat, so I press my palms against my eyes, pushing the feelings away. I'm playing a battleship game in this house—every item I encounter is a potential emotional ship-sinking bomb.

I clear my throat and turn my attention back to Ethan. He's leaning back against the counter so casually that I assume he must have done it a million times before, sipping his coffee from my ugly green mug. I lean against the counter across from him. My legs don't stretch nearly as far. We study each other as we sip our coffee.

I'm annoyed that he still looks so good to me.

It's not just because he's extremely fit. He doesn't look like the lanky teen I remember. While he doesn't have the physique of a weightlifter or someone who spends all his free time in the gym, he does have the body of someone who works hard every day. Combined with his naturally broad shoulders and thigh muscles that fill out his jeans, I find that I unfortunately like this older Ethan even more.

"Your refrigerator didn't have power for a while, so be careful with whatever you eat from it," he warns, waving my ugly mug in the general direction of the refrigerator.

"I'll probably throw it all out."

He shakes his head. "What? No. Just taste test it."

"I'd rather not gamble with food poisoning." That's just what I need besides the grieving and stress and nightmares. Vomiting.

He hands me his coffee mug—because we both know that if he tried to sit it down on the counter, it would spill on its uneven base—then grabs a fork from the drawer closest to the sink. There was no hesitation, no rummaging. He knew exactly where to find it.

Then he opens the refrigerator and takes a bite from the lasagna Maria left for me. Cold. Right from the tray. He sticks his fork into it and digs out a lump of congealed saucy, cheesy noodles.

"Oh, that's disgusting," I gag. "You're doing it wrong. That's not how you eat lasagna."

"Did you make this?" He turns to me, eyebrow raised in speculation. He's leaning on the refrigerator door, and I think I hear it groan in protest.

"No, Maria did."

He throws his head back in laughter, and I bristle as it bounces off me. He has a big laugh, no holding back. The kind you can hear through walls. Most people are too cowardly to laugh like that. In normal circumstances, I would have loved it—the contagious unbridled joy, filling this melancholy place. But today I feel a little fragile, so it's too loud and so annoying.

"What's so funny?" I snap. I don't enjoy being the butt of a joke I don't understand.

"Well, it tastes fine. This old thing is super insulated. It stayed cold in there. You can eat it." Then his voice drops an octave, and he leans closer to me as if he's letting me in on a secret. "But Maria made it with jarred sauce."

He says *jarred sauce* the same way my mother says *drugstore make-up*.

"OK, so?" I look at him like he's crazy.

"Ma does not use sauce from a jar."

I throw my hands up in frustration. "What does that mean?"

"It means, *'Screw you'* in Italian grandmother. Or I made you this food because I felt obligated to, not because I want you to enjoy it, and I did not put any genuine effort into it like I do for my own family."

"No, you're definitely wrong. She was happy to see me," I lie for some reason, and hand him back his coffee.

I hate the smug smile pulling at the corner of his mouth like he sees right through me.

"She would never back down from helping a neighbor in need. It's what we do around here, take care of each other. You have to in a community this small and isolated. But she stopped short of putting effort into making you a nice meal."

"I don't believe you."

He opens the fridge again, leans on the door, and peeks in. "It's a disposable pan," he says, and shuts the door definitively like it's the nail in the coffin. Like he is right, and I am a moron.

"So? I don't have to wash it, and I can just throw it away. How convenient and thoughtful of Maria."

"Pans are like a calling card," he explains.

"The ones serial killers leave at crime scenes?"

"No. Not like serial killers." He closes his eyes and pinches the bridge of his nose again, looking a little like he's going to laugh, and a little like he's in pain.

"An old-fashioned calling card. If it were Maria's pan, you would have to return it, and while you were dropping it off, she would invite you to stay for a chat or dinner. Rinse and repeat."

"How do you know?"

"I've had the pleasure of eating Maria-cooked meals most of my life. Don't you remember? Her son, Joe, is my best friend. I lived with them for a while."

I will never forget the blonde in the herd of dark-haired boys running around next door when we were kids. I spent most of my summer visits with Uncle Rowan reading on the porch instead of exploring the wilderness with them and my brother. Ben would come home covered in dirt, his friends in tow, all sunburned and breathless with stories about their adventures. I had been way too shy to talk to them most of the time. Especially this one, with his big laugh and flirtatious smile. Most of the times he came over, I would flit away like a scared butterfly. But that didn't stop him from talking to me long after the others gave up trying.

Then I hear fat feline footfalls as Frank bounds down the stairs. He rubs himself against Ethan's leg with a loud purr. I furrow my brows at the cat.

"I guess you inherited Frank, too." Ethan bends down to rub Frank's head. Frank seems delighted at the attention.

"If you want him, he's yours. Otherwise, I'll have to take him to a shelter."

Ethan snaps upright, picking up Frank and covering his ears as though he doesn't want him to hear.

"Are you allergic?"

"No, I just don't really like cats."

"*You just don't really like cats?*" he echoes with disdain. He's not trying to hide how much he dislikes me now. He's letting it all show. "What is it that you don't like? The companionship? Unselfish love? Soft fur?"

Frank is now reclined comfortably in this guy's massive arms, getting his belly rubbed and gazing up at him adoringly.

"You know, cats carry diseases. And they will eat their owners minutes after they die. Even if they have a full bowl of food available," I scramble, trying to defend myself.

"You sure know a lot of cat facts for someone who claims to dislike cats. I guess that answers my question about whether you are single."

"How does that have anything to do with being single?"

"I'm right, though, aren't I?" he asks with a knowing smile.

"Fine. Yes. Moving on—some people say cats are witches in disguise."

His eyes sweep over me, taking in every detail. "You do look like a superstitious sort of person."

"What does *that* mean?" I bristle.

"Do you honestly believe—" he starts.

"No, I don't honestly believe that," I interrupt. "But I have enough creepy shit happening in this house already. I don't also need a cat lurking around... if you can even call him a cat? He's part toad for sure."

"So, you'll trash Frank with the rest of Rowan's things because you think he's ugly and might eat you in the unlikely event that you die here?"

"I'm not *trashing his things.* And if you and the cat like each other so much, why don't you take him home with you?"

I'm not leaning on the counter anymore. Somehow, I'm closer to Ethan, halfway across the space between us, my arms firmly crossed over my chest.

"I would be honored to care for my friend Frank, but this is his home. He would just come back here as soon as he got the chance."

Frank is staring at me. I think. I can't actually tell where he's looking.

"He's... spooky," I say.

"You are also spooky," Ethan retorts, like it's the most obvious thing in the world.

It wasn't the worst thing I've heard, but it stings more today. I look down at my clothes, suddenly self-conscious. I will admit that I have the pasty complexion of someone who spends too much time indoors, and this contrasts dreadfully with the black hair I inherited from my father. I've been crying all morning, was awake half the night, and I'm wearing a ratty sweatshirt and sweatpants because I'm clearing out a drafty old house. And I guess I *am* reciting gruesome cat facts.

But that's not a nice thing to say to someone, so my cheeks are burning in anger as he closes the remaining distance between us.

"You two are a perfect match." He carefully places Frank at my feet, and Frank runs as far away from me as he can get.

"I think you should leave now."

"Gladly."

Then he's gone, and I'm alone in the house again.

I throw away the lasagna and get back to work, starting with rotating the laundry—but I can't find the laundry basket *anywhere*.

CHAPTER FOUR

"Mom, everyone here hates me. The neighbor. The cat. The repair guy. I'm fairly sure the house hates me, too. I couldn't get the front door to open. The lights wouldn't turn on and the coffee pot wouldn't work because the electricity was out. One of the bedroom doors is locked and I can't find the key. And just before I called you, a tapping sound started deep in the house—I can't figure out where it's coming from."

When I told my mom about the fireplace, she didn't believe me. Like the police officers, she said I must have sleepwalked and built the fire myself. With so many people telling me I'm wrong, I'm starting to doubt myself, too.

With my phone propped up on the sink, I scrub the bathroom floor, which is the best way to release all your anger. I imagine every little tile is Ethan's face. My entire day has been spent cleaning, sorting, and organizing myself to exhaustion, and I've gotten angrier and angrier as I go. I'm not sure why I'm so mad at him in particular. I think, on a different day, I would have had fun bantering with him if I wasn't juggling the fear and the lack of sleep and the grieving. But he just infuriated me instead and this floor is being punished for it.

"Well, that's nonsense. A house can't hate you," Mom replies. "It's a house. An old one. They make noises. You're projecting your feelings."

I stop scrubbing little imaginary Ethan faces and look at her. She is staring at her tiny reflection in the corner of the video call screen instead of looking at me, like the queen in a fairy tale, obsessed with the mirror. Her expertly highlighted hair is swept up in a glossy bun. I can see her high cheekbones underneath one of those moisturizing disposable sheet masks. It cost $400. I only know this because she just told me—she frequently does this as a justification for putting up with Roger. They are a classic Beauty and the Beast story. Except in this version, he stays beastly.

He forgets our anniversary and ignores me most of the time, but look, I got to go to a 10k per plate charity luncheon today and sit next to some B list celebrities, so the emotional abuse is all worth it.

I wonder if she believes me, now that he is showing her more of his true colors. At their engagement party, while my mom was sparkling and joyful, chatting with guests, Roger slid up beside me. He whispered gross, unforgivable things about how he was looking forward to getting to know me better now that we would all be living together. Then he grabbed my ass, his movement hidden by what was disguised as an innocent embrace. Frozen in terror and not wanting to make a scene, I told my mom and Ben about it later.

They accused me of lying to get attention.

"I know how bad you're feeling and how much you miss Rowan. I do, too," she continues. She's finally looking at me now. She may have a lot of the same regrets that I do, but it's hard to tell if she's being genuine or not.

"You're grieving, and that's OK, Millie."

"Ethan spent so much time here recently that the cat *loves him*. It runs and hides from me because I'm a stranger. And he knows where all the dishes are in the kitchen."

"The cat?"

"No, Mom, Ethan. Meanwhile, I can't even remember the last time I had an actual conversation with Rowan."

"See, darling, you're jealous."

I let out a sigh. "Maybe you're right."

"Why does Ethan know where the dishes are?"

"I'm not sure." I was too wrapped up in my own drama to prod him for details. "But I think he and Rowan had been fixing up the house together. The work they've done looks amazing."

"Oh, good. I'm glad Rowan didn't let the place continue to deteriorate. It was such a dump the last time we visited. And it will appraise higher, so we will make more money off the sale."

"The renovations aren't done—" I start, but her attention has already shifted before I can show her the condition of this bathroom.

"Be careful, darling. We hardly know anything about Ethan. I know his mom died young, and Rowan was a friend of hers, so he had a soft spot for him."

"He made me feel bad about clearing the place out."

"Well, someone has to do it before we sell! What are we supposed to do, keep a shrine?"

"That's what I said."

"I found a realtor for you, so don't worry. We'll get the place sold and you back home ASAP. She's going to stop by in two days. Her name is Vanessa, and she seems quite capable." By *I found a realtor,* I know that she actually means, *my assistant Chad found a realtor.*

"Then this will all be behind us, and you and Ben can have a nest egg for your future. Roger can help you invest it. I'll talk to you later, darling. My timer went off. I've got to take this thing off." She picks at the corner of the sheet mask, and it peels away like a wet membrane—an alien shedding its skin. Gross.

I disconnect and resume scrubbing the dirty grout, and Ethan's face, into oblivion.

***

I have a nightmare again.

Instead of the music, I'm followed through the house by a *tap, tap*. When I wake up, it's still in my ears.

In a quiet house, the tapping is deafening. I'm used to being insulated by the backdrop of roommate noise, and the hum of the city outside. Here it's only Frank and me, so any extra sound is ear-splitting, and acute.

Fear courses through my veins. Fear and *dread*. I don't want to do this thing. Get out of bed and once again acknowledge that my uncle is dead.

I could stay here and stare at the ceiling. Simply never get out of this bed. I could stay here until the end of the world, staring at the pretty purple walls while the square of light cast from the window traveled down the wall. It would eventually travel across the floor, fading away into the darkness.

I glance at my phone screen. It's just past seven. At least I slept through the night. But rather than feeling rested, I feel worn out and hollow, haunted by an open attic, a locked door, Ethan's derision, and my melancholy.

I close my eyes and wish myself home, back to my apartment, crowded by the bustle of Sarah and Ben. All their noise and mess and conversation. The scurry of them coming and going. The symphony of my days.

I call Sarah, but she doesn't answer.

Frank is what finally gets me up. He's meowing on the other side of the door. I open it to let him in, but he bounds away, stops, and turns to look at me. Like he's waiting for me.

"Playing 'lure the human,' huh? You must be hungry."

I follow him downstairs to the sunroom, which overtakes the octagonal corner of the house beneath the library.

I fill his little fish-shaped ceramic bowls with food and water. He rewards me with a bump of his head against my hand, then eats.

Most of the white spindled porch is wrapped around the exterior and open to the air. But this one corner is enclosed, with huge windows, optimal for enjoying breakfast with a view. I imagine the ladies and gents in fine clothes, drinking tea from beautiful porcelain cups and watching the lake. But now it's only Frank, sun-bleached wicker furniture dusty from disuse, drooping house plants, and his food bowl.

"You're still creepy, Frank. But I'll admit that I am glad you are here this morning." *I don't feel so alone.* "Were you the one making that tapping sound earlier?"

Frank crunches on his food.

"I think I'll tackle the dining room today," I tell him. A buffet full of stuff and ugly art-cluttered walls surround the mismatched dining tables. I think most of it was here when Rowan bought the place, and he never got around to sorting through it all. It's very *1980s grandmother.* There's too much plaid, an alarming amount of dusty ceramic ducks with blue scarves, and mismatched salt and pepper shakers. Nothing in there will remind me of my uncle. Simply a satisfying day of filling boxes for donations, I hope.

After pulling on my boots and sweater in the lobby, I head out to my car. I open the trunk and wrestle out one of many zip-tied bundles of flat-packed moving boxes I'd picked up at a hardware store on the way here.

As my trunk slams closed, I spot Frank sitting on the porch. "Hey, I don't think you should be out here," I call out to him with a frown. I shouldn't have left the door open.

I lean the bundle of boxes against my car, and try to chase him inside, but he slips past me, tail lifted jauntily. I pull the front door shut.

"Frank! Get back here!"

He doesn't run; he struts purposefully, looks at me, then dashes across the yard. Just like with his food bowl, he wants me to come along, too.

Well, I can't let him get lost in the woods. I frown.

As soon as my feet lift to follow him, he turns and bolts, disappearing into the tree line.

I check my pocket to ensure I have my phone, then nervously follow this damn cat into the forest.

"Frank!"

I spot a glimpse of movement, a little shadow up ahead. He's slowed down and walking with stubborn purpose, barely out of reach, down a cleared path through the dense evergreen trees. Rowan must have used this path often.

"Frank!" Does he have a microchip? He isn't wearing a collar.

He suddenly picks up speed, and I sprint after him as he slips out of sight, my boots pounding on the ground. I follow the path through the trees until suddenly the skyline opens up, and I'm on a one-lane gravel road. It winds around the property, leading to outbuildings, before meeting up with the main road.

Frank is a few yards ahead, sitting in the middle of the road. Waiting for me.

"You know exactly where you're going, don't you?"

He looks up at me—or maybe at the trees—with his eerie yellow eyes.

"Why is there a shortcut through here, Frank?" The trail leads in the direction of the west end of the property, where I know there's nothing but forest and an old cemetery.

He stands up and starts walking again.

"Why am I talking to a cat, Frank?" I sigh.

My father always encouraged me to be curious. But curiosity killed the cat. Am I the cat in this scenario?

"OK. Fine. Lead the way."

Gravel crunches under my boots as I follow him down the road for a while, and when he's confident we are heading in the same direction, he slows to walk companionably beside me. He darts off now and then to the roadside, chasing after stirring leaves or squirrels, but always makes his way back to my side.

It feels good to stretch my legs out here. To fill my lungs with sharp, chilly air.

It's overcast, the sky is unsure if it wants to break into a storm. Oak trees reach from one side of the road to the other, their barren branches meeting above me like the arches of a cathedral ceiling. A breeze swirls the leaves at my feet, tossing their jeweled tops and pale bellies across the gravel and bringing the smell of damp soil and decay to my nose.

Birds and bugs are mostly silent, long since left or burrowed somewhere for the colder months. Some stubborn, leggy wildflowers still bloom white along the gravel roadside, defying the cooling weather. They are beautiful, and I wish I knew their names. I think about taking some back to the inn with me for some color and cheer, but I can't bear the thought of picking them just to have them slowly die in front of my eyes in the house, little petals dropping and shriveling one by one onto my windowsill.

After a while, I spot a gap in the trees along the side of the road.

A wrought-iron fence with pointed balusters surrounds a small clearing with stone headstones. *Starling Cemetery* is emblazoned above the open gate that Frank runs through. I can tell at first glance, by the pointed spire shapes of the headstones, that the cemetery must be well over a hundred years old. Like the paths that led me here, the graveyard is well-tended.

The Starling family were the ones who originally built the inn, and they lived there for generations. It's not uncommon for historic rural homes to have a family graveyard.

But why was Rowan bringing his cat so often that he needed a shortcut through the trees? If it was so important to him, why did he never bring me? I feel the disappointing sting of another question that I will never have the chance to ask him.

My curiosity about the cemetery wins out over my melancholy. I haven't been here in so long—I was just a child at the time, double dog dared by Ben to step inside the gates. I'd only stood there for a moment before running away.

Now I step through the rows, respectfully avoiding the graves, walking only on the lanes between them. I study the headstones for the first time, one by one, as I pass them. Most are from the early twentieth century, with letters and numbers worn down to near imperceptibility by the elements. Most have the Starling surname.

So much local history, nature, art, and symbolism are tied intrinsically together in a graveyard. As part of my undergraduate public history internship, we helped restore some old headstones. During a sweaty summer week, a few students and I wet the stones with water, then used a soft brush to gently remove any thick dirt or lichen. After most of the surface debris was gone, we resprayed the stones again, this time with a pH-neutral biological cleaner that our professor assured us was safe for cleaning headstones. Then we would gently scrub again, using toothbrushes to clear the little nooks in the inscriptions and details.

After the stones were clean, we would snap pictures on our phones and upload them to a database of cemeteries across the United States. I took it a step further than my classmates, combing through local records to add as much information about the deceased as possible to the virtual memorials we were creating. Removing the grime and flora, looking at the freshly restored stone, and wondering about the stories of the people lying beneath is an experience I'll never forget. Not to mention the digging in the archives to find bits of information published about their lives and sharing what I found online. Everything I was doing felt sacred, somehow.

I wish I could come here with Rowan and share all that I know now. For a moment I mourn the conversations that we won't ever get to have.

I stop in front of a traditional upright headstone that stands out from the others.

It is new, the granite still glossy. There's a small vase built into the side, holding a bundle of drooping wildflowers. I trace my fingertips across the name and dates.

Catherine Starling

1970 – 2002

She died when she was only 32. So close to my age. She was buried surrounded by her ancestors, and there is some comfort to be found in that.

There are few things as grounding as walking in a cemetery. Knowing that you'll be reduced to dates and names on stone one day.

Where will I be buried? Will I be reunited with my father in that cemetery with the rolling hills and towering centenary trees outside Chicago? Or maybe I'll be buried in a city I haven't visited yet, next to a husband I haven't met. How strange to think about that—there could be someone out there that I haven't met yet, that I'll live a lifetime with and lay for an eternity in the ground beside, until our bones are dust and our headstones are covered in lichen that some intern will scrub off. I hope.

Or maybe I *have* met him, and I just don't know it.

Or I could be like Catherine, in the ground by 32.

Frank butts his head against my leg, breaking my spell of pondering mortality.

"Do you know who she is?" I ask him, gesturing to Catherine Starling's headstone.

I wonder what her hopes and dreams were and if she achieved them. Her grave is standing apart from the others. No spouse. I stand up to look at the back of the headstone for more clues. It's inscribed with a passage of poetry.

I was a child, and she was a child,
In this kingdom by the sea,
But we loved with a love that was more than love—
I and my Annabel Lee—
With a love that the wingèd seraphs of Heaven
Coveted her and me.

It's unmistakably Edgar Allan Poe's *Annabel Lee*. I remember Rowan reading it aloud, telling me it was Poe's last poem, likely written for his wife.

Rowan loved this poem.

I glance at Catherine's birth date—the same year as my uncle's.

***

I have the dream for the third night in a row. This time, there's a cat in it.

This same cat wakes me from my fitful sleep and lures me downstairs to serve him breakfast. Afterward, he sits by the door, ready for his morning walk. I appreciated the dose of nature last time and decide to join him again.

"Let me just grab a granola bar, Frank," I tell him and head to the kitchen. It's tidy now; nearly everything is packed and sorted. I'd spent the entire day yesterday in a whirlwind of cleaning, listening to my favorite true crime podcast, and only pausing to text my mom and ask if she remembered someone named Catherine Starling. She hasn't answered me yet.

Today, I will search local newspapers for an obituary. And I'll keep packing, trying to avoid the grief. It's like having a wound. You can sometimes carry on and forget about it until you accidentally brush against it, and it sears so painfully, it's unbearable.

"It will have to be a quick walk, Frank. A realtor is stopping by today."

As I step upstairs, I hear a soft scratching, dragging sound. I whip my head around, trying to figure out where it's coming from. Step by curious step, I follow the sound into the lobby.

I freeze.

It's coming from the front door. Whatever it is, it's right on the other side. I glance at the lock and breathe a slow, silent sigh of relief when I confirm that it's tightly fastened.

Frank is sitting beside me with his ears trained at the door. I'm glad I'm not the only one who can hear it.

I stand far back, putting the lobby check-in counter between myself and the door, and I listen. The unsettling sounds go on for ten long seconds, with purposeful pauses and clicks. Frank and I wait soundlessly, listening, watching for a few tense moments until the sounds come to a stop.

Silence.

I let out a breath, then slide out from behind the counter and tiptoe to the door. With my phone in my hand, I open the door, unsure what I'll find.

But there's no one there.

I step out a few feet onto the porch and look around, searching for what made the sound.

Nothing.

A big empty porch, my beater of a car in the driveway, the forest, sun rising over it all. I take a deep breath of unforgivingly cold morning air, and I can feel myself shivering from the inside out.

There's nothing here. So, what made those sounds?

I rub my hands over my arms, trying to smooth out the goose-bumps.

I turn to go back inside, my eyes lifting to the door. Then I gasp, my hand flying to my mouth. On a narrow strip of trim, sandwiched between the top of the door and stained-glass transom window, is a nearly illegible series of letters, numbers, and crosses.

That wasn't there before. I squint, trying to make out what it says, but the light-colored text on the light wood background puts it beyond my comprehension. I drag a chair over and stand on it, looking closer.

I can only decipher some O's, perhaps an M, and the number 2. When I reach out a nervous hand, it smudges, white dust clinging to my fingers. *Is this chalk?* But what does it mean? Who put it there and why?

It feels like a curse, if you believe in that sort of thing. Which I don't.

I whip my head around, trying to see into the forest. Whoever wrote above the door is long gone.

CHAPTER FIVE

I'M STANDING ON A chair with a rag in my hand, scrubbing the letters and numbers off the door, when I hear a car pull up behind me. I turn to see a little lady with a pristine blowout climbing out of her car. She dips into her backseat to wrestle out a cellophane encased gift basket nearly as wide as she is tall.

"Hi, sugar!" she calls out with a bright white smile and a bouncy voice. "You must be Millie. I'm Vanessa Brighton of Vanessa Brighton Realty. Your mom hired me to help you list this home. And wow, what a home it is!"

I step down from the chair.

"Hi, Vanessa. It's so nice to meet you. Thank you for stopping by. I'll give you the tour. Sorry about this," I say, gesturing to the smudges. "It's a prank or something. I'm not sure."

"Oh, no worries, sugar, it doesn't need to be all cleaned up for just me. Welcome to town!" she replies, handing me the basket. "This place is *gorgeous*."

"Thank you for the basket. I still haven't gone to the grocery store if you can believe it." I've been finishing off my granola bars and the last of Rowan's unexpired pantry items.

"Oh, I believe it! I bet you've been so busy with a big old place like this. I can't wait to see it all!"

She follows me through the house, going from room to room, with the clip-clop of her heeled booties. When I was younger, I wanted to be a polished lady like that. The kind that wears lipstick to the grocery store. But I usually reserve that effort for a night out or special occasions.

"As you probably know, it used to be an inn. Based on the architecture, it must have been built in the 1880s, by the Starling family, but I don't know much about it other than that. I think my uncle bought it in the late 1990s."

She runs her hand over the check-in counter with appreciation.

"It makes no sense to have an old counter in the foyer of a regular house, but no one has removed it over the years. My brother and I loved playing with it and all the room keys when we were kids."

"Oh, that's so sweet. I bet you have lots of great memories here."

My chest warms. "I do."

Vanessa stops her hand just before the bowl of apples. Then she reaches in and picks one up. I almost stop her because I don't know where they came from. But before I'm able to, she takes a bite. I cringe.

She's fine. It's just an apple. I'm being silly. Paranoid.

"How charming. Can you imagine all the people who came here through the years? So many stories. So many memories." She takes another bite of the apple, and her face is lost in reverent imagination as her gaze floats up to the 13-foot-tall ceilings. I decide I like Vanessa Brighton from Vanessa Brighton Realty.

"There must be," I agree. "I haven't researched the place very much yet, but when I know more about the original owners, I will let you know."

"That would definitely help it sell. Folks love a good story."

I lead her up the staircase and we pause on the switchback to the second floor to admire the bird in the stained-glass window.

"There are eight rooms up here. A few of them have ensuite bathrooms that have been more recently added. One room has been used primarily as an office or library. All have fireplaces."

She *oohs* as we explore the restorations upstairs, the glowing board and batten trim work, the warm maple floors, and Rowan's book-lined office.

"I can't get all the doors open," I admit, watching her closely. "Or all the doors closed." I nod to the attic.

She'd be sick already if the apples were poison or something. She's almost down to the core now and showing no signs of distress.

Because they are apples. Just apples.

It's all in my head.

"The keys are missing to one room." I explain.

"How very mysterious! Well, I'm sure they will turn up soon. If they don't, I'll send my locksmith over to change them."

I take her downstairs to the sunroom filled with plants that are starting to perk up under my care, a few sun-bleached wicker chairs and tables, and wall-to-wall windows overlooking the lake. Her longest pause and biggest *ahh* is at the view from here—the impossibly blue lake and craggy beach below.

"The kitchen needs work," I tell her, leading her back inside and down the kitchen stairs. "It's one of the few parts of the place that isn't original. They built it as a service kitchen to prepare food for guests, so it's large, but hasn't been updated since the 1970s."

We concluded our tour in the dining room. Vanessa pulled up a chair at one of the three oak and cane tables. I sit across from her, and the chandelier flickers overhead. The marble fireplace is topped with gauzy lace, and I make a mental note to take it down and put it in one of the donate boxes as soon as Vanessa leaves.

"What a *gem* you've got here, sugar," she says, eyes bright. "I've always wanted to see the inside of the old Starling Inn."

"It truly is a gem," I agree. "My uncle loved this place."

"Are there any outbuildings on the property?"

"Yes, but I'm not sure how many or what condition they are in. A conservatory. There's an old orchard as well."

"I'll have my office work on valuations for you. We'll send an inspector over, and a surveyor to finalize those details."

"Thank you."

"Your mother said you were looking to sell as soon as possible?"

I nod. "She is the executor as Rowan's next of kin. She thought it was best to sell the property and split the profit three ways, between herself, my brother, and I."

"Well, there is more than one path forward here. We can make a stipulation that the property is being sold as-is, with the sellers making no repairs. It will appraise for significantly lower than what the property is worth, but the positive part of this would be that it wouldn't require any work from you. The land parcel itself is quite valuable—nearly twenty acres with expansive lakefront views, beach access, rocky outcroppings, and lots of trees for privacy, but you're not too awfully far from town," she ticks off each feature with a manicured nail.

"You would only need to pack up personal belongings or things you wish to keep—maybe have an estate sale—then go home! I'd take care of the rest for you until you sign the papers at closing. Your target buyer would be an investor. They would make some needed updates to the house and sell for a significant profit. Or bulldoze and build something new."

There's a sinking feeling in my stomach. I hadn't even considered that.

"What's the second option?" I lean across the table and ask.

"*You* can be the investor, sugar, if you have the means. Finish the updates to the house yourself—well, hire a contractor. You have an enormous opportunity here; this community has a lot of vacation rentals," she explains. "People love the white picket fences, the ice cream shops, and the beach access."

Could I see this place as an inn, once again? I try to imagine my purple bedroom in an online rental listing. It isn't hard. Marketing buzzwords come to mind: *Stunning Victorian architecture. Waterfront views and beach access. Small-town charm. On-site library. Park-like grounds. Unwind from the city.* All at once, feelings of excitement, anxiety, and hope flood my thoughts at the possibilities. I wonder if my mom would be up for it.

"So, you can turn this old place into the showstopper it can be, then you can rent it out to vacationers and make quite a lot of profit for yourself."

If there is one thing I know about my mom, it's that she values money.

"I don't have the money for all of the upfront repairs it would need before that could happen," I admit. "But the thought of it being destroyed makes me feel sick."

"Do you know anyone who might be an investor for you?"

Roger might. But my skin crawls at what he might ask for in exchange. "Do you have any other ideas?"

"Well, maybe just some minor, less expensive updates could draw in a different sort of buyer. If you could make some basic updates before you list it for sale, it would at least be desirable to a larger market. We have some local home shoppers, of course, but the town is so small. Most of our potential buyers will be from out of town and people who are relocating aren't looking for a project that needs *this* much finishing—that's intimidating to someone trying to start somewhere new."

I look at Frank, who's watching us closely from his perch on an upholstered chair near the table. Where would he go if his house was torn down? A century of history would be erased. My little bit of history. Even considering the disconcerting few days it's been, the thought of the house being damaged in any way makes my chest hurt.

It doesn't matter, does it?

"I'll talk to my mom. I think we should make some basic repairs to get the house ready for sale. And I wonder—could we put in an application to have the house listed in the National Register of Historic Places? It would protect it from demolition."

"Millie! That's an amazing idea. You could get some preservation incentives that way, and it would add interest and authenticity to the place for future buyers or renters. Plus, I think your neighbors will appreciate it."

"What do you mean?"

"All of our hearts break a little when one of the historic properties along the lake gets wrecked and replaced with a cheap ugly McMansion by an out-of-towner."

I wonder if that's why Maria had her hackles up with me. She assumed I'd sell to the highest bidder, take my money, and run.

"The restoration project started upstairs was beautifully done," Vanessa continues. "But even simply getting rid of the excess furniture and personal effects and adding a fresh coat of paint on all the rooms would do a world of good for listing photos. Do you know what I'm saying, sugar?"

I'm in total agreement with her. "How much do you think it would cost?" I ask her. "Would I need to be here for all of it? How long would it take?"

"The answer to all those questions is entirely up to you. If you'd like, I can put you in touch with a contractor. He can do an inspection and work out some details and numbers for you," she explains.

"That would be helpful, thank you."

She fishes a Vanessa Brighton Realty monogrammed notepad and pen out of her binder and starts writing down a phone number on the table between us.

"I know *just* the guy," she says, smiling one of those be-tween-us-girls smiles. "He's local, reliable, and he does beautiful work. I think he might have done some work here."

Then she leans in closer like she's telling a secret.

"And you can appreciate the view while he's working," she says. "If you know what I mean."

I look down at the number. It looks familiar.

"His name is Ethan."

Fuck.

***

This is the fifth course by Professor Smith I've taken. Studying history in college is, simply put, listening to stories about interesting people doing interesting things in the past, and Professor Smith is the *best* storyteller. Sure, there are the investigative skills one develops while researching and writing an absolute life-halting number of papers, but it's the storytelling that I love, that hooked me in the first place and made me declare myself as a history major. I *needed* to hear every story and uncover every mystery that I could.

Professor Smith is sitting in what appears to be her basement, probably hiding from her children. I nosily eye the room behind her while she talks into the camera at our class. I spy a washer and dryer, a pile of unfolded laundry. I still haven't adjusted fully to the switch this semester to online classes. It's so strange to see her in her own house instead of pacing in front of a podium in a lecture hall. I feel like I'm seeing behind the magician's curtain.

She doesn't like it either—the spark has gone out of her voice; she doesn't have the same crowd-fueled vigor that a natural performer has in front of their audience, that electric feedback loop.

I desperately miss being side-by-side with my classmates and listening to the lecture. I miss the smell of the old hall—pencils and lemony floor cleaner. Drinking my expensive sugary coffee and scribbling notes in my spiral notebook while sitting on fifty-year-old desks that thousands of students have sat in before me. Observing my classmates around me, wondering where they come from and what part of history fascinates them the most.

"By the end of the week, I need you to submit proposals for your thesis topics," Smith concludes. I close my laptop as the class finishes.

I still haven't decided what I'll write my paper about. I lean back in my chair and stare at the millwork on the ceiling, searching my brain for something to jump out at me, a new question that needs answering. Nothing comes to mind yet. I'm too tired, too distracted by this house.

I pick up my phone and walk out onto the porch for fresh air and a chat with my best friend. I want to shake away my cloudy mood. Get some perspective about what's been happening and try to decide what to do next. Best friend chats are the best for that.

I circle around the wraparound porch until my phone shows enough bars to make a phone call. I spot the familiar Adirondack chairs I'd spent my summers in, but with their paint flaking off, they look more splintery than comfortable. I sit on the cold deck boards instead and gaze through spindles at the lake.

Sarah doesn't answer right away.

"Hey! How are you?!" She sounds rushed, as if I've interrupted her from doing something important.

"Do you want me to call back later?" I ask. "Is that Ben I hear in the background?"

"No, no. Now is fine. Yes, it's Ben. Ben's fine. We're all fine. How are *you*? Do you want me to put you on speaker so you can talk to him at the same time?"

I frown, confused about the frantic weirdness in her voice.

"No." Ben will tease me for sure. "I've had a rollercoaster few days, though."

"Tell me all about it. I want to hear everything."

I pull my sweater tight around myself for comfort and warmth and start at the beginning. Maria's wary eyes. Electrical problems. Bickering with Ethan. The locked door. The cemetery. The deep, persistent sorrow and guilt as I pack Rowan's life away, erase him, room by room.

"I know how much you loved your uncle. But you don't have to get this all done right away, either. Give yourself some time to deal with your loss. Let yourself grieve."

"It's not only that. I mean, yes, I've been grieving, and I think your mind can probably play tricks on you, but this is so overwhelming. I haven't slept properly in days."

"What are you talking about?"

"I've been having these crazy recurring nightmares. It's making me see things, I think."

In hushed tones, I tell her about the temperature swings, the fire, the attic door hanging open. Waking up in the middle of the night and feeling unsafe and calling the police, who probably got in their cruiser and laughed at me. Then the chalk on the door today.

"I don't think grief causes hallucinations, Millie. And besides, you said the realtor saw the chalk?"

"Yeah, she did. And the police saw the fire in the fireplace, which I definitely did not make."

She pauses before continuing, her voice uncharacteristically low and serious. "I think you should come home, Millie. It sounds like someone has access to the house. Or it's haunted. Neither option is good."

I thought the same thing but didn't want to admit it. It was too chilling to imagine someone in the house, doing who knows what while I slept unknowingly behind my bedroom door.

"The house can't be haunted." My laugh comes out all strangled and crazy sounding. "I don't know what to do about it. I've already called the police, and they didn't help."

"I don't like this. Please come home."

"I will. Just not yet. There's so much to do to the house still, and I need to do some local research. I think maybe I can save this place if I submit it to the National Register of Historic Places." She wouldn't understand. I'm not sure I fully understand yet—that I feel mired here by unfinished business. It's stronger than any of my fears. "I'm waiting to hear from the funeral home about Rowan's ashes. Then there's the memorial to plan."

"You don't have to do it all alone. Come home. Wait a few weeks, then Ben and I can join you and help over Thanksgiving break. To-gether, we'll pick up where you left off."

"I can't let the house sit here empty for three months, spend a week, then leave again. Especially if we're right that someone has access to the inside. Maybe they are trying to frighten me. I need to figure out why." My resolve tightens. "I can't run back home and leave the house compromised."

"I never met him, but I can say with certainty that your uncle wouldn't want you risking your safety."

"You're right, he wouldn't. I'm going to get the locks changed. Maybe install a security system."

She sighs. "I don't like this. Be careful."

"I will," I promise her.

***

My fingertips skim the headstone.

"Catherine Starling, Catherine Starling, who are you?" I sing. But no one can hear me, just the sick yellow moon. Even the bugs are silent tonight.

I leave the cemetery and make my way through the forest, nightgown trailing behind, catching on brambles. My bare feet are scratched and bloodied from the forest floor.

I pause at the foot of the stairs leading up to the porch.

My eyes dart to the inn's windows, but they are impenetrably dark, like the eyes of a skull. I wonder if there's anything in there, looking out at my pale face.

From inside floats the sound of someone playing the piano—a slow, sad melody. It's a macabre soundtrack as I glide up the porch stairs, one bare foot in front of the other, hand sliding up the fresh and glossy railing, the train of my soiled nightgown following me, dusting over my bloody footprints.

I reach the front door. The gilded plate announcing STARLING INN is glowing, lit by gas sconces flanking the door. Inviting beds lie within—beckoning.

My pulse quickens as I pull chalk from a pocket in my nightgown.

The piano picks up its tune again, a little erratic now.

With unnatural, jolting movements, I graffiti nonsense words on the door.

CHAPTER SIX

"Good morning, Morticia." Ethan is carrying a white bakery box and bringing in a lot of cold air with him. "I'm glad you reached out."

Morticia? I'd hope we could put awkwardness behind us and start off on a new foot today. But we're starting with insults instead, I guess. He's not wrong. My dark circles are out-of-control from exhaustion, my usually sleek wavy locks are all fluffy.

"Well, you look like a Civil War general," I fire back, attacking the easiest target, his unkempt beard.

"That is not an insult," he smiles slowly. "Thank you?"

"Well, calling me Morticia isn't a real insult, either. She's amazing. But you?" I try again, without much confidence. "You look like a pirate who's been lost at sea."

"You're bad at this, swamp witch," he says, pushing past me into the house. "I would *love* to be a pirate."

I put my hand to my chest, pretending to be wounded. "Being called a swamp witch would only *truly* hurt my feelings if it hadn't come from a redneck wannabe Tormund Giantsbane."

"Literally any resemblance to Tormund Giantsbane is a compliment. You fail again, Bellatrix Lestrange."

"But you understand that beards are supposed to make you look handsome, not homeless? You're clearly doing it wrong."

He winces. Maybe I've bruised his pride a little with that remark. But I'm on a roll, I can't resist.

"Maybe if you shave it off, you'll finally lose your virginity," I continue.

He bursts out laughing, surprised.

"I'll have you know that ladies love this," he says, running his fingers through his beard.

"No, they don't. Well, this lady doesn't."

"You're clearly not a lady."

"I set you up for that one, didn't I?" I let out a resigned sigh, then lead him down to the kitchen.

Last night, after getting off the phone with Sarah, I texted him an apology and requested his help. He said he would be over first thing in the morning. Sure enough, his black truck rolled up in the driveway before the sun was fully up.

I'd like to know why he can drop everything to come over here on such short notice, twice in the same week. If he's a contractor, shouldn't he have other contracts? Why isn't he busy? Maybe he's a bad contractor. Maybe it's the slow season. Is that a thing for contractors?

But he came highly recommended by the only other two people I know in the town. Against my better judgment, I am going to roll with it for now. And he came bearing gifts this time.

"Breakfast?" He holds up a pastry for me out of the box he's left on the kitchen table.

"You shouldn't have."

"You seemed hungry the last time I saw you."

"That's a weird thing to say."

He scratches his beard thoughtfully. "Well, it's true, you did. Are you going to tell me what you called me over here for?"

"I'm sorry we got off on the wrong foot," I start.

He smiles at me, surprised. "I'm sorry, too. I am having a hard time. I wasn't as kind as I could have been. You're not spooky. Well, maybe a little bit."

Our eyes meet over the kitchen table, and I feel a truce forming between us.

"It's hard for me, too. Sorting through Rowan's things and thinking about the future of this place without him in it." I admit. "I'm really struggling."

"I can see that," he says gently. "Just let me know how I can help."

"That's the other reason I called you. I want to fix a few things before we sell. I know my uncle has had a lot done already, but the realtor suggested a few more things before we try to list the property for sale," I summarize her advice for him. His face is guarded, difficult to read as he listens.

"What did you want to get started on today?" he finally asks.

"Can you fix the attic door? It doesn't want to stay closed." This is from my list, not Vanessa's. But I'm wondering if the nightmares will stop if I don't have to look at the open attic every day.

He finishes a croissant. "Probably just a latch. That's a quick fix, no problem. What else?"

"New locks on the exterior doors."

"That's a good idea. It probably hasn't been done in thirty years. Do you want me to pick up standard style and get them installed quickly, or do you want to wait a few weeks for the period-appropriate sort to come in? We would have to special order them."

"The nicer ones. I'm going reach out to a security company to install cameras soon. Thank you—" I start to say, then sink my teeth into a buttery croissant and completely forget what I was talking about.

My brain stops working, and my eyes close involuntarily. "This is so good," I murmur around the mouthful.

These are not grocery store croissants made in a factory that taste like air and have the texture of paper. These are boutique bakery croissants that a professional got up at the ass crack of dawn to make with their hands and cold butter. Layer after layer of flavor folded together and baked into flaky perfection, now melting in my mouth. I know the difference because Sarah drags me around to bakeries and has described the details to me passionately.

"See? You needed it." He's leaning on the table in that obnoxiously casual way again, legs outstretched, a satisfied smile on his face. I can feel his eyes watching me bask in croissant bliss. I'm feeling my claws retract.

"So, how exactly do you know your way around my uncle's kitchen?" I break the shared silence.

"He was friends with my mom. And when I became the neighborhood stray, he and the Russos stepped up. Maria was my guardian, but I spent a lot of time with Rowan, too. I'm sure you remember—he was always looking out for me." He trails off, then grabs a croissant.

I consider asking him about his parents, but I don't want to pry and disturb the peace we've found.

"I recently moved back," he continues. "I've been helping him work on this place for a few years. None of which you were around for," he adds pointedly.

"Well, I'm here now." I don't let Ethan see how much his words sting. "And I want to make amends if I can."

"Cheers to that. Let's get to work," he says, brushing his hands on his jeans.

"After I finish this croissant."

***

The attic doorway looks small when Ethan's in it. He repaired the latch as quickly as he predicted he would. But to my dismay, he continues through the opening. First, he's a headless torso, then only jeans. I flounder for a moment, temporarily distracted, realizing how nicely his butt fills out those jeans.

Then he's gone entirely and I'm in the hallway alone.

"Are you coming up?" his deep, muffled voice calls from overhead.

"I think I'll stay here," I shout back.

His head pokes down through the opening. "What? Are you *scared*?" There's a touch of sarcastic disbelief in his question. "You are definitely more terrifying than anything up here. I think witches are pretty high up on the supernatural food chain." He disappears again.

I sigh. "Fine, give me a minute."

I tell my feet to move, but they don't. My chest feels tight. Residual terror from my nightmares is making my fear impossible to control.

"Come on, Millie. It's just an attic. You're being silly," I tell myself, clenching my fists so hard I press my fingernails into my palms. A few moments pass, and I still don't move, but I can hear his footsteps above as he explores.

Then I hear a thud, like something heavy falling to the floor. Scuffling sounds. A strangled shout.

My feet *finally* listen this time, and I sprint up the narrow staircase through the doorway like my life depends on it. I step into a dim, spacious room with rafters peaking above.

"Ethan?" I call out, my heart hammering.

No response.

The air is musty and thick. Sunlight streams in through an octagonal window. I walk around claustrophobic clusters of boxes, furniture, and abandoned tchotchkes—artifacts of people who lived and stayed here over time. Cast aside remnants of their lives.

"Ethan?" My voice squeaks.

Movement catches the corner of my eye, and I spin around to watch as he stands up from between a pile of tall boxes. He's looking down at something in his hands, but I can't tell what it is because his back is turned to me.

"There you are. Are you OK?" I ask. "I thought I heard you shout for help."

He turns slowly, and I can see his solemn face and the outline of something small cradled in his hands.

It's a head. It's a fucking head.

I scream.

Ethan screams.

I scream louder.

Ethan screams and tosses the head at me *and for some reason I catch it.* I scream again as soon as it hits my hands, then I immediately drop it.

It hits the floor between my feet with a thud and rolls, coming to a stop against a trunk a few feet away from me. It's illuminated by a shaft of light, and I can see now that it's just a mannequin head. A horribly creepy one, with a brown comb-over of painted hair, eyelash-lined blue eyes, and a too-wide, forever smile. I shudder.

A few feet away, Ethan is bent over, his face red from laughter.

"You scared me, you asshole," I say through gritted teeth.

He takes a moment to collect himself. He has to catch his breath.

"I got you to come up here, though, didn't I? And isn't it nice to know you have a bit of a heroic streak? You came *racing up here* to save me."

I'm speechless. I stare at the mannequin head, and it stares back at me with painted and dead wooden eyes.

"Besides, it's payback," he continues, then tilts his head upward as he steps around and studies the trusses, like he's figuring out how they were put together over a century ago.

"Payback? For what?" I start rummaging around. The attic is not so bad. It was so much worse in my head. I wonder if my nightmares will stop, now that I know what it looks like. Now that it's no longer a mystery, maybe my imagination will stop filling in the blanks with horrible things.

"For that time I asked you out on a date and you shot me down mercilessly," he answers, turning toward me, arms crossed across his chest. "Don't you remember?"

What?

"First of all, I can say no to a date for any reason, especially as a sixteen-year-old girl."

"Fair point," he says, holding up his hands in surrender.

"And second," I continue, then stop, biting my lip. I don't finish my sentence because I've suddenly decided that saying it out loud would be a huge mistake.

"I don't remember," I lie.

That last summer I visited, my eyes strayed to him more often than to the pages of my book or the blue water. I watched his skin get darker and golden as the summer stretched on. I remember that his hair was longer, curly and blonde, sometimes falling into his eyes. He looked like the outside of one of those Abercrombie & Fitch bags that Sarah and I would giggle over after we went shopping at the mall.

One afternoon, about a week before I'd be heading back home to Chicago, I watched him through my sunglasses as he'd left Ben and the others down at the dock. He walked up the steep rocky trail from the beach to the shaded back porch where I was sitting alone. I was wearing a black spaghetti strap tank top, my feet tucked beneath me, a glass of iced tea on the table beside me, its sides frosted with condensation. My hair was pulled high in a bun to keep the lake wind from whipping it into my face.

He leaned against the porch railing across from me, his hands in the pockets of his swim trunks.

"What are you reading?" he asked me with a dimpled smile. It was too much, that dimple. He was perfection to me. I hadn't always felt this way with him, just for this past year.

So, I preferred to watch him from afar.

He knew it. He'd catch me watching and he'd share a wink meant just for me. I would look away and blush and pretend I wasn't staring.

"*Jane Eyre,* like always," I answered, setting my book down in my lap and with the voice of a mouse that I desperately wished at that moment was a lion. "Is that what you climbed all the way up here for? To ask me what I'm reading?"

But then the other guys had noticed he was missing, and they started climbing up the trail behind him, shouting his name.

All my senses were overwhelmed by his nearness—my heart loudly thundering and my gaze fixed on the water droplets on his chest. I could smell his suntan lotion and the sun on his skin and my senses were screaming at me to get closer, closer—so loudly I could barely hear him when he asked me out.

"Millie?"

The balloon in my chest burst, rendering me numb. Because I knew immediately he couldn't possibly be sincere. I was a sophomore. He was a senior. I was gangly and so shy I could barely even talk to him. And he was... so far out of my league. It was a joke, I'd decided. It must be some sort of joke or bet.

A cruel prank on the weird girl.

So, I faked a laugh and told him no. My cheeks burned over the whoops and catcalls of his approaching friends as I turned and went inside. My mom picked Ben and I up the next day.

I pull myself back to the present and look around the attic, dust motes floating through the air, caught in shafts of light streaming in through the window.

"You weren't actually asking me out on a date. You weren't serious."

"Oh, I wasn't? You seem so certain."

It would be humiliating if he found out how much I used to like him. I shouldn't have been crushing on him so hard that summer. It was my last peaceful summer with Rowan, though I didn't know it at the time.

The familiar feeling of sick guilt floods my stomach.

"I'm going to get to work," I say, opening the nearest box. "You don't have to stay."

"I want to help. I'm going to be busy—in and out of town and catching up on orders—for the next couple of weeks, but you've got my undivided attention today."

My first instinct is to push back, and tell him no, I don't want him to stay. But I could use the extra set of hands.

"Fine."

I kneel in front of a steamer trunk so large I could fit inside it. Its metal riveted edges are coated in dust, and the brass latches stick when I pry them open. It's mostly empty inside, except for a paper box at the bottom. I pull off the lid, finding a white satin banner neatly embroidered with a golden star.

"What is it?" Ethan asks, reaching in.

"Get out of here with your dusty fingers. It looks like a window hanging for a Gold Star Mother."

"Gold Star Mother?" he asks, peering over my shoulder.

"They are a support group for women who lost their sons at war. This one looks quite old. I'm not sure which war it's from. Maybe World War I? Or World War II? Let's start a new pile for stuff I want to donate to a museum."

We quickly figure out a flow and fill the silence of the attic now and then by bickering with each other and wondering aloud about the lives of the old things we come across. Items that I want to donate to a Goodwill go in a mostly empty shed outside, which I'll clear out with a rented moving truck another day. Items to trash go in a pile next to the inn, for a later trip to a dumpster.

There's an obscene amount of holiday decorations, mostly Halloween. Ethan explains these boxes are where he found the mannequin head, which he leaves on the porch railing, scaring the shit out of me a second time when I walk past it.

With each layer of stuff we move, there is an older layer underneath, like an archaeological dig site.

I find a box marked *FRAGILE* filled with old stoneware jugs and glassware. I pull a few interesting pieces to repurpose in the house later; the rest I decide to donate.

We find a Jenny Lind cradle that still rocks, with intricate spindles that Ethan points out the craftsmanship on. It's too old for anyone to use safely for a child today, so donation isn't an option. But I can't bring myself to throw it away. I briefly think about selling it at an antique store. That doesn't feel right either, so we leave it where it is for now.

Then we find boxes and boxes of moth-eaten extra linens, laundry bags, broken foldaway beds, old hats, and empty silk-lined suitcases.

Leftovers and discards from when this used to be an inn. Things guests left behind.

My hair gets frizzier, and the attic gets tidier. We make pretty good progress, bit by bit clearing the place out, finding treasures along the way.

"Oh, a hair wreath!" I hold up the oval frame for him to see. He steps over and leans in to examine the delicate brown flowers woven around each other along a vine. They are lacy, intricate, and strange, protected under a dusty bubble of glass.

"Hair... wreath?" He steps back to the vermin chewed box of newspapers he's leafing through.

I shake my head at him. "You should trash that box."

"But it's all so old?"

"The local historical society probably has microfilm copies. They won't want our mouse-chewed copies. But this?" I hold up the framed wreath. "This is one of a kind. Families would save hair from their deceased loved ones, and have it made into a memento. The fabric backing is usually made from the same fabric that lined the deceased's casket. And do you see how the design is in a horseshoe shape?" I ask.

He nods.

"They left it open ended so that souls could escape."

"Morbid."

"Yeah. But kind of beautiful, too, right?"

He furrows his brow at me.

"Families made these to memorialize their loved ones," I say, looking at the lacy arrangement. I want him to see the beauty that I do. "They created art like this, and death portraiture to remember them by. It was fashionable for Victorians to be obsessed with death and the macabre."

"Why?" He leans in to look again, giving in to his curiosity.

"A few reasons. One was that there was a lot of death back then—the mortality rate was crazy high. But mostly because Queen Victoria's husband died young and tragically, so she memorialized him in tragically cool ways. She wore mourning clothes for forty years and froze her house in time. She made her servants lay out his clothing each morning, long after he was dead. And anything the queen does is fashionable, right? So, Victorians started their own grandiose mourning rituals to be like her."

"That is fascinating. How do you know all of this?"

"My dad used to work in a museum. He was a cataloger. He would research artifacts, write about them, and build special boxes and enclosures to keep them safely stored. When I was a kid, he would take me behind the scenes to see artifacts up close. He would drive me around to tons of museums and libraries. After he died, I continued going on my own, sort of to remember him, I guess. But I also loved it, old fascinating things catching my curiosity then researching to learn more about them and who made them."

He tilts his head, appraising me. I set down the frame. It was made for the house and should stay in the house—a piece of its story. I look around for what I want to tackle next.

"It's not hard for me to imagine little Millie traipsing around museums," he says with a crooked grin. "Same scowl on your face, same messy hair."

"Well, it *is* hard for me to imagine young *you* in a museum. What were you doing instead? Playing ultra-masculine sportsball?"

"Something like that."

"Gross."

"Yes, exercising outdoors with a bit of friendly competition is so gross."

"You mean banging into each other, sustaining head injuries, and getting dumber with every game?"

"Millie." In an instant, his face switches from fake wounded pride to dead serious.

"Did I hurt your feelings?"

"Yes. But that's not why I stopped you. Hold still, there's a spider in your hair."

"I am not falling for your tricks again," I say, waving him away.

"No, really. I swear. I'm not messing with you. Hold still, I'm going to brush it off."

I freeze. He's either a superb liar, or there truly is a spider in my hair. Did I just feel eight spindly legs tiptoeing across my scalp, or was that my imagination? I shudder involuntarily and close my eyes.

"Get it off. Get it off. Get it off." I sound like a broken record, but I can't help it.

"I will, I will, hold still, you're OK." I hear him close the distance between us, then I feel his fingers thread through my hair, gently tugging through the strands.

"When I was a little girl, my brother told me once that spiders lay eggs under your skin at night, and when you wake up, you'll have little spider babies hatching on your face," I whisper.

"Well, I don't think that's true, but it sounds exactly like something Ben would say. How is he doing?"

"Good. I think. We don't really talk the way we used to," I reply, opening my eyes to watch Ethan pivot, his hands cupped together. With great care, he sets the spider down and places an overturned cup onto it.

"Coast is clear. I'll put him outside later."

"Thank you." I pull my hair up into a bun, so I don't get any more hitchhikers.

"There are boxes of old books over here. Where should I put them?"

"Rowan's office—the library, I mean. It will take a while to sort through it all. I want to do it somewhere more comfortable than up here."

"Oh, you don't think it's comfortable up here?" he asks, looking around.

"It could use some better lighting," I laugh, and pick up one of the book boxes. It's heavy. With great effort and complaining, I lug it down the stairs and drop it in Rowan's office. From the spines of the books I saw, some were old enough to be original to the house.

Ethan and I pass each other on the stairs, in the hall, and in the office again and again and again.

I'm very aware that he took off his flannel and is wearing a pair of well-worn jeans and a white cotton undershirt.

Each time we pass each other, I have to tell myself to look at my feet or the ceiling or *anything*, so I don't rudely stare at how nicely he is filling out that shirt. But I peek anyway—time and again, catching sight of strong, flexing arms. Big, confident hands.

I think, maybe, he's doing the same thing. Not looking, or looking down at his feet, lashes dark against his cheeks.

It's the afternoon when we get to the last box. We're both sweaty and out of breath, covered in dust. We were so focused that we worked through lunch.

"Last one," I announce to the tidy, mostly empty attic. Ethan is standing with his hands on his hips, watching.

I pull the lid of the last box open, and I'm a bit disappointed that it's anticlimactic—a bunch of old rusted tools.

"Trash," I declare. I take a picture of the attic and send it to my mom.

"Please don't." Ethan sounds pained.

"It's rusty, dangerous trash," I say. "Don't touch it, you're going to get tetanus."

"I won't get tetanus. Some of it can be cleaned and restored. This is an old block plane." He holds it up like it's made of gold.

"Then you take them," I insist.

"Are you sure? You can restore them and sell them for a decent amount."

"Yes, keep it, please. It's the least I can do. Thanks for all your help today."

"You're welcome," his voice trails off, distracted as he looks around the nearly empty space, contemplating. "Does the attic seem bigger than it should be?" he asks finally.

"What do you mean?"

"The master suite is over here," he says, striding over to me.

"And this is the hallway." He steps away, focused and purposeful, counting his steps.

"The library."

I nod, watching him take long strides from place to place as he maps out an invisible blueprint.

"My room, the guest rooms are over there," I add, pointing.

"Yeah. So, what's this unaccounted-for area? It's too much for spacing between walls," he adds, hands on his hips.

"A secret passageway?" I ask sarcastically.

"A secret passageway," he echoes, eyes bright.

"How can you be sure?"

"I'm not. Only one way to find out."

***

"It must be around here somewhere," I say, gently lifting books and figurines from the shelf one at a time and setting them back down, looking for a mechanism that would unlock a hidden door. We've been in the library for almost an hour, searching, lifting every volume.

Ethan started on one side of the shelf, and I started on the other, and we finally just met in the middle.

"Maybe the switch isn't on the bookshelf," I conclude.

"Where else would it be? We know the entrance has to be on this wall." He moves away and starts peeking behind paintings and wall ornaments. "Besides, the secret switch is always on a bookshelf."

"I have an idea," I say as I sit down in Rowan's chair and run my fingers along the underside of the desk. "This piece looks old enough to be original to the house."

"And it's bolted to the floor, so it doesn't move." Ethan starts pacing around the desk.

"What if the switch is here, so the occupant can pop the door open whenever they are sitting here working?" I ask.

My fingers catch on a metal knob on the underside of the desk, hidden within a drawer.

"You find something?" Ethan asks, drawing closer. I take a deep breath and crank the knob.

We both turn toward the unmistakable click of an unlocking door. One of the bookshelves is slightly ajar.

"No way," Ethan says incredulously. I follow him to the bookshelf and watch as he pulls it all the way open with a reluctant creaking. Beyond it is nothing but darkness and stale air.

"Secret passageway? Really?"

"Secret passageway. Really."

My phone flashlight shines into the space. Together we stare at a narrow hallway with bare floorboards and wood lath and plaster walls, disappearing into the hidden depths of the inn.

"Ladies first."

"No way. You first," I fire back. "What if there are spiders?"

"We've already established that spiders love you. But fine, I'll go first. Need to check if the floor is stable."

I watch with nervous excitement as he takes careful steps, checking the floorboards for rot. Then he turns back toward me. "Seems safe enough so far. Come on."

I follow his cautious steps through the narrow hall. We disappear into the walls of the house, its claws catching our clothes now and then.

"Oof."

Ethan stops walking abruptly, and I run into his immovable back. He quickly turns and reaches out to steady me, his hands gripping my biceps.

"Are you alright?" Ethan asks, a smile in his voice.

"Yeah, sorry," I say, tilting my face up. He's standing only a few inches away, and I realize once again just how tall he is. He smells like wood smoke. It makes me want to lean in closer.

For an instant—and it's probably my imagination—his eyes drop to my lips.

"Ethan?"

"Yeah?"

I take a bashful step backward, putting some distance between us. "Why'd you stop walking?"

"Oh, right. I saw something."

His phone's flashlight beam shines on an unmarked envelope, tucked against the wall where someone carefully hid it long ago.

I watch as he scrubs his empty hand on the front of his jeans, then picks up the envelope and hands it to me gingerly, like he's trusting me with an egg he's afraid to break.

There is a little bundle of paper inside, neatly folded, yellowing with age and covered in thin, looping cursive script.

"It looks like an old letter, but I can't be sure yet. I'm going to bring this out into the light so I can see it better."

"Good plan," he says. "I can see the end of the passageway so I'm going to check it out."

"Shout if you need me."

"Oh, are you going to run to my rescue again?" he calls after me.

"You wish!" I shake my head at him as I leave the passageway.

I close the envelope and set it on Rowan's chair. Then I find the nearest sink. Methodically, like a doctor about to perform surgery, I wash the dust off my hands and find a rag to clean and dry the desk. Only then do I open the unmarked envelope again, reaching inside to pull out the small rectangle of tightly folded paper.

Frank watches from a bookshelf, still as a statue, as I hover over the thin, brittle pages. Slowly and gently, I unfold them.

"Damn it," I mutter, feeling resistance as I try to open the pages. If I force them open all the way, I suspect they will shatter along the fold lines. I can only see a quadrant of the first page, and it's clearly a letter. The letterhead has an upside down, hollow, red triangle. I can't make out the words yet.

After a quick trip to the kitchen for supplies, I set a glass casserole dish with tall sides on Rowan's desk and use my water bottle to fill the bottom with a bit of water. Frank is following me around, curious about the commotion. Ethan joins him after a while, equally curious, his arms folded across his chest as he watches me.

"It's a trick I learned at the archives," I explain. I set a cookie rack in the water, making sure the top of the rack stays dry and only the bottom of the rack has contact with water. Next, I carefully place the bundle of folded paper on the cookie rack, suspending them above the water. I stretch plastic wrap across the top of the dish so that it's airtight. "The ambient humidity will help the fibers in the paper relax. In a few days, I'll be able to open the letter without damaging it."

"That's cool, swamp witch."

"Did you find the end of the passageway?"

"I did, but it's stuck shut. I think it opens into the back of one of the bedroom closets."

"That's cool, ZZ Top."

Ethan laughs.

***

I collapse on the green couch in the living room and open the crinkling cellophane paper that covers the gift basket from Vanessa Brighton of Vanessa Brighton Realty. I spy a log of salami, crackers, bubble bath, wine, and cheese spread in a jar.

"Thank you, Vanessa," I say aloud as I bite into a cracker stacked with delicious, salty, preservative-filled things. I hold up the sleeve of crackers and jar of cheese to Ethan in offering.

"Please don't eat that for dinner."

"What? It's the five food groups. Grains, dairy, meat, and... fruit?" I hold up the wine bottle.

"You forgot about vegetables."

"No one cares about vegetables, Ethan."

He shakes his head at me before shrugging his coat on.

"More for me, then." I twist the cap off the wine and drink straight from the bottle. My legs are too tired to carry me all the way down to the kitchen for a glass.

The groove between Ethan's eyebrows deepens.

"Do you want me to build you a fire?"

"No!" It comes out more sharply than I mean it to, my eyes darting to the hearth.

He lingers for a moment with his hand on the doorway. But then he leaves, still shaking his head, holding the box of old tools we found in the attic like they are beloved trophies.

I hold up my wine bottle to the mannequin head.

A toast to progress made.

To one room empty and done.

To fears faced.

And a friendship rekindled.

A friend who provided a spectacular firework show of brawn and dimples that made me forget, for a moment, the heaviness of my situation.

My head falls back on the couch cushions and the silence of the house surrounds me once again.

I call Sarah, but she doesn't answer.

Ben still hasn't answered the picture I sent him of the inn the first day I got here. But that's not out of character for him.

It is out of character for Sarah. I wonder if she's alright.

Not talking to her makes me feel... unsettled.

But if she could talk to me, what would she say? I would tell her about all of Ethan's help today. She would ask if this was the same Ethan whose name I used to doodle on my middle school notebook? With blushing cheeks, I would tell her yes.

She would ask if he was still cute or single because she is forever trying to set me up.

"He is more than cute," I would confirm.

She would say, "This is an unexpected twist in the Millie's-lost-her-mind-and-fled-to-Michigan-saga."

"No kidding," I would agree.

And she would end with, "Be careful. You still don't know what's causing the disturbances in the house. You shouldn't trust anyone."

I *should* be more cautious. I shift on the couch, smile fading from my face as unease settles over me. I'd gotten swept up in his easy smile and my past crush, so focused on what we were doing, I forgot for just a moment about how tumultuous and strange the last week has been.

My head snaps to the left, in the direction of a *tap, tap, tap*. The settling of old lumber? It's louder than that, though. A staccato beat, slower now. I set down the wine bottle on an end table that has the carved legs of an octopus.

I follow the sound to the wall and place my ear against it, beside a framed painting of a hunting dog.

The sound stops.

There's a hair protruding from the plaster, inches from my face. I pull at it. It's coarse and black. *Whose hair is this?*

I try to free it, but it breaks, leaving a thick strand between my fingers. I get a letter opener from Rowan's office and chisel away at the spot until there's nothing but the wooden slats underneath.

***

My fingertips skim the walls, feeling the ridges and bumps in the pattern of the velvety floral fabric wallpaper.

I pause at the top of the stairs, and I pull at my gown, its eyelet-laced throat cinched, seams scratchy at the wrists.

Lightning flashes bright and draws my gaze out the windows. There's a thunderstorm, black and raging.

From the drawing room floats the sound of someone playing the piano—a slow, sad melody. It's a macabre soundtrack to my glide down the staircase, one bare foot in front of the other, hand sliding down the railing, the train of my nightgown trailing behind.

I reach the bottom of the stairs. I open the door to the storm. Through the garden, down the trail, a cliff is waiting for me.

Sharp rocks bite at my feet, trying to stop me. Rain stings my eyes.

But the sound—what is that sound through the deafening wind?

I stand at the edge of the cliff. Rocks skitter down to the beach in a tap, tap, tap.

The piano stops playing.

Tap.

Tap.

Tap.

***

Is the tapping what awakens me, or was that part of the nightmare?

I don't know.

I do know that it's still dark outside but there's no chance I'm falling back to sleep.

So, I settle on the pink tufted sofa in my bedroom, laptop perched on my lap.

First, I search for upside down triangle symbols on letterheads, trying to find clues about the little bundle Ethan and I found in the secret passageway. But after paging through useless results, I give up. My answer isn't on the internet. Or if it is, I can't figure out the right search words to use.

Determined to learn more about the grave Frank keeps leading me to—a grave my uncle must have frequented because the path was well-worn—I type 'Catherine Starling' into the search bar. A buzzing fly darts near, attracted by the glow of my bright screen in a dark room. I swat it away, irritation simmering beneath the surface.

I scroll through a few pages of bloated results before finding her and a database of cemeteries.

Catherine Starling (1970-2002)

Birth: June 15, 1970, Charlotte County, Michigan

Death: August 29, 2002, Charlotte County, Michigan

Burial: Starling Cemetery, Charlotte County, Michigan

Tap, tap, tap goes the house and I shiver.

The virtual memorial has two images. The first is of the headstone, topped with snow. Whoever entered the information on this website had snapped an image to accompany their data entry. But the second image snags my attention—a studio portrait, maybe a school photo, of a young woman with blond feathered bangs.

"Hello, Catherine," I murmur to her electric blue eyes. I scroll through the rest of the page. There's no link to an obituary, no information about her death.

Strange.

I open a new tab and navigate to the local newspaper's website—*The Charlotte Report*. The website is clunky and full of annoying pop-up ads. I ignore the headlines and scroll to the bottom of the page, searching for the site's older archived copies. I pull up an issue from August 2002, the week she died. I scan the digital copy, the fly crawling across my screen, until I find her obituary.

There's hardly any detail in the paper—only the announcement of her death and details for the service.

The Starling family held her wake here at the inn.

Probably in the parlor? I think about the formal room beneath me, with its heavy curtains, and overstuffed floral couch.

After closing the laptop I settle fitfully on the sofa.

I know that before the funeral home industry existed, people were laid out for their wakes at their own homes, often in parlors. I'm sure Catherine wasn't the first, or only, person to have a wake at the inn. But I hadn't thought about it happening here before. To me, that room is full of memories of Ben—playing hide and seek with him, listening to him play piano. Now, every time I enter it, all I will think about is wakes. A corpse and their mourning family.

When sleep finally takes me again, I have a nightmare, but in it, the attic is fastened tight. I stand frozen in front of Room 3, unable to move anything but my eyes. I watch and I wait as the *tap, tap, tap* echoes in my ears.

CHAPTER SEVEN

THE PAST TWO WEEKS have been a blur. Some days, I work with conviction. I conquered the guest room closets one day. The living room next, carefully packing the pictures from the mantel. Bit by bit I clean, sort, pack, and toss. The rooms start to empty of things, filling instead with tidy stacks of boxes, and furniture labeled with sticky notes.

Donate.

Trash.

Keep.

Rowan's room has been the hardest to pack. I've started and stopped more than once. It still isn't finished.

Other days, I glide through the house like the wraith in my dreams, listless.

Like today. I can't decide where I want to get started, so I wander from room to room in an exhausted fog.

Until I get caught by the wallpaper in the stairwell.

Once upon a time, this wallpaper was stunning, to be sure. But now, it's nagging me with its ratty appearance. Persistently pulling my eyes each time I walk past it.

It's decorated with hand-painted, nonsensical twisting vines and forest creatures with wicked eyes. The pattern is interrupted by dis-integration and missing swaths. I lift my fingertips to it, and they are coated in powdery decay. I want to rip it all down so badly. Just use my nails and pull away great big strips. I imagine them littering the stairs like skin shed from a snake.

But there's a process to these things. Safety measures that need to be taken. Old wallpaper is made from who knows what—that green is so vibrant, it's probably arsenic, blisteringly poisonous.

I can't rip it down. I can't reveal the clean plaster beneath.

So, I stand and watch the light slowly move across it, unable to remove my eyes. Unable to focus my mind on accomplishing anything. Until the sun sets, and the wallpaper is cast in shadows, and I'm set free.

CHAPTER EIGHT

"Sorry, Frank. I don't think we'll make it to the cemetery before the rain starts this morning." I bite my fingernails—not that there is much fingernail left. China and knickknacks rattle in the dining room cabinet as thunder rumbles outside.

I truly am sorry; our walks in the peaceful, cold dawn are often my favorite part of the day. After weeks of broken sleep, waking in a sweat with my heart racing, I grasp onto those walks like life-preservers, a bit of daily distance from this house to help keep me sane.

I'm exhausted. My nerves are on edge from this incessant *tapping* sound, and my muscles scream with every movement. There have been other things—strange things. Things I'm afraid to say out loud because then they'll be spoken into reality instead of remaining as something that exists only in my head. So I shake it off and tell myself, *No, Millie, it's only your mind playing tricks on you.*

Like this morning, I set down my coffee cup on the dining room table and got up to go to the bathroom. When I got back, it was in a different spot at the table, scooted a few feet to the right, sitting in a puddle, like some of the coffee had sloshed out.

Who moved my mug?

Not ghosts, because ghosts aren't real. Are they?

They can't be.

If they were real, my dad would have reached out to me. I'm sure of it. He would have never left us without saying goodbye if he had the chance.

Plus, I'm making a career of old things, spending time in cemeteries and old places, cataloging precious pieces of the past. I have yet to see a ghost.

My coffee is probably in a different spot because I'm so tired. I must have moved it before I left the room, then forgot.

But yesterday, when I was dusting the parlor, I heard footsteps upstairs. "Nice try," I'd said. I didn't even stop my dusting. "You won't fool me again. I know that's you, Frank."

But then Frank croaked at me. He was sitting right next to me, and when we tiptoed up the stairs together to investigate, there was no one there. Just a tingle down my spine, a frantic beating in my heart.

I need to get some sleep. Restful sleep, without nightmares.

I pull my sweater tight around myself because I can't ever seem to get warm. Then push aside the dusty brocade drapes to look outside at the dark clouds above. My face fogs up the glass on the window, and I stare at the opaque circle until it starts to fade, sparking a memory.

At the first sign of a summer thunderstorm, Ben and I would beg Rowan to race us across the yard to the glass-walled conservatory. It smelled like roses and damp Earth inside, the air thick and heavy. Then the storm would unleash, and I remember the raindrops beating so loud on the arched glass ceiling that we could hardly hear each other talk. The storm would strip all the color from the world, turning the sky gray and blocking out the sun, but we'd be lit up inside our glass palace with golden lanterns and crimson roses. It felt like being inside a little jewel box.

Ben and I would use our breath to fog the glass walls and draw on them. I loved watching raindrops race each other down the glass, loved watching the clouds swirl above us, trees twisting with wind outside while we were protected within. It was magical.

I could use some magic today. I want to step back into that memory and bask in it. So, I find an umbrella by the door, then pull on my boots and my black wool peacoat and twist my hair up into a bun.

"You coming?" I leave the door ajar for a moment, watching Frank. He stares, unmoving from the threshold, unwilling to step outside into the thick air, noisy with the frantic chirps of countless birds and the roaring swirl of wind-stirred trees and loose fallen leaves.

"I'll be back soon," I tell him as I pull the door closed.

Strands of my bangs get caught and lifted by the wind to join the flurry of dancing leaves. My boots land on the flagstone steps in the lawn, leading down, down, down into the forest. I think about how many people have come and gone along this path, how many stories, how many steps. The Starling family and all the residents of the inn over the years. It's part of my story, my uncle's, and my brother's. It will outlast us, this trail of stones and dirt, and become a part of someone else's story. It looked not too different a hundred years ago, and I hope that will still be true a hundred years from now. I'll do everything I can to make sure of it.

As drizzle starts to fall, I can just barely see the spire of the conservatory standing tall through the treetops

Thunder rumbles overhead, and I pick up my pace.

Then I see the rest of it, our jewel box, and I hold my hand to my mouth in horror.

The once carefully latched door to the glass building is thrown open, and nature has crawled in and overtaken it. It looks like a beast got inside and lost its temper. My eyes linger on flowerpots, once filled with beautiful blossoms, now broken to pieces, dirt spilled. Dry brown leaves litter the floor like trash, collecting in high drifts in the corners. Vining plants, once contained in pots, have escaped, climbing up the glass like the tentacles of a sea creature, seeking breaks in the glass above. Benches where I once sat are tipped over. Some of the glass panels covering the walls and ceiling are busted out, now lying in dangerous, glittering piles on the floor. The intricate spiderweb of metal that served as the skeleton of the building, which once held the glass, is rusted from exposure to the elements.

The drizzling rain transitions into a steady downpour.

Humanoid shapes stand watch in the center of the building. I step closer, glass crunching underfoot. Once, this was a bright white, classical statue of the three Hesperides. But now, some areas are so densely overgrown with vines I can hardly tell it's a statue at all. It looks like a creature rising from a sea of thorny brown vines.

The rainfall is torrential now, intermittent pillars of water cascading through openings in the glass. I step around them until I reach the statue of the three sisters, unshed tears choking my throat. They are supposed to be guardians of the garden of Hera, guardians of our magical little garden under the glass, of my memories here.

But how can they be guardians, if they can't even see? I look around for garden shears to free them with, but they are nowhere to be found—the place is too severely ransacked.

I can't leave them like this.

Wrapping my fingers around the vines, I tug and pull, trying to uncover the figures underneath. Bit by bit I expose a white face, pocked by brown from the plants.

I sigh in relief as one of the sister's faces is revealed and she can see again. Raindrops are running down her upturned face like tears, and I realize I'm crying, too.

"I don't know why Rowan let this happen," I say, frantically moving to the next sister.

I pull and heave with all my might, ripping away all the vines I can, and my crying escalates to deep, scattered sobs.

All the tears I've been holding back are breaking free.

The thunder is loud and all around me, chased by flashes of lightning. My head is spinning and I start shivering violently as I pull vines from the third sister. I pull and pull, but it hardly makes a difference. My hands are too weak, the vines too stubborn. Tears run down my cheeks, blurring my vision.

I've always told myself that I had grit. But I guess not enough.

I can't catch my breath, so I sink down onto the concrete floor, curling my knees to my chest.

"I'm sorry, I'm sorry, I'm sorry," I say to this beautiful place, which has suffered the neglect it didn't deserve.

I look down at my hands; they are blood-streaked and torn. Red rivulets fall into the rainwater at my feet.

I sink my head down onto my knees and stay there, shaking, listening to the thunder and watching the rainwater turn pink with my blood while my nightmares play on repeat.

***

"Max?"

There's a voice on the wind. I lift my head from my knees and try to blink my surroundings into focus. I don't know how long I've been here. But the rain has slowed to a drizzle and sunlight is triumphing.

The rusted metal arms of the conservatory ceiling are spinning like a kaleidoscope, and there is an enormous black dog standing a few steps away from me, his brown eyes fixed on mine.

His paws and belly are splattered in mud, his glossy black coat glittering with raindrops. He's looking at me like he doesn't trust me, his pointed ears on a swivel, not sure if they want to point toward me or the voice in the distance. His narrow snout drops to the ground, sniffing and inching closer. I draw my knees up closer to my chest. He lets out an uneasy bark and I flinch away from the sound.

His eyes are eerily intelligent, and I am reminded of the scene in *Jane Eyre* when Jane gets caught off guard by a dog. It rises up out of the darkness at night, when she's alone on the trail, and she fears it's the monster from the folktales her nursemaid used to tell her.

"Are you the sort of monster that leads people astray? Or the kind that guides the lost?" I croak. My head feels thick and foggy.

He wags his tail half-heartedly.

Both of our heads turn as we hear the crunch of boots on glass. The dog's posture relaxes, and his tail starts wagging as he looks toward the direction of the sound. Then he lets out a bark.

We listen to footsteps on glass coming closer.

"Millie?"

In a rush of movement, Ethan kneels next to me. His warm hands push the wet strands of my bangs off my face.

"Millie." His voice sounds strange, absent of his usual joviality. "What happened? Are you hurt anywhere? Should I take you to the hospital?"

His bright blue eyes are full of worry—his intense gaze searches my face—and I feel like I can breathe again at the sight of them. Some of the tightness in my chest recedes.

My cheeks flush in embarrassment. I wish he wasn't seeing me this way.

"No. I had a panic attack. I've had one before. I just need a moment," I explain, my voice weak and shaking. I push his hands away and lay down fully on the ground and shut my eyes, wishing the world would stop spinning.

I hear him hesitate as he considers what to do next. Maybe he's wondering if he should push me, insist on taking me somewhere. But then he does the last thing I would have expected. He lays down beside me, his arm barely touching mine.

And for a few short moments, or maybe an eternity, we let the drizzle fall on us while I try with all my might to pull the pieces of myself back together. In those moments, I fight a whole war.

Then, I open my eyes and watch him watching me. He looks so worried, his forehead crinkled up in concern. I draw strength from his closeness, the rhythm of his steady breaths. We lay there until my breathing starts to slow down, sounding more like his.

Eventually he sits up, and I do, too, mirroring him.

"How did this happen?" he asks, voice rough. With painstaking care, he takes each of my hands in his own to examine them. I watch his jaw flex as he looks at the lacerations across my palms, red roping slices on my fingers.

"The vines." I nod toward the statue of the sisters, my voice constricted. "I couldn't get them off." I sound crazy.

Maybe I am crazy.

"Come on, let's get you back to the house," he says gently.

He stands up and tries to help pull me up by my arm, but my legs are stiff from the cold ground, so I stumble a little.

In a blink, he's sliding his arms around me and scooping me up. My head rests against his shoulder, cheek brushing his athletic jacket, damp from the rain.

"How did you know where to find me?" I ask.

"I didn't." His voice is a deep rumble against my ear, warm and reassuring. "Max and I were out for a walk in the woods. He started barking and took off in this direction. I followed him to you. Do you want to tell me what you were doing out here and why you did that to the vines?"

I take a moment before answering him. "I used to watch thunderstorms in the conservatory with Rowan and Ben. I came out here to do that... and then... it was so different from what I remembered. Everything is destroyed and overgrown. It was just too much. Too much on top of a few days of too much. So, I started having a panic attack," I explain, voice wavering. I can still feel the dark claws in my brain; the tightness in my chest. "I still am."

He glances down at me.

"Millie, I need you to close your eyes and picture yourself somewhere peaceful. What's your favorite place?"

"Why?"

"This works, trust me."

I let out a reluctant breath.

"The porch in the summertime."

"Tell me all about it." I can hear the smile back in his voice, relieved that I'm participating.

My words are clipped at first, but then they grow stronger. I tell him about blue skies, white puffy clouds, summer wind whipping across the lake and teasing my hair as I sit and read my book. I'm lounging in a low-slung Adirondack chair, and Rowan is there. We drink iced tea in fancy cut crystal tumblers and talk about silly things and important things, while the sun turns our cheeks pink, and we stare out over the glittering water. I catch Rowan up on my dreams and wishes and gossip about family. We watch my brother play in the lake with friends, the echoes of their laughter traveling up to us on the warm wind. It's a perfect day.

As I picture it, I feel the reassuring beat of Ethan's heart. The rhythm of his steps through the forest. His deep steadying breaths. Some of the chill in my bones gets chased away as he cradles me against his warmth.

I look up at him with a clear gaze. His eyes are fixed ahead on the trail, determined. There are raindrops in his beard. I can feel his arms around me, squeezing me tight.

My panic is gone.

Embarrassment, though—that's in full force. I feel all raw and jagged and weird. We're almost at the inn now. Max trots ahead of us, past the last of the trees, their trunks dark from the rain, and up the flagstone steps to the house. He goes onto the steps of the enclosed back porch, taking a double step to skip over that one broken stair.

"Will you come inside with me?" I ask. He feels like an anchor—like if he lets go, I'll float away, disappear into a nightmare again.

"I'm not letting you out of my sight," Ethan says tightly, then the porch door swings behind us, closing with a bang. "Let's get some of these wet layers off." He sets me down in the sunroom.

Max shakes, and cold drops of water fly everywhere, splashing sun-bleached cushions on wicker furniture.

It's so hard to take a coat off when it hurts to use your hands. Especially a soaking wet wool one. I struggle for a few humiliating moments.

"I need help," I say, defeated.

Ethan pulls off his wet outer layers and is beside me in a moment, peeling off my coat one arm at a time, then dropping down on one knee to pull off my boots.

"Thank you," I mutter to the top of his head.

"Max, you're all muddy. Stay here, I'll be right back." Then he opens the door into the inn for me.

CHAPTER NINE

Stiff from the cold, I climb the winding stairs up to my bedroom. Ethan pushes past me into the bathroom and starts filling up my tub with steaming hot water. My pretty bathroom, with white marble floors and a gorgeous clawfoot tub in the middle, looks small with him in it. I think about sinking into the warm water, and bite back a moan. I'm cold all the way down to my bones.

"Get in, get warm. I'll be right back. I'm going to get the first aid kit and some firewood."

He pulls the bathroom door shut with a click and I listen to his footsteps recede. I start to grab my shirt to pull it over my head, but bending my fingers makes the fresh cuts on my skin flex and bleed.

Tears of frustration spring to my eyes as I try to unbutton my jeans. It's impossible. Each movement brings debilitating pain. I'll be up here for hours if I try to get undressed. I feel pathetic.

I hear footsteps up the stairs. Creaking floorboards in my room. Then the thump of logs being piled on the floor followed by the strike of a match.

Choice one is for me to get undressed myself, agonizingly slowly, continuing to open all the cuts on my hands. Choice two, stand here shivering in wet clothes, possibly for the rest of my life.

Or... my nerves flutter in my stomach at the thought of choice three, as I listen to Ethan building a fire on the other side of the door.

Can I ask him to undress me? Completely platonically.

Should I trust him?

As far as I know, Ethan's moral compass always points due north. I remember how hard he tried to keep my brother and their friends out of trouble. One summer—Ben couldn't have been more than thirteen—he and the youngest Russo son, Tony, stole fireworks from a fireworks stand. Before Rowan even found out about it, Ethan made Ben and Tony return what they stole and apologize to the shop owner.

I can't think of a single memory where he's been anything but the most trustworthy. He won't take advantage of me. I'm sure of it.

But can I trust me? Am *I* going to behave?

I feel a swoop low in my belly, remembering how I felt as soon as he found me—knowing in that vulnerable moment that everything would be OK because he was there. I can still feel where his hands pressed into my body while he carried me here, the brush of his fingers on my face, his eyes on mine.

"Um, Ethan?" I call through the door, swallowing any pride I have left after the embarrassment of my day. And my nerves, which are entirely because of the way I'm realizing he makes me feel, and not because I feel unsafe.

"Yeah?" His answer is muffled.

"I need you to help me get undressed." I look at the crystal doorknob and think about how bad it will hurt to touch it. "You can come in."

"You need me to do *what*?" I can hear the smile in his voice. He's opened the door only a crack so he can hear me but is still standing on the other side where he can't see me.

"I still have clothes on," I assure him. "I can't take them off."

He opens the door all the way and leans in the doorway with crossed arms. His eyes are full of concern. Over his shoulder, I can see a small fire in my bedroom hearth. It's crackling merrily, casting an amber glow and filling my room with the fire's warmth.

"Will you help me? But you'll have to do exactly as I say. Like keep your eyes closed when I tell you to."

"Yes, of course."

"No more talking."

He nods, lips pressed together.

"Come here."

He steps into the bathroom, wool socks on the honeycomb tile, and stands facing me in the small space. The faucet is roaring as it fills the tub with water, the steam curling out and fogging the mirror.

"If you are uncomfortable at any moment of this, say something, and I'll stop," he starts to say.

"No talking," I command softly. He presses his lips together again. I think if he isn't allowed to look at me or speak, this should go totally fine—be totally platonic.

"Unbutton my jeans."

With his eyes on mine and nowhere else, he takes a step forward and drops his hands to my waist. He accidentally brushes his thumb against my abdomen.

I inhale sharply.

"Sorry," he apologizes softly, sincerely, before undoing the button. He smells like rain and wood smoke, and I can see that his eyes aren't simply blue—they are hazel with a little bit of copper in them. I wonder if he ever feels butterflies in his belly. Probably not. He just causes them in innocent, unsuspecting women.

"Zipper. And close your eyes."

He shuts his eyes, his handsome face stony with focus, hair damp and plastered to his forehead from the rain. But why am I even noticing? I shouldn't be feeling this way, not after what I just went through.

But I'm only human, and he's breathtaking. Maybe I'm feeling it *because* of what I just went through? I feel my jeans loosen and I listen to the sound of him pulling my zipper down.

"Put your hands on my belt loops and pull my jeans down halfway."

Eyes still closed, his hands glide across my hips until he finds the loops by feel. He has to lean in even closer to me as he works the waistband of my damp jeans down over my butt to my knees. My face is nearly against his chest, and I can feel the blush rising in my cheeks as I take a deep breath in.

"OK, give me a second," I say.

He opens his eyes and takes a step back, putting his hands in his pockets and adding a bit of distance between us. He's pointedly looking at the floor, and not at me.

I sit on the edge of the tub, black panties against the enameled iron, and jeans encircling my knees.

After a deep swallow I say, "Pull them the rest of the way off."

He has to drop to his knees to do this next part. I watch him glance up at my face as he shimmies the wet fabric down my legs and off my ankles one at a time, my socks going with them, his fingertips dragging across my skin.

Then he stands, and his eyes drop to my lips. I can see how fast his chest is rising and falling.

My breath hitches.

"Millie—" His voice is tender.

"No talking. Close your eyes," I snap, and take another moment to compose myself.

He does as he's told, and I study the shape of the millwork instead of the shape of his shoulders, telling myself to recite the pledge of allegiance. I cool my jets—he's only doing this because he's kind. I need help, nothing more.

I step toward him and guide his hands one at a time to the hem of my shirt.

"Take my shirt off," I say, my voice a whisper.

He slides it up over my torso and chest, past my head and catches my hair, then drops it on the floor.

I shiver from the cold and adrenaline as I stand there in only my black cheeky panties and matching bra. My eyes dart up to his face, where his eyes are still shut tight. His breathing is a little ragged, his chest rising and falling even faster than before.

It would be so easy to stand on my tiptoes and press my lips to his. I spin around so my back is facing him.

"Open your eyes and unhook my bra."

I wait a moment, but nothing happens. He didn't hesitate the other times I gave him an order, so I peek over my shoulder at him.

Goosebumps erupt all over my skin as I watch his eyes climb up me, catching on my lean legs, my plump butt, the black straps of my bra, and the curve of my neck. He is biting his lip, his hands clenched into fists at his sides.

I feel lightheaded. It has nothing to do with what happened outside today and everything to do with the hungry way he is looking at me in this moment.

"Do you know how to unhook a bra?" I dare with a raised eyebrow. "Maybe if you shaved your beard, you would get more practice."

That snaps him out of it.

"Sorry," he murmurs, shaking his head. His eyes are dark, his voice pitched lower than normal. He steps closer and I shiver as his breath caresses my shoulder. He unhooks my bra, taking the utmost care to not touch any of my skin.

Then he's gone, shutting the door tight behind him.

***

I'm discreetly submerged under milky water and lavender-scented foamy bubbles, courtesy of Vanessa Brighton and her bougie gift basket. Just my head and hands are visible, hanging over the side of the tub, when Ethan softly knocks on the door.

"I'm sorry to bother you. We need to bandage your hands up."

"You can come in."

He settles on the floor next to the tub and takes my hand in his. I expect my body to react to his touch but the spell from before is broken, and we are both clear-headed.

"This is going to hurt, I'm sorry." He swipes hydrogen peroxide over my palm and fingers. I wince at the bubbling sting. He notices and blows gently on the peroxide until I feel the sting receding.

"What got you so upset today?"

"Do you always go for walks in thunderstorms? It seems like a bad idea," I deflect.

"No. I thought we would be able to get a quick run in between the rain showers. We headed out as soon as it started to let up. Max gets wild if we skip our morning hike."

"I should probably go for more runs," I say. But I don't mean it. I loathe running. I would rather keep my soft bits soft than torture myself.

"Millie. Stop stalling."

"It's dumb, though."

"So? Tell me anyway."

I let out a resigned sigh.

"Well, I am graduating soon, and I don't know what I'm going to do next and it's freaking me out. History lives in words and objects that are tangible and categorized and archived. It's all about things that have already happened—I suppose I am someone who struggles with the abstraction of the future and what comes next. I can find the answers to most questions in a book or online, but not the future. I'm a planner. I'm a creature of habit. I've been living in the same apartment with my brother and best friend and going to the same campus for five years. I had so much upheaval after my dad died. We bounced from house to house to house. I finally made a little home in my apartment, and I guess, thinking about parting with it, with my roommates, was weighing heavily on me."

I pause for a moment, then continue, "And I'm worried that I won't be able to get a job after graduation, so every snide remark that my stepfather said about my irresponsible choice to be a history major will come true. I'll have to move back in with my mom and stepdad, and...we don't get along. I avoid him so much that I've hardly seen my mom the last few years. I mean, she and I didn't have the best relationship to begin with, but now it's even more strained." I stop, embarrassed that I've trailed off.

"None of us know what comes next, Millie," Ethan says. "Trust yourself that you'll figure it out."

"You sound like you're speaking from experience."

"I never thought I would find myself moving back to this town. It was completely unplanned and unexpected but I am so much happier for it."

I lean over the tub and watch him spread antibiotic ointment over my hand with a cotton swab. I want to ask him about his past, but before I do, he interjects. "Enough about me. Go on. What else is bothering you so much?"

I push through my discomfort. Somehow, talking to him like this feels as intimate as him undressing me earlier.

"I've been fighting with my brother for so long that I can't remember what we're fighting about. The last few months, he's barely been able to look me in the eye. The energy in our apartment is all weird and awkward. Since the day I got here, I've wanted to talk to him about this place, but he won't answer my messages and I don't know how to fix it."

I take a shaky breath and get to the heart of it. "And Rowan died," I say, my voice breaking.

"Rowan died," Ethan repeats. "It's so hard to say out loud."

We sit silently together in a moment of reverent grief.

"My days feel sort of disconnected from reality because of it. Like it's too terrible to be true, and I'm living in an awful alternate reality."

Ethan nods, then kindly looks away from my face while I cry.

"I don't know if his death was an accident or if it was on purpose and I think about it every day. I can't get it out of my head. And I'll never forgive myself for not spending more time with him while I had the chance. The regret is..."

I trail off, searching for the word.

"It's suffocating," Ethan whispers.

It does feel like it's stealing all my air, making me sick with panic. "I wonder, if I had been here, maybe it wouldn't have happened."

"Hey," he says, turning to look at my face. "There's nothing you could have done. If he did go over that cliff on purpose, then it is a choice that he made. It was not your choice. The guilt of it should not fall on your shoulders. I *was* here and it didn't make a difference."

He takes a breath, then continues, "I think about that weekend all the time. I play it through to the end, rewind and pause on the uncomfortable parts, the parts where maybe I should have said something different or done something different. And I obsess over it. But for what? I'll never get any answers this way. Nothing good will come of it—it's going to eat me alive until there's nothing left, the obsessive wondering. So, you have to make a choice not to. You have to forgive yourself. Do you hear me, Millie? You have to forgive yourself. Or choose someone else to blame, to protect yourself. You can blame me if you want to. But there's nothing you can do to undo it."

Tears start rolling down my cheeks again.

"The grief will never go away completely. It's in us forever. It's part of who we are now. But it does get easier. Someday, it will feel like part of the story of who you are. Instead of the whole story."

"How do you know all this?"

"Because I say it to myself all the time."

"Does it work?"

He shrugs, turning back to my hand. "Some days."

I let my tears fall until I don't have any more. Ethan sits beside me in comfortable, silent support. I stare at the chandelier above me, and I notice little figures on it. I can't tell what they are from this far away. Little fairies, probably, or birds.

"When I was standing in the conservatory, I realized this isn't my home anymore. And without it, I don't have one. Not really. I love this place," I admit to him. "I love the character it has in its ugly rooms. The creaking floors and beautiful finishes and marble fireplaces in nearly every room. The glass knobs and heavy wooden doors. The ornate beauty and whimsicality that you never see in new houses these days. Just look at this tub. Look at its little feet! Lion paws. If you pick any place in the house and sit down awhile and stare and study, you'll see something new each time. Did you know the fireplace grate in Room 5 has fairies on it?"

He shakes his head.

"It does. They are hiding in the flowers. None of the other fireplace grates has that. Some of the corbels have—"

"Gargoyles."

"Yeah! There are at least seven I've counted. Scowling and laughing at us."

"Twelve."

"Twelve? Huh. And that little bit of stained glass on the stairway with a crow."

"It's a starling."

"Oh, yeah, that makes sense. See, every day I'm in this house I see something new, I learn something new. Every corner tells a story. And I have so many beautiful memories here. So, part of me *needs* to be here and knows that I'm doing the right thing by taking care of Rowan's affairs for him and this house. But another part of me just can't handle it—I can't handle being here when Rowan isn't, erasing evidence of him room by room."

The silence stretches between us, and I watch bubbles pop and swirl on the water.

"Is it possible to hate something and love something at the same time?"

The *tap, tap, tapping* pushes into my ears, that spooky staccato beat.

"Absolutely," he says with conviction.

"I think I hate it here as much as I love it. Sometimes I feel like I can't breathe. I've never been so on edge in my life. I can't sleep. I've been seeing things." Hair in the walls. A locked door. Finding items in different places than where I left them.

I turn my head to look at him. He's sitting with his legs stretched out in front of him, crossed at the ankles. My hand is draped over the tub and resting in his. He paused mending it long ago but neither of us moved apart.

"Ethan, I think this place is haunted."

He should laugh at me. I brace myself for it. There's no such thing as ghosts, he should say. But he doesn't.

"You know what chases away ghosts, right?" he murmurs in that deep voice.

I shake my head, tears shining in my eyes.

"Laughing, good food, sunshine, spending time with people you love, keeping yourself busy with something that brings you peace." He pronounces each word slowly, like they are sacred. And I suppose they are, really.

"And warm bubble baths?" I ask.

"And warm bubble baths."

CHAPTER TEN

Ethan stands up and moves to the other side of the bathtub. My gaze follows him as he sits on the floor and takes my other hand in his and starts cleaning it.

"This one is deep. I'm making a butterfly bandage for it, but the rest are superficial scratches and should heal quickly."

"How do you know how to do this?"

"My girlfriend was an ER doctor," he says.

"Was a girlfriend or was an ER doctor?"

"No longer my girlfriend, still an ER doctor," he clarifies.

"Got it."

I hide a smile. I don't have any business feeling happy that he doesn't have a girlfriend.

"And I've had plenty of practice with your uncle. He turned up at my place drunk with a huge gash on his forehead, blood all over his face, bottle of whiskey in his hand."

"That doesn't sound like Rowan at all."

"How much did you know him as an adult?"

"Not as much as you, apparently. Why is that? Tell me."

His gaze moves from my hand to my face. He starts to talk, then pauses with a shake of his head, like he's changed his mind.

"Millie, it's such a long story. And it's someone else's sad story. Enough heartbreak for today. You should be focusing on yourself right now. Do something that helps you relax and get well."

I pull my hands back.

"I promise I will tell you everything, just not right now."

He's keeping something from me. What, though? There are so many mysteries in this place, and I can't figure out how Ethan fits into them.

I hold my hands up in front of me and study his handiwork. I'm all cleaned and bandaged and waterproofed. I bend my fingers, and it hurts considerably less. I flash back to the moment when I did all this damage to myself. I was so completely lost in my head that I didn't feel it happening.

He crumbles up bandage wrappers and tosses them in the trash. Snaps the first aid kit closed, and steps toward the door.

"I'll be right outside for a while, fixing the broken stair on the porch." He starts to pull the door closed. "I'll check on you before I leave."

"Hey Ethan?" I ask, before he shuts the door all the way.

"Yeah?"

"Thank you."

I try not to think about the level of despair I'd be in right now if I woke up on my own at the conservatory and had to hobble home on shivering legs, pull myself out of wet clothes with painful bleeding hands, then sort through all these feelings alone.

"You're welcome. Text if you need anything. You should try to get some rest."

Then he's gone, and it's only me and my thoughts and this bathtub, warming me to my bones.

Back in my apartment, the cheap acrylic shower bathtub enclosure isn't deep enough for me to submerge my whole body. Plus, the water gets cold after ten minutes, so I have to keep refilling it with hot water every so often. Then, I would step out of the tub and into a cold bathroom, shivering my way into pajamas. I've done it a total of one time and decided it wasn't worth the trouble.

But this clawfoot tub? It is deep enough for me to sink my whole body all the way in. It's made from cast iron, and it is retaining all the heat from the hot water. So, I sit and soak and float and breathe in the lavender until I feel my stress melting away, the stiffness leaving. I stare at the gilded chandelier above me as I wash away my troubles and the crazy events of this morning feel like a distant memory.

I can't get his blue eyes out of my head, or the relief I felt when I saw him. Would I have felt that way if it was anyone else? No, I don't think so.

I'm almost uncomfortably hot when I finally haul myself out of the tub and gingerly towel off. It hurts my hands but is bearable. I step into my room, which is blissfully heated by the fire. I stretch in front of the hearth and thank Ethan mentally. Again.

The room swims around me, and I feel dizzy with exhaustion, the crash that comes after a panic attack and the nights of broken sleep. If only I could sleep in this godforsaken house.

I hear a quick buzz of power tools coming from outside my window, the sound of Ethan cutting a new stair tread. I notice that the blinds are propped open to let the sunshine in.

I feel the bed shift slightly as Frank jumps in. He nudges my hand, like he's checking on me. I guess he isn't so bad after all.

I wonder if I'll be able to sleep easier knowing that I'm not alone. Reassuring bright light streaming in from the windows. I don't bother getting dressed before I dive under the covers.

***

I wake up feeling rested and clear headed for the first time in a week.

And hungry.

I roll over and grab my phone off my nightstand to check the time.

3 p.m.? I can't believe I slept for six hours straight.

Still no messages from Sarah and Ben. But one message from Ethan.

Ethan: Call me when you wake up.

He answers on the first ring.

"Hey, how are you feeling?" he asks, his voice wrapping around me like a hug.

"Rested. For the first time in days," I admit.

"Good. You scared me today."

"I scared me, too."

"I checked on you before I left, and you were still asleep. I didn't want to wake you. But I had to head home to meet a client."

"Thank you, Ethan. How'd you get so good at taking care of people?"

He doesn't say anything.

"You just shrugged, didn't you?"

"How did you know?"

"You do it all the time. Ethan fixes something, shrugs. Ethan helps me clean out the attic, shrugs. Rescues me in an amazingly kind, grand gesture, shrugs. Like it's no big deal."

"It's not a big deal."

"Yeah, it was. Most people would not have done what you did today. Thank you. And thanks to good boy Max, too."

He changes the subject. "I'm installing the new locks on your house tomorrow morning."

"Thank you."

"How else can I help you feel safe?"

"Did you hear the knocking sound when you were here? Like that tapping sound—it sounds like it's coming from the walls." I'm almost afraid to ask, because if he says no, what does that make me?

"Yeah," he says, and I let out a sigh of relief. "That's water hammer. Old pipes with pressure built up in them can make knocking sounds. We can fix it. Have to drain all the pipes in the house and it should stop. If it doesn't, we can put a water arrestor in. Did you know Joe Russo is a plumber? We can call him tomorrow and see when he can stop by for a better look."

Just old pipes. Water pressure.

"I appreciate all you've done for me."

Silence stretches between us.

"I'll see you tomorrow morning. Don't do anything stressful tonight and take care of yourself."

***

I pour myself the last glass of shitty gift basket wine, and head back up to my room. That's harsh—it's not shitty. For drinking alone after a weird day, this wine is hitting just right.

I pull an old bodice-ripper of a romance novel out of my bag and bring it to my tufted sofa along with my sandwich.

I sit cross-legged and try to get lost in a book. A perfect sugary confection of a story, comforting and heart lifting and familiar and a guaranteed escape from my current circumstances. Reading romance novels is one of my favorite forms of therapy.

But it's hard to stay focused on the pages. Despite the main character being described as lanky and brunette, my mind keeps replacing him with a beefy blonde.

I push my book aside, pull out my phone, and spend a while searching before I find him on social media. He only has one account, and he stopped updating it about four years ago. There aren't any pictures of himself. A few artsy architectural shots of interesting buildings. Lots of pictures of Max's familiarly pointy-eared profile. And... bugs? A ladybug on a metal handrail. A spider suspended in a tree branch, dew sparkling on its web, the city skyline unfocused in the background. A centipede on concrete.

"Weirdo."

He was tagged in a few pictures by @dremily. I click on her account and find a picture of Ethan with a stunning girl tucked underneath his arm.

I scroll through her perfectly framed shots of healthy, brightly colored food. A clip of her running in a marathon for charity. More pictures of Max. Her arms around girlfriends at a bar, dotted with an occasional picture of Ethan in the city, looking suave in sunglasses. She's always smiling brightly, one of those people who radiates. There's a video of her in scrubs, talking passionately about her career. In the holiday pictures, she's surrounded by a whole complete family, all of them as lovely as her. It seems like she's killing it in life and she's doing it with the silkiest, straightest hair.

Something flares in my chest. Am I jealous?

There are no recent pictures of her and Ethan. But there isn't a new guy in her life either.

I turn off my phone.

It doesn't matter that I like him. I'll be selling this place and leaving soon. Besides, he probably thinks I'm unhinged, with all this fainting in the conservatory and talking about ghosts.

CHAPTER ELEVEN

A KNOCK SOUNDS AT the front door, and it can only be one person.

And I'm buried under blankets on the couch like a groundhog. I was trying to finish my book, which I've finally sunken into. It's late morning but I still haven't gotten dressed. I'm doing what Ethan suggested and letting myself take a break from the packing and cleaning and classwork and emotion bombs.

I jump off the couch like it is lava for some reason and try to toss my loose messy waves into something presentable. When I pull the door open, I'm blushing furiously and probably *look* like I've been reading a romance novel.

He's wearing a smirk and a tool belt low on his hips. I suddenly feel shy.

"How are your hands?" Ethan asks, following me inside. I sit back down on my cozy couch nest.

"They hurt. On the mend, though, thanks to you."

"I have the locks in my truck. I can get started now if that's OK with you. And I wanted to drop these off, too," he says, holding what looks like a bag of groceries. I spy the box of croissants on top and greedily reach in. I flip open the white lid to grab one, then sink my teeth in with a groan.

"Are you going to bring these every morning?"

"Probably," he says, blue eyes flickering to mine. "How's your brain?"

"Better," I answer truthfully around a mouthful of croissant.

He spots the book I left on the couch. The muscled fellow missing his shirt on the cover is a clear indicator of what it's about.

I not-so-smoothly push past him and pull a blanket over it in a desperate *nothing to see here* way.

A polite person would not say anything. I meet his eyes and silently plead with him not to. Of course, he can't resist.

"So, this is how you cheer yourself up?" he asks, putting his hands on his hips. "Do you have a real boyfriend or only imaginary ones?"

I didn't know how this morning would go after all the intense intimacy yesterday. I suffered a mental break, unloaded all my grievances, and asked him to take my clothes off. I was certain that today would be awkward.

But right away he's goading me into our familiar banter. I silently thank him for it and rise to the challenge.

"No boyfriends, real or imaginary. Though, I did have Stephen to keep me company." I gesture at the mannequin head we found in the attic, whom I've named. He is now propped up on the lobby desk, a grotesque receptionist. The longer I look at Stephen, the less I hate him. He's kind of dapper, reminding me of a caricature of a handsome man from vintage print ads.

"Were you up late last night, drinking cheap beer and banging doe-eyed country girls in the back of your pickup truck while you listen to shitty country music?" I continue, with my hand on my hip, my voice saccharine sweet.

"That is so specific and unnecessarily harsh. I feel like you thought about that one for a long time. But I don't drink or listen to country music."

"I did, yeah, thanks. It came to me a few days ago but you were so nice yesterday, I didn't get to use it."

"But you've been thinking about what goes on in the back of my truck." His eyes are dark on mine, and a slow smile is spreading across his face. I hate that he knows what I look like in my underwear.

"What? No," I stammer. "It's just so stupid and big. The Earth is dying, you know. You should be more eco-conscious."

"The lady doth protest too much." He turns toward the kitchen stairs. "I can't haul 10-foot boards in the back of a tiny car like yours."

"Stop bothering me. Aren't I paying you to work on this house?" I follow him down the stairs to the kitchen, where he is unpacking a bag of groceries into my fridge.

"You aren't paying me yet actually. I haven't sent you an invoice."

"Oh, yeah. Why are you here again?"

"Masochism," he starts, then changes his tone to something more serious. "To check on you. And I don't know. Rowan would want me here, helping you. You seem like you need it. Or maybe I am having a hard time letting go of this place. I'm at your whim for the next few weeks, 'til the memorial."

"Is that why you're putting vegetables in the refrigerator? Because you think Rowan would want you taking care of me?"

He finishes unpacking the bag, turning to look at me, his hands in his coat pockets. He *really* looks at me, head to toe. I'm wearing an oversized t-shirt that stops mid-thigh. No bra. My hair is tossed over one shoulder. My cheeks heat under his gaze. I'm not presentable. He should have texted first, and I would have gotten dressed.

I can tell he wants to say something, but he breaks eye contact first.

"Um," he starts, clearing his throat, "I'll get started. Replacing the locks on the doors. It shouldn't take too long."

***

I pull on jeans and a sweater and join Frank for a walk to the cemetery. I linger longer than usual, taking in the names on the headstones.

"Who are you, Catherine?" I ask, running my fingertips over her name. I think about the history of this place, the generations of this family on this land. I wonder what triumphs and hardships they faced, and how they shaped their local community.

As I walk home, I work through whether I could write my thesis about them, about the Starling Inn. I have to do the research anyway, to find out if the house is historically significant enough to be on the National Register of Historic Places. I might as well kill two birds with one stone. I would need to find enough primary source material. The ledgers we found in the attic would be a good start.

As soon as the Inn's spotty Wi-Fi is within distance, I send an email to the local archives, requesting an appointment.

"I have to head out," Ethan says as I step up onto the porch. "The keys are on the lobby counter." It's only noon, but he's finished replacing locks already. Hopefully, this deterrent will keep my poltergeist away.

"How much do I owe you?"

He hands me the receipt for the locks. No invoice for his time. I push for him to bill me for his services, but he waves me away again.

"Why are you doing this for free?"

"I'm not, I'm prepaid."

"By Rowan?"

"Yes."

"In that case, you could have taken the money and gone. No one would have known."

He shrugs a mountainous shoulder. "What's next, boss?"

"Painting. And one of the bedrooms upstairs—it's locked, and I can't find the old hotel key. I was wondering if you could break it open?"

"I can bust it open, but it would damage the door. Which I would rather not do. Why don't we wait awhile and see if the key turns up first? It's bound to, with all the sorting and cleaning you're doing."

"Can't you pop it off the hinges?"

"Yeah, if they were on the outside of the door, but they are not."

"Right. Do you know what's in that room?

"Not exactly. It's been locked for as long as I can remember."

"Don't you think that's strange? Mysterious?"

He shrugs again but I can tell his nonchalance is feigned. There's an edge in his tone when he says, "I don't think there's a mystery there. Just a stuck door, and a room full of old junk."

"OK." I back off, acquiescing at his tone. But what does he know? And why is he hiding it? "We also need some plaster repaired in the hallway. I thought I saw something."

"What do you mean you saw something?"

"Hair? Sticking out of the wall. I was trying to find what it came from, and... I damaged the wall," I admit.

"It's horse tail hair. I'm surprised you didn't know this, Miss I-Know-Everything-About-History."

"I don't know," I bristle, and vow to read up on Victorian construction and architecture, "everything about history, asshole."

"Builders used to mix horsehair into the wet plaster to add strength, and to prevent cracking. It was common at the time this place was built. Speaking of cracking, are you sure you're alright?" he asks me again, changing the subject, his brows bunched.

"I'm fine," I assure him, biting my lip. "Mostly just embarrassed."

He steps a bit closer, and gently takes my hand in his own, his gaze raking over the bandages there. Mine are cold from my walk, and his are so warm. "There's no reason to be. I'm here anytime you need someone to talk to."

"Thank you, Ethan, for everything."

"You're welcome, Millie." I like how my name sounds when he says it. "I'm going to head out. I have an order to finish this afternoon. But I'll see you tomorrow."

***

I open a guest register with the year 1924 on the cover and flip to a random page. There are hand-drawn columns spanning across both the cream-colored pages. Date checked in, date checked out, room number, guest name. Cafeteria. Guest signature. Notes. Bisecting the columns are rows and rows of names and numbers. A tally of the amount owed, and the amount paid.

I run my finger across August 15, 1924. John Conte, Room Six. Cafeteria—$154. Hotel—$200. I wonder who John Conte was, and what he was doing in town for a month. His signature is practiced and tidy. I flip through the pages, wondering at each entry. The last guest visited the inn in 1957—a Miss Elizabeth Howe.

The Starling family owned the Inn from the date it was built until my uncle purchased it from them about twenty years ago, but this is the last date it was in operation. I suppose they only used it as a residence after that.

Scanning over the guest registers, I see there's one that stands out from the rest. It's thin, the cover decorated with filigree. I pull open its pages, expecting the same guest information and find something entirely different.

Mrs. Tabitha Lowe on the 3rd of November 1920 attests to unnatural cold spots in her room.

Mr. John Frank accounts a persistent flickering of lights in the dining room on the 12th of December.

Ms. Basil, the scullery maid, reports the daily relocation of her laundry basket.

Goosebumps rise on my arms and legs, skittering up my neck.

"It's not real, Frank. It's probably marketing to attract people to the Inn. People who craved supernatural encounters."

Battling with myself, I shut this ledger for now. It's morbidly fascinating, but I know if I read it all I won't be able to sleep. I turn back to the hotel registers and continue note taking until the sun is near setting, then I pause to make myself dinner.

When I open the pantry, my eyes widen in surprise. It's all mason jars and handmade goods, like what you would see at a farmer's market. I open the fridge. There's a carton of eggs in an unbranded box and half-gallon of milk in a glass jug. Garden fresh vegetables. I was so distracted by him when he was unpacking that I didn't notice.

I grab a mason jar of natural peanut butter, the oil still floating on top. I stir it up and slice up a loaf of crusty fresh bread. There isn't any jelly but there is a jar of apple butter, so I make myself the first and best peanut apple butter sandwich I've ever had. I thank Ethan silently as I take a bite of the salty, sweet, crunchy, cinnamon sandwich.

Ethan is hiding something.

But he's also so incredibly kind. He's taking care of me in small ways and big ways. Should I prod and uncover his secrets?

No.

I surprise myself. I don't want to figure this out. I trust that he will tell me in time. When he's ready. I owe him that much.

After I finish eating, I head upstairs to my room to sort through the next box of books we found in the attic. This one is mostly filled with business ledgers—dusty, thin-spined accounting books. A business history of the Starling Inn documented in volumes over time. The leather covers are crumbling to velvety dust in my hands, and they emit a strangely sweet smell from red rot.

My phone dings, and I reach across to it, my heart lifting in hopes that it is Sarah or Ben. But it's not. Just a text from my mom, reminding me to request extra copies of Rowan's death certificate from the coroner for insurance purposes.

I add this to my mental to-do list, mute my notifications and keep working.

CHAPTER TWELVE

I JOLT UPRIGHT IN bed, spurred by the deafening, terrified, and high-pitched scream of a woman outside.

I thought it was all over. But with a revelation that I can feel deep in my belly, I admit that it's all real. The nightmares, the terrors, the attic, the locked door, and blazing fire. Symbols on the doorway, cursing me, marking the house for something.

I stumble out of bed and run to the window, searching for the woman who screamed. I can barely make out the edges of the forest illuminated by the porch light, trees twisting in the wind.

She screams again, and I jump. All my nerves are telling me to do something. There aren't any words but it's shrill and panicked, like she's crying for help.

But I can't see her.

As I pick up my phone from the nightstand, I think about calling the police but remember how they had laughed at me last time. They wouldn't get here urgently. Officer Thickneck would roll over here in a lazy hour or two, ready to stare at my cleavage and tell me I'm a fool.

I dial and put the phone to my ear, pacing the room and flipping on the lights.

"What's wrong?" Ethan asks in greeting, his voice husky from sleep.

"I can hear someone outside," I say, pacing the room. "They sound hurt. I'm not sure what to do."

"It's just a fox, city girl. It woke me up, too."

"No way. It sounds like someone being tortured."

"It's definitely a fox. They've been bothering us for a while. I can put a trap out."

While he talks, I stop pacing. I sit back down on my bed and open my laptop to search for clips of foxes. I find one and press play. He's right. The horrific caterwauling out my window is just a fox.

"Why, cute little fox? Why are you so strange and screamy sounding in the middle of the night? Wait, you're going to trap it? Don't kill it."

I stand up and start pacing again.

"No, I'm not going to kill a fox. Trap and release. Somewhere far away from here. Far, far away."

"You're close enough to hear it, too? Where are you?"

"About a mile from you, in one of the outbuildings."

I freeze.

"When you said you lived next door, I thought you meant at Maria's."

"No. I'm on your property. I thought someone told you already, or it would have been the first thing out of my mouth when I came over."

"I had no idea."

"I'm so sorry, I hope I'm not making you uncomfortable. I'll be gone before you list the property. I'm applying for jobs all over the country and planning to relocate."

"OK. That was a lot of information." I should feel more alarmed by this. That he lives here, close by, and we're so isolated.

But still, part of me is relieved that he's not too far away if I need him. Because weird things keep happening here and he's my answering-the-phone-on-the-first-ring friend. Rescuing me in the rain, taking care of me friend.

There is still something that he is holding back, but I feel like I can trust him anyway.

I blow out a breath. "Anyone else live here that I don't know about?"

"Just me and Max," he reassures me. "Millie. I know you're dealing with a lot, and I don't want you to worry about me being here. Please don't let it bother you or affect any of your plans. If I don't get a job offer fast enough, I'll stay at Maria's or Joe's."

"Which outbuilding?"

"Do you remember the apple orchard?"

"Of course." There weren't many apples. It was all wild and wicked and overgrown, branches snagging at my clothes when I was a kid.

"There's a building next to it—used to be used for apple storage and processing."

"I remember. Rowan said he thought they used to make hard cider there."

"Yeah, we found a sill, too. So not only hard cider. Moonshine. Anyway, the building hadn't been used in the last fifty or so years, so Rowan told me to set up my wood shop here after I started helping with the inn, to make the project go smoother. About a year ago, I converted the second floor into an apartment. Stop by tomorrow if you want. I'll be working in my woodshop, but you are welcome to show yourself around."

I soak in the details, grateful that he's finally opening up a little. I have so many questions.

"I would like to see it all again. It's been so long," I say as I turn off the lights in my bedroom, and get back in my bed, cuddling up around my phone.

"Are you OK? Do you want me to come over?" He's not laughing at me for once. His voice is low and gravelly with sleep, and listening to it feels intimate. His bedroom voice. His pillow talk voice.

I think about him in the room next to mine, only a door and a wall between us. My pulse quickens in response.

"No need. I'm feeling a little silly now. Just a fox."

"Don't feel silly. You can call me any time you are scared."

"That's most of the time. I'd always be on the phone with you."

"I don't mind."

His words settle over me like a blanket.

The silence stretches between us for a few heartbeats. But I don't want to hang up yet. I'm full of all the questions I want to ask him. And I don't want to be alone in the house again. I want someone on the phone a little while longer.

"Ethan, what's in Room 3?"

He lets out a sigh, low and breathy. "Oh Millie, it's a long story."

"So, you *do* know," I push.

"I've never been inside, but I know."

"What is it?"

"Good night, Millie," he says, and his voice is velvet as he deflects me. "Or should I call you Nancy Drew?"

"Ethan—"

"Good night. Watch out for foxes." He's chuckling when he disconnects, that low rumbling laugh. The sound replays in my head until I fall asleep.

***

"Did you hang up my coat?" I look down at Frank. "Who hung up my coat?"

I never retrieved it from the back porch, where Ethan had helped me shuck it off after that rainy day in the conservatory. It should still be there, in a damp musty pile on the floor. But it's hanging on the hook in the lobby, dry, right next to the front door.

I look around, unsettled, before shrugging it on.

Frank and I skip the cemetery this morning, and instead we find a break in the trees that I know will lead us to the apple orchard.

It's different than I remember. Pruned clean, less crowded than it used to be, and about half of the trees are now sparsely laden with apples. I walk through one of the tidy rows toward a two-story out-building.

It's painted a fresh bright white with contrasting black trim. The double doors are rolled open to the sunshine. I pause when I catch sight of Ethan. Cabinets line the wall behind him. I spot the stationary machines vented with ductwork, and several workbenches on the well-swept concrete floor. Max lays in the grass like a guardian, eyes and ears fixed on Frank and me, but Ethan hasn't noticed us yet.

He is building something, but I'm too far away to tell what it is. Measure, mark, measure again, cut, inspect. He's concentrating deeply, moving with confidence. I recognize the look on his face. It's the same look I have when I'm centered in yoga. Focused. A meditative ritual.

He's wearing an unbuttoned gray waffle knit Henley, the sleeves pushed up to reveal muscled forearms. A sawdust-speckled black apron protects his front and holds his tape measure. He has a pencil he keeps using then stashing behind his ear. He's wearing earbuds and I wonder what he's listening to.

His beard is a little unkempt, but I don't hate it.

Not really.

Not at all.

I'm under a spell, watching him in his element. He moves over to a bank of wood storage, where the pieces are arranged neatly, and searches for something. He inspects board after board before finally finding what he's looking for. From where I sit, they all look identical, but he's meticulous. He begins the process of measuring, marking, cutting, and inspecting, his brow furrowed in concentration. He bites his lip now and then. I feel like I could watch him do this for hours.

I walk closer so that I'm in his line of sight. He spots me and smiles, and I feel happiness swell in my chest.

Max stands up and wags his tail at Frank. Ethan takes his earbuds out.

"Good morning, Laura Ingalls Wilder," I call out as I walk toward him. "Thanks for all the jams and stuff."

"You're welcome. I see you survived a walk through the woods, city girl. Were you terrorized by any foxes or other adorable woodland creatures?"

"That's not fair. I don't think most people would know foxes sound like that." We're inches apart now, and I'm smiling like a fool. "Hey, did you hang up my coat for me? In the inn?"

He shakes his head. "Why?"

"Oh, it's nothing."

"Did it hang itself up?"

"Yeah," I frown uncertainly. "Maybe I did it and forgot?"

"Maybe. Or maybe not. You wouldn't be the first one to experience strange things at the inn."

"Show me your place," I say, determined to change the subject. The sun is shining, and the morning air is crisp. I want to escape for a moment. I don't want the strange occurrences darkly tumbling around in my mind. Instead, I want to think about bright and beautiful things.

"Welcome to my wood shop," he says with a flourish. "I have to finish this for a client today, but please feel free to snoop around. I'll give you a full tour another day. There is a fresh pot of coffee upstairs."

"Well, if you insist."

I step up a set of stairs at the back of the wood shop, following them into a modern, studio loft apartment. When I breathe in my mouth waters—it smells like coffee and leather and Ethan.

The dark, exposed wooden beam ceiling is balanced by floor-to-ceiling windows overtaking one wall, flooding the space with light. I peer out over the orchard, over the red and orange and gold forest, dotted with evergreens and black branches bare of leaves. I wonder if you could see the inn from here in the winter when some of the tree cover is gone. I bet it's magical in the spring, with the orchard trees blooming, white petals fluttering by.

I turn back to the room. A cast iron wood stove takes up one corner, still giving out residual heat from a morning fire, and Max's bed is right next to it. A navy duvet-topped king-sized bed takes up the other corner. The living room has warm brown leather armchairs and minimalist tables arranged atop a woven rug and wood floors. I wonder if he made any of the furniture himself. Judging by the few pieces I saw in his shop, he definitely has the skill to. There are no hangings on the walls, but if there were, they would be overshadowed by the view out the windows.

The kitchen is sleek with glossy countertops and industrial light fixtures. It's meticulously tidy, not a dish in the sink. Adjoining the kitchen is an equally glossy and equally tidy bathroom.

I want to snoop forever. I want to examine the contents of his bookshelf and refrigerator and medicine cabinet, but politeness doesn't allow, so I pour myself a cup of coffee and reluctantly head back downstairs.

"What do you think?" he asks when he hears my footsteps, but he doesn't look up from what he's working on.

"It's nice." It's much more than nice. It's a cozy masculine retreat. I have the strongest urge to settle in his armchair with a book and take a nap. I wouldn't even mind the racket of the wood shop below—it would be a welcome change from the eerie quiet of being alone at the inn.

"Did you do all this yourself?" I ask. "Last time I was here, it was an unfinished barn and loft filled with old tools."

"I had some help, but yeah," he says, eyes fixed on his work.

I step through a side door into a room filled with rough shelving, loaded with pickled vegetables, jams, two crates of root vegetables, honey, blocks of unsliced natural soap, and plastic-wrapped bakery items. Way more than one person could make, or more than any one person would need. Also, barrels and barrels of apples.

"What is all of this?" I call out to him.

"I barter goods for services sometimes. People don't always have money to pay, and I don't need it anyway. Plus, I have a lot of apples to get rid of, from August through December, since I started restoring the orchard."

"How did you do that?"

"I cut down blighted trees, pruned the others. It took a few seasons, but they started producing again. I started taking them to the farmers market every week to sell. The other regular vendors and I all trade goods with each other. At first, I would split the sale profits with Rowan since they were on his land. But as it turns out, he was banking all the checks I gave him. Then he used that money to help buy me my first saw. I was just an apprentice to another woodworker at the time.

It was a steppingstone for me. One thing led to another, and now I have my own wood shop. And my own apprentices."

I step out of the storage room and back out into the wood shop. I'm running my hands along a chair that is slowly taking shape.

"Well, *you* have a lot of apples to get rid of," he adds, correcting himself. "This is all yours now."

I shrug uncomfortably. "It seems like you've made quite a life here."

A life that can change dramatically on my whim. This is his home, his livelihood, but as soon as I say, or as soon as I sell, he has to leave.

I rethink our interactions with this new bit of perspective. Rescuing me in the rain and listening to me rant endlessly about my troubles. Answering the phone the second I call, every time. Working for free. Bringing me food. Being exceptionally kind and helpful and charming. Letting me snoop through his place.

"Is this why you've been helping me? You don't want me to sell?" My voice wavers with uncertainty.

"What?! No." He takes off his black apron, hangs it up, then removes his work gloves.

"No," he says again with conviction, and steps closer, his hands on his hips. We're only a breath apart now. There's the littlest dusting of sawdust on his shoulder and I stop my hand from reaching up and brushing it off.

"So, are you a tenant here?" I ask, trying to figure this out.

"No. Sort of. It's complicated. But this is not real life," he says, gesturing around. "This is all a fantasy. A temporary one. As much as I love it, it isn't sustainable on its own, and I'm on your property. I've been applying for jobs in the city. I meant it when I said I'll be gone before you sell. I have an interview next week. And the improvements I've made here will help the property appraise higher for you. I'm giving the shop equipment and most of my client list to my apprentice."

I look around the shop. "That hardly seems fair to you."

"It's the fastest way for me to move out. And it's on the condition that I can use them any time I want, when I come back into town."

"You don't seem like a job-in-the-city sort of guy."

"I'm an architect."

"Oh. Like Rowan?"

"Yeah."

"Have you thought about staying, buying the whole place?"

"I have. But then I picture my future and… I don't know what I see. I just know that I don't want to be a lonely old man, stuck here like Rowan was. I want a family someday. I don't want to be tied to this place the way he was."

He's interrupted by a car pulling up behind us, blaring music. I turn to see a Jeep roll to a stop in front of the shop. Ethan seems to notice then how close we are standing to each other and takes a step away from me.

We watch a woman swing herself out of the driver's seat. She has warm brown skin and is wearing a vintage band tee and jeans that hug the sort of curves I've always wished I had. "Ethan?" she calls out with a gorgeous smile.

"Mae." He waves to her. "Come on in. This is Millie. She lives at the inn."

"Hey," Mae says, and I see my reflection in her aviator sunglasses. She looks from me to Ethan and back again with raised eyebrows.

"I'll give you two a minute," I say, and step out into the orchard. I grab a basket from his shop floor on my way, and take my time moving through the trees, picking some of the lower hanging fruit. The apples are cold from the night before and glistening with dew. I take a bite of one, crunchy and sweet. I eat a few and fill my basket before I finally turn back toward his wood shop.

The first thing I see is Mae leaning over his worktable, getting herself as close to him as she possibly can without touching him. He's staring at a piece of paper she's holding out and biting his lip, his arms crossed, that pencil stashed behind his ear. Her gorgeous, joyful laugh rings out at something he's said.

I have the strongest urge to shoo her away.

But what do I care if this girl is flirting with him?

Come on Millie, be real. You're leaving. It doesn't matter who he flirts with.

Though, really, I think it's mostly one sided, the more I observe. I step just a bit closer, my basket in hand, and listen.

"I'm not taking any new orders."

"Look, I know you're booked out for like a year." Mae's tone is whiny. "But this is for my *sister*. You know how important she is to me, and I wanted to know if you could do this one little favor for me, pretty please? I'll make it worth your while."

I leave before I can hear his response.

CHAPTER THIRTEEN

Ethan: My lady, my dearest Millicent, you blowhard.

Millie: What do you want, Ethan?

Ethan: I feel compelled to invite you on a journey with me to the General Store on the morrow.

Millie: WHAT

Ethan: I need your aid, your fine tastes, to procure paint for the walls of the inn.

Millie: Are you talking like this because I called you a Civil War general? Are you asking me to go to the hardware store with you?

Ethan: If you wish to accompany me, I shall escort you astride my black stallion.

Millie: I think that means you're picking me up. What time?

Ethan: Huzzah! I shall arrive at half past 8.

Millie: See you then.

Ethan: I wait with anticipation to lay my eyes on your pale, corpse-like skin, my dearest Millicent, terrible in your beauty, with hair as black as tar. Your smile so bright, sharpened and ready to feast on children.

Millie: You are ridiculous. If I could paint this whole place by myself, I would.

Ethan: Ah! She wounds. I shall take my leave. I look forward to more sparking words at first light.

***

"I thought you said we were going to the hardware store?" I stare at the end cap of an aisle stocked with instant noodles, duct tape, eyeglass repair kits, and condoms.

"This *is* the hardware store. And also, the grocery store." Ethan grabs a shopping cart, and as I watch him, I am reminded of those videos of bears doing human things.

I grab my own cart and start loading it with groceries under the watchful eyes of taxidermied ducks mounted on the walls.

It feels so claustrophobic in here. The windows are blocked by fishing gear, and the low ceiling holds yellow, fluorescent bulbs not bright enough to illuminate the short shelves, crammed full of goods. None of the aisles are labeled with directional signs. I wonder if they don't need labels because the locals come here so much that they know where to find things. I've never been here before. My mom and Rowan usually drove us to the next town over to go shopping. Now, I guess I know why.

"This way, dearest Millicent." Ethan strolls past me with the cart, which has a loud, wobbling wheel.

"Are you going to do that out loud in public?" I whisper-yell at him, then follow him reluctantly into an aisle with box hair dye, paper towels, and canned vegetables. All the surfaces are off-white. The shelves, the floor, the walls. I wonder if they are supposed to be that color, or if they are just dirty.

"Our General Store is a startling sight, I admit," Ethan continues, "but do not fret, sweet Millicent! We shall procure the goods that we are seeking. I am certain of it."

His voice is always a touch too loud without trying, but right now he's projecting on purpose and curious heads are turning our way, staring.

I'm dead. I've died of embarrassment, right here, right next to the lifejackets.

"Is that a British accent, Ethan?" asks a woman in clothes that are too small for her and hair that is too big for her. "I always wanted to go to London."

She's not in our aisle, but the shelves are so low we can see each other over them. She's standing by the peanut butter and dog food.

"What do you want to go to London for?" asks the flannel-clad man beside her, who looks as tired as his wife looks sunbaked.

"No, no, I fare not from London, my friend. 'Tis a filthy place, full of Redcoats!" Ethan declares.

"Redcoats?" the woman asks, her brows furrowed in confusion as we walk away.

"Something isn't right with that one, I told you," grumbles her flannel companion.

"It's a shame, because he makes such beautiful tables," she adds, shaking her head.

I reluctantly catch up with Ethan, who has stopped at a glass-covered deli counter.

"Hank!" he shouts at the counter of meat.

"Ethan!" A beaming man, a black apron tied around his rotund belly, pushes his way through a set of swinging double doors.

"I need a five gallon of primer, whatever paint the lady chooses, and two of the day's special sandwiches."

"Sure thing! I'll get started on the sandwiches. Here's the paint catalog."

"Thank you, fine sir," Ethan says, swiping the booklet and passing it to me.

"You order all these things at the same counter?" I ask, as Hank disappears behind a swinging door again. "Isn't that like, a health code violation?"

"Perhaps."

I page through the booklet before circling a few dramatic, period appropriate hues—deep emerald, rich chocolate, vibrant ochre, and sultry maroon, with a bright warm neutral for the narrow lobby and hallways, then set it back on the counter. "I'm not eating anything that comes over that counter. And can you please stop with the accent?"

He leans in close, eyes twinkling down at me.

I swallow.

"And miss this magnificent sight, you squirming with discomfort? Not a chance."

Hank appears again and hands us two paper-wrapped sandwiches over the counter. "Here's your lunch. The boys will get the paint mixed and load it in your truck."

My eyes plead with Ethan to say something normal in response to this nice man.

"Stupendous! Heartfelt thanks!"

"Sure thing," Hank says with a laugh, like he has heard far weirder things from him. And I am somehow not surprised.

"Oh hey, are you the girl staying at the old inn?" Hank asks.

"Yeah, that's me."

"Listen, I'm a bit of a paranormal investigator," Hank rests his meaty elbows on the counter.

"Is that right?" I blink at him.

"Yeah, me and the guys, we've got a club."

"A club?" I ask. Because that's all you can do in a situation like this, when you're completely dumbfounded. Just keep repeating what the other person is saying, a pleasant look on your face.

Ethan is grinning from ear to ear.

"I've always wanted to visit the inn. It's so old, I'm certain it's haunted. I'd love to visit, do an investigation. Now, your uncle, he didn't like the idea and he always told us no and I respected that. But now I'm wondering..."

"Now you're wondering?"

"Could the guys and I stop by sometime with our equipment? I'd love to take some readings. I'd share everything with you, and my nephew, he's got us a YouTube channel now."

"A YouTube channel?"

"Yeah, we can't settle on a name, though. My wife likes Boo Busters, but I think that sounds too juvenile."

"Mostly Ghostly. Spook Troupe!" Ethan shouts.

"Spectre Inspectors!" I join in.

"Boy, you guys are good," Hank says.

"Dude, Where's My Ghost?"

"Hunting Hauntings."

"Afterlife Investigations."

"Ghost Gobblers!"

I can feel Ethan's eyes on me as I let out a laugh. I can't remember the last time I laughed.

"Sure, you can bring your club over," I say to Hank the sandwich maker and paranormal investigator. "In a few weeks. I'll let you know. We are working on getting the place cleaned up right now."

Hank punches the air victoriously. "Thanks Millie! Can't wait to tell the guys!"

***

"You're doing it wrong."

"What do you mean, I'm doing it wrong? I'm painting."

"No, you should edge around the trim first, and use the angled brush, not this one. If you're going to be painting a bigger section of the wall, use the roller, and go in like a *W* pattern, not… whatever it is you're doing." He closes the distance between us, his front to my back as I'm facing the wall, and puts his hand over mine on the roller.

Then I start to fear that my deep inhales are a little too loud to be secret and my body is liking his near warmth way too much.

We've been working since this morning. First, I carefully took pictures of each room. Then we clear out enough of the living room furniture to paint the walls. Then Ethan patched a few small holes in the plaster. After a quick lunch break of Hank's admittedly delicious sandwiches, we started priming. Tomorrow, we'll cover up tired peach with a stately navy blue.

Three days later, we're still painting. We fall into a comfortable routine. Every morning, I go for a walk with Frank to visit the cemetery. When I get back, Ethan is waiting at the house with breakfast for us. Then, room by room, we tackle the house. Pulling down framed items, sorting them, deciding which to keep for staging, putting most in the shed for donation. Pushing furniture we want to keep to the center of the room, away from the walls. Carefully packing items of Rowan's that we want to keep. Then Ethan patches more holes in the plaster. We eat lunch. Then we paint. And paint. And paint some more, the windows flung open for fresh air.

We talk about everything and nothing. I talk more this week than I think I have in a month. I tell him about how Sarah and I met and how disappointed and frustrated I am that she hasn't been answering me beyond a few perfunctory texts letting me know she's alive. How I think my mom is a boring stereotype—she married someone she hated because he had money, and she was beautiful. I tell him about getting chickenpox when I was a kid and how I'm still driving my dad's old car. I'm rewarded with smiles and stories of his own. He tells me his favorite writer is Stephen King or Wendell Berry or Terry Pratchett, but it changes depending on his mood, and that he and Joe used to pretend they were soldiers in the woods.

And we banter.

I don't know why I keep arguing with him. I think, maybe, I just don't know how to act because I'm conflicted.

I like him.

So much.

So devastatingly much.

But we're prepping this place for sale. *In a few weeks, I will move on*, I tell myself for the thousandth time. So, I can't tell him how happy it makes me when I see his truck in the driveway. It's easier to be prickly sometimes and send out no-flirting-allowed signals.

I shouldn't encourage my delusions, my secret wishes.

But it's getting harder and harder to do that.

"What are you listening to?" he asks me as I toss a set of dusty curtains into his truck bed. He's wearing a black shirt today. He's all sweaty and dirty and he's wearing paint-flecked jeans and it's doing things to me.

I, on the other hand, look like a pig. I'm wearing gym shorts and an old t-shirt of Rowan's and have my hair in a bun on the top of my head. Well, it was in a bun when we started this morning, but now I think it's a fuzzy mat. I don't look hot when I get all sweaty and dirty. Why is life so unfair? Thankfully, I don't *smell* like a pig. But it's probably only a matter of time—I'm testing my deodorant to unfair limits.

But it's for the best, I assure myself. *Schlub it up. Don't let yourself feel sexy in front of him. Don't let your guard slip.*

"A podcast my friend Sarah and I are fans of."

"About what?"

"Murder."

He sets an old lamp with a pleated shade down on the driveway and leans in to look at me. He has this way of leaning in and looking down at me with those blue eyes—it makes me feel like the most interesting person in the world.

Who am I kidding? I don't stand a *chance* of holding out.

"I thought you were listening to music. You've been casually listening to grisly murder stuff this whole time?"

"Um, yes." I push past him, back inside, bracing myself for a *what is wrong with you* talk.

He grabs my arm and stops me. "Give me one of your earbuds, you little weirdo."

I watch him slip it into his ear, a crooked smile on his face.

"These ladies curse a lot. Is that why you listen to it? To increase your vocabulary?" he asks as he follows me back inside. I can still feel the spots where his fingers wrapped around my arm.

"Just listen," I say, exasperated.

And by the end of episode one, he's guessing who the murderer is.

By episode three, he's whistling the main theme.

"Come here, you have paint on your cheek," he says. I step closer and he cups my face like he's going to kiss me. My foolish little heart goes *pitter patter*. Then, I feel the pad of his thumb swipe slowly along my skin, lifting away the paint.

He wipes it on his jeans, a little speckle, part of the constellation of flecks and drips on his work jeans, like *Millie was here.*

***

The house is so big, so eerie, that I can't get comfortable until Ethan is there in the morning with his easy smile, bakery box in hand. As soon as I wake up, I'm out the door with Frank for our morning walk, and we don't go back inside until Ethan's arrived. After he leaves, I pour over the ledgers, taking notes, researching until I fall into uneasy sleep. A week later, we've mostly finished painting, and I've proudly sent before-and-after pictures to my mom. Now, I'm working on my thesis and trying my hardest not to get attached.

"Millie! Come here," I hear his voice muffled through the wall of Rowan's office, where I'm sitting with my laptop.

"No. I'm busy," I call back, eyes still focused on my screen.

"You'll want to see this, come here."

I groan and push my chair back.

I find him in Room 5. The pink room. This one was always my mom's favorite because of the four-poster bed and the fancy floor to ceiling mirror. I never liked it in here, with its lace doilies. It reminded me of being inside a dollhouse. Packing it up helped, and so did a fresh coat of neutral paint. Now when I walk in, the first things I notice are the millwork and the view of the forest out the window.

Ethan is crouching in the corner of the room. He has part of the carpet pulled back in one corner and I can see the wood floor that was hidden underneath.

"This looks like it's in pretty good shape. Want to help me rip all this carpet out today? It should go quickly."

"Oh, yes! Show me how."

"There is a layer of carpet, then a carpet pad to cut through. Then we'll need to rip out lots of little nails and staples and tack strips that will be left in the floor. Sometimes there's other floors on top of the hardwood but in this case, I think we're going to be lucky, based on what I've found in other rooms. Also, the floor might be covered in glue or paint or scratches or whatever, but I'll bring a sander in to buff it all off another day."

He takes off his dumb looking safety glasses and puts them on my face, then hands me a crowbar and a pair of pliers.

"I need your muscles, Millie. I need your fury."

"What for?"

"It makes the very tedious job of ripping out staples and carpet tack strips much more fun."

"Oh."

"Think about whatever makes you maddest."

"You, then?" I fire back, taking the respirator he's handing me.

He smiles. "Any lovers who scorned you? Voodoo dolls you had to make?" He slips respirator loops over his own ears before he starts slicing into the carpet with his knife. I watch as he uses a crowbar to loosen the section and rolls up and throws away one section at a time with gloved hands.

"I *should* have made a voodoo doll. I dated a guy for a few years that I met as a freshman. I thought it was serious. It was for me. Until he cheated on me." I feel my cheeks burning bright with anger and shame. Even after all this time, it still stings. I knew he wasn't my forever person. But because the breakup lent so much credibility to every insecurity I have.

"It's not a big deal. That's what college is for, right? Experimentation?" I continue. This is not really what I believe, but I tell myself this to feel better. To convince myself it wasn't me, it was him. "But sometimes I do wish I'd stabbed a little doll that looked like him through the heart."

Ethan stops and pulls off his respirator so he can talk. "My little witch, college is for experimentation if you didn't promise to be faithful to someone." It's clear from his tone that this is a breach of morality for him—his voice is all deep and frustrated for me.

I smile to myself. I like this feeling. Ethan defensive on my behalf.

"I'm going to continue pulling the carpet out of the way in strips. Then you'll come after me, like this." I watch, transfixed, at his practiced hands gripping the crowbar, muscled forearms flexing as he pries up old nails.

"Your turn." He hands me the crowbar. "Make sure you don't miss any, or when I come through here with the drum sander it will tear up the sandpaper pad."

We both pull our protective equipment back on and get lost in the work.

As Ethan cuts sections of carpet and rolls them up, stuffing them into trash bags, I follow, ripping out tack strips, nails, and staples. My pile of sharp, crooked metal grows.

With every annoying staple and nail I pull out of the wood boards, I think about how much of a dick Trevor was.

That he hated how I stopped going to parties with him.

That we had different interests, and he didn't want to know mine.

"You're the worst, Trevor!" I grumble at a particularly stubborn staple, my voice muffled by the respirator.

"The worst!" Ethan agrees. His eyes look a little sparkly as we survey the progress we've made. It's been less than an hour, and most of the carpet is gone.

I can't muster all that much rage at Trevor. When I found out he cheated on me, I was humiliated more than anything else. I knew we weren't a good match, and we probably should have broken up much sooner.

What else makes me mad?

My mind jumps to Ethan first, but let's be honest here, what I feel for him is getting less and less rage-filled each day.

I think about my mother telling me I should straighten my hair and wear brighter colors. But I never will. I haven't stopped wearing black since my dad died. My grief is part of who I am now. I can't feel so sad on the inside and lie on the outside with a bright pink sweater.

I think about my mother telling me to find more normal interests instead of dusty old boring ones, that maybe I'd be able to keep a guy tied down then.

That did it.

I can hear blood pounding in my ears as I rip out more floor staples.

Bit by bit, the carpet disappears, and the warm colored, dusty wood floor is revealed underneath. I run my hand over the boards, feeling the bumps and divots, the wood worn by centuries of traffic. The carpet is rolled into bags and tossed into the back of Ethan's truck. I take out every tack I can find. We work side-by-side in focused, near silence. When I lean back and admire our work, I'm breathing a little hard and smiling a lot at the warm wooden floorboards, seeing sunshine for the first time in decades. I take a picture of our progress and send it to my mom, Ben, and Sarah.

I push the sweaty hair off my face, remove the goggles and respirator, and break our silence.

"Your turn. If I had to talk about my past, you do, too. Tell me about your ex-girlfriend. What happened? Was she horrible? Anything that makes you want to smash things?"

He sits down to rest, his back against the wall. I set my crowbar down and take a drink of water before sitting next to him.

"I met Emily at a gym right when I moved to Chicago. She's amazing, the most inspiring person. We were happy for few years.

But then..." He pauses, collecting his thoughts. "Have you ever had a moment, like an out of body experience, when you suddenly had so much clarity that it changed your life?"

I shake my head. "I'm not sure what you mean."

"I was on the subway and a nice older lady was making small talk with me. As I was telling her about myself, it felt like I was talking about someone else's life and not my own. It wasn't until that moment that I fully realized how unhappy I was."

"What were you unhappy about?" I ask as I rub my knees and shins, which are aching from kneeling on the hard floor.

I watch as he stretches his legs out alongside mine. "Everything. I knew almost from day one the lifestyle wasn't for me, but I didn't want to disappoint Rowan by quitting, so I stuck it out as an architect for a year after graduation."

"That's a long time to be unhappy." I hand him my water bottle, offering him a drink. My eyes get caught on the distracting bob of his Adam's apple as he swallows.

"I hated the city," he continues. "I thought things would get better after I graduated and started working. But they didn't. I hated my commute. I hated my routine. Up at 5 in the morning, drop the dog off at daycare, ride the subway for an hour, work a job I hated for a boss I hated sitting at a gray desk for ten hours, make a bunch of mock ups for clients, actually get to finalize designs for a fraction of them but never build things with my own hands, deal with aggravating workplace politics, ride the subway for an hour again, pick up the dog from daycare, order takeout and eat dinner alone because Emily and I worked different schedules most of the time."

His gaze has drifted out the window, unfocused.

"On her days off, we tried to see friends, but it was all *her* friends. I didn't make very many because I was always working overtime to try to get ahead at the firm. I didn't have time to meet new people. We fought all the time about stupid stuff that doesn't matter because we weren't right for each other. I missed the Russo family Christmas twice. I wasn't here when Rowan needed me. I was a robot and all that existed was work. I desperately wanted to take my dog for a walk in the woods every morning instead of on concrete."

"That does sound miserable. You should love your work. I hope to find a job I love someday."

"Or if you don't love it, you need the work-life balance or a paycheck big enough to make the job worth it. I wasn't checking any of those boxes. I hit a point when I just felt like, *what is all of this for?*

He rubs his hands over his face as silence fills the space between us for a few moments.

"And Emily," I ask? "What happened there?"

"She was pressuring me to propose. I knew if we got married it would be the same every day, my whole life wasted on the subway and twice monthly shitty dinner parties. We would've had kids that we wouldn't have time for—they'd have parents they hardly knew. I was so depressed. I missed my family, the trees, the lake. I spent my childhood outside, without a lot of structure, you know? As soon as the school bus let us off, we were out in the woods. I felt like I was suffocating in the city. Like a bear in a cage. I was frustrated all the time and lashing out at her."

"So, you broke up with her."

He shook his head.

"Something came up, and I needed to move back here. I asked her to come with me, to see if we could make it work here—a fresh start. But she didn't want to. She didn't want to leave her career. I don't blame her; I shouldn't have even asked her to."

"I'm sorry, Ethan," I say, reaching out to touch his hand. He surprises me by lacing his fingers in mine and not letting go.

It feels exactly right.

"Don't be. I'm not. It's for the best—we're both happier. Emily is doing great, probably better without me. It's not a sad part of my story. It helped me figure out what I need to be happy. And my dog likes me now at least."

"So that's when you started renovating the inn with Rowan and opened the wood shop. It seems to have brought you some sort of peace."

"It does bring me peace," he says, turning to smile at me. "How can you tell?"

I look down at our hands, where's he's caught my fingers in his. I swear I can feel my heartbeat in my palm, pressed against his.

"Your focus when you are working—how steady and meticulous you are. The beautiful things you create," I say, thinking of the times I spent watching him work. "It radiates out of you, and your peace is contagious. I've definitely taken it for granted. I was such a nervous wreck the first few days I was here. Then, after spending time around you, I started feeling better. You're like one of the sleepy happy pills my mom takes that she swears she isn't addicted to."

He closes the small bit of distance between us—leaning closer as he listens—and I feel nervous flutters in my belly, my cheeks blushing pink.

"Will you have dinner with me later?" His voice is so hopeful.

"No, we can't." I drop his hand, then cross my arms to hold my heart in, to keep myself from saying anything else.

"Forget it, I'm sorry," he says before standing up, stepping away from me. I climb to my feet, my eyes following the disappointed set of his shoulders.

"I thought... there might be something here." His voice trails off as he runs his hands through his hair, uncertain.

"Ethan. Don't apologize. You're not wrong," I say to his back. He freezes as he listens, then turns to look at me over his shoulder. "There is something here."

I watch the familiar smile slide back on his face as he steps toward me and then all the oxygen leaves the room as he braces his arms against the wall, boxing me in. I tilt my head up at him as he studies my face and I try to remember how to breathe.

"You *do* like me. Explain why you won't have dinner with me."

This close, I'm overwhelmed by him. His eyes are so kind, and his lips are so kissable, and he smells like laundry detergent and fresh air, and I can feel the warmth coming off his chest, I just want to snuggle in so bad I feel dizzy.

He wants to kiss me. His breathing is as heavy as mine and he can't take his eyes off my mouth.

But this is dangerous territory. A slippery slope straight to heartbreak.

"Because I'm leaving, Ethan." My self-preservation instinct was screaming at me to *abort, abort, abort*. I'm already grieving Rowan. How much more heartbreak can I handle?

He steps back, letting out a long, frustrated sigh. I immediately miss having him so close.

"If you won't go to dinner with me, then dance with me," he says.

"What?" I let out an exasperated laugh. Of all the things I thought he'd say in this moment, that was not on the list.

"Just dance with me. It doesn't have to mean anything else."

"There's no music." I wave my arms at the music-less room.

"So? We have a dance floor. And we've been bumping into each other all week on accident. Let's bump into each other on purpose. It doesn't have to mean anything. I just want to hold you for a minute."

He's not wrong. We've been like magnets, gravitating toward each other. Hands lingering when he hands me something. Brushing past each other in hallways. On purpose or on accident, I don't know. Probably a little bit of both.

"So that's what it's like, dancing with you? Getting bumped into?"

"You should try it and find out," he dares me.

I want to.

I want to, so very badly.

I close my eyes and take a steadying yoga breath in. After a slow exhale I open them again and with resolve say, "I need to go work on my thesis."

My responsible side wins this round. It always does. I push past him and go to my room. He doesn't follow me.

CHAPTER FOURTEEN

"Are you the one who keeps moving my coffee?" I ask the death certificate of John Starling Sr., which I have pulled up on my laptop. From my research so far, I've learned that he was born into a wealthy family in 1863 and invested well—steel—and his wealth boomed during the Gilded Age. He commissioned the inn to be built in the 1890s as a summer retreat for himself and his family and their friends. He had one son, John Jr., who inherited the inn on his father's passing, and two grandsons. I wonder whose desk I'm sitting at right now. I had always thought of it as Rowan's. But it was probably picked out by John Sr.

In 1911, John Sr. died of heart disease, according to the death certificate. No mysterious circumstances. *If* you believe in ghosts—and that mysterious circumstances cause hauntings—it probably isn't him.

Do *I* believe that?

I don't know.

My phone vibrates and my heart jumps into my throat, hoping it's Sarah.

I'm immediately disappointed. It's a notification from the security system I had installed. The cameras must have picked up some movement outside. So far, I've only seen wildlife on the cameras—birds, deer, foxes, and raccoons. Max and Frank. I open the notification to immediately dismiss it, which has become a habit.

But I balk when I see what the front porch camera picked up.

There's a person hunched over in the yard, making jerky movements.

I stop breathing and raise the phone closer to my face.

They are too far away—deep in the morning fog—and the camera is too low resolution for me to make out any distinguishing features except that they are wearing a hooded coat.

There's something long in their hand. A stick? I watch as it moves up and down, then the figure hoists it over their shoulder.

A shovel.

They push it back down into the ground again.

Someone is burying something in the yard, in the early hours of the morning. The sun has barely risen.

With a gasp, I push my chair out from the desk and stand up, far away from my phone, like the person can see me through the screen.

Frank's ears are flicked back, agitated at me for disturbing his peace. He's lounging on a leather armchair in the corner of the office in a shaft of morning light.

The doors are locked, I assure myself. And the security system is armed. If someone tries to get in, the alarm will sound, and police will be notified.

I'm as safe as I can be.

I should call the police anyway, to report someone trespassing. I step closer to my phone and peek at the screen.

The figure is gone.

***

"Is that *an axe?*"

I pull my coat tight around myself as I find Ethan stepping out of his truck, looking *enraged.* His hair is a little messy, his shirt a little wrinkled. The laces of his boots aren't tied. I must have woken him up.

"It's the first thing I saw on my way out, so I grabbed it," he explains, his voice rough from sleep.

Max jumps out next and he's on high alert, picking up on Ethan's mood. His hackles are up, tail lifted, and ears pointed up, pacing circles around us letting out little *ruffs.*

"Which way?"

"They were over in that area." I point to the corner of the yard, close to the tree line—and close to the trail that leads to Maria's.

"Stay here?" Ethan asks me before he and Max set off purposefully.

I shake my head and follow, jogging a little to keep up with his long strides. His posture is tense, and he looks absolutely menacing cutting through the fog, the axe on his one side and Max on the other.

Max finds it first. My heart thunders in my chest as he lifts his nose from the ground, and his warning bark pierces the air.

"Should have brought a shovel," I say, as we all stare down at the pile of disturbed grass and dirt.

"Dig, Max," Ethan orders. I shiver and wrap my arms around myself.

Max happily rips apart the spot with his paws. Clods of dirt and grass fly through the air. Ethan and I lean over, anxiously watching for what might be revealed. I hear Max's nails scratch against something hard.

"Stop, Max." Max sits, and looks at us expectantly, his tail wagging.

Ethan plants the axe in the ground beside him, then crouches down and picks up a dirt-covered object, smaller than his palm.

"What is it?" I ask, leaning over his shoulder.

"I'm not sure." He brushes off the dirt and hands it to me, his face drawn tight.

It's a figurine made of clay. It's been worn by time, so the features aren't sharp. Maybe a woman in a dress, or a man in a robe. I can't tell, except the hair and the garments are long.

It had been buried face down. Purposefully oriented with its feet to the sky.

"Who would bury this here? Why?" Ethan looks distraught. He stands up and spins around, looking at the tree line.

"I don't know. But I'm going to figure it out," I vow.

Max whines. I rub his ears. "Good boy."

***

"Why do you keep bringing these?" I ask, polishing off my morning croissant. It's a few days after I saw the mysterious figure in the fog digging in the yard. I filed another police report. They kept the little figurine as evidence and said they would be in touch. I've been waiting to hear back.

Ethan's been jumpy, checking in even more than usual. Finding every little reason to stay longer.

He doesn't want to leave me alone here.

And I'm so grateful for it.

"Well, it started as a peace offering to you. But I keep going for the baker, obviously. I can't stop showing up now, Oscar will be devastated. He's writing a book, you know. Every day he bounces ideas off me. I have to show up to hear what happens next. You are funding the next great American novel with your bakery habits, Millie."

"Pleased to be of service."

"Also, you won't come to dinner with me so I'm going to bring food to you every day instead."

I smile at him shyly.

We fall into comfortable silence in the kitchen, sipping our coffees.

"I can't help you much today. I really do have to work on my thesis. I have to submit a draft to my peers soon."

With all the work on the house, it had fallen off my priority list. The only efforts I've made have been pouring over the old ledgers, creating a family tree, trying to piece together the story of this place. My first draft should be further along.

"I'll stay out of your way. I was planning to work in the office."

It's the last room we need to paint. We're keeping it green for Rowan, replacing the mossy green with a fresh coat, a deeper hue. It's also the best room for Wi-Fi. And the big desk is in there, my favorite place to set up my laptop.

I let out a dejected sigh. "I was also planning to work in the office."

"Do you want me to come back another day?"

"No! Don't go. We'll stay out of each other's way."

So now Ethan is kneeling on the floor, painting the wall along the baseboards, moving around the room with an angled brush. With each careful stroke, the last of Rowan's green office walls are replaced with primer.

He's moving so agonizingly slowly. I think he wants to linger here so I feel safe. I also know that he's having a hard time with the guilt that comes from erasing pieces of Rowan from this house.

Or maybe he's just patient.

When I paint, I move twice as fast, messing up here and there, cleaning paint drips off the trim with a rag or touching it up later. But it takes me twice as long as him, fixing mistakes from hasty work.

There's something kind of mesmerizing about watching him paint. He's wearing a t-shirt again, stretched deliciously over his shoulders.

What am I doing?

I shake my head and force my eyes back to my laptop screen.

Thesis. Starting with a summary of the tourism industry in Michigan in the early twentieth century. Yes. Right. I stare at the cursor blinking on the document, my few paragraphs of words there.

My eyes bounce right back to him.

When you tell yourself not to think about something, it will be all you can think about. In that dreamy involuntary place, I float. I think about blue eyes focused on me. The smell of wood smoke and coffee and clean laundry. Strong hands, gripping. I think about how my name sounds when he says it, the feel of his shirt beneath my cheek. The way his eyes crinkle at the corners when he laughs. The way my breath left my body when I watched his eyes climb up me that day in the bathroom.

I watch his hands, expertly gripping the brush, his strokes long and confident and meticulous. The same hands that so carefully mended mine after he found me in the conservatory. The same hands that unbuttoned my jeans, unhooked my bra. The same hands that hoisted an axe in my defense.

Shamelessly, I wonder what it would feel like to have those hands cradling my hips or sinking into my hair.

I bite my lip as my eyes slide down the pronounced veins in his forearms.

"How's it going up there?" he suddenly asks, and I jump, my cheeks flaming red. He didn't look up from his painting, but I can hear the hint of a smile in his voice.

"What do you mean? It's going fine," I say, my voice higher pitched than usual.

We share a slow smile, and I'm certain he knows exactly what I'm thinking about.

"You are not clickety clacking with as much purpose as usual." He sits back on his haunches, sets the brush down on the rim of the paint can.

"Clickety clacking?" I ask, eyebrows raised.

"When Millie is focused and productive, fast clickety clacks. When Millie is feeling contemplative, slower and quieter typing, scrunched up face."

"I don't scrunch up my face when I type."

"You definitely do."

I shake my head. "It doesn't matter. I was... reading. Doing research," I lie. "You can listen to music if you want, if you don't want to listen to my typing."

He stands and stretches, and I unabashedly admire the view.

"It doesn't bother me. I'm just curious. What are you writing your thesis about? I guess you finally decided?"

"I did. For the course requirements it must be about early 20th century American history."

"Lot going on then."

"Yes, there was, but what hasn't been written about a ton already? I wanted to find something new that no one's written about, something that fascinates me. So, I decided to write about the inn. The Starling Family. I have to do the research for the National Register of Historic Places application anyway. I need to prove that the inn has historic significance."

He tilts his head, looking at me curiously.

"What exactly are you writing about the Starlings?"

"I think it's going to be partly biographical about the original owners. I'll be exploring the ups and downs of the inn throughout time.

But I'll tell the story with a backdrop of the vacation influx to the lake that took off in the 19th century and early 20th century. I'll be examining how the industry affected changed the area and this family in particular."

"Can I read it when you're done?"

"Yeah, of course."

"I'm looking forward to it. Do you need a coffee refill? I'm heading downstairs," he asks.

"Yes, actually. Thank you." I hand him my mug and his warm fingertips brush mine as he takes it. I don't think I've ever been so aware of someone else's fingertips in my life. How does he not have any paint on them? Magic.

He's back moments later, setting the coffee next to my laptop. I take a sip, and it has a splash of non-dairy creamer. It's exactly the way I always make it for myself.

"Ethan?"

"Yeah?"

He leans in, shifting his bright blue eyes to mine, and I think about all the things that I want to say.

How grateful I am for him, deep in my soul.

How much it means when I see him arrive each morning, because I, and the house, feel a little less haunted with him here.

How badly I want to take what we have, this beautiful blooming friendship, and push on to something more.

I lean in, too.

I could kiss him. I want to kiss him.

I want to tell him that every day that I spend with him is making it harder and harder not to.

"I'm going to go get some air," I say instead.

***

"What are you doing?" Ethan asks with a bashful smile, and I can hear the hitch in his breath. He's just walked into the sunroom and I'm in downward facing dog pose, my palms on the floor, my back arched. I've pushed some of the wicker sunroom furniture out of the way, and I'm working through yoga poses, soaking in sunshine like one of the plants lining the walls.

I'm wearing my favorite yoga outfit. Black spandex pants and a matching bra. It's supportive in the front but plunging and strappy in the back. Most of the skin on my top half is on display. I was stiff at first, but after a few difficult poses, I'm warming up. I stand and transition into warrior pose, arms outstretched, strong and beautiful.

"Yoga. What are *you* doing? I thought you were painting upstairs."

He has the same look on his face right now that I have when I watch him push heavy furniture around.

Dazzled.

"Um," he stutters. "I wanted to give you some space to work in the office... seemed like you needed it... so I thought I'd pause painting and replace the lock on the sunroom door. I miscounted and didn't buy enough last time..."

His eyes land on everything around the room but me.

"Do you mind if I do this? I can go back upstairs." He looks un-characteristically shy as his words trail off.

"Go ahead."

He pulls the door open to work on it. I can feel unseasonably warm air rush in from outside. It's been a steamy few days in the midst of a chill fall.

I hold warrior pose for three more breaths, then sit down, legs outstretched. I lean forward, grabbing my feet. I can feel a delicious pull in my lower back as my forehead dips down and touches my shins. The extra tightness in my muscles from all the work we've been doing, coupled with a few weeks of no yoga, is a little painful and satisfying at the same time. I roll over onto my back. Press my heels into the floor and lift my pelvis off the ground. Bridge pose.

Ethan starts to say something. Fails.

"What was that?" I ask innocently. I can't help the smile that spreads across my face. If he was doing bendy shit in front of me in tight fitting clothes, I might die. He's holding up better than I think I would in his position.

Sarah and I joined a yoga class a few years ago, and while she dropped off eventually, like she did with every one of the million hobbies she ever picked up, I took classes for years. Eventually, I felt confident and disciplined enough to practice at home a few times a week. All I need is a patch of sunlight and my yoga mat.

I should've started doing yoga the day I got here, I chide myself. I probably would be sleeping better and wouldn't be so anxious. Maybe a little more of this would have kept the panic attack at bay. I focus on my breaths, centering myself, losing myself in the poses, trying to pass into that space that's meditative.

But with Ethan here, I'm about as far from Zen as you can get. My heart is pounding like a herd of horses, and I feel like I'm on stage. I can feel his eyes on me, hot on my skin, and the order of my poses doesn't make any sense because I can't concentrate.

I stand up. I can hear the pause of his tools. He works a little, then watches, then works again, like he's battling himself.

My lips curl in a smile as I transition into another pose.

I'm not used to having an audience. I like it.

I can't find the nerve to look at him, so I keep focusing on my moves, watching him in my peripherals, my skin prickling in the most tantalizing ways.

I take a deep breath and ground one foot for balance, then lift the other foot into the air to grab with an outstretched hand. My other hand stretches out strong in front of me, following my line of sight, out the windows and to the lake, where waves are crashing against the craggy shore. Lord of the dance pose. I love this one. It makes me feel like a ballet dancer. I hold it for several breaths, then let go.

I ground both feet to the floor, heels together, and bend in half, my head nearly touching the floor, my butt in the air. I peek at Ethan through my shins. He's upside down and he's concentrating his hardest on the door.

I plant my hands on the ground. Then lift one foot in the air, then the other. I'm suspended in a headstand, all core strength and balance keeping me aloft.

"Show off," he murmurs.

When I stand back up, he's given up on his project. He's just watching me with his arms crossed.

"Have dinner with me. Just dinner, it doesn't have to be anything else," he asks again.

I should tell him no. I should be pushing him away. I don't want to start something and have it fall apart. I don't want something else weighing heavily on my heart when I go home. I repeat this to myself almost every time I see him. A self-protective mantra of sorts.

But right now, I'm so tired of my mantra.

I'm tired of making careful, smart, responsible choices.

I want to make a selfish choice. I deserve it, don't I? After all this darkness.

Every part of me wants to get closer to this person in any way, in every way that I can. So, I decide to finally listen to myself. With bare feet and a resolute smile, I close the distance between us. Just dinner can't hurt, right?

"I have one more question first." I stop in front of him, my arms crossed.

"Ask me anything."

"That day when we were teenagers, and you wanted to take me out on a date—were you being sincere? Or were you making fun of me?"

"No, I was not making fun of you. I would never do something like that." He's clearly horrified at the thought. "I was so into you it took me all summer to muster up the courage and I had a whole first date planned."

"You did? What was it?"

"Yes, the used bookstore then ice cream."

"I love both of those things so much," I say, squeezing my eyes shut for a moment. "That would have been the perfect first date."

Responsible Millie loses this round.

"My answer is yes," I say what I've wanted to say from the beginning. Since the first time he asked me that summer, so many years ago. He stares at me for a moment, eyebrows furrowed, like he isn't sure he heard me right. Then my chest fills with warmth as I bask in the incredulous smile on his face.

"Let's have dinner," I say again. "But it's not a date. It can't be a date. That would be so catastrophic to my heart."

"Not a date," he agrees, smile fading, eventually slipping away. I miss it. "Tomorrow night."

"Not tonight?"

"I have a commissioned piece to finish. So, I need to head back to my shop, and I won't be here tomorrow morning."

"Oh." My heart sinks a little. "OK."

"See you tomorrow night."

CHAPTER FIFTEEN

After my morning walk with Frank, I find myself drumming my fingers on my laptop, too restless to focus on my thesis. I can't stop thinking about dinner tonight with Ethan.

My gaze drags across the hallway, lingering on the door to Room 3.

Before I know it, I'm leaning against the wall of the secret passageway, dust settling on my shirt. My face is illuminated by the glow of my phone screen as I watch videos on how to break open a door.

Step one. Check to see which way the door opens by looking the hinges. If the door opens toward you, kicking it down is going to be next to impossible.

I shine my phone flashlight at the hinges and we're in luck, the door opens away from me.

Step two. Step away so that you have enough distance to throw your body weight forward into the kick. If you don't step back far enough, you'll bounce off the door.

I take two big steps back from the door, further down the passageway.

Step three. Pick your sight where you want to put your foot. Aim your foot as close to the doorknob as you can. The intent is to separate the locking mechanism through the softer wood on the other side. But don't kick the lock itself, you'll break your foot.

Step four. Using a front kick, drive the heel of your foot into the door. Keep your balance by grounding your other foot down into the floor.

"You've got this, Millie." I brush my bangs out of my face, then take a deep yoga breath in and throw my forward momentum into a kick at the old wood door. It gives inward a little but doesn't open.

I wonder if I'm a wimp. Or maybe the door in the tutorial I watched gave way easier because it was a modern and hollow core with a short deadbolt. This door is older, completely solid, more resistant.

I square my shoulders, ground my left foot, and try again.

On my second kick, it bursts open with bang, and slams into the back of a closet with a satisfying puff of dust and splinters.

"Fuck yeah!"

My cheer falls away as I step through the door.

It's a time capsule.

My footsteps are muted on mauve carpet, coated in a layer of dust. *Everything* is coated in a layer of undisturbed dust. I'm the first one who's been here in years. Decades maybe.

The closet doors are flung open, and about half of the hangers are empty.

The room is soft and feminine, accented with muted pastels. The air is sweet and stale. Hairs stand up on the back of my neck as I spin slowly around, taking in the abandoned bedroom.

A canopied bed takes up most of the room, adorned with a striped comforter above a ruffled bed skirt. Next to the bed is a salmon pink corded rotary phone atop a white nightstand.

The walls are plastered with floral wallpaper that the room's occupant did their best to cover with tacked up band posters and pictures cut from magazine pages. In one corner, the wallpaper has been ripped away. I imagine a grounded teenager, sitting on the floor, picking and picking at the paper.

The desk beneath the window is piled with high school textbooks and notebooks. The chair is pulled out, a pair of canvas high-top tennis shoes lounging untied on the floor.

I flip one of the textbooks open to see the list of handwritten names and checkout dates of students on the inside cover. Written in blue pen, with a little heart above the "i" is *Catherine, 1986.*

My eyes flit to the dresser. The drawers are open, and clothes a mess. Dust-thickened cobwebs span between the hairspray and perfume canisters cluttering the top. And above the dresser is a mirror, with a picture tucked into the corner. Catherine in a puffy-sleeved dress, with her arms around Rowan.

Her face is so familiar, and I think, *how did I not notice this right away?*

Some instinct of mine is screaming at me to get out. Get out of this private place.

So, I listen.

***

The sky is pitch black by the time I get to Ethan's for dinner. Max met me on the trail when I was about halfway there. He must have heard me coming and dashed out to escort me—such a gentleman.

We find Ethan at the edge of the orchard, setting a picnic table. White lights are strung in the trees above, casting a soft twinkling glow down, creating shadows on his face.

"Milady!" he calls out when he sees me. "You look lovely."

"Thank you. This looks like a date."

"Nonsense, this is how I treat all my friends."

I don't have it in me to tell him what I found yet. I want to take a moment to recognize and appreciate the effort that he clearly put into this night before I bombard him with my discovery of Catherine's room.

And maybe this is it. The moment he'll tell me all on his own. I should give him a chance to tell me on his own terms, shouldn't I?

"Did you put this together?" I ask, lifting my eyebrows at the antipasto with olives, mozzarella, sliced tomatoes with basil, prosciutto and a baguette, all arranged beautifully on a platter.

"I so badly want to take the credit for this, but no. I was planning on grabbing takeout, honestly. But Maria heard what I was up to and shoved a basket of food at me as usual. This I *did* make though—would you like some fancy apple juice?"

"Why, yes, I would."

He fills my cup. I sip cold cider, tart and sweet.

"You were with Maria this afternoon?" I ask.

"Yeah, I was dropping off a tiny table and chairs set that she commissioned for her grandkids. I hear that it will host many tiny tea parties."

"Well, that's adorable."

"So are they. Three girls, Joe's kids. Maria wanted me to stay for dinner. When I told her why I couldn't, she put this together for us."

"Honestly, I'm glad you aren't cooking me an amazing meal right now. It'd be too much. You're so good at so many things, it would be overkill really."

"What things do you think I'm so good at?" he asks, leaning across the table, shamelessly fishing for compliments.

I hold up my hand and start ticking things off, happy to oblige. "Rescuing me, helping me talk through my troubles, building things, painting things, fixing things, growing a beard, being handsome, being tall, looking really good in jeans, answering the phone in emergencies, and orchards? Orcharding? Offering wise life advice, making me laugh, and planning romantic evening picnics."

When I finish, he's looking down at his hands bashfully.

"I am a bad cook, though, it's true. I haven't had a lot of practice. When I was living in the city, I ate out most of the time. We didn't have time to slow down and cook together. And since I've been here, I eat with friends and family a lot. I don't want to cook for only myself so it's grilled cheese most of the time."

"I don't believe that you'd be a bad cook if you put your mind to it. You probably cook the same way you do everything else."

"And how's that?"

"With great attention to detail."

"And you? Are you a good cook?"

"I'll have you know that I am *the best* at making grilled cheese." I take a sip of my cider. "I can follow a recipe just fine, if I prepare first and take my time. But my best friend, Sarah, is so talented. She's studying to be a teacher, and I know she'll be good at that, too, because she has such a big heart—but I can't help feeling like she's missing her calling. She's got that creative skill; the *I can look at an uninspired pantry of mismatched things and make an amazing meal* skill. And she's an incredible baker—that's her real passion."

"I can tell you miss her."

"Yeah. I really do. This is the first time in years we haven't seen each other every day." I push my disappointment about Sarah away. I don't want her ghosting me to ruin my mood. Which is almost *happy*, I'm surprised to discover.

We eat in silence for a while, polishing off a jug of apple cider and most of the antipasto tray. It's predictably divine. As the night goes on,

I find myself unconsciously leaning closer and closer across the table, hand on my chin while I listen to him talk.

"The other day, you said you were a stray. What happened to your parents?" I ask him. I know the answer already, but I want him to tell me his story in his own words.

He looks up at the stars, mulling.

"If you don't want to tell me, I understand," I add softly.

"There's something I need to talk to you about. I should have told you a long time ago. I'm just trying to figure out where to start."

I sit up straight, refocused. "Go ahead," I encourage him.

"Well, like you, I'm a member of the dead parent club," he finally says.

"I'm so sorry, Ethan." I raise my glass and clink it against his. "Your mom or your dad?"

"My mom..." He spins the glass slowly, watching the cider swirl inside, gathering his thoughts. Then he looks me in the eye, ready to unload all his truths.

"Her name was Catherine Starling. Rowan was in love with her. For years. They were high school sweethearts."

"But Rowan never talked about her," I say, trying to fit this information about my uncle into what I know about him.

"Because it was agony for him. He wouldn't talk to me about her either. He couldn't move on to the next stage of grief. He stayed firmly planted in denial and anger."

I let that tumble around in my head for a while before I speak.

"That makes you a Starling. My thesis research is about your family."

He nods.

"I never knew, because your last name is different. Why didn't you tell me sooner?"

"I didn't want you to feel uncomfortable or like I had any claim to the property. I wanted you to make whatever choice you were going to make about selling or not, without me or my circumstances factoring in."

"I don't think I fully understand."

"Ah, let me start at the beginning." He finishes his drink, setting it down on the table before training his blue eyes on mine. They are catching the reflection of the string lights and sparkling at me.

"My mom grew up here, at the inn. But her parents were terrible people," he finally says. "When my mom was around eighteen, she got hit for what she decided would be the final time, and she left. She got in a car with some friends and drove to California. She wanted Rowan to go with her, but he wouldn't—he tried to talk her out of it. She left anyway, and he stayed behind because he had already been accepted into college."

"What happened in California?"

"About what you would expect to happen to a naive teenager with no money or support. I don't know the details. I only know she was back in town not long after she left, pregnant with me, and dealing with a dormant drug problem."

His eyes meet mine again.

"She battled it." I can see some pride in the set of his jaw. "She tried so hard to be a good mom. She had periods of sobriety, times when she held a job and remembered my birthday. She had dreams, like reopening the Starling Inn. I try to focus on those memories instead of the others."

He reaches down to rub Max's ears. The dog had inched closer and closer to Ethan as he talked, as if sensing he needed extra support.

"She wanted to reopen the inn? So *that's* why Rowan bought it?"

"Yeah, when my grandparents lived here, they didn't run it as an inn. They just lived in it. My mom grew up here, totally enchanted by the place. She told me once that she felt like the house was alive, or maybe even haunted. It was as if someone was protecting her, showing her where to hide."

"From what?"

"My grandparents," Ethan says sadly.

I draw my arms around myself.

"Years later, my grandparents wanted to retire to somewhere warm, but they refused to give the place to my mom, or any of their money. I guess they didn't trust her because of her history of substance abuse. So, Rowan bought the place from them, and they disappeared to somewhere warm for retirement. He had been living in the city for a while at that point. He was a successful architect, and they didn't realize he was the same gangly dude who took her to prom."

"Wow. Then what happened?"

"He wanted to reconnect with my mom. Be her white knight and lay all her dreams at her feet. Grow old with her here, running a grand, reopened inn together," his voice catches.

"That's so beautiful and romantic." Also, generous and everything good I remember about Rowan. My heart aches for my uncle.

"I was about twelve and I still remember the phone call. Rowan telling her he'd bought it, he was moving back home, and they could start over with each other. My mom had been completely sober for nearly a year, and they had been reconnecting. So, we started planning to move into the inn. After living my entire life in poverty, in a series of shitty apartments, it felt like a fairytale."

"Cinderella marrying a prince."

Ethan nods. "He needed some time to tie up loose ends with his job, then he'd be coming home. But a few weeks before we moved, I started noticing the signs again. She was having mood swings. She got fired for missing work. She wasn't buying groceries or paying the bills, but our money was always gone. I came home one day from school, and she was passed out on the couch, a needle still in her arm."

"Oh Ethan—" I reach across the table for his hand.

"I called Rowan for help. He dropped everything and flew in as soon as he could. But it was too late—she was too far gone for either of us to save. She was combative when he confronted her and tried to intervene. She snuck off and overdosed a few days later."

His voice is steady, like he's talked about this many times before. Like it's a sad story from long ago that happened to someone else.

"Do you remember when you asked me if you could love something and hate something at the same time?"

I nod.

"I loved her, but I hated her, too. In that moment, when she threw away our future, and abandoned me, I truly hated her."

I can see it now, her choices still weighing on him all these years later. This is why he spoke to me with so much conviction about forgiving myself about Rowan's death. Because he was dealing with it, too—not only from Rowan but also from his mom.

"I'm so sorry, Ethan." My voice is thick with tears.

"It would have been a lot worse if I didn't have a support system. The Russo family stepped in to foster me, so I was able to move in with them to finish school here."

"I'm so sorry for what you lost. And I'm so sad that they didn't get their happily ever after." I think about the silhouette of a woman's form drawn over the mantel. "She was his *Annabel Lee.*"

I can tell by Ethan's expression that he doesn't know what I'm talking about.

"Frank took me to her grave. Every morning after breakfast, he waits by the front door. He slipped out one day and I followed him to a cemetery. I think he and Rowan probably went for a walk there together every day to visit her grave and Frank was keeping up the habit. The inscription on her headstone—it's an Edgar Allen Poe poem called *Annabel Lee*."

Ethan takes a shaky breath, "Yeah, Rowan chose the inscription on her headstone. I was just a kid at the time. I didn't know what to put on my mom's headstone. I haven't read the whole poem."

"It's about two young people who fall in love by the sea. A beautiful girl who dies, and her lover wastes away thinking about her."

Our knees accidentally touch under the table and neither one of us tries to move away.

"I know how hard it is to lose a parent. A part of me always felt sort of incomplete after my dad died. Full of what-ifs," I say after a long pause. "I imagined all sorts of what-if futures. On the worst days, that's what I would do. Reimagine the day, but this time, imagine what it would have been like if my dad was there."

"I'm sorry, Millie. I wish I could have met your dad."

"I wish I could have met your mom."

We sit in silence for a while and drink our cider while the stars twinkle above us, watching.

"What about the rest of your family? Your grandparents? Are they still in your life?"

"Rowan and the Russos are my only family. My mom was such a disappointment to my grandparents, I guess I was an extension of that, so they weren't in my life much. I was the physical reminder of their greatest shame. They died a few years back. But when they passed away, they left their money to me—they invested most of what they made in their sale of the inn to Rowan. But I don't want it. I always felt like it was his money or my mom's. I couldn't ever spend it on myself. It didn't feel right. I've been putting it back into the house and property."

"So *that's* why you've been helping me get the house ready to sell without letting me pay for any of it."

"Yeah, and other reasons." A bit of his heaviness lifts away and he winks at me before continuing. "Rowan sunk his savings into buying it for my mom and me. He couldn't afford to keep it up after a while. A building this old always has something to fix. After my mom died, he couldn't bring himself to sell it. I thought he was going to drink himself to death, angry and alone, the house crumbling around him. So, I left the city and moved back here."

I look down at my glass, a lump in my throat.

"I don't know how much of that side of him you knew, so I didn't want to talk about it. I don't want to change your perception of him."

"I feel like I hardly knew him at all. He never told me about Catherine. And you seem to remember him so differently than I do."

"Because he was his best self around you. He adored you and Ben like you were his own kids. You chased all his sadness away and he felt relief when you visited, his grief lifting away like a weight. He told me so."

I let the gift of those words settle over me and I take a moment to collect myself, sipping on my drink and watching Max and Frank eat moths that dared flutter too close to our island of light in the darkness.

"How long have you been living here?" I ask.

"About four years. I mean, I told you before, it wasn't much of a life I was living. I wasn't happy. Then Rowan called me one day and he sounded... awful. Wrapped up in the past, lost in his head. I was worried about him, and I came home. I saw the spot he was in, stuck with this crumbling place and getting more depressed and lonely day by day. I couldn't talk him into selling and moving. So, I tried to give him something to hold onto and talked him into chasing my mom's big dreams for her, because she couldn't. We were going to restore the inn together. I thought it would give us both some purpose for a few years. So, I moved here and opened the wood shop. Converted the barn into my house. We put ourselves to work. We buried ourselves in it. I used the money my grandparents left me to fund most of it. It felt like the right thing to do."

"And did it work? Did it help him?"

"For a while it kept him busy. Rowan did all the design work. He made plans for a kitchen redesign, but we never got that far, obviously. And he designed my barn conversion, too. We subcontracted plumbers and electricians and a few other specialists, but I did a lot of the finishing work. All the woodwork."

"It's so well done," I admit. "I like how my room felt the same as it did when I was a kid, but better. Like you updated it but kept the soul of the room. Or maybe it feels like what it is supposed to look like when it was first built, instead of the layers of terrible design choices stacked on top of each other over the years, fighting against each other."

"Thank you," he says with pride. "I took months to strip all the paint off the doors and trim. I fixed the staircase, too, and remade any broken spindles to match the original. It took weeks."

"It looks beautiful. All of it. I can tell so much care went into every bit of work that was done. How much did you accomplish?"

"We finished a lot of the big pieces already, like the staircase. Replaced the roof. Luckily, my ancestors built this place without sparing any expense, so the bones are still solid. We did have it tuckpointed. Repaired some of the windows. Then we started working upstairs. Renovated the upstairs bathrooms. We ripped up so much carpet.

So, so much carpet. And refinished the wood floors underneath. But there's still a lot left to do."

"I'm glad he had something to keep him happy."

"Distracted at least. But his depression never truly went away. He had good days and bad days. He didn't get the help he needed. I told him to go to therapy, but he wouldn't. I never stopped worrying about him. I spent as much time with him as I could. I didn't ever want him to feel like he was alone."

Silence falls between us again.

"I'm adding another thing to the list of things that Ethan does well."

"What's that?"

"Unfailingly loyal, takes care of the people that he loves."

A half-hearted smile chases away some of the sadness on his face.

"Ethan?"

"Yeah?"

"What exactly is left to do on Rowan's wish list of improvements to the inn?"

"He wanted to entirely restore it to its original grandeur, paying homage to the style of the period as much as possible. We didn't want to make any changes that someone would have to undo because they quickly fell out of style. We wanted to restore the craftsmanship that it was built with. Like the old tile for your bathroom? Do you remember it? I think my grandparents added it in the '80s. And it was all busted up and worn."

"I remember."

"We replaced it with tile Rowan specially ordered from a company that has been in business for over a century manufacturing the sort of tile that would have been original to the house. So, it is brand new, but it doesn't look out of place. We wanted to continue doing that sort of restoration work. He liked keeping busy with that sort of thing. The designing and researching. You and I these past few weeks have checked so much off of the to-do list. We finished painting most of the rooms. You've done so much work clearing out clutter. Now that you and I cleaned out the attic, I want to put more insulation up there. The next big thing Rowan thought we would move on to was the kitchen. He drew up plans for it, but we didn't get that far. And we wanted to change a few of the light fixtures from awful 1980s grandma to something more..."

"Tasteful," I finish for him.

He nods. "I think the last thing, the icing on the cake, will be to paint the exterior."

"What color do you want to paint it?"

"I'm not sure."

I trace the bevels on my glass with my fingertips.

"You would be able to walk away from all of this? Years of work, time and money you've put into this place? Where's your anger?" I ask.

"It's not my choice. And I want what is best for you. That's what Rowan would want. He would want you taken care of. Your future is so much more important than a building."

"But... Ethan. I can't just leave. You and Rowan were in the middle of something. I can't sell it and give this place to someone else and force you to leave. It's a part of you. It's part of Rowan."

And part of me, too.

"Maybe, if we are able to see your mother's dreams realized, to see Rowan's wishes fulfilled, we'll have some sort of closure. I want to stand in my jewel box again and see blooming roses. I want to sit on the patio and feel the sun on my face, peace in my heart."

His gaze rests on me, cautiously hopeful.

"I think if I leave now, with this place half-finished and broken, casting you off, I'll be haunted by it forever. The guilt will never leave me. But maybe if we finish Rowan's list together, I'll be able to forgive myself. Maybe I'll be able to move on then."

"You want to stay?"

"Not stay. I don't see how I could stay." I would have to buy out my mom and Ben, which isn't possible. And would I even want to? I don't see myself as an innkeeper, business owner. "But I can hold off the sale for a while longer. I want to see Rowan's list finished. I just need to speak with my mom about it."

"Are you sure?"

"I am. What's the downside? I have someplace to stay a while longer. You're adding more value into the property, so we'll get a higher sale price. I know the work you do is good because I've seen what you've done already. There's no risk for me. And together you and I can make sure it's the best package for a buyer. Give the inn the best chance we can. As long as you are OK with putting more money into this place?"

He nods. "Like I said, it doesn't feel like my money. It's an account separate from my savings."

"I want to help. Will you show me how? Like you did when we were painting?"

He stands up and comes around to my side of the table, wrapping me in a hug so tight it squeezes the air out of my lungs.

***

Ethan stands behind me as I unlock the door to Room 3. I hear his intake of breath as I swing the door open.

He steps around me and slowly takes in the room, and I know he immediately understands what we are looking at. He and Rowan knew what was behind this door, and they kept it closed, didn't want to see it, didn't want to face it.

I watch as he drags his fingertips over the dresser, leaving finger tracks in the dust past artifacts of his mother's teenage years. Exactly as she'd left it, the day she left for California.

He sinks down onto the edge of the bed. With his elbows on his knees and his face in his hands, he crumples into himself.

For the first time since I've met him, his shoulders look small.

"I'll give you a moment." I put a reassuring hand on his arm before stepping away.

He catches my hand. "Where are you going?"

"I thought you might want a moment alone?"

"Get over here."

He pulls me down into his lap and wraps his arms around me, burying his face in my hair.

CHAPTER SIXTEEN

32nd Infantry Division, American Expeditionary Forces

My dearest,

You are an ocean away, but I hope against hope that when I turn a corner it may be to run into you. It's foolish, I know, but the woods and bluffs here look not too different from our woods, so my heart looks for you around every branch and boulder.

Oh, my dear, I just could not help crying as I read what you had written. The tears rolled down my cheeks as I thanked God for having given me such a gift that you are, and the little treasure that you are carrying. Dearest, be safe, take care, if I should lose you both I dare not think what I should do for I love you so much and want to be reunited with you both with all my heart and soul.

I know you worry about what your family will say. Worry not because my heart is your heart, and I will make you my wife. I could be happy anywhere with you. We will be happy, yes, truly happy, away off, far from the bother of human uproar, away from the inn, hidden in some place of grandeur. Imagine, a room warmed by a fire and love, filled with books, and you and I reading together to our child. We are all tired, for it is after a strenuous day, walking by the lake under the bright sky, and oh how we are enjoying it and are happy as happy can be.

And if I don't return? I can't bear the thought of leaving you and my child alone in this world. But my dearest, you are strong, and my love for you both is deathless. The memories of the blissful moments we have spent together shall keep us both sustained until we meet again. Never forget how much I love you, and if my last breath escapes me on the battlefield, it will be your name.

Yours,

L

After time in the humidification chamber, I was finally able to open the letter Ethan and I found in the secret passageway.

It is a letter from a World War I soldier to his sweetheart back home.

I snap a photo with my phone so I can zoom into the tricky text and lessen handling of the fragile paper. I read the letter again and again, unpacking details and looking for clues.

I can tell now that the upside-down triangle with the circle around it is an icon for the YMCA. With a bit of quick research on my phone, I learn that they provided paper for soldiers at their canteens in France. Morale is one of the main factors that can help or cripple an army. So, when the U.S. joined World War I, the YMCA set out to work alongside the U.S. Army to keep up morale—feeding soldiers, providing comfortable spaces for them, and keeping them entertained. The canteens they ran were set up everywhere that soldiers were, and were stocked with doughnuts, soda fountains, hot chocolate, parties, pretty women, and stationary like this to write home with.

My eyes rest on the 32nd Infantry Division printed across the top of the page. I turn to the internet once again and learn that the Division was formed from Army National Guard units in Wisconsin and Michigan. By May 1918, when the letter was written, the 32nd Division was on the front line in France. It was during this brutal six months of front-line combat throughout France that the Division earned the nickname *Les Terribles.*

Notably, it was the first Allied Division to pierce the German Hindenburg Line of defense, and the 32nd then adopted its shoulder sleeve insignia—a line shot through with a red arrow—to signify its tenacity in piercing the enemy line. Soldiers in the 32nd Division still wear this red arrow patch today.

I move on to my next clue. The handwriting is the practiced script of a well-educated person. Not only the beautiful poetic content, but the handwriting itself. In 1918, states only required students to attend school through 8th grade. It was usually the wealthy families who pursued education past that, while the rest went to work. Most soldier handwriting is clumsily formed. So maybe he was an officer or affluent.

Did he survive?

Did they see each other again?

Is this the soldier whose mother had a Gold Star banner in the attic?

"Hey, Ethan!" I yell as loud as I can. I'm not sure exactly where in the house he is but I know he's here somewhere, working on something.

Frank runs through the door like he's the one I called.

"Hello friend, care to join me?"

Frank jumps in my lap and purrs as I read.

"Yeah?" Ethan calls from the doorway, his pencil behind his ear, his sleeves pushed up, tool belt on his hips. He's been quieter than usual today, distracting himself with work, last night weighing heavily on him. We haven't talked about our plan of attack for Catherine's room yet. I wonder if he wants to pack it all up himself, or if that will be too painful for him. I want to help, but not without him asking me first. For now, the door is staying shut.

"I opened the old letter we found in the secret passage. Do you want to read it?"

He steps over to where I'm sitting and leans over the table, brows knitting together as he reads.

"Well, did he survive?"

"That's what I was wondering."

"Did they see each other again?" His face is scrunched up, and he sounds kind of wrecked about it. I'm glad I'm not the only one.

"I hope so. I need to do some research. I was hoping to start with you. Do you have any family stories about a soldier? Your great-grandfather wasn't one. A cousin or something?"

"No. You think he's a Starling?"

I nod. "Someone who lived here is more likely to stash something in the walls than someone who was just passing through as a guest."

"But he could have been dating a Starling, or a resident at the inn?" Ethan asks.

"Maybe. Let's rule out Starlings first, then we will cast a wider net. We know he was likely born between 1890 and 1900, because he was old enough to be a soldier in 1918 but young enough to be unmarried. So, I'm going to search for World War I soldiers who lived in this county whose name started with the letter L. And just cross our fingers that the L didn't stand for a nickname." I tap my fingers against my chin in concentration, as I think through our options out loud.

I open my laptop and navigate to the State Archive website and enter the search parameters into their database of soldier records.

"You found him," Ethan says over my shoulder a few minutes later. I click on the record, and he reads it out loud. "Louis Starling. Born August 7, 1895, in Charlotte County, Michigan. Inducted in November 1917."

"An officer," I confirm, looking at the text. "Stationed at Camp MacArthur, Texas for training. Then deployed to France in January 1918. But the record is incomplete. It usually includes discharge dates, and if he was wounded or disabled," I say, staring at some blank spaces in the record.

"So, what do we do next?" Ethan asks, eyes bouncing from the screen to me.

"Since the state record was incomplete, we can see if the federal record still exists. But I've run into problems accessing them before. All federal military records are stored at the National Personnel Records Center in St. Louis. It had a big fire in the 1970s and some records were destroyed. Some partially, some completely. They have technicians who scan the fragments with special equipment to try to piece the information back together. We could try to reach out to them and put in a request to see if they can pull any more data for us, but that could take a while. I wonder…" I say, looking up at Ethan. "If the census has some clues for us."

"Census?"

"The 1910 and 1920 census records for the inn should show him listed as a resident here."

Ethan pulls up a chair next to me.

I save a copy of the soldier record in a new folder on my laptop, then navigate to a free genealogy website and enter the address of the inn. Moments later, a black and white census record pops onto the screen, and Ethan leans in closer to view the digitized script. We see Ethan's great-great-grandfather John, and his great-great-grandmother Mary, listed. On the next lines of the census are their son John Jr. and his wife Eliza with their two sons, George Starling, age four, and Louis Starling, age eleven.

"There he is—Louis Starling. Your great-grandfather's brother."

Ethan runs his fingers through his beard.

I navigate to the 1920 census. Louis isn't on it, only George and his parents.

"So, by 1920, Louis either moved away from home after the war—"

"Or died," Ethan interjects.

"Yeah, or died. So many American doughboys died during World War I that nearly every town in the nation has a little war memorial tucked away somewhere. And your family, being affluent, surely would have done something to commemorate him. Do you know of any war memorials in town?"

Ethan shakes his head no.

"Let's see if we can find a newspaper article about him. Soldier deaths were always published in local papers, usually with a lot of details. The *Charlotte County Record* has been digitized by your local historical society. Let me pull it up."

"How do you know all this?"

"Internships. And I was doing research on your mom," I admit, blushing. "I wanted to know why my cat kept leading me to her gravesite every morning."

"*Your* cat?"

I smile, noticing the slip up. "Yeah, yeah, Frank is *my cat*, I guess."

After scratching Frank's ear, I pull up a cemetery database and show it to Ethan. I enter Louis' name but nothing relevant comes up.

"This is a pretty comprehensive database. So, if we aren't finding him here, he isn't buried in an easily accessible cemetery in the United States. And soldiers are usually buried in military cemeteries, which are well documented. So, my guess is that he could have died overseas, and his body was never recovered. Or he is in a small unlabeled plot somewhere."

"Is my family cemetery on here?"

"It is. Do you want to see it?"

He nods, so I type in Catherine's name. She pops up in the results, next to her grandparents, great-grandparents.

Ethan stares at her picture, wordless.

"She looks like you," I say softly. "I'm sure she would be so proud of you."

He clears his throat after a moment. "You were saying... about the newspapers?"

"Oh yeah, we can try to find a newspaper article. If Louis died overseas, it would have been big news for the town. Some newspapers published a column every week with updates on their soldiers," I explain, navigating to the historical society's website.

"A death would have definitely been mentioned. Oh, no."

"What?"

"Editions of this local newspaper printed prior to 1950 aren't online. But it's OK—I'll just have to go to the library to access those. I already have an appointment there for thesis research at the end of the week."

***

"Hello, old friend. You're just as lovely as I remember," I say softly as I park my car. The public library's domed roof towers over all surrounding buildings, reminding me of a church. It's on one end of the town square, bracketed by hair and nail salons, antique stores, and sleepy restaurants. It looks grandiose against its neighbors.

I step through the vestibule and breathe in the familiar smell of books, floor polish, and wood furniture and follow signs for the local history department. I pass a group of giggling kids on their way in for story time in the children's section, and a retired old woman holding a cloth bag, heavy and laden with books.

This beloved place is a temple to books, all wood paneled and gleaming brass. Vaulted ceilings and stained-glass windows. I haven't been here in years, but it reminds me of another I've been to.

"Is this a Carnegie library?" I ask the librarian perched on a stool at the reference desk in the local history room. She has her hair pulled into a bun, and clever eyes behind gold-rimmed glasses. The sleeves of her shirt are pushed up, revealing a delicate black hieroglyphic tattoo on her forearm.

"It is!" She smiles warmly at me as she looks up from her work—a laptop and a tidy pile of glass negatives. "It was built in 1905. Of the 1,600 or so that Carnegie had built, this is one of the 700 remaining. The architectural details are some of the best in this part of the state. If you're interested in that sort of thing, take your time wandering around."

"I haven't been here in ages. You must love coming to work here every day."

"I do. Is there something I can help you with?" she asks, taking off her nitrile gloves, gently setting them down on her desk.

"I hope so. I'm Millie Atwater. I sent an email about coming in to do research on the Starling Inn, and the family that owned it. I was hoping to look at some newspapers today."

"Thanks for coming in, Millie. I'm Lucy. I've got the newspaper ready for you. We also have the Starling Family Papers in our special collections if you'd like to look at that."

Jackpot.

"That would be amazing."

"I'd be happy to help you access that. There's not enough storage space in this cool old library, so it's stored off-site. It does take a few days to have it couriered here. I'll put in your order today and it should arrive later this week."

"That's no problem."

"Great. Please place your jacket and bag in the lockers. Only a pencil and laptop at the table. No food or drink. Have a seat and I'll be over with some paperwork in a moment."

I pack away my belongings as directed then choose one of the four heavy wooden tables in the room, each topped with a brass and green glass lamp. When she walks over to my table, I show her my ID and sign the papers she brings over, promising not to steal or damage anything.

"And please keep the papers in the order that they are found in the folder," she adds. "If you need copies, let me know. Do you mind me asking what the purpose of your research is today?"

"Not at all. I'm working on my master's thesis, which has some overlap with another project. I'm hoping to get the inn added to the National Register of Historic Places. But I don't know where to begin with the application process. Do you have any suggestions?"

"I've never done it myself, but let me see what I can find out for you. In the meantime, I've got your newspaper microfilm reels loaded up on that computer in the corner. Have you used a microfilm reader like this before or do I need to show you how?"

"I've used one before." I remember learning in my internship that archives often reproduce newspapers on microfilm for long term preservation and accessibility. Newspapers are printed on the cheapest, lowest quality paper. As a result, they decay quickly, their acidity harming any other papers they touch, leaving brown discolorations. Newspapers can last a few decades—microfilm, we think, should last 500 years or more.

"I am going to go look up that NRHP information for you."

"Only if you have the extra time." I know these places have shoe-string budgets, impossible backlogs and workloads.

"I truly don't mind," she says warmly. "It's a quiet day, not many researchers. And you are momentarily saving me from the monotony of cataloging an agricultural collection. I learned there's a threshold for how many old pictures of pigs I can catalog in one day and I reached that limit about an hour ago. I'm happy to help you with your research for a little while."

"Thank you so much for all of your help."

"Let me know if you need anything," she responds with a friendly smile, then heads back over to her computer.

I sit down at the microfilm computer and use the mouse to scroll through the pages for any news or an obituary about the Starling family. As my mouse scrolls, the microfilm on the machine beside me stretches from one spool to the other, sandwiched between glass, with a pleasant whirring sound.

They are all gossip, old newspapers. Social media before social media. Who's in town and who visited whose house when. Who died, who was born, who left, who traveled to the town. Step a foot out of line, it would be in the newspaper for your neighbors to read. Or do a good deed, something interesting, and get to brag about it in a column. Sometimes I would skim the headlines, sometimes I couldn't help but read the whole article. I get lost in it.

Wishing with all my might I could use "ctrl+f," I spend an hour skimming headlines, hunting for the word Starling. I found a few hodge podge mentions of the inn, mostly unremarkable, but I downloaded and printed each one, lingering on one about a seance hosted there.

I showed it to Lucy.

"This is so cool!" she says, pouring over the newspaper clipping.

"Was it normal to host seances at inns?" I ask her. "Or is this unique to the Starling?"

"Not unique," she says. "I would need to do research to back this up, but I believe they would host them anywhere that a large group of women could gather. There were surges in spirituality and seances following wars. Families lose soldiers during the wars, of course, abruptly, without the chance to say goodbye. So, they turned to supernatural encounters to try to connect with them one last time. There was a burst in the popularity of seances and ghost sightings after the Civil War. It was sort of a fashionable thing to host, too. Something *a bit* more interesting to do with your friends than sit and talk to each other and drink tea."

"A bit," I agree. I look down at my buzzing phone to see my mom's name on the screen. "Excuse me, Lucy, I have to take this. Thank you for your help today."

"No problem. Thank you for visiting. I'll let you know when the Starling Papers arrive. See you soon."

I call my mom back after I step outside, cold wind and overcast sky a stark contrast to the amber warmth of the building I was just in.

"Hey Mom," I answer carefully. Seeing Ethan with these remnants of his mother's life is breaking my heart. I want to try to be better with my own mother, try to mend things.

"Millie," she says, and her voice is thick with emotion. "Rowan's ashes are ready to be picked up."

***

We set Rowan's ashes on the mantel, where the sketch of Catherine used to be before I'd packed it away.

The ashes are startlingly heavy, and encased in a glossy, wooden box that Ethan made. The second my eyes shift away they are pulled back to it. A horrible, undeniable truth.

Ethan sinks down beside me on the couch, and for the longest time, we sit in silence.

"I feel like we should say something," I say, the moment hanging between us.

"Yeah. I'm still working through what I want to say for the memorial. I'd rather save it for then I think. But we can't say nothing," he agrees, and I can see the pain on his face. "It feels..."

"Like we just put a box on the mantel and not the remains of someone we love. I know."

"Yeah." He puts his hands on his face, rubbing his eyes with the heels of his hands. "But I don't know what to do."

"I have an idea. I'll be right back," I say, and trot up the steps to Rowan's office. I quickly find *The Works of Edgar Allan Poe* on a bookshelf. The gold letters stand out against the black spine.

Moments later, I'm settling in my seat again. I carefully open to *Annabel Lee* and hand the book to Ethan. He looks down at the old, speckled pages, contemplative, before looking at me with a nod. This feels right for Rowan.

Then he takes a deep breath and starts, his voice gruff, his face lit by firelight.

It was many and many a year ago,
In a kingdom by the sea,
That a maiden there lived whom you may know
By the name of Annabel Lee;
And this maiden she lived with no other thought
Than to love and be loved by me.
I was a child and she was a child,

In this kingdom by the sea;
But we loved with a love that was more than love -
I and my Annabel Lee;
With a love that the winged seraphs of heaven
Coveted her and me.
And this was the reason that, long ago,
In this kingdom by the sea,
A wind blew out of a cloud, chilling
My beautiful Annabel Lee;
So that her highborn kinsman came
And bore her away from me,
To shut her up in sepulchre
In this kingdom by the sea.
The angels, not half so happy in heaven,
Went envying her and me -
Yes! - that was the reason (as all men know,
In this kingdom by the sea)
That the wind came out of the cloud by night,
Chilling and killing my Annabel Lee.
But our love it was stronger by far than the love
Of those who were older than we -
Of many far wiser than we -
And neither the angels in heaven above,
Nor the demons down under the sea,
Can ever dissever my soul from the soul
Of the beautiful Annabel Lee.
For the moon never beams without bringing me dreams
Of the beautiful Annabel Lee;
And so, all the night-tide, I lie down by the side
Of my darling - my darling - my life and my bride,

In the sepulchre there by the sea,

In her tomb by the sounding sea.

When he's finished reading, we sit for a moment in silence.

I'm full-on weeping now, the hot tears on my cheeks mirror images of his. He opens up his arms and I settle into his lap, lay my head on his shoulder, where it fits perfectly.

"How do we go on without him?" Ethan asks, and I can hear the desperation in his voice, just under the surface.

"We don't. The memories we have don't leave us. Rowan will be with us still in so many ways. The way your mom is still with you. The way my father is still with me. I just wish... Poor Rowan and Catherine. I wish they could have been together."

"Maybe they are together now."

"Yeah, maybe."

I think about broken glass and Ethan's comment that I'm not the first person he'd rescued in the conservatory and connect it with Rowan and Catherine's story.

"Hey Ethan? Is Rowan the one who wrecked the conservatory?"

"Yeah. He would get blackout drunk sometimes. Usually just be sad and pass out. Sometimes he'd get angry. Her birthday was the worst."

"I can understand that I guess. It's so unfair, what happened to him. He had the right to be angry."

"I disagree. He should have tried harder to move on."

"Like you did? You must have demons, too. But you don't seem burdened by them."

"Oh, I definitely am. I fake being in a good mood all the time. Sometimes I forget I'm faking it. Except when I'm with you. Then it feels real."

"You lose your mom, your girlfriend, and your job. You come home to start over, and you blessedly find some peace and happiness and spend lots of time with your dog. But it's about to get wrenched away because the man who was almost your stepfather died, then this angsty asshole," I say, gesturing at myself, "shows up on this doorstep, orders you to do menial tasks and insults you and your beard many times a day."

He smiles despite the tears.

"I'm so sorry that I was so mean to you in the beginning. I take it all back," I continue.

"Don't be sorry. I love it when you're mean to me."

"You love it?"

"Yeah. Sometimes I act like I can't hear you, or that I don't think you're funny at all—I act totally stone faced. But then I'll go outside and laugh my ass off. I can't do it in front of you. Your ego would be too big. You'd be insufferable."

"But, how are you even able to laugh?"

"Well, a decade of therapy. And choosing to learn from the people that I've lost and not waste a second of my life. I've been there, I've lost my temper, but then you come out of it and don't feel any better, you know? Getting angry makes you feel better for a few cathartic moments but then it all floods back worse than before."

He rubs his palm across his face and takes a solid breath in and out. I watch him, mesmerized.

"I don't want to be a tragic love story like my mom and Rowan. They aren't here. I can sit here and cry about projects he never finished with me, or I can finish them myself and enjoy it because he can't. I'm not going to punish myself because he's dead. I'm going to flirt with this weird, pretty girl that fascinates me because I don't know when I'm dying or having my life pulled out from under me again. Laughter is one of life's joys and I'll always be chasing that. So please don't ever stop making me laugh."

"I won't," I promise him. "I have the same philosophy. But I think instead of choosing joy, like you do, I choose distraction. I'd rather organize this cabinet for the fourth time than think about what is making me sad."

"Why do you think you do that?" he asks. He's twirling some of my hair in his fingers and I have to concentrate on stringing words together instead of getting wrapped up in the feeling of his hands in my hair.

"I remember that during the first week after my dad was gone, I set timers three times a day to remind us to eat. My dad was more of a nurturer than my mom ever was. He did all the shopping, cooking, laundry, and signed the permission slips. When he couldn't do it anymore, I took over. I managed everything for Ben, myself, and my mom. My mom seemed to check out of reality for a few years."

I start to feel the tears rising up, constricting my throat. I cough them away, focusing on his hands twirling my hair instead.

"I'm sure they both appreciate you. You're a warrior, Millie."

I shrug, trying to look nonchalant, when I feel anything but. "We would come here in the summers, and Rowan would take on the responsibilities and let me feel like a kid. I was always sad when my mom came to pick us up, take us to her newest boyfriend's house."

"We both lost so much when we lost him."

I nod into Ethan's shirt.

"It's OK to cry. You don't have to be the tough one anymore."

I laugh because it's such a sweet and cheesy thing to say, but tears spill over with it, and for a while Ethan and I just hold each other, and I feel his tears, too.

"You think I'm pretty?" I finally ask him, my voice thick.

"You know I do. I tell you all the time."

"It doesn't count if it's in Civil War prose."

"My darling, Millicent," he says grandly into my hair.

"Please, no," I beg.

"You're beautiful." I feel his chest rise and fall as he breathes in deep, then the soft weight of his lips as he kisses the top of my head. I wipe my eyes with my sleeve.

"Millie?"

"Yeah?"

"I want to kiss you so badly. But it can't be like this. I want to kiss you for the first time on a beautiful night, not a sad one."

"Deal."

CHAPTER SEVENTEEN

"WHAT DO YOU MEAN you're doing major renovations on the inn? The last time we talked—and in all the messages you've sent—you said you were doing the bare minimum. Just enough to sell!" My mom says, her voice is icy, edged with panic. "What changed?"

Frank is ready for our walk and impatiently staring from the doorway—probably at me, but maybe not. It's hard to tell.

"It was already in progress." I fill her in on the details Ethan shared with me. "I'm staying around until it's finished. We shouldn't sell until Rowan's list of projects is done."

I hear my mom say a quick, cheerful goodbye to her spin class gals. Then she is back to hounding me again, whisper-yelling into the phone. "You worship him, and you shouldn't, Millie. He was a depressed, lonely, angry drunk. I'll never understand why he bought that dilapidated property. I got his autopsy report back. The coroner said—"

"I don't want to know, Mom," I interrupt. "I really don't. And he bought the inn for *love*," I snap back. "He was in love with Catherine Starling. He bought the inn for her. But you knew this story, didn't you? You knew who Ethan was. Why didn't you tell me?"

She barks a condescending laugh, like that was the dumbest thing anyone has ever said. I get out of bed, set my phone to speaker mode, and start pulling on clothes.

"Because Catherine Starling was *also* a drunk, and she pulled Rowan down with her. I never understood what he saw in her. She was a terrible influence on him—she got him into so much trouble in high school. Your grandmother, God rest her soul, cried tears of relief when Catherine broke up with Rowan and ran off to California. We had some peaceful years without that trainwreck in our lives."

She takes a deep breath before continuing. "And then he spent his entire savings on that place, sacrificed his career, and moved back there for her."

I hear her car door slam.

"Then she has the *audacity* to die after everything he did for her! And instead of selling that money pit and moving on, he stayed put. He got angrier, drunker, and poorer every year until he was completely unrecognizable."

"That's not how I remember him at all," I snap, patting Frank on the head before I walk downstairs. I'm comforted by him walking alongside me, his little paws making soft sounds on the wood floor.

"Well, he hid that side from you, honey, you were a child. And I do thank him for that. But the reality is that he was a deeply troubled man who wasted half of his life pining after a woman that did not deserve him. Millie, I couldn't even get him to come and visit us for the holidays. He loved the memory of Catherine more than he loved us, I guess. A healthy person would have dealt with their grief and moved on with their life."

"Like you did, Mom? You abandoned your kids for weeks at a time and dated a whole football team worth of dumb jocks to erase the memory of my father, until finding one rich enough to latch yourself onto permanently. I guess that's what Rowan could have done, yeah. But he was *heartbroken* and busy taking care of us while you were occupied."

I hear a sharp intake of breath, like she's been punched. I should feel happy that I broke through her shell, but I don't. I feel sick instead.

"And how's that working for you? Are you happy?" I challenge her.

She doesn't answer me for a moment.

"I don't see you complaining about the life Roger, and I have provided for you," she finally says, with a carefully controlled voice. "I'll be damned if my daughter gets sucked into that place and lost the way Rowan did. You are coming home tomorrow. We will have lawyers and realtors tie up loose ends. You. Are. Done."

"No," I press the red hang up button and my phone makes a pleasant *bloop* sound as we disconnect. I frown, thinking of the avocado-green phone in the kitchen and how much more satisfying it would be to hang up on people with that thing.

I feed Frank, slamming down his little water bowl.

"Sorry," I apologize to him. "She brings out the worst in me."

He butts his head against my hand, like he's proud of me. Or maybe he just wants me to scratch his ears. I suppose having a cat isn't so bad.

"What are we going to do today, Frank?"

I look back down at my phone and shoot a text to Ethan.

Millie: I think we should take a break from working on the house today. I'm not feeling it.

Ethan: Same. Can I still spend the day with you?

Millie: I'd like that. What do you want to do? Something fun please. Something distracting.

Ethan: I have an idea. Come over when it stops raining. Wear clothes you don't mind getting dirty.

***

It's magnificent outside. The forest is glittering, with sunlight bouncing off raindrops clinging to tree leaves and blades of grass. The trees have been slowly turning for a few weeks now, but after yesterday's cold rain, today is a vibrant, breathtaking explosion of fall color. Impossibly bright yellows contrast against the dark, rain-soaked trunks, while leaves drift down like golden confetti.

Frank and I walk to the cemetery, mud pulling at my boots. Along the way, I hear the trees swaying and whispering, and I wonder if they remember the other couple, the one in the letter.

Catherine's headstone is dark with rain. I think about the things my mom had said. She was a hurricane that disrupted Rowan's life, but I bet if he were here, he'd say he'd do it all over again for her. He'd do anything for the people he loved.

I called him once when I was a freshman in high school. I wasn't doing well in art class. He talked to me on the phone for hours about my classwork and art. We sent sketches back and forth in the mail until I was confident enough to succeed in class. When it came to helping someone he loved, his capacity for help was endless.

When Frank and I emerge from the orchard, we're greeted by the sight of Ethan hauling things around outside—barrels of apples, buckets, and worktables set up on sawhorses in the grass. He looks a bit rumpled and worse for wear: his shirt is wrinkled, his eyes dark, and his smile slower than usual. His sleeves are pushed up, revealing forearms that are...obscene.

"Come here, will you?" he grumbles at me.

"What?" I ask innocently, my gaze darting up to his.

For a moment he says nothing, but he is watching me strangely, almost wryly, and then he says, his voice quiet, "Millie, stop pretending that you don't like me. I usually love to play along. Just not today. Get over here."

I close the distance between us and let myself sink into his hug.

"How are you?" I ask against his shirt.

"Last night stirred up a lot, you know?" he answers, and I can hear all the emotion in his voice.

"Yeah, I know."

After a moment, he pushes me back to arm's length and searches my face. "How are *you*?"

"It's hard talking about Rowan's death. Makes me relive it and all the feelings I had when it first happened. I had a hard time sleeping last night," I admit. Though thankfully the nightmares still haven't returned.

"Me too." I can see shadows under his eyes. "Let me get you an apron."

He steps away and is back a moment later, tying one of his work aprons around my neck. I'm swimming in it. He lingers a moment longer than he needs to as he ties the knot.

"What's the apron for? What are we going to do today?"

"Well, I have four barrels of apples left that I need to do something with before they rot. How does making apple cider sound?" He steps back, smiling at the sight of me in his apron. I probably look ridiculous, like a kid wearing her dad's boots.

"When I told you I keep myself busy to relax, you listened," I say.

"Of course I did. It works for me, too. Plus, this is fun, you'll see," he says. "We have to chop these up and mash them in the cider press. Strain the solids out, add yeast, bottle it, and wait a few weeks. Easy."

"Easy?" I tilt my head. "Wouldn't it be easier to just to buy the cider?"

"But we would be sad and boring today, the cider wouldn't taste as good, and you wouldn't have the pride and sense of accomplishment of drinking cider you made with your own hands, which is the best feeling ever."

"Alright, I'm up for trying. How do we do this?" I watch his eyes drag up my exposed neck as I pull my hair up into a bun.

"Would you rather chop apples or press them?" he asks, pointing to a wooden, barrel shaped contraption. It has a metal crank wheel, and is emblazoned with an S.

"What is that thing?"

"That's the cider press. It grinds up the apples and presses their juices out. I found it here when I was clearing the place out. It was probably my great-grandfather's. Still works perfectly."

"That's amazing."

"Yeah, it is. Needed a little bit of cleanup and it was good to go. This is the third season I've used it—it's a hundred years old and works as well as anything modern I would be able to buy."

"I'll chop," I say.

He leads me over to a station he's set up in the grass—a few rough boards laid over sawhorses, topped with knives and a cutting board, and a barrel of apples on the ground. He shows me how to cut out the core and rough chop the apples then throw them into a smaller bucket. We work side by side in silence for a while, listening to the chops of our knives on the cutting board.

"My mom finally called me back," I say finally. "She wants me to leave now and let realtors and lawyers sort out the estate."

"What do you want to do?" he asks carefully.

"I'm not finished here yet," I say with conviction, peeking at him out of the corner of my eye.

He smiles, a sweet secret smile, the first one of the morning to reach his eyes.

"She was not a fan of your mom, or Rowan's choice to stay here after she died," I explain.

"I understand that."

I put my knife down, turn, and look up at him. "You do?"

"Yeah, she was trying to protect him, right? She wanted what was best for him. There are good intentions at the heart of that judgment."

"But doesn't it make you mad?"

He shrugs. "A little. But people have said worse. They don't understand that each of us can be more than one thing. My mom was funny and generous and had a big heart. It's your mom's loss that she didn't get to know that side of her. It says more about her than my mom. People can be more than simply the bad choices they've made in life."

He picks up the bucket full of chopped apples and brings it over to the machine, pouring in the apples and cranking the handle. I watch as the apple pieces are mashed to bits, separating the fiber and juice.

"A lot of people are like that. Forward focused, they only see what's on the surface, make their judgments and move on," he continues.

"Rowan was the opposite," I say. "He saw that Catherine was troubled and wanted to save her."

Ethan nods in agreement. "He believed that people should be seen for more than what they appear to be on the surface. If someone is troubled, we shouldn't look away with judgment, we should dig in harder and find out why."

I pull another apple from the pile and Frank weaves between my ankles.

"I'm not sure where I fall on that spectrum. A little more judgmental than I should be, probably," I say, thinking about Ben. I wonder how he's really doing. We haven't connected in so long, not since the engagement party. It still stings that he didn't believe me after Roger harassed me.

I don't want to be Rowan and my mom. I don't want to drift apart from my brother.

"I like you just how you are," Ethan says, handing me a glass of fresh pressed juice. "But if you want to be better, learn from the people we've lost and make your changes now. Can't leave unfinished business with the people you love."

I take the glass and my fingers cling to the outside, sticky with the cloudy, amber-colored cider. I close my eyes as I take a drink of the unfiltered, fresh juice. It smells like fresh apples, thick and tart and complex with layered flavors, sweet being the most prominent one.

"This is so good," I say at him over the glass.

"A little better than the grocery store kind, huh?" he asks as he watches me with a satisfied smile. "I'll send you home with some, but it's unpasteurized, so I'll turn the rest to hard cider."

"I've never seen you drink. I didn't think you did?"

"I don't. I make it for other people."

"Why don't you drink? Your mom?" I ask, even though I know the answer.

He nods. "Have to set a good example for Max."

We work in quiet focus together for a while, until my hand starts cramping, my feet start getting sore, and my mind is blissfully blank of anything except for apples and Ethan's forearms and the autumn breeze on my face.

"Hey, Millie, what book are you reading?" Ethan breaks the comfortable silence.

"Oh, some cupcake romance books, you know," I say, waving off his question, a little bit embarrassed with my answer.

"Cupcake romance books?" he digs in.

I set my knife down. "Like if books were food. A fantasy series with multiple viewpoints, that takes years to finish, I'd call that a banquet.

Sometimes I'm in the mood for that. Complex, satisfying from start to finish. After you finish a great book series like that you have that weird disappointing floaty period of having to transition back to the real world where there are no dragons. I appreciate books like that. But sometimes I am tired, and I want *instant* gratification. I grab the cupcake. Not a fancy posh cupcake, but the mass-produced grocery store kind. I binge them. So sweet it hurts your teeth and you're slightly ashamed but also so happy."

"I like that analogy." He pauses before saying, "Now you're supposed to ask me what I'm reading."

"Ethan, what are you reading?" I ask and he smiles like he's won the lottery, which makes me feel like I'm floating.

"Will you think less of me if I say James Patterson?"

I burst out laughing. "Potato chip book. Nice for reading when you want your brain to coast. But terrible for your body, an addictive habit. He works off a formula and you know exactly what you're getting when you pick one up. I get it. I'm surprised, but I get it."

"I'm just kidding. I'm not reading James Patterson. But I've been waiting for you to ask me what I'm reading for like ten years."

"What are you talking about?" I put my hand on my hip and direct all my focus his way.

"That same day I mustered up the courage to ask you out on a date I asked you what you were reading. Do you remember?"

"Yeah. *Jane Eyre*, like always back then."

"And what food would you compare *Jane Eyre* to?" he asks. I study the way his shoulders move under his shirt as he cranks the apple press.

"A chef's table. Innovative for its time—many people try to recreate it but fall short. Timeless. When you read it, you learn things about writing. Or when you eat it, you learn things about food. You learn things about yourself, all the books that inspired it, and the books it was inspired by. It's the same with a chef's table and food. Connecting those lines into the past and future. Everything is derivative of everything else. But sometimes, once in a while, a writer, a chef, a creator will come along, taking what we know and adding something so compelling that we feel the ripples of it generations later."

Ethan finishes cranking the press and turns to look at me.

"I started reading it that summer," he says carefully, like he's trying to tell me something important.

"You did? Which summer?" I'm confused.

"When you told me you were reading *Jane Eyre*. I thought you were so cool, casually reading the classics. The only thing I was reading at the time was my assigned summer list for school and I hated it all. I felt like such a fool when you asked me what I was reading, and I didn't have anything interesting to say. And I wanted to impress you, to have something to talk to you about when I saw you again. So, I read *Jane Eyre*. It took me a few tries. A few years. But I finished it."

"That's sweet, Ethan. And what did you think of it?"

"It was too long. Kind of weird. It was spookier than I thought it would be. But I liked the setting. And I liked Jane."

"What did you like about her?"

"Her quiet strength and steadiness. Her convictions. She was the one everyone could always lean on. I was rooting for her when she left Rochester on their wedding day. I didn't like Rochester—"

"Was it the cross-dressing as a fortune teller?" I laugh.

He smiles. "Definitely didn't hate him for that. Jane shouldn't have come back to him after she ran away from the wedding. He lied to her. That's unforgivable"

"He does do some unforgivable things. That's the point. He's not a likable character. But in the end, Jane saw his faults and accepted them, and he accepted hers."

He shrugs. "It didn't feel like a happily ever after to me."

I feel the need to defend my favorite novel.

"Each time Jane and Rochester talk they chip away at each other and try to get behind all the walls they built around themselves—their class differences, their trauma. Hidden beneath all of that, they are finally able to be their true selves with each other. When Jane leaves him, they never stop pining for each other. That's why it's the best love story. Because they can both be kind of hard to love. Neither one of them is perfect. She's kind of cold, carrying childhood trauma, and he's a stereotypical Byronic hero and a bit of a mess, but they love each other so deeply anyway. They see each other's truths. If she was an unflawed character, if he was a perfect prince charming, the story would be sort of boring. It would be a cupcake book. Nothing memorable. Not a chef's table."

"Ah, so this is a book that helps people learn things about themselves and each other."

"Yeah."

"I agree with that. Listening to you talk about it is helping me learn about you." His blue eyes are fixed on my face.

"What are you learning?" I ask, my voice breathy.

"That you see people. You see beneath the surface," he says, and I look away, blushing at his attention.

I distract myself from those blue eyes by moving on to chop my next apple. But it's mealy inside. I drop the knife and step away with a shudder as a little worm crawls out, startling me. Ethan's by my side in an instant.

"Sorry we wrecked your home," he says to the worm, then gently scoots him off the cutting board and into the grass.

"Let's trade places for a while." I shudder. "I prefer my apples dewormed."

I take his spot, and he takes mine. I start turning the press, watching the apples separate into amber juice and nearly dry pulp. "Do you do all this work every year?"

"Yeah, but it was a community event last year. Everyone showed up with their own buckets and jugs and we spent the day taking turns at the different stations. Rowan and I appreciated the apples not going to waste and the neighbors appreciated the free cider and pulp for their chickens."

"Was Mae there?" I try to sound indifferent but fail.

"She was." He smiles down at the cutting board. "Why do you ask?"

"Are you doing it this year?" I ignore his question.

"Rowan usually organized it, so, no. Maybe I'll be able to bring myself to pull it all together next year." I see the visible drop of his shoulders.

"What's the next step?" I steer the conversation back to safe territory, even though we're nowhere close to starting the next step.

"Apples have fermentable sugar on the inside and naturally oc-curring yeast on the outside. So, all you have to do is press the juice out, bottle it, and let it sit for a few weeks and it usually turns into hard cider. But it tastes better if you take a few extra steps. After we get it into the sterilized carboys, I'll add yeast and enzymes. This should be a good batch because we had a good year with the apples."

I tilt my head in question, encouraging him to continue.

"The orchard conditions during the summer months will actu-ally impact the chemical composition of the apples and change how the finished cider ferments."

"Oh, interesting. How'd you learn all this?"

"The internet and trial and error—half of what I made became hard cider and the other half I accidentally made vinegar when I was trying to do it the old-fashioned way. So, now I do it the modern way, using a particular yeast that works well with cider."

"You know," I add. "Johnny Appleseed isn't a famous folk hero because apples were a tasty fruit. It's because he was bringing alcohol and potable beverages to the frontier through cider."

"Millie." My name tumbles out of him in a laugh. "I lured you over here because I needed free labor, but little did I know I'd be getting historical anecdotes." He says it in that way that sounds like he's both making fun of me and really fond of me at the same time.

"Lucky you."

"Did Johnny Appleseed actually wear a pot on his head, and why?" He cocks his head toward me.

"You know, I'm not sure, but if you give me enough time I will find out."

"I'm sure you will. Do you know anything about cider being made here, on the property?" He tosses a piece of apple to Max.

"The cidery was probably not a part of the inn business if that's what you mean. A lot of settlers and rural folks had orchards for making their own hard cider for their household."

I'm buzzing with sugar and sticky with juice when Ethan finally calls it quits. All the sadness from last night, all the anger from the phone call with my mom, has dampened throughout the day. Being around him is like a balm for my troubles. Maybe it's the fresh air and working with my hands. Or maybe it's the laughing and deep conversation and silly conversation and being made to feel like I'm the most interesting girl. Oh, and the out-of-control forearm porn.

"Will you come to dinner with me?" he asks as I hand him my apron, just like I hoped he would.

"Yes!" I don't want to let go of all this warmth I've gathered in my chest. "Yes," I say less manically.

"I didn't expect you to say yes. I'm so happy you did. I have to finish up here and change and shower. I'll pick you up around 5?"

"That works for me. Where are we going?"

"It's Nonna's birthday. Maria is hosting."

CHAPTER EIGHTEEN

"Ethan!" Three little dark-haired girls—mirror images of each other—are running full tilt as soon as we step out of the woods and onto Maria's manicured lawn. The first to reach him jumps into his arms and he twirls her around. She's exploding with joy and laughter, and I can't say I blame her or that I had wanted to do anything different when I saw Ethan tonight.

He showed up on the inn's doorstep with a tucked-in shirt, fresh and shy like a prom date.

After a relaxing bath to soak away the sticky apple juice, I'd put on a casual black cotton maxi dress and paired it with a cardigan and my boots, which I'd had to wash the mud off. There weren't enough choices in the little duffel I'd brought along. I left my hair down and naturally wavy. The outfit was nothing special.

But when I opened my door to his knock? He stuttered.

"Are you his *girlfriend*?" one of the little girls asks me.

"Um," I say, my cheeks going pink.

"You're so pretty!" the second girl interjects.

"Are you going to hand out candy on Halloween? Rowan always handed out Halloween candy and let us explore his spooky house."

"Give them some space!" I'm rescued by a handsome, dark-haired guy. He's wearing jeans and a friendly smile, and a T-shirt that says

"Rad Dad." There's a bit of glitter on his arm. I wonder if it's the remnant of a craft earlier in the day.

He and Ethan embrace.

"Joe, do you remember Millie?" Ethan asks, turning to introduce me.

"Of course, it's nice to see you again, Millie," Joe says, leaning in to hug me next, squeezing me tight like we're long-lost best friends instead of being barely casual acquaintances a decade ago.

"I've heard a lot about you over the years, especially recently from this one," he says, nodding at Ethan. "And these three are my daughters. Rosa, Maria, and Ava."

"It's nice to see you again, too. Your girls are beautiful."

"Thank you, yes, they are. They take after their mother, thank God."

I laugh. If Joe is ugly with his olive skin and warm brown eyes, I can't imagine how gorgeous his wife must be. He's the self-deprecating humor type I suppose.

"My condolences on your uncle's passing," he says politely.

"Thank you."

"How are you holding up?"

"I'm alright. Trying to keep myself busy. Which is not hard to do, lots to get done still at the inn."

"Ah, that cursed, damned place," he mutters under his breath.

"What?" I ask, taken aback at his sudden consternation. "You think it's cursed?"

"Well, not really, I don't. But some of my family thinks so, yeah. It's an old family superstition, but the profanities just slip out sometimes. I'm so used to hearing them."

"You all should stop by sometime. It's not feeling as cursed anymore," I say, looking over at Ethan. But he's been overpowered by the three girls, who are taking turns getting twirled around by him. We hear eruptions of giggles and "my turn, my turn!"

"We will. I'm glad to hear it," Joe says to me. "You better be hungry. Come with me."

He leads me inside Maria's home—a cozy craftsman bungalow that is impossibly clean and adorned with pleated floral curtains and the remnants of four boys growing up there. Well-worn furniture is covered with starched lace doilies. My eyes linger on a graphic, bloody crucifix hanging on the wall, more prominent than the small television.

Joe leads me to his brothers, Dominic and Tony. They are unabashedly warm, welcoming, and passionate huggers. There are common themes in our small talk. Ethan is part of their family, and they want to know my status with him. Each of them offers their condolences for Rowan. Then, in whispered tones, with wide eyes and shaking heads, they ask about the spooky old inn—the haunted house I live in.

I think they are truly afraid of it.

"Wait. Have any of you been inside the inn?"

Joe nods. "Always liked Rowan. Stopped by a few times, to help with this and that. My mom didn't like it, though. She was always waiting back at home, praying for us."

"Why are you all so nervous about it?" I remember Maria on the day I arrived, how she wouldn't take her eyes off it while we stood outside.

"Ethan didn't tell you the story about the inn being cursed?" Dominic asks.

I shake my head and look around for him. "What?! No. Where is he anyway?"

"Ethan is distracting my children outside. Please allow me these few moments of freedom from their adorable and exhausting clutches," Joe says.

"We've got to tell her the story," Tony says, elbowing Joe in the side.

"Yeah Joey, you tell the story best. You do it," Dominic adds.

They lead me to the dining room. Joe pulls out an upholstered chair covered in clear plastic for me before sitting down on the opposite side, his hands folded on the table in front of him. Dominic and Tony sit on either side of him. Between us all on the table is a sliced loaf of bread and small bowl of olive oil.

"It's just an old story," Joe starts.

"I *love* old family stories, especially when they are about buildings I'm currently living in. In fact, I'd call myself a professional old family story listener."

With a grin, Tony slaps the table, making me jump. "You're *perfect*, Millie. Listen to this."

With a practiced tone, Joe begins. "My great-grandmother, Nonna's mother, used to work at the old Starling Inn as a maid when she was young. It was a big operation back then."

"People came from all over the world to stay here, can you believe that, Millie?" Dominic asks.

Joe, aggravated at the interruption, side-eyes his brother.

"So," he clears his throat and begins again in a slightly louder tone. "My great-grandmother, Nonna's mother, she was proud of her job—not a lot of women had jobs back then, but she needed to help support her family. My great-great-granddad was a bricklayer, a new immigrant, you see? So, the family didn't have a lot of money."

"And the inn was right next door and needed a lot of hands to run it, so it made sense," Tony interjects.

Joe bites his finger while glaring at Tony.

"Go ahead Joey," Tony nods at him.

I press my lips together to stop myself from laughing.

"Right," Joe begins again, speaking even louder now. "So, my great-grandmother, Nonna's mother, she started helping out when she was young, doing the laundry and cleaning rooms and such at the inn. She loved working there and meeting fine people—and not so fine people—from far and wide." Joe spreads his hands apart when he says far and wide.

Both brothers nod.

"They say she had a big laugh—"

"And a kind heart, Joey, everyone said she had a kind heart," Dominic interrupts.

"Hey! Who's telling the story here?" Joe asks.

Dominic and Tony put their hands up in surrender.

"As I was saying, my great-grandmother, Nonna's mother, she had a big laugh, and a kind heart," Joe pauses and looks at Dominic and Tony before continuing, as if daring them to interrupt again. "And she put on her apron with pride each day. When she was a teenager, her days away at the inn got longer and longer, and she started to return home wistful and smiling."

I see Ethan blur past the window with a little girl bouncing on his shoulders. He backtracks and catches my eye. He raises an eyebrow at me, like, *Are you OK in there on your own?*

I wave him away and put my hand on my chin, leaning toward Joe.

"Her parents asked questions that she never answered. She got pregnant," Joe's eyebrows furrow. "The father never came forward to marry her. She died of heartbreak only a few years after the baby was born."

The brothers all lower their heads, and Tony makes the sign of the cross.

I clutch my hands to my chest. "Poor thing."

Joe smiles sadly. "So with her mom gone and her dad never having come forward, Nonna was brought up here in this house by her grandparents."

"She's celebrating her hundredth birthday this week!" Tony chimes in again.

"A hundred," Dominic echoes. "Can you believe that, Millie?"

"Let me finish the story!" Joe interrupts, cutting off any reply I might have had. "Nonna warned the family to stay away from the inn because it was cursed by the devil. It's where her mother got pregnant and was abandoned."

"That's such a heartbreaking story, thank you for sharing it with me," I say.

"There's more," Tony says. "Keep going, Joey. Tell her about Dad."

Joe continues, more solemn now. "You know all about the sadness with Rowan and Catherine, I suspect?"

I nod.

"Nonna also blamed that on the curse. Then my dad, God rest him, he was a plumber, and he did some work at the house with Ethan and Rowan a few years back. He died of a heart attack right after."

Once again, all three brothers lower their heads in unison and Tony makes the sign of the cross.

"I'm so sorry for your loss."

"Thank you, he was a good man. It was almost three years ago now and we still all feel like we're getting used to the idea of him not being around anymore. I still pick up the phone to call him because I want to tell him something. Old habit."

"I feel that, I really do. Did he die *at* the inn?" I ask carefully.

Joe shakes his head. "No. People die of heart attacks all the time, I know. Surely, it's a coincidence and has nothing to do with the inn, but—"

"But you can see why we don't like that place so much," Tony says while tearing off a piece of bread.

"I can definitely see that. Curses and haunting rumors have been born on much shakier ground than your stories. You really do have bad luck with the inn," I say, and Joe smiles at me. "Well, I hope it's all over now."

"Amen to that," Dominic says.

I tear off a piece of bread and dip it into the bowl of olive oil, just like Tony did. It tastes more complex than any olive oil I've ever tried—bright, grassy, bitter.

"Could I talk to Nonna?" I ask them. "I found an old letter and I want to ask her if she knows anything about it."

"Yeah, of course—I'll warn you, though, she's getting a little salty in her old age and her memory is not the best," Joe says.

****

They lead me to an ancient, tiny lady, with milky eyes and a puff of wispy cotton candy hair. She's sitting in a beige recliner, with a multicolored crocheted blanket in her lap. One of the bedrooms in the house has been turned into a little apartment for her. She's listening to a baseball game on the radio.

"Nonna!" Joe says. She pats his cheek fondly with a hand gnarled by arthritis. "This is Ethan's friend, Millie. She lives over at the inn."

Her other hand is curled in her lap around a beaded necklace. No, a rosary.

"Nice to meet you," I say with a smile. "And happy birthday. We almost share a birthday! Mine is on Halloween."

"Your birthday is on Halloween? You must have had awesome birthday parties!" Dominic says.

"The Feast of All Souls is soon, you know," Nonna croaks, her eyes on her rosary.

"Pardon?" I ask.

"Feast of all souls is the time we pray for the departed. We pray to release souls from purgatory."

"Oh, interesting," I say, my voice rising an octave.

"I pray for Ethan that day. He's trapped in that house. It's his purgatory. It trapped his mother and my mother. It trapped Rowan. And my son—he died of a heart attack after he visited. All who set foot in that cursed house, they get trapped. Take care or you'll get trapped, too."

I take one step backward toward the boys. This was not a good idea.

"Come on now, Nonna, that's nonsense," Joe scoffs, but I cut him off.

"What do you mean, Ethan's in purgatory?"

Her lips are moving but she isn't speaking, her hands shift to the next bead in silent prayer. After a few moments, her eyes meet mine.

"He was doing so well, moved to the city, beautiful fiancée, everything was going according to plan. And now he's stuck here. Doing what? Picking apples?" She spits the last two words. Then she turns her eyes on me. "You're next."

I step back so fast I bang into Tony, but she hardly notices, her fingers moving from bead to bead on her rosary. *Fiancée? Ethan didn't say he was engaged—*

"Jesus Christ, Nonna," Tony mutters under his breath.

"Don't take the Lord's name in vain, Anthony," Nonna reprimands.

"Nice meeting you, Nonna," I say, and decide that this is the perfect time to find Ethan.

"*Sorry*," says Joe as he follows me into the narrow hallway. "I did try to warn you."

"No need to apologize, I understand," I say nonchalantly, but my heart is beating fast.

Like my thoughts have conjured him into existence, Ethan crowds into the hallway with us, having finally escaped the triplets.

"What have you cool kids been doing?" he asks as he slides his arm around my waist.

"Oh, just scaring the hell out of your date, no big deal," Tony says quickly.

"Don't tell me you told her the whole curse story."

Joe rubs the back of his neck and looks at Ethan with a guilty expression.

"Damn it, Joe. I left her alone for like ten minutes."

"*Twenty* minutes and she asked to hear it," Dominic adds.

"I did. I asked Joe to tell me," I admit.

Ethan looks down at me in this crowded little hallway with that big smile of his, and suddenly it feels like the sun is shining on me, and all my thoughts vacate my head.

"Ethan, is that you I hear?" Nonna calls out.

"Joe. Tony. Dominic. May I trust you to not terrify this woman in the few moments that I speak to your grandmother?"

Joe shrugs. "Yeah, I mean, we'll try, but no promises."

Ethan throws his hands up.

"We're needed in the kitchen, anyway. I just heard Mom."

They shuffle toward the kitchen and Ethan walks into Nonna's room, and I'm left lingering in the hallway as I decide to watch instead of following him.

"Happy birthday, beautiful." Ethan leans down to kiss Nonna on the cheek. She beams at him, and they small talk for a while—I miss all of it, too distracted watching her hand moving bead by bead up the rosary.

I give them privacy and turn my attention to pictures hanging in the hallway. There are individual portraits of the boys, probably senior photos, including one of Ethan. Then a more recent picture of what must be Joe's wedding. It must be the same day as the picture on Rowan's mantel. Beneath them all is a second row with pictures of the granddaughters.

Ethan's arms slink around me, and I bask for a moment in the easy familiarity of it.

"This got so weird, so fast," he said. "I'm sorry about all of the curse talk."

"I'm fine, really. I'm thinking it all over." And how Nonna said Ethan had a fiancée, I don't add. "The family story is so sad. Do you know if they ever tracked down Nonna's father? Have they done a DNA test?"

"I don't think so."

I turn back to the pictures in golden frames, lined up in proud rows. "You've got some real Shawn Hunter energy here," I say, nodding to his picture. He's young, wearing a black jacket.

"Who?"

"You know, from *Boy Meets World*. Wholesome family dynamic. Two best friends, one good boy and the other one from the wrong side of the tracks."

He shakes his head.

"You've never seen it? Well, I know what we're doing this week. We're having a '90s sitcom watch party."

"Fine, but only if we do it the authentic way, which is topless," he says.

"What? I've never heard of a topless sitcom watch party. That's not a thing."

"Sure it is. Dominic?" Ethan leads me into the living room. Dominic meets us there, holding a beer.

"You're only supposed to rewatch '90s sitcoms topless, right?" Ethan asks.

"That is correct," Dominic agrees, not missing a beat. "Shirts not allowed, bras optional."

I roll my eyes.

"See?" Ethan says, turning back to me. "Topless '90s sitcom party at my house tomorrow night."

He says it with all the authority and conviction of a judge, and I honestly cannot tell if they are messing with me or not.

"Can I come?" Dominic asks, smiling from ear to ear.

"Fuck off, no. Only Millie is invited."

"Fine. But you have to play that '90s sitcom drinking game, too. Take shots any time a nerd gets shoved in a locker, or someone walks into their neighbor's house without knocking, or someone has a dream sequence. Oh wait, I forgot, Ethan doesn't drink," Dominic says.

Tony chimes in from the other room. "Yeah, I guess instead of taking shots, you remove a piece of clothing."

"Boys, behave," Maria calls out from the kitchen. "And get a plate. Food is ready. Then go outside—it's too crowded in here."

I tense up at her voice and Ethan notices.

"What's wrong?"

"Nothing, it's nothing." But I clam up a bit before we get to her, remembering her weirdness the last time I saw her.

"Um, do you know if she has any issues with me? You know, the lasagna thing..."

"Let's get to the bottom of it."

"Now? Right now?"

He pulls me into the kitchen, and I'm distracted by the feel of his hand in mine. We're enveloped in the smell of roasted garlic and heat from the stove that's been working all afternoon.

"Hello, Maria, thanks for having me."

"Millie, it's good to see you, glad you could be here. You first, you're the guest," Maria says, and hands me a plate. I'm herded toward a countertop filled with trays and trays of stuffed shells, garlic bread, and a big bowl of salad topped with artichoke hearts, thinly sliced onions, and shaved parmesan, and a tray of seeded cookies.

"This looks amazing, thank you," I say, filling my plate.

"*Mangia*," she says with a smile. Her short black hair is pushed back with a headband, and an apron that says *kiss the chef* is tied tight around her waist. "I make extra for everyone to take home. I hope you brought Tupperware."

"I didn't!"

"Then you take mine and return it next time. I worry about you in that big old place. It's not good for anyone to be alone for too long, especially not in a place like that."

I watch as she touches her fingertips to her forehead, chest, and each shoulder—making the sign of the cross.

"I am doing OK now, thanks for asking."

"I left a blessing on your door. And I buried St. Joseph in your yard."

My heart summersaults in my chest.

"The chalk above the door? The figurine buried in the yard? That was *you*?"

She nods. "I buried the figurine when I thought you were selling—I wanted St. Joseph looking over you during such a difficult time. And I was glad to hear you aren't selling to a contractor right away. We thought we'd have developers for neighbors, building a high-rise complex or who knows what. But you're staying!"

I glance at Ethan. This is it, then? This is why she was acting weird this whole time?

"Well, I'm not staying permanently—just long enough to try to finish what Rowan and Ethan started."

She waves her hand at me. "Nonsense—if you were going to leave you would have done it already, and with Ethan to keep you company, who would leave? That would be crazy."

I mean. She's not wrong.

He's got his forearms out again.

"Well, I do have good company," I agree. He's smiling and pretending not to eavesdrop while loading his plate with pasta.

"Ethan, you look thin in the face. You are exercising too much," she insists, and puts cookies on his plate on top of the pasta.

"That's what I said! Did you know he goes for a run every morning regardless of the weather? Saw him out in a thunderstorm once," I add.

"Running in the rain? What? You will slip and fall. You will catch a cold."

"I'm fine, Ma," he says with a groan. "I don't need *extra* cookies. I'll take one cookie like everyone else. I have to run every day with you feeding me this all the time."

She tuts at him and waves us to the dining room, slipping three more cookies onto his plate.

"Do you call her Ma as a shortened form of Maria? Or because she's been a mother to you?" I ask, setting my plate down on the table. Ethan pulls up a chair next to me and our knees touch beneath the table.

He shrugs before twirling pasta around his fork. "Both, I guess. I called her Mrs. Russo for the longest time, and she told me to call her Maria after I moved in, but that felt weird. I never called her mom—that for my actual mom—but calling her Ma felt comfortable. All the boys do, too."

"How long did you live here?"

"About five years. After my mom died, until I went to college."

"Because you didn't want to live with your grandparents."

He nods, gesturing around. "Look at this place. Look at all the love."

I listen to the giggles of the girls while I eat buttery pasta and crusty garlic bread.

"Look at this food. Sometimes I feel so angry about what happened to me. But then I think, this is the best family I could have fallen into."

"Damn right it is," Joe says, dropping his plate on the table. "You're so lucky to have us."

One by one they fill the table around us and we get lost in good food and conversation and warmth.

***

Tony builds a bonfire on the rocky beach, and we gather around it to drink ice-cold beer from coolers as the soft purples and blues of twilight give way to the deep blues and blacks of night, with stars popping up one by one like little pinpricks in the sky.

Everything feels hazy and magical. There's something about sitting around a bonfire and drinking beer on a cold night—our breath frosting out in front of us—that brings out people's best, truest selves.

I collect every embarrassing story about Ethan that his adoptive family is willing to tell me. My cheeks literally hurt from all the laughing.

Long after the girls have fallen asleep inside with their grandmother, I get to talk to Joe's wife, Liz, who's as sparkling and lovely as I would have expected.

"Maria buried a tiny St. Joseph in my yard. And wrote over the top of my door. Some symbols and letters and numbers. Something about blessing the house and keeping the devil away," I tell her.

"She does the chalk thing every year to all our houses. The priest blesses the chalk, it's a whole thing. It's a little forward, I'll give you that. But it comes from a good place. She's trying to protect you in the way that she knows how to."

She pauses before continuing, "She was happy to hear from Ethan that you wanted to stay awhile and weren't selling right away to a developer. I think that blessing on your door was a bit of gratitude. She saw the smiles coming back to Ethan's face. He was devastated after Rowan died, you know. We didn't see him for a few days. But then he popped up again, talking about this gorgeous girl—you pulled him out of a dark place, Millie."

"I don't know about that. He's pretty grounded in who he is—he doesn't need me."

"You're not giving yourself enough credit. He was quiet for once, if you can believe that. Can you imagine Ethan quiet?"

I shake my head.

"But he's smiling today! It's because you're here."

Moments later, he's reaching his hand out to me. I grab it and he pulls me up and steals me away from Liz.

"Come with me."

"Where?"

"It's a surprise."

He grabs a lantern from the beach, then we walk deep into the forest, until I can barely see Maria's house in the distance, the light from the windows beaming like a lighthouse calling you home.

"Welcome to my fortress, milady," he says, gesturing at boards nailed to a tree trunk, disappearing up into black rustling branches above.

"Um, I don't know if this is safe."

"It's safe. I built it. Even twelve-year-old Ethan knew his way around a construction site. Come on." I watch him climb up the planks and none budge, so I follow, cautiously, one hand after the other, my feet scrambling to make purchase on the rough boards.

He extends his hand to pull me up the last few rungs. When I get to the top and he hoists me onto the platform, I forget to take my hand out of his. We stand there a moment, inches apart, me looking up at him and him looking at me. He's just barely lit by the lantern, and I feel dazed like a deer in headlights, being so close to him and so alone.

Get it together, girl. I shake my head and step away, looking around.

Ethan flips on a switch, and twinkling, battery-powered string lights brighten the treehouse around us.

"What is this place?" I ask him.

"Joe and his dad and I built it after I moved in. They were happy to take me in, but they didn't have much space for me. Slept in a room full of bunk beds."

"Like summer camp."

"Or an army barracks."

"That sounds crowded."

"It was. They all made me feel like a part of the family, from the moment I met them."

"And still today," I say.

He nods. "Still today. Joe and I spent a summer building this so we could spend a lot of time out here to stretch our legs and get some space away from the younger kids."

"It's incredible. I've always wanted a treehouse," I admit.

"You should have come out to play with us when you visited. Ben would sometimes. He's been up here."

"I should have. But I was busy reading and sunbathing. And, of course, being way too smart and cool to hang out with a herd of boys I hardly knew."

His laugh echoes out into the night, and I feel so clever to make him laugh.

"Fair."

I see a set of suspicious hatch marks on the wall.

"What are these?" I ask, my voice rising to a scandalous accusatory octave.

"When we were teenagers, we would bring girls to hook up with."

My jaw drops in mock horror.

He pulls a blanket out of a bin and wraps it around the both of us, cozy in a little cocoon sitting on the floorboards. I stare at the perfect geometry of his face. I think about the kindness beneath, and I wonder how I got so lucky.

"I wanted to bring *you* up here when we were teenagers but never got the chance to ask you because, tragically, you shot me down."

I'm being given a second chance. A do-over, from when I rejected him all those years ago.

"Oh? And how many other girls did you bring up here, Ethan?" I ask.

"A few. None as pretty as you." His eyes are dilated, fixed on me like Frank's when he's ready to pounce on a skittering leaf. I shiver and it has nothing to do with the cold.

"And how did you get them to kiss you? What sweet words would you say?"

"I would tell them they were the prettiest girl I ever brought up here, then I would challenge them to a game of truth or dare. Worked every time," he says with a mischievous grin.

He means so much to me already, in the few weeks I've been here. I've learned about myself because of him. He's pushed his way into my chest and settled into my thoughts. I'm starting to look at the world in a new way.

Already, thinking about leaving him here, going back to Chicago, is making me feel panicked. And we haven't crossed that boundary yet, the one we are carefully keeping, past friendship and into something more.

If we do?

"What are you thinking about?" he asks. He's tracing the faint lines on my palm where my scratches were.

He didn't even touch me that day, not with romantic intent, and it's still one of the most erotic moments of my life. Ethan sliding off my jeans? I'll remember that moment forever. The feel of the cold tile beneath my feet, the sound of the running bathtub, his steady presence making me feel safe in such a vulnerable moment. The tempo of his breathing, his flushed cheeks, sharp blue eyes, raindrops clinging to his beard. As long as I live, I'll never forget it.

And if we did this for real? If I let myself sink into this thing I have with him? I'll be *devastated* when I go. I'll be picking up the broken pieces of myself for who knows how long.

I've had enough tragedy in my life. I don't want any more.

"Ethan. I'm leaving. If we do this, it will wreck us both. Well, I can't speak for you, I guess. But *I* will be wrecked. It's going to be hard enough as it is, leaving as friends. I'm going to miss you so much when I go home."

"I know," he says, voice low. He raises my hand to his lips, pressing a kiss to my scars. "But don't give up on us before we even have a chance. Look at you. You're worrying about how much you'll miss me, and you haven't even left yet. Doesn't that tell you something? There's something here between us. A big chance. For a best friend, a great love. It is worth figuring out. It might not be a simple path, but we're so intertwined now," he continues, looking down at our joined hands.

It is worth figuring out, I admit to myself.

"Truth or dare?" I ask him.

The slowest, sexiest smile spreads across his face.

"Truth."

"What's your favorite color?"

"Brown," he answers without pause. The color of my eyes, which he is staring into so intently. I tell myself it's a coincidence—not everything is about me.

"No, black," he changes his answer. "Truth or dare?"

"Truth."

"Why did you really decide to stay here these last few weeks?" he asks. "Why didn't you list the place and leave?"

I thought about this awhile before answering. "Besides the guilt and grieving, you mean? Rowan always helped me feel so grounded. I think I've been missing direction. And a home. I came back here looking for that feeling again. It's not too different from the reason you came back, I think. And then I got caught up in *you* and the renovations and didn't want to leave."

"And did you find it? Direction?"

"You're helping me find it. Or you are at least helping me figure out how to be at peace in each moment I'm in. Thank you for that. Truth or dare?"

"Truth," he says.

"What's your favorite food?"

"Cold lasagna, with a beautiful, intimidating woman watching me eat it, disgusted." *OK, maybe everything is about me.* "Truth or dare?"

"Dare," I say.

"I dare you to put your hand on my chest," he says.

I lift my hand to his chest, and I can feel his heart thundering as fast as mine is. He holds my hand there, gripped beneath his, as I ask, "Truth or dare?"

"Truth."

"Why do you keep finding new jobs to work on at the house? You could have stopped days ago. You keep drawing out projects longer, even though you have so much work to do at your shop. I've literally watched you painting in slow motion."

He laughs again and I congratulate myself.

"I like you, Millie. I like our days together. I like listening to you talk about whatever you are studying that day. I like working alongside you. I like watching you play with your hair while you're concentrating. I like how you cut to the heart of everything I say, like you've got me figured out. I like making sure you've eaten breakfast, and I like trying to make you blush." I glance away, overwhelmed. "Just like that," he continues, sweeping his thumbs gently across my cheeks. It's dark out here—my cheeks must be flaming red.

"You're so beautiful, and kind of sad, and I want to take care of you. I think about that day I found you in the conservatory all the time. You looked like a broken butterfly. I was so terrified—it pops into my head sometimes and makes my chest hurt. I want to do everything I can so that you never feel that sad ever again. Or, at least, never feel alone," he corrects himself. "I want to share your sadness with you, so you don't have to bear it alone."

He's sitting so close I can smell his soap, spicy and warm. I want to lean in and breathe him in forever. He sees me looking at his lips.

"Do it," his voice comes out thick and husky. "I dare you."

Dear reader, I kissed him.

Time stops and I catalog every detail. My heart is pounding like I've jumped off a cliff. He kisses me exactly as I expected he would. Reverently. With a viciously slow pace, he savors me.

He pulls away, brushing his nose against mine and dropping his lips to my collarbone. He leaves a trail of kisses all the way up to my jaw, before finally sinking his lips to mine again. As he murmurs my name, I can feel the scrape of his stubble beneath my lips and my breathing goes from nonexistent to fast and shaky.

Ethan is kissing me.

Ethan is kissing me.

Then, his phone buzzes, but he ignores it. A short pause. The buzzing resumes for a second time, and he groans in frustration, the most devastatingly sexy sound, then pulls away from me, the air sudden and cold between us. He fishes his phone out of his pocket and the sparks in my bloodstream fizzle out.

Emily.

I can see his phone screen and it says Emily.

Nonna's words claw at me. *Fiancée.*

He'd lied to me or hadn't told me the whole story about his relationship with her at least.

"Millie, I'm so sorry. I have to take this. I'll be right back," he says and stands up. I'm left in a half-empty blanket cocoon.

He drops out of the treehouse and steps out into the woods to speak to her, his cellphone a little square of light I can make out between the gaps in the floorboards.

I wonder why his ex-girlfriend is calling him at 10 p.m., and why it's important enough, private enough, for him to walk away from me to take the call.

It doesn't matter.

The spell of the evening is broken and I'm thinking straight again. I climb out of the treehouse, and weave my way through the woods, following the light from Maria's house until I find Joe sitting outside.

"Hey, can you walk me home?" I ask.

CHAPTER NINETEEN

I cry all the time now.

I used to fight it, battling against that uncomfortable welling up in my throat. I'd swallow and push and wish it away. I'd clench my fists so hard to stop it that I would leave half-moon circles from my fingernails in my palms.

But now it wells out of me in an uncontrollable downpour. It's like the crying in the conservatory broke a dam open and now the tears are unstoppable.

Scallop-edged platter Rowan used to pile Ben and I's pancakes on? Epic weeping downpour.

A bright aqua, purple, and pink 1980s era puff coat that I found in the coat closet and I'm pretty certain is Catherine's? Tears everywhere.

Crying is healthy. It means I've made progress. I'm letting myself grieve and feel all my feelings. *I think*.

I cried last night, after Joe dropped me off at my door and made sure I got inside safely, with a huge plate full of leftovers. I put the leftovers in the fridge and patted Frank on the head and sank onto the couch and just lost it.

Because that kiss devastated me. It knocked me off my trajectory. Well, not just the kiss—everything with Ethan, culminating in that kiss.

Two things are true.

One, I am falling for him. In a way that I never have before. My past relationships pale in comparison to the blossoming start of this one.

And two, I'm leaving, sooner rather than later if my mom gets her way.

This fact is breaking my heart and getting harder and harder to accept every day.

A full half of my heart doesn't want to leave anymore and I'm panicking about it. I don't know what to do.

I just know that I want to drink coffee with him each morning, watch him work, and hear his big stupid laugh. I want to sit on the porch with him each night and listen to him talk about his day. I try to imagine myself going back to campus and just going on with my life, selling this place out from under him and new owners taking over next door to the Russo's, and I just *can't*.

Frank is slowly suffocating me to death, sitting on my chest with his face pressed against my face. He jumps off me with a sassy hiss as I sit up from the couch. I'm still in my outfit from last night, mascara and cat hair making my eyes feel like they are full of sand.

I pick up my phone to call Sarah and talk this all through with her. Then I pause, because I don't know if she'll answer. What is going on with her? I hate the distance she's put between us.

There's a flurry of texts Ethan sent last night, and a reluctant smile inches across my face as I read them.

Ethan, 10:00 p.m.: I'm so sorry for taking that call. Where are you? I need to explain.

Ethan, 10:05 p.m.: That bad of a kiss?

Ethan, 10:15 p.m.: Millie, I promise to never kiss you again. Will you please answer?

Ethan, 10:17 p.m.: I need to know that you aren't lost in the woods or something.

Ethan, 10:20 p.m.: Joe told me he walked you home, so I know you're OK. I guess you're freaked out. I'm so sorry if I moved too fast, or if anything I said upset you.

Ethan, 11:00 p.m.: Please don't shut me out. I'll take it all back if you want.

Ethan, 11:00 p.m.: I think you're ugly.

Ethan, 11:01 p.m.: I hate the color of your eyes.

Ethan, 11:02 p.m.: You're a terrible kisser.

Ethan, 11:02 p.m.: Your hair is outrageous.

Ethan, 11:03 p.m.: I'll never play truth or dare with you again.

I type a response to Ethan and delete it twelve times. I pour myself a glass of water and don't drink it. My brain is so scrambled, I need to wake up and get my thoughts in order. Frank's nudging at me for breakfast and our morning walk. I fill his bowl and brush my teeth.

I'm tying my shoes for our walk when I hear the doorbell ring and frantic knocking.

My heart leaps in my chest and I tousle my hair as I jog to the door.

I bite some color into my lips and pull the door open, ready for a heart-to-heart with Ethan.

"Surprise!"

Ben steps inside, wraps his meaty arms around me, and lifts me off the floor in a hug that knocks all the air out of my lungs. Sarah is right behind him, hopping up and down, impatiently waiting her turn. She's wearing the purple sweater she was in the process of knitting the last time we video chatted. Ben gently sets me down and Sarah rushes in.

"Surprise! Happy Birthday!" Sarah squeals. It's been way too long since I've hugged my best friend. She's a little rumpled from a road trip but she smells like vanilla and memories, and I get a little choked up, because she's the best person and I love her so much.

"Come in, come in," I order, holding the door open. Then, I remember that she's ghosted me for the last few weeks, and I block her path.

"Wait a minute. *Why the hell* haven't you two been talking to me?" I don't hide the anger and hurt in my voice.

She looks over her shoulder at Ben, her face drawn.

"Let's get inside and we'll tell you. I'll tell you everything, OK? Please, Millie."

She looks... scared.

I look back and forth between them. They are acting so weird. I'm not sure what is going on, but I won't get an answer if I shut them out.

I step back from the doorway again, and with a dramatic sigh of relief, Sarah pushes inside.

"Millie, you've been eating breakfast again, I can tell! You look amazing. Your face is filling out."

Unlike me, Sarah had a completely normal childhood with two supportive parents, and she is soft and shiny and perfect as a result. Her parents were elementary school teachers, and it shows—she is all empathy and softness held together with a razor-sharp brain.

Her face isn't perfectly symmetrical like the rest of us boring people. I think it makes her look more interesting. My eyes want to linger longer. "I don't want to look interesting, Millie. I want to look pretty," she told me once. But she is. She doesn't always see it, but she is.

She probably said more words in the last five minutes than I had uttered in the last five days, and it never seemed to make her get exhausted the way it did me. Or that's how it usually is anyway. But these last few weeks have been different. Ethan is making me different. It dawns on me then that I don't have trouble finding things to say when I'm around him. I don't get exhausted with him the way I do around most people. He's in that special place that only Sarah resides, the I-never-get-tired-of-talking-to-*you* place. Being around him fills me up. While being around most people drains me, he's like tinder, sparking something alive inside me.

"I can't believe you came all the way here." Even though I'm mad at her, I've missed her and love her so much. "In a car with him, no less." I gesture at Ben, who is slowly walking through the living room behind us, overcome with memories in this place, I'm certain.

Sarah and Ben never quite fit together the way she and I did. They were always competitive and annoying, arguing and one upping each other. We used to play board games sometimes, but it usually ended in me tapping out with my eyes rolling at those two trying to destroy each other.

Sarah studies my face. "It's your birthday weekend. Of course I showed up. I will bake you a cake, like every other birthday. I will bake you a cake every October 31st until we are both dead. Or until my fingers are arthritic and then my grandchildren will bake you cakes. This is going to be the best weekend of our lives."

"You say that every time."

"And I mean it every time."

"I didn't think you were going to show up this time. Why haven't you two been answering your phones? I needed you, and you weren't there."

"I'm so sorry, Millie. I hope you can forgive me some day. There's a lot I need to catch you up on," Sarah says worriedly.

"Yeah. There is." I say pointedly, frustration in my tone. "Let's go set your stuff down first, I'll show you your room."

"What's this?" Sarah points at Stephen, the mannequin head, his forever saccharine smile grinning up at her from the lobby counter.

"There's a lot I need to catch *you* up on."

"Hey, old girl," Ben says, looking up the staircase, a dreamy look on his face. "Looking good."

"That's not nice, she's not that old," Sarah starts to defend me.

"I'm talking to the house," Ben corrects her. He takes the lead and guides Sarah up the stairs, then through the hall room by room, pausing in each to see the changes since he'd visited last.

Sarah is in love. Moved to tears. She's never had a nondramatic reaction about anything in her life. But she's *extra* with this house, all gasps and wide-eyed wonder as we walk around, her fingertips dragging across surfaces like she simply cannot stop herself from caressing it. I point out the starling in the stained glass, and the hidden gargoyles—I can find ten now. I need to ask Ethan where the other two are.

Her head is on a swivel, not wanting to miss a single detail.

"This is your room." I unlock the door and hand her the key to Room 5. It's sweet and bright like her. She sets her bag down on the freshly refinished floor and spins in a slow circle, looking at the room with big, round green eyes.

"I'm sorry it's a bit of a mess. We haven't put it entirely back together yet. As you saw, a lot of the rooms are a bit of a mess like this—it's a work in progress."

"Do you need any help putting it back together?" Her eyes sparkle with possibility, and she clasps her hands together in front of her chest, like she's begging me.

She owes me. But she also loves interior decorating.

"That would be helpful," I admit. "I could use your eye. The realtor is sending a photographer to take listing pictures eventually. Most of the rooms are painted now, but we need to stage them. If you want to come to the shed with me later, you can sort through the old furniture.

Maybe we could run to the thrift shop in town, too." I look over at Ben.

"And Ben, if you want to stay in your old room?" I ask my brother, who is lingering in the hallway, a duffel bag in his hand.

Sarah and Ben look at each other, then back at me, then back at each other.

"Um," Ben starts to say. "Millie, there's something we need to talk about."

"I know." Whatever they are going to tell me can't possibly be good. It's driven a wedge between us all. I feel so overwhelmed with their surprise arrival and I'm still on the rollercoaster of emotion from last night. "But can it wait? I need to take a bath and drink some coffee. I'm still in last night's clothes."

"Yeah, of course," Ben says, running his hands through his hair, fidgety. He peeks his head in his old bedroom right next to mine.

"So many memories here." His voice is soft and kind as he peeks at me from our respective doorways. "Do you remember when we were kids, and we were too scared to sleep in this place so you would come to my room in the middle of the night?"

"Yeah. We would hide under the covers with a flashlight. Like in a tent. And I'd tell you stories until we both fell asleep." Ben reaches out and pulls me into another bone-crunching hug. "You smell like a fireplace, go take that bath."

Sibling relationships are so bewildering. How can you be such strangers with someone you love so much, with someone you've shared childhood with, whose soul you know as well as your own?

"CAT!" Sarah interrupts, with an ear-splitting screech. "It's nice to meet you in person, you weird little thing."

Frank stares at her a moment, then runs away as fast as he can with a scramble of kitty claws on the wood floor.

***

I follow Sarah's laughter and Ben's assertive baritone down to the kitchen and it's so unexpectedly heartwarming to have this place crowded with people and to be able to chase their voices again.

I'm still mad at them. But I've missed them so much. I'm quickly learning that when love goes that deep, people can wound me, and I'll find it in myself to forgive. Whatever it is, I'll forgive them. They're here now, after all.

Ben brings in plastic bags full of groceries from the car and sets them on the kitchen counter one by one. Sarah pulls her apron out of one of the bags. It's white with little watercolor flowers on it. Then she starts pulling out her ingredients.

"Have a seat." Sarah nods her head at the kitchen table, and I follow, squishing the water out of my hair with a microfiber towel.

"Are there big bowls and measuring cups and stuff?" she asks me.

"Yeah," I say. "I packed up a lot of the kitchen stuff for donations. There were duplicates of most stuff that was donated, and some old appliances that we trashed. I think it was cabinet junk from the owners before Rowan and he never bothered to clear it all out. But I did leave a few items. Just in case someone wants to buy the house furnished."

Sarah opens a cabinet, and her jaw drops at a set of vintage glass Pyrex dishes, a set of ceramic soft pink mixing bowls.

"Oh hello, my pretties." She strokes them lovingly and selects a few.

I set baking tools for Sarah on the Formica countertops and sit down to watch her work.

"That's cute, is it new?" I ask, nodding to the apron.

"Thanks, yeah it is," she says, and her voice is wary. Scared.

Why?

I watch her closely as she concentrates on measuring her dry ingredients. She fills the measuring cup and scrapes the excess flour off the top with the back of a knife.

There's a smudge of flour on her cheek. Ben reaches over and brushes it away tenderly. My eyes narrow.

"I bought it for her at a farmers market we went to last weekend."

Ben does not go to farmers markets. Ben does not gently brush flour off Sarah's upturned cheek.

"What is going on?" I ask them, and I'm doing something scary with my voice.

Sarah takes a deep breath, like she's mustering up the courage to say something. She sets down her whisk and locks eyes with me. "Ben and I are together."

"*WHAT?*" I'm shouting a little and I hate it. I never shout.

"It's not what you think it is," she says in a panicked rush, her eyes wide. "It's not just a hookup."

"I'm in love with her." Ben stands behind her, his hand on her hip in silent support. Like he's daring me to put up a fight. They both stare at me, waiting nervously for my response.

I sit there in shock, my eyes flitting back and forth between them.

"We didn't start dating on a whim. I've had a crush on him for years. And the last few weeks, with you here and the apartment to ourselves..." she says in a rush, then looks at Ben and doesn't finish.

"Not something you've been keeping from me for a few weeks but something you've been keeping from me *for a few years*. And with me out of the way, you two were able to connect. So that's why you two weren't answering my calls lately?"

Sarah makes herself quite focused on mixing cake batter.

"I knew if I talked to you, you would realize something was up and I didn't want to tell you about it until we knew what we were doing. Until we knew if it was going to last or not."

"So, what, you have always wanted to date, and I have been a big cock block all this time?" I ask, my grip on the tabletop tightening.

Ben says, "Yes, definitely," at the same time that Sarah vehemently says, "No!"

"Sarah. I understand why *he* would want to date *you*. You're a strong, perfect, butterfly princess. A talented, sparkling dolphin. But, honestly, what are you doing? Don't you have any self-respect? You know he has a revolving door of girlfriends."

"Millie! Stop slut shaming. You're better than that. And why are you always so hard on him?"

"I love and support you, too, Millie," Ben adds, his voice is heavy with sarcasm. "This is why we didn't tell you earlier. We knew you would be an absolute jerk about it. A judgmental asshole like always."

"That's not true," Sarah says. She pushes away from him and starts buzzing around the kitchen like a nervous bee. "Well, I guess it is, sort of, yes. I knew you would be uncomfortable with it. That's why we waited to say something. I wanted to be sure Ben and I weren't just a fling. And I wanted it to be the right time."

"So, my birthday was the right time?"

She shakes her head, eyes wide. "Well, of course not, but we both wanted to come and see you, help you. We wanted to tell you in person."

"*And* we'd moved on to the next step in our relationship and didn't want to hide it from you anymore," Ben finishes for her.

My gaze falls on him and I'm speechless. He's staring at her like she's the sun. They've liked each other for years? How did I not see it sooner? I must be so self-absorbed to have missed it. I'm an obstacle, standing in the way of them being together. How many times have they lied to keep this from me?

"Can we talk? How are you feeling about this?" Sarah asks me as I sit there in stony silence, willing myself to calm down, battling all the feelings rising up in me.

"How do you think I feel? You've been lying to me for years. You must think so little of me. And I can't deal with this right now, anyway. I was on my way out of the inn when you showed up. I'm in the middle of something."

I have to get to Ethan.

I stand up and push my chair away from the table. Ben reaches out to put his hand on my shoulder, but I brush him off.

Sarah has tears in her eyes, and I can't stand to see it.

"Sarah and I want to move in together," Ben adds.

"Ben, you don't need to spring that on her now!" she cuts him off.

I stop in the doorway. "So, I'm out a best friend, a brother, and an apartment."

"That's a bunch of dramatic bullshit and you know it," he says, his jaw clenched. He was always the best jaw clencher and now I know why Sarah was offering him chewing gum all the time. Ugh, gross.

"Why can't you be normal and happy for us?" He's hurt.

I look at Sarah, searching for a kind word, some support, a sign that it isn't unreasonable for me to be upset right now.

"You are really hard on him, you know," she adds gently.

There's nothing quite so satisfying as slamming a solid old door. The weight. The noise.

The modern ones are so quiet.

The resounding bang follows me into the forest, Frank on my heels.

***

There's sharp uneasiness crowding my chest at the thought of Ben and Sarah.

I should be happy for them. I will be—it's just going to take some time to move past the initial shock.

I want to see Ethan so he can wrap me in one of those hugs that blocks out the world and makes me feel safe and treasured. I want to bury my face in his neck and breathe in deep.

Honestly, what was I even thinking, walking away from him last night? I should have stayed and asked him about the phone call, listened to what I'm sure was a completely reasonable answer and then kissed the hell out of him because he is simply the best.

I pick up my pace to a jog. I'm full of restless energy.

I want to talk to him about Sarah and Ben and have him help me sort out everything I'm feeling in that way he does.

There's a misty fog out, creeping through the underbrush, not yet burned away by the late sun, and I can feel the damp air twisting in my lungs with each deep breath I take.

I don't know exactly what to say to him yet about our kiss last night. I'm not sure what the next step could look like for us—if we could even take one. I do know that leaving last night and not letting him explain was a mistake. And I know that what once felt like a choice before doesn't anymore. My feet carry me. My heart compels me. Like gravity or other forces of nature. I know that when I think about him, everything else fades away.

I pick up my pace.

In the trees, I spy movement. A set of black, pointed ears.

"Max," I call out with an uncontrollable smile, and Frank runs off trail to greet him. Soon, his cold nose is booping my hand.

Ethan's not far behind. He's wearing his hiking boots, jeans, and the same athletic jacket that he was wearing when he carried me out of the conservatory. His hair is a little messy and I have an irresistible urge to make it even messier.

"Hey," I say, searching his face. He looks tortured.

"Hey," he echoes. His boots stop toe to toe in front of me, his hands planted firmly in his jacket pockets. His words come out all in a tumbled rush, like they've been rehearsed. "I came over to beg for your forgiveness and promise to keep my hands to myself from now on. I must have crossed a boundary, and I'm so sorry. How do I fix this?"

It's one of those moments, like when you're riding a rollercoaster, perched at the top about to go down. That fear response. You hold your breath. Your fists clench. Your heart thunders, flooding you with adrenaline. And then you fall.

I jump on him and wrap my legs around his waist. He stumbles back a step... two steps... three steps... then braces himself against a tree, hugging me tight. It's so good to see him, I let out an involuntary sigh. It hasn't even been a whole day, but I've had one kiss, so I'm an addict now.

"I don't want you to keep your hands to yourself. I love your hands, Ethan. I am so, so desperately into you."

I bask in his radiant smile for a moment before I drop my lips to his. My unbound hair surrounds us both like a curtain. I fill all my senses with him, and he is *so* delicious. Coffee and pine and fog and Ethan. I feel the cold bite of wind on my ears and lean into his warmth, soaking up all that I can get. Every thought in my brain is obliterated by the sensation of his tongue on mine, supple and demanding and skilled and the sound of the groan in his throat.

After basking in his kisses forever and not long enough, he pauses.

"Good morning." He pulls away just a fraction and I open my eyes. "Why didn't you answer your phone? I thought you were mad."

"I freaked out and bailed. I'm sorry," I tell his handsome face. Then I lay my head on his shoulder, so I have the courage to say all the things that I want to say next. It's a little easier if he isn't looking at me.

"I like you. So much," I admit with an incredulous whisper. "I don't think I've ever liked anyone as much as I like you."

He's tracing his hands up and down my back, encouraging me to continue.

"And I was kissing you last night, realizing this and finally admitting to myself how much I like you, and then you got a phone call from Emily, and I was embarrassed about how big my feelings are."

His hands stop roving.

"We haven't set any boundaries," I continue. "And I'm only here short term, and you're planning to move away, so of *course* you are going to be connecting with people from your past."

I pull back to look at him. "But Ethan, whatever this thing is between us, even if it's temporary, I don't want to share you. With Emily. Or Mae."

He shakes his head. "Mae and I are just friends. And the phone call was because I told Emily I am moving back to the city and looking for a roommate. She was going to ask around for me. It was at a weird time because she works hospital shifts—she'd just gotten off work."

"That wasn't a booty call?"

He sets me down and I feel his gaze tracing the lines of my face thoughtfully. I feel the ground beneath my feet, the cold air biting my ears and his warm hands on me.

"No. Not a booty call. I have no lingering feelings for her. I wouldn't be pursuing you if I did."

"Nonna told me you were engaged."

"I've never been engaged. Nonna doesn't always have the facts straight—you might have noticed she is 100 years old and sometimes details escape her. It's only you, Millie, and I don't want to share you either. And stop reminding me how you being here is temporary. I already think about it *all the time.*"

I answer him by sinking my fingers into his hair and pulling him closer, kissing him with everything I've got.

"You make me feel safe. You chase all my nightmares away," I pull away just long enough to tell him. His hands sweep up the side of my neck and he kisses me again in response and I'm drowning in sensation.

The pace of the kiss shifts—more demanding, deeper, rougher. My toes curl in my boots as his hands slide inside my coat. Then they are gripping my hips, the bare skin of my back, my waist, brushing the band of my bra.

I gently bite his lower lip and he gasps into my mouth, pressing into me harder. Then he gathers up my hair in his fist and pulls my head to the side for better access to my neck and jaw.

He spins so I'm against the tree, then drops his lips to my neck, above my thundering pulse. Being this close to him, there's no way to miss the hardness between us, the length of it settling against my abdomen, swelling with every stroke of our tongues.

I twist subtly against him.

In response, his hands drop to my ass, grinding me closer just once, before pulling back with a reluctant groan. He moves his hands from my hips to my face, directing my attention back to the kiss in the most commanding way.

Then he plants a chaste sweet kiss on my nose. He takes a step back, but our arms are still entwined, and I forgot how to breathe.

I take in the sight of him at this moment, hot and flustered, his hair messed up from my fingers running through it, breathing heavy, dark eyes, jaw clenched, and his hands in fists at his sides. He pushes me away and rubs his neck as he stares at me with a goofy grin. His body language says he doesn't want to stop, but I think his brain is winning out because he takes another step back.

My eyes drop to the button on his waistband.

He closes his eyes and shakes his head. "No. No, slow down."

I growl in response.

"You are so hot. You little raven-haired succubus." He coaxes some of my fury out by leaning back in for gentler kisses. Slower and slower, he winds me down, until finally, he places his forehead against mine. We stay like that for a moment, until our breathing slows back to normal.

"We are not hooking up for the first time in the woods," he presses. "Second time, maybe. First time, definitely not. First time, there will be candles and shit. And condoms. Which I don't have any of, as I was on my way to apologize to you about boundary crossing."

"But what about..." I look down at the front of his pants, which are badly bent out of shape.

"What, this?" he asks, looking down, too. "Millie, I've been hard since the yoga thing. I can survive a little while longer. At least until our topless '90s sitcom watch party."

I burst out laughing. "That's not a thing. And anyway, it is going to have to be postponed. Sarah and Ben showed up this morning. To celebrate my birthday weekend."

"What? Happy birthday!" he shouts to the forest, and tips me back for an extravagant and unfortunately chaste kiss.

"If they are in there, why are you out here?"

"I got into a fight with them, and I stormed out to find you and tell you about it. Apparently, they are dating."

"So, you weren't jumping me all fiery because we kissed yesterday, and I've been pining after you and texting you nonstop? You're mad at your brother and friend and you're taking it out on me?" His face reads part hurt, part amusement.

"No! Well, maybe a little. Like ten percent mad at them, but the rest is all you. They were telling me all this life-altering stuff and I could hardly focus because I needed to see you so badly after bailing last night that I couldn't think straight."

"Go home," he orders me, and tries unsuccessfully to untangle us. The jaws of life could not pry me away from this magnificent creature. "Hey, as much as I enjoy you using my body as your emotional punching bag, I think you need to talk to them and sort this out. Besides, there's no way I'm making out with someone who ditches their family."

I bite my lip.

"No regrets, remember? Don't leave unfinished business with the people you love."

"You're obviously right, like always. It's annoying."

"It's my greatest pleasure to annoy you, milady. Do you want me to come in there with you?"

It's so tempting. I know he'll charm them immediately. Smooth out all the awkwardness of our fight for a while. But it would only be postponing it until later.

"No," I sigh. "I need to work this out with them on my own. Can I see you tomorrow?"

"You damn well better." He kisses me again, a short, sweet, to-be-continued kiss, complete with a go-get-them-tiger slap on my ass.

I'm smiling like a moron after I turn around. I'm all loose boned and wobbly. He's right, of course. I need to talk to them. It doesn't seem insurmountable anymore.

***

It smells like a chocolate sugary confection in here. Cake is coming out of the oven soon. Sarah is sitting on the couch, and I drop down next to her, sinking into the cushion. She looks at me warily at first. But then, she notices. My eyes are probably a little glassy, my lips a bit too pink. She raises her eyebrow at me, her mouth forming a little *o*.

"Millie?! Spill!"

"I was with Ethan," I say, and I can't stop the smile spreading across my face. I literally put my hands on my cheeks, but it does nothing because my smile is out of control. "But we'll talk about him later. Let's talk about you first."

"OK. Where to start?" she asks herself. "Wait, I have something for you." She jumps up from the couch and is back in a moment, a soft black bundle in her hands.

"You made a whole sweater this month?" I ask with concern, examining the sweater.

"I made it in two weeks, Millie." Her eyes are crazy. "I was sort of tortured, seeing Ben around all the time, and not, you know. So, I was always knitting to keep my hands busy. And then after we... you know. I haven't been knitting anymore. Look at me. I'm just sitting on the couch like a normal person and my hands aren't moving."

"So, this is your sexual frustration sweater."

"Yeah. I taught myself cables!"

"Beautiful cables." I fold the sweater back up with care.

"Thanks," she says, missing my sarcasm, or ignoring it. "Do you remember junior year of high school when your mom was dating that football player and she took us to his house for a barbecue, but it was actually a raging party?"

"Yeah, I drank too much sangria and threw up like, an hour in," I say. "It's gross thinking about it now, actually. What the hell, Mom?"

"Right. Underage drinking is not great. Also, too much sangria is *never* a good idea. Anyway, I, um, I kissed Ben that night in the pool," she says, biting her lip. "I had a crush on him for years but from that moment on I was completely in love with him."

"Completely in love?"

"Yes. Then, at your mom's wedding, we danced, and he admitted how he felt about me and..."

She pauses, tucking her silky strawberry blonde hair behind her ear.

"Go on."

"We hooked up that night."

"Oh, that's why you weren't there when I woke up in our hotel room. You told me you were grabbing breakfast before I woke or something? You were actually with Ben all night?"

"Yeah," she says sheepishly. "But we decided it couldn't ever work. I made him promise not to tell you. Then I deleted his number from my phone and told him not to call me. We hardly talked for years. Until you wanted us to all room together."

"That must have been difficult," I admit. "To keep all of that a secret."

She reaches her hand out and grabs mine.

"We didn't want to hurt you. So, we pretended like neither one of us had feelings for each other and that it was a one-time thing. And honestly, Millie? It took a toll on both of us."

"What do you mean?"

"I could not stop thinking about him. It's been tearing me apart. First, it was denial, then a slow unraveling. I've been a nervous wreck about it. I keep myself too busy, so I never have a second to think about him. With too many credit hours and hobbies and jobs. And Ben? He—"

"Got blackout drunk like every weekend and hooked up with a lot of other girls to try to get Sarah out of my head," he calls from the next room. He's trying to give us space to talk to each other but can obviously hear our conversation.

"What about Johnathan?" I ask, remembering the guy she met in her scuba diving class. Vegetarian Johnathan. Super nice. Lots of freckles. They were cute together, matching wholesome sunny energies and green smoothies.

"Yeah, I dated other guys, but I only wanted Ben. It was *always* him. It was *only* him. I don't know how else to explain it to you except that no guy really mattered except for him and when I wasn't with him, I was crawling out of my skin."

"I'm familiar with the feeling," I admit, and her eyes light up with curious joy for me.

"We ignored it for a long time," Ben says, wandering his way into the room. He sits down on the other side of the couch, sandwiching me in the middle. "For you. Because we love you."

"But then you left to come to the inn," Sarah continues. "It was just the two of us in the apartment together for weeks, eating dinner together every night and bumping into each other in the hallway after he got out of the bathroom with only a towel around his waist, his skin still a little damp from the shower, smelling like toothpaste and all the years of built-up sexual tension between us." She's biting her lip, and her eyes are all misty as she stares at my brother over my shoulder me.

I shudder. "I think I can accept the two of you dating but you *have* to spare me the details."

"Deal. Are we all OK?" she asks, squeezing my hands in hers.

"Yeah, of course. I need a minute to get used to the idea. And I wish you would have told me sooner. I feel terrible that you felt like you couldn't trust me with this. I'm sorry. I will try to be better."

"No, *I'm* sorry," she says. "For keeping this from you for so long. No more secrets."

"No more secrets," I agree. "Do you have anything else to confess?" I ask jokingly. But to my surprise, she answers, and stars light her eyes.

"I'm going to drop out of my teaching program when this semester is over. I am going to go to culinary school instead. Ben and I want to open a bakery together someday. I've been working on recipes, and he's been working on a business plan."

"When the inn sells, I'm going to use my part of the inheritance to help with startup costs," Ben adds, and I can see the pride in his eyes, this dream of the future between the two of them.

When the inn sells.

My plan to stall the sale just got more complicated.

"A baker. That's amazing, Sarah. Startup won't be easy. But if you want it to happen, it will happen. I have so much confidence in you."

"And me?" Ben asks.

"You too," I admit. "But guys? I don't want your sexual frustration sweater." I place it gingerly back in her hands.

"I can see why you might say that," Sarah admits.

CHAPTER TWENTY

My phone wakes me up when the sun has hardly risen fully in the sky.

"Hello?" I answer groggily.

"Twenty-five years ago today, my water broke while I was waiting in line at the grocery store, trying to buy candy for the trick-or-treaters. I terrorized the poor cashier! I nearly broke your sweet dad's hand, squeezing it so hard, but he never once complained."

"You don't have to tell me the story *again*," I say. She tells it every year.

"Happy Birthday, darling."

"Thanks, Mom."

"Are Ben and Sarah there?"

"Yeah, they came in yesterday."

"Good, good. I know they'll make sure you have some fun today."

"Did they tell you..." I trail off, not sure if I should continue.

"That they are together? Yes. I think it's natural, don't you? I was so happy to hear it."

I rub the sleep from my eyes. "I guess so. Yeah."

"Don't be mopey about it, Millie."

I roll my eyes.

"I've been thinking about what you said," she reflects, "about wanting to stay longer and complete Rowan's wish list."

"Oh?" I sit up suddenly and push my hair out of my face.

"Do it. Finish it," she says, and I can hear the resolution in her voice.

It's the best birthday gift I could have ever wished for.

***

We spend the next day decorating the inn with Halloween treasures from the shed—posable skeletons and tarnished candlesticks now adorn the dining room. Creepy old dolls that were in our donation pile are now perched in the front windows, staring outside. I put a devil's mask on Stephen's bodiless head and found a witch hat for myself. Scratchy tunes float from Rowan's old record player which Ben set up in the drawing room. Sultry French lyrics serenade us and our spooky decor.

"Happy birthday, Millie," Ben says, carrying in a black and white polka dot box with a sparkling gold bow. I step down from the chair I'm standing on to string paper bats from the millwork.

"Aw, thanks, Ben."

"She picked it out," he says, his eyes resting sweetly on Sarah, like she's the only thing that exists. She finishes setting up candles along the lobby counter, lighting them one by one, before she turns to look at me, a huge smile on her face.

I tear the box open and pull out a vintage, black velvet dress. My hands stroke the fabric involuntarily. It's so lovely and so completely me that it takes my breath away and I forget what to say.

"I found it a few months ago and knew you had to have it. Plus, I figured that you didn't have anything to wear for Halloween, since you weren't planning to be here this long." Sarah hurries over, her cheeks dimpling as I pull her into a hug.

"She's a champion gift giver. It's like a sport to her," Ben interjects, his eyes still on Sarah. I want to say, *Ugh, I know, she's* my *best friend*.

"Thank you. I love it. How do you think it will look with a witch hat?"

"Amazing! Let's go get dressed!"

Getting ready for a party is as much fun as the actual party. We talk about boys while perfecting each other's hair and eyeliner, just like when we were teenagers. While we work, I catch her up about Ethan and his connections to this place. I confess how much I like him but leave out the parts where I'm thinking less and less about selling the inn, my mind frantically sorting through ways I can stay.

Because now her fate is tied to it, too. Sarah and Ben opening a bakery? What a beautiful dream. And they have enough grit to make it a reality.

After my Sarah perfects my hair and makeup, she steps out of my room to put on her costume.

I pull on the velvet dress and it fits like it was made for me. It has a plunging sweetheart neckline, and the sleeves stop at my wrists. The hem rests on the floor. There's a long slit in the front that lets one of my slender legs peek through.

When I head back downstairs, Ben's already changed into his costume and Sarah is still missing.

"You look awesome, Millipede." Ben kisses my cheek, and I smile at the use of my childhood nickname.

"Thanks. You look like... a wolf?" He's wearing a grey tracksuit, a knit cap adorned with a pair of pointed furry ears, and sharp plastic teeth. The tip of his nose is painted black.

"Yeah, it's a couple's costume," he says, blushing. Ben never blushes. I'm beginning to appreciate the changes my friend has made in him. "You'll get it when you see Sarah."

I catch sight of myself in one of the windows. It's dark outside and my reflection shines back at me. The dress fits perfectly, clinging to me in all the right places. It's the sort of dress that gets you tipped backward for a kiss, the whole room pausing to watch. My hair is twisted into a low bun, and I've got smoky eyes, sultry lips. I can't take my eyes off myself in this thing. Ben helps me pin a witch's hat on top of my head.

"Ta-da!" Sarah says as she makes her way down the stairs. She's little red riding hood, in a flowing red cloak and tulle skirt.

"You look so cute!" she says.

"*You* look so cute!" I echo back. Ben is speechless, just smiling like a sweet fool as he reaches for her hand.

"Do you think so? It's our first couple's costume. I made the whole thing. Probably over-thought it."

She's interrupted by the chiming of my phone, which is sitting on the lobby counter right next to her. She picks it up for me and stares down at the screen.

"It's from Ethan. It says, *For your birthday, milady, I'm going to help you fulfill that kink*." Her voice trails off and she looks back up at me with a bemused look on her face. Ben scowls.

"What the eff? Millie, does he always talk like that? Because he sounds like a creep. Oh no. There's a picture incoming—is this going to be a dick pic?"

I run over and slap my phone out of her hand, and it clatters to the floor. We both scoop it up and she fights me for it in a blur of tulle and velvet, but I win because I've always been a bit scrappier.

I unlock my screen.

No. Oh no, he didn't. My hand shoots up to my mouth in horror. Ethan is sporting thick sideburns, connecting a robust mustache. His chin? Shaved clean.

"What is it?" Sarah asks.

"This is so much worse than a dick pic," I say.

I send him a text, my thumbs a flurry.

Millie: You look like Ambrose Burnside. What did I do to deserve this?

Ethan: Everything, babe. See you soon.

***

The multi-tiered cake is barely frosted because I don't love icing. There's a chocolate ganache sandwiching the layers of chocolate sponge and cute meringue ghosts on top with faces doodled in chocolate. Sarah, in her fluffy tulle like a fairy godmother, is putting the final touches on it in the kitchen when a knock sounds at the front door.

"Trick or treat!" I hear tiny voices calling from the doorway, accompanied by frantic banging on the door. Ben steps down from a ladder where he is stringing spiderwebs next to my bats. Frank sits below, tail flicking, wanting to paw at it all.

"Oh good! I didn't think we would get many trick or treaters out here," I say, as Ben pulls the door open and the girls spill inside, bringing all their joy and giggles with them. Joe and Liz follow.

"Hi, Millie, hope it's OK we stopped by!" Joe says, leaning in to hug me. I am realizing that I love hugs from Joe. He hugs me like he means it, squeezing all the air out of my lungs and lifting my feet off the ground a little. I can't help but smile forever afterward.

"Of course it is! I'm so glad you did. Come in, come in," I say, ushering them through the door.

"A princess," I say, looking at their costumes. "A fairy, and a..."

"A ninja pirate!" Rosa says triumphantly, kicking the air.

"Whoa! Well, ninja pirate, there is cake in the kitchen if you want some. Sarah is finishing up the decorating now." The girls disappear into the house, chasing Frank, all blurs of bright color, noise, and sparkles.

"You should have seen her last year," Liz says, out of breath. She looks like she ran a marathon moments ago. Her hair is up in a bun, fuzzy pieces escaping at odd angles. I can't help but wonder how long it took to get three girls into costumes. "She was a refrigerator! Ninja pirate was so much easier to make. No batteries or moving parts."

They follow me inside and I watch with a full heart as Joe and Ben are reunited for the first time in years.

"Do you want to stay? We are having a little party. Ethan should be here any minute."

"No, we've got to take the girls around trick or treating. Thank you, though. We were going to ask if you wanted to come drive around with us and see the neighborhood. We weren't sure what we would find when we stopped by. We couldn't stand the thought of you sitting over here alone tonight."

"That's so kind of you."

"Rowan used to make a big deal out of Halloween," she continues, her eyes landing on the paper bats. "He would decorate the house and read scary stories in front of the fireplace to the kids."

"I didn't know that," I say, touching my hand to my heart. "That explains all the decorations we found. Thank you."

"For what?"

"It's a sweet memory. I can picture it so easily. It feels like a gift." I can see Rowan sitting in the armchair by the fire in the living room, chairs pushed aside to make room, little costumed ghouls and goblins and fairies and superheroes sitting on the big carpet, their eyes wide with fear as Rowan reads animatedly. Frank the cat sitting stoically at his feet.

"Aw. You're welcome. I've got plenty more memories. Whenever you want to hear them, you let me know. He was a sweetheart. We all miss him."

There's another tap on the door, and Liz smiles at me knowingly. "I'll go round up the girls and we'll get out of your hair," she says, and disappears into the house, following the sound of giggles down into the kitchen.

I can barely spot Ethan through the stained glass of the grand door. He's facing away, draped in a white sheet. He turns around as he hears me pull the open the door and—

I freeze.

He's clean shaven, smiling bashfully at me.

I can actually see his face for the first time since we were teenagers. And he is all chiseled cheekbones and perfect geometry, golden like prince charming. There's a swarm of butterflies in my belly. I want to run to him and throw my body against his, but I also want to run away from him very fast at the same time.

I step aside so he can come in. As he passes through the doorway, he drops a kiss on my cheek, whispering in my ear that I look beautiful. He's wearing a white sheet like a toga. The hard ridge of his collarbone and part of the pad of muscle that stretches down over his chest are on display, along with both sculpted arms. His forearms are out of control.

"Were you expecting the burnside beard?" His voice is velvet, and his eyes are warm, and it all feels a bit like a dream.

I nod.

"You probably thought I was going to show up in a full Civil War re-enactor costume. Embarrass the shit out of you."

"Yeah." I'm dazzled, only one syllable at the moment.

"Good." He's chuckling and the sound soothes all my jitters. "What do you think?" he asks, gesturing at his beardless face.

"I like you better with a beard," I say, and cover the bottom half of his face with my hands. Any excuse to touch him, really. I'm shameless.

"No, without," I decide, lifting my hands away again to study his face.

"No, with," I say. "Because without one you look like a vampire extra from a Twilight movie."

"Ah, not even one of the main cast, damn."

"And what do you think?" I ask, gesturing grandly at my gilded self. The dress. The hair. The makeup.

"You're breathtaking, Millie."

My cheeks flame, and I burst into a smile. "That was nice! I didn't know we were playing nice tonight."

"I'm on my best behavior—it's your birthday. I can't believe it's on Halloween. So on the nose."

"I don't want you to be on your best behavior," I tell him.

"Well, in that case, I think I like you better without the dress."

He holds me at arm's length, looks me up and down appraisingly, and shakes his head. "No, with."

Then he finally decides, "Definitely without," and leans in, his lips against my ear.

I'm laughing again. I'm always laughing around him, and it takes the power of a thousand suns not to run away with him, find somewhere to finally unleash all this pent-up energy we have for each other. Dark corners, upstairs, his truck, the forest, I don't care. I just want all his skin on all my skin. I'm breathing fast, my lips apart. His eyes are dark, and he knows *exactly* what I'm thinking.

"But first, milady," he says with a ridiculous accent that makes me snort in laughter because apparently, I am now one of those girls who snorts with laughter. "I have something for you."

He laces my fingers in his and pulls me outside, toward his truck. He lets go of my hand to drop the tailgate. I instantly miss his touch, his warm palm against mine. I wrap my arms around myself to guard against the cold. As he steps aside, I can see that in the back of his truck are two perfect Adirondack chairs.

"You told me they were part of your happy place. They were broken, so I fixed and re-stained them for you. I wanted to try to recreate the feeling for you, give you some peace for your birthday," he says gently. "I know Rowan's not here, so it's not the same, but I thought you could take them with you when you leave to help you remember—"

I throw my arms around him, tears choking my throat. "Ethan, this is one of the kindest things anyone has ever done for me."

"I'm glad you like them." I can hear the pleased smile in his voice.

"I like *you*." I squeeze him as tight as I can.

"I like you, too, Millie—you have no idea how much."

"So, show me."

He tilts my chin up and kisses me, the loveliest kiss, and I melt into him and think this is maybe the best birthday. Any other birthday after this, without him, is going to be a bit of a letdown. I try to shake away the negative thoughts, but they clamber and crawl into my mind, unbidden. That this beautiful connection I've found with him is fleeting. That I don't deserve these nice things happening to me, not really, and he is *so nice*.

"What's wrong?"

"The usual," I admit, with a deep, sharp breath. "I am thinking about how perfect this moment is and how I don't want it to end.

Next birthday—no matter how great the cake Sarah makes me is—I will have an Ethan-shaped hole in my life, and I'll be so sad."

"Who says I won't be in your life?"

"The chances are pretty unlikely. I don't know how you could ever forgive me for selling this place. I know you say it won't bother you, but it's your *home*—you'll be angry with me. How are you not angry with me?"

"It's not that I'm not angry, Millie." He says as he lifts the chairs out of the truck and sets them on the ground one at a time. "Of course I'm angry. But not at *you*."

He slams the tailgate shut with a bang before he turns back to me.

"You're not?"

"It doesn't make any sense for you to do anything besides sell this place. I'm angry at fate, I guess. It's not fair that he died, after that tragic life he had. He should have grown old. I wanted to see him happy, or at peace, at least. He should have aged gracefully here. But he died, and we all lost." Ethan says as he moves the chairs onto the porch. "Of course I'm angry. But not at you. I'll never blame you."

I follow him and sit down in one. He crouches down in front of me and takes my hands in his.

"I promise. Next birthday, if you want me there, I will be there. Regardless of where you are or where I am in the world. OK? And there's nothing to forgive. You're doing what you have to. I've started over before and I'll do it again. Don't worry about me."

"Anywhere in the world?" I press.

"Or in the next world. I'll even be there for your birthday party on the moon, spooky girl."

"Uncle Ethan! Uncle Ethan!" He stands and turns as the girls come tumbling out of the house, Liz and Joe right behind them.

"What are you, a ghost?" asks Rosa, coming to a stop in front of him. She stares unabashedly at his shaved face, her eyes wide.

"No, it's a toga."

"That's not a very good costume," says little Maria. "Why does your face look so weird?"

"It does not look weird! I shaved my beard. This was the best I could do on short notice," Ethan fires back, his hands on his hips.

"Should have been a ghost, put the sheet over your head," says Ava. He picks her up and hangs her upside down, tickling her belly until she screams in laughter and drops her fairy baton on the ground.

"Why aren't you out trick-or-treating?" Ethan asks her upturned feet. "Why are you here pestering me?"

"We *are* trick-or-treating! This was our first stop and now we are going to Nonna's," she says, upside down.

"Have fun! Get lots of candy," I say.

"Oh, we already did," says little Maria, holding up her bag. It's full. Ben must have emptied our entire candy bowl for them.

"Little Red Riding Hood gave us some cake, too."

***

Sarah rushes into the lobby as Ethan and I step back inside. She's waving enthusiastically, like an embarrassing mom at their kid's football game.

"Hello, Ethan! So nice to meet you," she says as she stands up to give him a hug.

"So nice to meet you," he says, his voice trailing off in uncertainty, as she still hasn't let go of the hug. She's wrapped around him like a koala bear.

"Oh my goodness. No wonder you had such a silly big beard. How do you go out in public with a face like that? Big, strong arms like these?" She's patting him appreciatively on his one exposed arm, like an old auntie would do. "Do women swarm you like thirsty bees?"

"Sarah, please—" I beg, mortified. But I shouldn't have worried because Ethan is beaming down at her, not at all put off by her weirdness.

"Well, look at you! You are so adorable, I want to put you in my pocket."

She giggles and Ben gently pulls her out of the way. "I apologize for my girlfriend, she's a few drinks in. Good to see you again, man."

It's so weird to hear Ben refer to Sarah as "girlfriend." It's going to take a while for me to get used to it.

"Good to see you again, too. How have you been?" They do that man handshake back slap thing and are clearly delighted to be reunited.

"We may have had some libations already," Sarah admits, and burps a cute little burp. She offers me a glass. It's bright green and tastes like licorice and is, naturally, on theme.

"Why *did* you shave?" I ask, running my finger down Ethan's jaw. I'm not usually one for public displays of affection, but I can't help it with this man.

"I have a job interview tomorrow, so it was time for the beard to go. And I couldn't waste the opportunity to torture you," he explains carefully.

Job interview.

Selling the inn.

The end of all of this.

My stomach churns.

"Oh yeah? Where at?" Ben asks politely.

"Sarkas and Ladlow Architects. Rival to my old firm, actually."

"Dinner is ready," I say with a tight smile, changing the subject.

Sarah had artfully arranged candles, old glass bottles, and brightly colored maple leaves she'd gathered from outside on each table. The grand chandelier hanging in the center of the room flickers as we pull out our chairs and sit around the table like aristocrats of old.

"Do the lights always do that?" Sarah asks, eyes uncertain.

"Yeah," I admit. "There are a lot of flickering lights in this place, honestly. You'll get used to it."

Her eyes widen as she stares up at the chandelier.

"So this place really is haunted?" she asks.

"Maybe."

Sarah's gaze falls questioningly on me. I can tell she wasn't expecting me to say that. She knows I never believed in that sort of thing.

"But enough about ghosts. I want to hear about you and Ben," I say, as I pull a slice of pizza onto my plate.

While we eat pizza beneath a flickering light, Ben and Sarah tell us their love story and we tell ours. Ethan's left hand never leaves my knee.

Ben and Sarah seem giddy with relief now that their secret is out.

"I'm just happy that you two are so happy," I finally concede.

And it's true because I love them. But my heart is squeezing tight because my world's a little off kilter. I'll forever feel like a third wheel with the two people who are most important to me in my life. I can't help but wonder how things are going to change. What happens if they break up? I shake the feeling away. I tell myself to do what Ethan would do. Relax and be happy for them and enjoy this time we have with our loved ones.

"Happy birthday, Millipede," Ben says softly.

"Millipede?" Ethan leans back in his chair, crosses his arms, and looks at me appraisingly. "Is that because of her exoskeleton?"

"No, my thousand legs," I roll my eyes and take a bite of pizza while Sarah dissolves into a puddle of giggles across from me, sinking into her chair.

"Millipedes don't actually have a thousand legs," Ethan adds.

"You made fun of me for knowing things about cats but look at you with all this insect knowledge."

"They're not insects, they are arthropods. Like lobsters."

"Why do you know so much about arthropods, Ethan?"

He shrugs. "I was the kid with the bug jars and the magnifying glass. I had this vintage book from the Starling library with pictures of local bugs in it and Joe and I would hunt in the woods for them."

"And then what? They died in their jars? That's a very serial killer look for you."

It's his turn to roll his eyes at me. "No, I didn't let them die in their jars. I would build them little habitats and study them for a while and release them."

"Oh, that's so cute, Ethan," Sarah says, her hands on her chin and her elbows on the table. "Did you name them, like they were your little bug friends? Do you still have bug friends?"

"I didn't name them. I do still like bugs. I want to put an apiary near the orchard. Now that the trees are finally blooming again. Bees are fascinating, and we could harvest apple blossom honey in the summer."

"That sounds divine," Sarah says dreamily. "Think of all the honey cakes and baklava and apple blossom honey sweetened tea."

"What do we do now?" I carefully change the subject away from his slip up, talking about the future of the inn. "I don't think we'll get any more trick or treaters out here."

"We can play hotel like we used to when we were kids," Ben suggests.

"How did that go?" Sarah asks.

"I was always the hotel guest, and Millie was the hotel porter and I would try to check in and get a key from the lobby. She was real mean, turned me away over and over. Sometimes it was because no boys were allowed. Once she told me only people who read books are allowed." He stares at me pointedly. "I read books, OK?"

"He does, he likes those ones about the wizard," Sarah says.

"Harry Potter?" I ask, confused.

"No, no, no, the other wizard named Harry—the detective one," Sarah clarifies.

"I know what we can do next," Ben interrupts us. "Sarah has a whole suitcase full of spooky stuff."

"Spooky stuff? Like what?" I ask, eyeing her with suspicion.

"A Ouija board! Can we set it up in the attic?" Sarah asks me, her voice manic.

I glance at Ethan for permission. If our hunch is right, this ghost is part of his family. He gives a brief nod, indicating that he doesn't mind.

And I don't want to disappoint Sarah.

"Let's do it," I acquiesce. "I guess we are having a seance."

****

We climb up the attic stairs in our fine clothes and sit down on dusty floorboards in the near pitch darkness. The rafters of the attic reach down around us like ribs of a skeleton. The air in the attic is still, silent, and heavy as we settle shoulder to shoulder in a circle in the heart of the house. Sarah positions candles in the middle.

I lean back, my palms on the floorboards, and Ethan does the same, his pinky finger touching mine.

"Actually, I don't know if this is a good idea. I've changed my mind," Sarah says after placing the last candle.

"Why?"

"Because it sounded fun in theory, but I'm legit scared—it's terrifying up here. I can hardly see anything, and there are definitely ghosts," she says in a rush.

"It's OK, babe. I'll keep you safe. But ghosts aren't real anyway so there's nothing to be afraid of," Ben says, lighting candles one by one.

"Yes, they *are*! I'll prove it to you."

Sarah takes a determined breath, pulls out the Ouija board, and sets it in the middle of us. Our faces and the board are barely illuminated, the rest of the attic pitch black beyond our ring of candlelight. The board is old, covered in an alphabet, each letter decorated with twisting curls and vines.

Involuntarily, I shiver, unease tickling up my spine. Ethan's eyes meet mine in the near dark, asking if I'm all right. I lean forward and drop my fingertips to the planchette in response.

If the ghosts are real, I want to know what they've been trying to tell me.

"Let's do this," I whisper.

One by one they follow suit, our fingertips crowding on the ivory-colored, heart-shaped planchette, our faces all drawing close together. It has a little window on it, so we can see the letters on the board beneath. Sarah's eyes are closed in concentration, Ben's brow furrowed, and his lips pouted out in skepticism. I glance over at Ethan, but his gaze is fixed on me. He's not paying attention to the board at all. He looks how he always looks. Cheerful and like he wants to take a bite out of me.

We share small, secret smile and look back at the board.

We sit in tense silence, waiting for the planchette to move.

One heartbeat.

Two.

Three.

"This is boring," Ben breaks the silence.

"Shhh," Sarah shushes him, her eyes closed tight. "We're waiting for the spirits to communicate with us."

"Come on, let's go back downstairs. My butt is falling asleep, and the floor is so dusty," he insists.

"No," she scolds, her eyes clenched tight in concentration.

We wait in silence.

I can't help but glance at Ethan again—he is looking at the board this time, his face contemplative. I wonder if he wishes for this to be real.

Do I?

What would I ask them, if I could, the people who I've lost? What would I say to them if I had the chance?

To my father.

To Rowan.

Suddenly, I wish it were real.

With a dry skittering noise, the planchette sweeps across the board. My gaze whips from Ethan to the board so fast I get whiplash. We're all watching the planchette, transfixed, as it stops, hovering over the letter B.

"B... what does B stand for?" Sarah asks, her voice a frantic whisper.

"Which one of you is doing this?" Ethan asks.

But the humor has drained from Ben's face, and I know Sarah wouldn't fake this because she wants so badly for it to be true. She desperately wants to have a real experience with ghosts. She's been obsessed with this stuff for as long as I remember.

The planchette jerks to the letter U. We all look at each other, back at the board, back at each other, back at the board.

The planchette moves slowly to the letter T. We all wait with bated breath for its next move. It jerks, indicating the T once again.

"B-U-T-T? Did the Ouija board just spell... butt?" Ethan asks, a smile in his voice.

Ben bursts into laughter, ringing out across the attic.

"Ben!" Sarah punches him in the arm.

"I hate you so much," I confess.

"Come on, there's no such thing as ghosts," Ben says defensively. "This is what Ouija boards are for. People playing tricks on each other."

"Well, *I* think they exist! Millie, what do you think?"

"I... I don't know," I say hesitantly, my voice trailing off.

"What do you mean, you don't know?" Sarah asks, leaning in closer.

"Well, if they are real, why hasn't Dad visited us?" I turn to Ben.

"Probably because if ghosts are real, they have unfinished business. That's what movies say, right? And he didn't have unfinished business. He knew we would be OK. He knew you would take care of us."

I swallow the lump in my throat. "Well, ask me again in a few weeks after I've solved all the mysteries of this place," I say, feeling all their eyes on me.

"I know you had some spooky things happen when you first got here but we need more details."

"I found an old ledger, with accounts of ghost encounters at the inn over time. If the ledger is to be believed, then hauntings started in the 1920s," I say, reluctantly.

"What?!" Sarah is leaning over the board to look at me. "Why wasn't this the first thing out of your mouth when I arrived? Why didn't you tell me sooner?"

"It is an old marketing thing. A former Starling proprietor inventing stories to draw people to the inn, people hoping to have a paranormal encounter."

"But what if it's real? What does the ledger say? What sort of ghost encounters did they record?"

"Doors opening and closing one by one, like someone was searching for something. Cold spots in rooms. Misplaced items. The sound of a man weeping. Footsteps. Flickering lights."

"Holy shit," Ben says.

"Has any of that happened to you?" Sarah asks.

"Not exactly. We had some electrical problems—" I admit.

"Which is completely expected in an old building," Ethan continues. "And an electrician has since fixed it."

"Yeah, but there was more than that. The first night I was here, I went to bed and there was no fire in the hearth. I had a nightmare and, when I woke up, there was a blazing fire that I hadn't built." I shudder, remembering how terrified I was. It freaked me out so much that I had compartmentalized it right out of life, pretending it didn't happen and refusing to think about it.

"That was me," Ethan says, turning to face me. "I thought you knew."

"What do you mean it was you? I called the police!" I round on him.

"I came over to check on you and the door was unlocked. I noticed that it was cold as hell so I built a fire before I left so you wouldn't be freezing through the night. I left a bowl of apples and a note with my phone number—it's in the bowl. I thought you knew because you texted me the next morning asking for help. How'd you get my number if you didn't get the note?"

"From Maria!"

"Ah. I'm so sorry, Millie, if you've felt unsafe this whole time from that."

I take a deep breath before continuing. "It's not only that—there's been other things. Like, I'm always cold. Clanging pipes, buzzing flies. Footsteps. Nightmares. I feel like half the time I set something down it's in a different spot than where I left it. I don't know if it's ghosts. But if it's not, what is it? Something about this place is making me senseless."

"Do *you* believe in ghosts?" I turn to Ethan. "I feel like you must. With all the time you've spent here. His family built the inn," I explain to Ben and Sarah.

He considers it for a moment. "The pressure in the pipes we fixed. The flies in the house are because we leave the windows open all the time."

"So, you don't believe?" I push.

"I didn't say that. I'm just saying... not everything is ghosts. But—" He takes a deep breath before continuing. His gaze is unfocused, lost in memory, his handsome face lit by candlelight, standing out in the dark attic.

"My mom told me a story. When she was a child, she had this little starling toy. A wood carving." We all lean in, listening to him. "She found it in the attic one day. She would play with it, and with her imaginary friend, Lou. She and Lou and the starling toy would have adventures all over the house. But then the next day, the starling would be in a different spot than where she had put it away the day before. She was sure her imaginary friend moved it, like he was playing hide and seek with her. He was showing her places to hide in her house, places where she would be safe."

"Like a secret passageway?" I ask.

He nods.

"A secret passageway?" Sarah repeats, her eyebrows lifted.

"My grandparents were not kind people," Ethan explains to Sarah and Ben, before continuing. "She stopped seeing her imaginary friend when she grew older, but the starling never stopped moving. She would leave it in the conservatory and find it on the fireplace mantel. Or she'd hide it in the attic, nested deep inside of boxes, and it would be on her pillow the next morning."

As his voice fades, I stare at him, searching for any hint of a joke. He's dead serious.

"I remember Lou." All our heads whip toward Ben, who looks shaken. "Yeah, that was the name of our imaginary friend when we played here as kids. Don't you remember, Millie?"

"Are you kidding me?" Sarah asks, her knuckles turning white as she grips Ben's arm.

I shake my head. "I remember that we had an imaginary friend, but I don't remember his name." And in this moment, I'm glad I don't, chills skittering up my neck. I reach out for Ethan's hand, my eyes wide. As he pulls my hand into his, I wonder if he is thinking the same thing I am, about the letter we found in the walls, signed with an L.

"After my mom died," Ethan continues, "it happened to me. I had it, the little starling toy. And I brought it to the house one day when I was stopping by to see Rowan. I put it on the porch railing. Rowan called me the next morning and asked me why there was a ratty old kids toy on his kitchen table. No one else had been here, only the two of us. I knew I didn't move it. He swore he didn't."

"He wouldn't have lied," Ben says.

Ethan shakes his head in agreement. "So maybe... maybe there is something here, haunting this place," his voice trails off.

"Something," I agree.

We sit in heavy silence for a moment.

"The Russo family, the next-door neighbors," I explain to Sarah and her saucer wide eyes, "believe pretty strongly that this place is cursed."

"What did Rowan think about all this?" Ben asks, sounding incredulous. "Ghosts and curses? Is this why he drank so much and..." he doesn't finish. The implication that he killed himself is unspoken.

Ethan cut him off, "Rowan was a passionate guy. His moods swung from highs and lows like a pendulum. And he was dealt a difficult hand in life—his downward spiral wasn't entirely because of the house itself. And the Russo's have some complicated family history here. I'm not sure about the rest. I don't have an explanation for it. Maybe there are ghosts. But I never felt unsafe here, for what it's worth."

"It's haunted. The explanation is that it's haunted. And you know how to clear a haunted house, right? Sacrifices!" Sarah says.

We all turn to look at her.

"I saw it on a TV show once. They had sort of a group exorcism. We'll build a fire and each of us will drop in something meaningful to us. Let's do it later tonight. We'll cleanse this place of ghosts."

CHAPTER TWENTY-ONE

I FEEL A SWIRL of nervous energy at the sound of tumbling click as Ethan locks my heavy bedroom door. It's not like we haven't been alone in my room before, but tonight feels different.

"I feel terrible for scaring you, I'm so sorry," he says, arms encircling my waist. Only the glass hurricane lamp on my nightstand is on, casting the room in a soft rosy glow, and the embers of a fire lend warmth to the air.

"I forgive you," I say, and I reach out to touch his face again. There's no tickly scratch of his beard. I run my fingertips across smooth, dimpled cheeks, a chiseled jaw. Down the curve of his neck, over the bump of his Adam's apple.

"If I had thought more about it, I think I would have figured out it was you. I was terrified of everything when I first got here. I jumped to conclusions. There's just something about being so alone that plays tricks on you."

"Do you still feel that way?"

"No."

"If there is a ghost here, it's…" he starts.

"Mischievous…" I add.

"But kind," he finishes.

"And related to you, apparently. So, it can't be *all* bad."

"You'd be surprised. Hey, ghost," Ethan says with a half-smile to the room, "if you're here right now, go away for a minute."

"What are you doing?"

"Protecting its innocence from all the things I'm about to do to you," he smiles with wicked intent. "I'm sorry to tell you this, Millie, but there is dust all over your dress."

"Oh no! I'm going to need help getting it all off."

"I hoped you might say that." His hands drift down to my ass, my legs, and back up, encircling my waist. I tilt my head to the side as his lips drop to my neck, planting searing kisses.

"Did you get it all?" I ask innocently, eyebrow arched.

"No, I think there's more dust right here." His hands rove upward, cupping my breasts.

"Oh, on both of them, really? Thank goodness you're here to brush it off." My heart thunders in response and I stretch with a luxuriant smile beneath his touch.

"I don't know, there's dust everywhere, you might want to take the whole thing off." Then, his hand hooks around the back of my neck and he pulls my mouth to his, and I kiss Ethan for the fourth time. I wonder if I'll ever stop counting. Or if I'll remember every one, each one sacred.

"I take it back, please, keep it on," he says, sliding his hands up my waist again, his lips resting against my ear. "You look so beautiful every day, Millie, but tonight, in this dress—"

"Not my sweatpants days, though. You're definitely lying—no one looks good in sweatpants."

He pauses his roving hands. "Every time you wear those sweatpants all I can think about is how I want to rip them off you. It's distracting."

"What? Why?" I ask, giggling as he pulls my earlobe into his mouth.

"I can't see the shape of your ass in them the way I can when you wear jeans or yoga pants. I'm frustrated all day long. I obsess about how easy it would be to pull them off. No zippers—"

"Oh," I say, breathless.

"But this dress," his fingertips trace the plunging neckline, "it makes you *feel* sexy and confident. And I can't stop watching."

He kisses me again, but this one is different from the others. There's no softness. No gentle, curious exploration. This time, he's plying my lips open with need, like he's been waiting for this moment for far too long. Like he's been holding back, keeping himself restrained, and he suddenly can't anymore.

I wrap my arms around his neck and deepen the kiss, pushing myself flush against him, testing the ways our bodies might fit together. His hands draw me tight against his body, lifting me onto my tiptoes.

My hands start roving all over him, lingering on those tantalizing bits of exposed skin. One hand slips inside his costume and my fingertips skim his muscular abdomen.

"Millie," he pauses, his voice so deliciously husky that goosebumps erupt on my skin. "Don't start something you aren't going to finish."

I pull him over to my tufted chaise. It's a piece of dainty furniture built for fainting ladies. He dwarfs it and I whisper a prayer to ghosts and gods and goblins that this thing will hold us both because I am not getting off his lap after I get on it. His head tilts back, and I hike up my dress and sink down on top of him. His hands dig into my waist as I lower myself onto his lap and press my lips against his.

Whatever I convinced myself of earlier, that this was all a bad idea, I ignore it now and let myself commit to this moment, commit to him. These feelings are bigger than any bit of reason that I told myself, any bit of hesitation I had.

I feel the press of our bodies contouring against each other, and I've never wanted anyone, anything, more than I want him in this moment.

His broad hand slides up the slit in my dress, up my thigh as I explore his neck, his chest, his collarbone with my mouth.

"Millie!"

Ethan's hand freezes at the sound of my brother's voice.

"The next ghost in this house is going to be Ben," I growl, contemplating the ways I can murder him.

"Where are you?! I want to eat this cake!" Ben shouts from downstairs. "We're going to eat it all without you! I'm going to blow out your birthday candles myself."

"To be continued?" I ask with a frustrated sigh.

"Not here," he says as he sets me upright and fixes my little witch hat.

"Not here," I agree.

***

The night devolves into laughing and party games and stealing kisses in empty rooms. We deal Lou the ghost in as a player in our round of rummy. He isn't very good, but I'm not either.

We move furniture out of the way in the drawing room to make a dance floor and build a fire in the fireplace. Each of us drops in something meaningful—Sarah's idea of an exorcism.

Ethan drops in a card with contact information for his biological father, because he says has all the family he needs.

Sarah drops in a tube of lipstick. "It's my favorite," she explains. "Lots of memories, and it has been discontinued."

Ben drops in a cocktail napkin. I can see Sarah's handwriting on it, and her smile for only him, so I don't press for details.

I drop in a note I had written to Rowan years ago, then found recently in his desk drawer. It was a perfunctory birthday card. When I read it, I ached with regret. It was so impersonal—I could have written it for my dentist. I burned it in apology and hopes that I am mindful and careful with the people that I love that I still have left.

I dance with Sarah. I dance with Ben. I tell them how much I love them while we twirl around the navy-blue room, listening to Rowan's scratchy records on the record player.

"Do you think Lou has anyone to dance with?" Sarah asks dreamily, her head on my shoulder.

"I don't think so. If he did, why would he be here, moving my coffee cup around and fiddling with the electric?"

"Poor Lou," she says sadly.

"Poor Lou," I agree. "I wonder why he's here, after all this time?"

"Well, it's obviously for love," Sarah decides. "What else could it be?"

"I suppose you're right."

"Of course I am. Love is the only thing worth haunting for," she says with certainty.

"Will you haunt me someday, if you die first?"

"You know I will. Do you promise to haunt *me* if *you* die first?"

"Promise. Or maybe we'll die at the same time and be ghost friends. We'll scare the shit out of people together."

"Especially Ben."

"Especially Ben. Speaking of which, where is that big dummy? I want to dance with him. I can't believe he spelled BUTT on the Ouija board." She steps away to find him, disappearing into the dining room where he'd slipped away to the bar cart to refill his drink.

"Is it my turn yet?" Ethan hands me a glass of water. "Drink up so you don't get a headache tomorrow."

I finish the glass and set it down on a side table next to a tasseled velvet lamp shade.

"Thank you," I say, grabbing his hand and pulling him out to dance. "Not just for the water. For everything. You're always taking care of me."

He slides his arms around me, and we start to gently sway to the music. One hand explores my back, the other holds my hand tight and strong.

"Thank *you* for letting me take care of you. It doesn't seem easy for you to allow someone to do that."

"It's not," I admit. "But I don't mind when it's you."

He kisses the tip of my nose. "Do you remember when you asked if dancing with me is like getting bumped into?"

"I did say that didn't I?" A blush spreads to my cheeks, and he studies it with warm eyes.

"So, what do you think? Is this better than what you thought? I can't have my reputation ruined."

"Mm, I'm not impressed yet," I lie quickly.

"Let's see if I can change your mind."

He tilts me backward and I can't contain the laugh that escapes as he pulls me back up again. Then his fingertips sweep up my back, tracing the curve of my neck, leaving trails of fire. He pulls me tight against him, and our bodies slide against each other to the beat of the music.

"What about now?" he whispers against my ear. My laughter is gone, replaced with resolve. Suddenly, the room feels too crowded. Too hot. I know he is feeling the same, I can see it in the heat in his cheeks and the way he can't stop looking at my lips.

I've made it my mission to turn off all the *Millie, don'ts* in my brain and just be. If I want to tell him he's handsome, I will. If I want to flirt with him, I will. If he says something that makes me laugh, I will not hold back.

I am done holding back.

I want to be with him.

"Fine, fine. You're a good dancer. I'll walk you home," I say, my voice a sultry whisper.

He stares at me for a long moment before nodding once, a mere resolute jerk of his chin. I can see my own resolution mirrored in his eyes.

When we slip away, Sarah and Ben don't notice—they are dancing softly in the firelight, their eyes only on each other.

***

Last night, walking home with Joe, the woods were terrifying. My phone flashlight catching on pale branches and getting lost in the deep black forest beyond. My instincts were screaming at me to run, to get inside. My arms wrapped my jacket close around me as I tried not to think about how everything in the woods could see me and my ultra-bright light, but I couldn't see them, deep in the darkness.

Ghosts and goblins and things that go bump. Wolves with glinting teeth. How many creatures were watching me, listening to my clumsy human steps? Each step I took felt disturbingly loud, dry rustling crackles of fallen leaves, the snaps of tree branches. All the while, I was ignoring Joe's kind reassurances and eating myself alive with anxiety about what to do about Ethan.

But tonight, the predator is beside me, pulling me forward, and instead of being scared, I feel alive with it all. Always with him, I feel so alive. Now, the music in my head is bold and soulful and throaty and defiant.

If there are creatures watching, I think, let them watch—look at this glorious beast I've caught. Look how we can't keep our hands off each other, our eyes off each other. There's absinthe on my lips and sugary confections buzzing through me, but more than anything else I'm intoxicated by *him*. He's laughing about something, that deep low beautiful sound that's become a balm to my soul. I am floating and giddy as I run beneath the moon. And oh, I can't stop looking at him as he leads me through the forest, fingers laced in mine, the light of his flashlight a spotlight on the ground, barely, just barely pushing back the night.

But it doesn't matter that I can't see him, because I've studied his face so much, I could fill in any blank spots. I feel like I could stare at him for hours, explore every millimeter with my hands and lips and still be hungry for more.

So, this is what Ethan looks like at night, hot-blooded after a party. I know what he looks like when he's focused on his work. When he's struggling under the unbearable weight of loss and grief. When he's laughing, and when he's relaxed, basking in gentle happiness. When he's bored, and when he's frustrated as hell. What will Ethan look like when he finally, fully lets down his guard, completely giving in to the frenzy between us? What will Ethan look like in the morning light with rumpled sheets around us?

I *have* to know.

Each step through the forest takes us one step closer to discovering every part of each other we haven't shared yet. My blood is roaring and every inch of me wants to touch every inch of him.

"Ethan. I can't wait," I tell him, breathless, and stop walking, reaching for him instead.

I pull our joined hands to my lips and one by one, kiss his calloused knuckles. With each kiss, I tell him how much he matters to me, how badly I want him.

"I can't either," he says, voice ragged with lust. The sound of it absolutely wrecks me. He grabs my face with his hands, and I stand on my tiptoes to meet him. I feel him curl around me, kissing me back so deeply and sweetly I feel tears well up inside me. Like always, his hands are part of the kiss, exploring, gripping, pulling me closer. He kisses me like we're in an action movie and he's about to do something deadly courageous. Like he's a soldier going off for war. Like I'm his dream girl and he's been waiting for this moment for years. Like he's suffocating and I'm his oxygen.

He's drinking me in and never letting me go. I feel like my legs are going to give out, so I jump on him, and he lifts me up. I wrap my legs around his waist and his hands grip my ass, holding me. His hips are still pressed against mine, making the bulge of his arousal unmistakable.

He drops his phone flashlight on the forest floor and we're in total, absolute darkness. I open my eyes to see him, but it's pitch black. It feels like we're floating in a starry sky, tethered only to each other. Sensory deprivation—only Ethan exists.

I love kissing him like this, with his face tilted up to me, my hands on his cheeks, our breath mingling. I kiss him until we're both senseless with need, his breathing coming in rasps. I press my nose to his nose, my forehead to his forehead, and try to slow down and savor this perfect moment and catch my breath.

"Millie, I need you. It doesn't matter if we're going separate ways for now. We'll make it work, OK? We'll do the long-distance thing. I don't care how hard it will be. I'll wait for you."

"You want to do the long-distance thing? So, this isn't a one and done deal?"

He laughs and my whole body warms with the sound. "You and I both know that I will never recover from this night. If we do this, I am yours completely and you are stuck with me. I'll go with you, if you want me to."

"You would come with me?" This is not a good plan. I know it's not a good plan. But I love hearing it anyway.

He nods against me in the dark, forehead rolling against mine. Something about not being able to see each other is helping him spill his vulnerabilities.

"Anywhere. If you want me to. God, Millie, can't you tell how badly I want you? How bad I've wanted you for so long?"

"You've been hard since the yoga thing," I repeat his line to him.

"I was lying. I've been hard for a decade. When we were both teenagers and you were outside sunbathing every day. I couldn't sleep the whole summer, thinking about you in that bikini."

"I think you're supposed to talk to your doctor for an erection lasting more than 48 hours."

He shuts me up with his mouth and soon we're both gasping for air in frantic breaths between kisses.

"My dream girl," he says against my lips. "I had such a big crush on you, but I felt like I didn't deserve you, with all my baggage. I knew I wasn't good enough for you."

"We could have been friends," I say, sad. "I wish we would have talked to each other."

I feel his shoulders roll in a shrug. "I didn't persist because I wasn't surprised when you rejected me. I thought you deserved better than me."

"But now you know me, and I have as much baggage as you do." I'm conflicted with wanting to slow down and listen to him opening up, and my impatience for him to finish talking so I can get my mouth back on his.

"More, probably. You're so messed up." I can't see his face, but I know his eyes are crinkling in the corners.

"Shut up."

"No. You're perfect, Millie. I haven't been able to think about anything but you, only you, every day since you opened that door."

And now we're finally here.

I catch his bottom lip with my teeth, and he groans, low and deep. I love that sound. I can feel it in my bones. I want to make him make that sound every day for the rest of my life. My hands are frantic and so are his, exploring, grabbing, two forces pushing against each other, and neither can get enough.

"Come on, let's keep going." He sets me down on my feet and I pick up his phone, lighting us both with the flashlight. He looks so vulnerable, a little dazed, completely infatuated with me. I drink it in and hope I never forget this moment.

"Catch me!" I don't know if it's the drinks or the moonlight or Ethan or all of it but I'm feeling wild. I pick up the hem of my dress, turn, and run, laughing through the well-trodden forest trail, stars bright and the world spinning.

"Millie!" he calls after me and starts running, too, chasing me and my heart pounds, pounds, and pounds. I am barely out of his reach, branches whipping past as I run down the familiar trail toward his house.

My heart races at the steady crunch of his footsteps behind me.

He catches me in the orchard.

The ground falls away and the sky spins as he wraps his iron arms around my waist and lifts me up.

He pushes me against a tree, bark poking me sharply in my back, my arms pinned above my head. He smashes his mouth to mine, his body to mine, breathing and pushing against me. I arch against him and moan into his mouth, as I meet the delicious hardness straining against his costume. He's lost in it, in us—he's devouring me, completely losing his composure. I want him inside me. We could, here, now. In seconds. I would only need to part my dress, push my panties to the side.

The anticipation is too much. I'm on fire with lust and it's devouring me.

"I can't make it to your place. It's too far. I want you right now."

I break our embrace to pull the costume off him, and he's left standing in only a pair of shorts. I explore his muscled torso with impatient eyes and fingertips and lips. I can barely see him, lit in the warm amber beams of light spilling from his porch in the distance. His chest is heaving with big breaths and his tenderness is gone, his laughter is gone.

Feral, lusty, smoldering-eyed Ethan—I've never seen anything sexier in my whole life. I give in to the impulse to lean in and smell the hair-dappled skin between his pectoral muscles. I taste the faint sheen of sweat covering his neck, his chest.

"Not the first time. Have to get to my place," he tells me for the second time. His voice is deep, shaking. He unzips my dress and I hear his intake of breath as it slips open, and he catches sight of my yoga toned body and black lacy bra.

He reaches for me, but I dance to the side, slip off the beautiful dress and hang it carefully on a branch. Then I turn and haul ass, running as fast as I can, racing to his workshop. I barely reach it when he plows into me and knocks the laugh out of my lungs as he lifts me up.

I get enveloped in his arms again as he pins me against his door with a thud, and it's even better this time, without shirts on. Lips on lips, skin on skin, heaving chests. He's such a warm contrast against the cold night. I run my hands over his shoulders, his arms, his back. I sink my hands in his hair and pull him closer, closer.

He sets me down and pulls my bra off, letting it fall into a puddle of fabric on the ground. My nipples are pebbled and I'm shivering from so much more than cold.

"You are so hot," he says, and I've never felt so beautiful. He begins to explore my skin the way I explored his in the orchard, hands and eyes and lips tracing every inch of me. No part of my exposed skin goes unworshipped. But it's still not enough.

There's an undeniable, throbbing ache between my thighs.

"I want all of you," my voice is a husky whisper.

He slides his hand inside my panties, and I shiver against him. When he slips a finger inside of me, I sink my teeth into his shoulder. My knees weaken and I brace myself against the door as he massages small circles on my most sensitive places, the most divine torture, and his name thunders through my veins like a drumbeat.

"Please," I whimper.

He untangles us, opens his door, and lifts me across the threshold like a bride, carrying me through the darkened woodshop up to his bedroom.

He drops me on his bed, and joins me a few moments later, after I hear the sounds of a crinkling wrapper. We get tangled up in his sheets, which smell like Ethan magnified and make my head spin with lust.

He's kissing me everywhere, down my chest, my belly—his hands are sweeping up my legs, cupping my breasts. He reaches the elastic of my panties, ready to pull them off, and pauses.

"Are you sure?"

"Yes, yes, and yes." I reach out to grab him, to pull him closer, but he moves away. "Ethan, I swear, if we get interrupted one more time, I'm going to die."

He switches the light on his nightstand, and I'm bathed in light. I blink my eyes shut.

"I want to see you," he says, kneeling on the mattress in front of me. He's smiling so sweetly, my heart feels like it's going to explode.

"Get over here," I pull him down to kiss me again, and he presses me down into the mattress, the most exquisite weight.

And then, I don't have to wait anymore.

CHAPTER TWENTY-TWO

I WAKE UP TO the beeping of an alarm and growling against my back.

Ethan untangles himself from me, snoozes his alarm, then rolls back over to pull me into a big snuggly naked bear hug. I feel my whole body sigh against him as he takes in a deep breath of my hair. It's sprawled all around us—it came undone sometime in the night.

He squeezes me tight in his arms and I am the little spoon, dwarfed against him. I snuggle back, starting to drift off again, blissed out, warm, and basking in that peaceful space between awake and asleep, our slow breathing matching each other.

I shouldn't be surprised to learn that Ethan is the best at cuddling.

This is almost as good as the sex.

The alarm beeps again.

"I'm up, I'm up."

He plants a kiss on my shoulder before he slips out of the sheets and silences the alarm on his phone again. I watch him stand and stretch, golden sunrise spilling in through all those windows and landing on his skin.

"I object." I pull the covers around myself, squinting at the sun. "This is too early and I'm cold. Why are you getting up this early?"

"Going out of town again for another interview, remember?" He calls from the bathroom, where I hear the shower turn on.

The word knocks the smile off my face, taking a dangerous swipe at the happy bubble I'm in. Before I can even think about joining him in the shower, he's out.

He's quickly pulling on dress clothes from the back of his closet. Somehow, watching him get dressed is almost as intimate as getting him undressed. Straight navy dress pants, white under-shirt. I sit up in bed, covers bunching around me, and watch him transform into someone I hardly recognize, the clean-cut guy in the picture on Rowan's mantel.

Ethan in a suit is a little bit formidable and outrageously sexy. All that height and posture. But it's more than the clothes. As he buttoned up the shirt, he lost his easiness, button by button.

"I'm sorry to rush out on you so early. Go back to sleep. Is it still OK for you to keep an eye on Max for me?"

"Yeah, of course. Remind me when you'll be back?"

"Three days," he says and leans down to plant a quick kiss on my lips. I try to catch his eyes, but they are closed off, focused on getting out the door.

"Good luck," I tell him reflexively.

But I didn't mean it, did I? In my head, I can't separate Ethan from this place. He's part of it and it's part of him and everything about this feels wrong.

***

"Good morning," Ben drawls as I step up to the porch.

"Sleep well last night?" Sarah asks. "We weren't expecting you back so early."

They are both grinning knowing grins, like Cheshire cats. They are sitting in my beautifully refinished Adirondack chairs, each holding a cup of coffee, steam rising in quick-fading whirls.

They weren't talking as I approached. They had already slid into that comfortable secure place in a relationship where they were simply enjoying silence side by side without the pressure to fill every moment with chatter.

"Um..." I say, because I'm still thunderstruck. Flashes of last night pop into my head unbidden and I can't control the ridiculous blush that takes over my face.

"So?" Sarah asks, eyes twinkling conspiratorially. She knows exactly what my blush means. She hands her coffee mug to Ben, who takes it inside for a refill and to give us some privacy. "How was it?"

"Absolutely amazing," I close my eyes for a moment.

"Really?!"

"Sarah. It was the best night of my life," I admit.

"Of course it was! And how are you feeling this morning? And where is he? I thought I'd make us all breakfast." She peppers me with questions as I sink into the seat Ben left open beside her.

"He's gone for a few days for a job interview. I'm confused about what the next steps are going to be and how we're going to make this work. And I'm worried that he didn't mean everything he said last night. Like maybe it was lust-fueled words. But mostly?"

I pause, savoring the bubbly feeling in my chest, the smile I can't get off my face. "Mostly, I'm happy. I can't remember the last time I felt this happy."

She squeals.

"I really like him, Sarah," I admit. Happiness, warm and sweet, washes over me.

"I can tell. You were laughing so much last night, Millie. You light up around him, and it's beautiful to see."

"What do you think of him?" I ask her.

"*Girl where do I start?* He's funny and kind and respectful and like, is so perceptive to your every whim, it was so adorable watching him wait on you hand and foot. Plus, he's like a... hot Viking cosplaying as a fit grandpa and you should bang him all over his woodshop. That's what I think of him," she finishes with a passionate flourish.

"Tried that, he wouldn't let me, something about splinters."

"Oh, God." Sarah bites her lip and closes her eyes.

"Is this a thing? Is this something you want?" Ben stands in the doorway, his eyes on Sarah. "If you have a woodshop kink, tell me and I will find a woodshop."

He hands Sarah her refilled coffee and a fresh cup for me.

"Ben, go away," I say. "There are so many doorways in this place, find a different one to lurk in for a minute."

"Fine. I was just going to say, I like him a lot, too. You could definitely do worse. Honestly, he's way more awesome than you. I'm not sure how you ensnared him in your clutches."

***

"Do you remember when you and Mom and I would all be in separate rooms doing whatever, and Rowan would turn up the volume on his record player obnoxiously loud? And we would drift down one by one to find him?" I ask Ben. After breakfast, we spent the morning working on my to-do list at the inn.

"He was usually in his office, drinking bourbon. He would nag at us for being boring and staring at our phones," Ben smiles ruefully.

"Then he'd teach us about the classics," I start.

"And give us bourbon," Ben talks over me.

"He did not."

"Yeah, he did for me."

"Well, regardless, I think you should take his music. Not me," I say, pushing the box of records across the floor at him.

"Are you sure?"

"Yeah, I'm sure. I know you'll appreciate it more than I will. Why don't you put something on for us right now?"

"There's something I want to talk to you about first."

"What?"

He takes a deep breath before beginning. "I'm so sorry Millie, for not standing up for you that night at the engagement party. Mom was just so happy for once, there was this illusion of everything being perfect. I didn't want to rock the boat, and I am *such* a coward. I hope you will let me make it up to you."

I stare at him, wordless. There is shame in the slump of his shoulders. I reach out and hug him. I feel his shoulders relax as he reaches around to return the hug, squeezing me so tightly it's hard to breathe.

"Thank you for apologizing, Ben. It means a lot to me." Ben's apology fixes something broken inside of me. I feel like I have my brother back. I hand him the box of records. He pulls one out and sets it to play.

So, with Rowan's favorite albums as our soundtrack, we spend three days staging the inn and getting to know each other again.

Ben loads his car with the mementos I'd set aside for him and Mom, and we've decorated the other rooms. We're down to the bare minimum of furniture, and only the most tasteful knickknacks.

But it needs something more, a final polish. And the wallpaper...

"I need help taking this wallpaper down," I say, standing on the stairs. "It's awful."

"It won't take long if we do it together," Ben says, leaning in close to study it. "It looks like it's only one layer. Let's go pick up a steamer and scrapers and face masks when we go into town."

"We'll order something *amazing* to replace it with," Sarah says. "I'm thinking of a modern floral pattern, something that works with all these bold wall colors!"

"They're dark, I know. But I wanted to do something period appropriate, and this is what it would have looked like. Victorians loved the drama. Dark walls, small rooms."

"Oh, don't get me wrong I love it. This inn is a *mood*. I am thinking through the decor. Maybe some rooms we will do period exact with the old furniture you've saved, and others we will add more modern pops in accessories. Like bright fabric bed linens. Gallery walls. Look." She pulls out her phone and shows me a few photos she's curated while we all crowd around her on the steps.

"Let's do it."

"Don't have to tell me twice."

Sarah pulls things out of the shed and repurposes them in ways I never thought of. Ben and I are at her beck and call, hanging an old picture frame here, adding a stack of books under a vase there. We redistribute the plants from the sunroom throughout the place. We spend half a day shopping, pouring through thrift stores and Target in the next town over. We buy new rugs, linens, and pillows. We center throw rugs on the floors. We arrange the carefully chosen remaining furniture just so. We hang old black and white photos of the inn, of the Starlings, in modern gold frames in the lobby. We add fresh cut flowers to the dining room, a stuffed raven to the end table in Room 5, and an old rotary hotel telephone to the dresser in Room 4.

I get to work on the front door, the one that sticks.

Some past painter had slopped paint over any exposed metal. I pilfer a screwdriver and utility knife from Ethan's toolbox, which has become a semi-permanent fixture here, and use it to cut a clean line in the layers of paint. After I remove the knob and plate, I dump them in a warm crock pot filled with soapy water. In the morning, I'll use a toothbrush to gently scrub all the paint off then reassemble it all. Fingers crossed, the intricate whirls and swirls on the knob will shine again and the door won't stick anymore.

As we work, I see it more and more, how good Ben and Sarah are to each other, and the knot of worry in my chest eases. The what-if-they-break-up-and-my-world-implodes knot is slowly being replaced with hopeful joy that this could work.

***

"Babe, you're so amazing, this place looks great," Ben says what we are both thinking, as we stand with our hands on our hips watching Sarah fluff a pillow.

Ethan and I did a lot of the groundwork. But over the past few days, she put frosting on the cake. It's welcoming, historical, and modern all at once.

"I hope the inn likes it," she says.

"Of course it does," I assure her.

It's gleaming, bright, proud, whimsical and weird, its original elements highlighted with care. New pieces added to help it shine. We're so close to finishing the renovation. Only the kitchen left, hanging new wallpaper on the stairwell, and painting the exterior.

I'm exhausted and elated all at the same time. It's Thursday night, which means Ethan should be on his way home.

"What should we do with Stephen?" Sarah asks. I look over at the head on the lobby counter.

"You mean you don't think he'll look good in the listing photos?"

"Nothing says 'buy this place!' quite like a severed mannequin head."

"I have the perfect place for him," I say, and tuck him under my arm.

***

The cheery notes of a piano pull me away from the book I'm trying to read to pass the time until Ethan's arrival. I can't focus—I keep re-reading the same paragraph over and over on accident. I set it down and stretch, then follow the notes of the familiar song.

Ben is bent over the piano keys in the drawing room, where he'd been packing up records and sheet music for himself. He doesn't look up as I come in—he's too focused on the song. There's a bottle of wood cleaner and a rag on the floor next to him. I nudge him with my hip, and he scoots over on the bench to make room for me, all without the song missing a note.

I put my hands on the keys to join in as he effortlessly transitions his song to *Twinkle, Twinkle, Little Star*.

"This is the only song I know how to play," I admit.

"I remember, Millipede." He starts adding complex chords around my basic repetitive notes and together we make something beautiful.

"You've always been so much better at this than me. I hated practicing but you stuck with it."

"It's the only thing I'm better at than you," he says with a crooked smile.

"What? That's not true at all," I argue. "You're the more talented one. Always with all the sports and friends and stuff. I should have pulled my nose out of a book more often and paid attention to the world around me."

"Millie, stop."

My hands freeze on the keys. He does, too.

"No, I mean, stop cutting yourself down all the time."

"I'm being honest."

"No, you're not being honest. You're echoing Mom. She picked a favorite child, and it wasn't you and she was awful to you sometimes. I know it's gotten better as we got older, but I still hear her voice every time you cut yourself down. It's not reality. The reality is that you are kind and brilliant and I love you and I feel so lucky to have you in my life. We shouldn't be so competitive with each other, that's Mom. We should be building each other up."

I don't say anything, because all my breath left me in a woosh.

"How are you, really?" he asks quietly, and goes back to playing a gentle melody.

"Today?" I take a deep breath and check in with myself. "Today, I'm good. Great, actually."

"Sarah said you had a panic attack."

"I did," I admit. "A few days after I got here. I hurt myself by accident, out in the conservatory. But it was so weird when it happened. I felt like I was in a fog—I wasn't sleeping or eating well, and I was seeing strange things. Ethan found me."

He stops playing, turning his head to look at me.

"I'm glad he was here for you, but what if he hadn't been? You have to take better care of yourself. You put so much pressure on yourself all the time. You don't have to. No one expects you to be perfect. If you worked half as hard as you do and messed up twice as much, we would still love you the same. Stop trying to prove something to yourself or Mom or whatever this is. Your mental health is more important."

I let my head fall softly on his shoulder.

"It's not only the mom thing or grief."

"What then?"

"We're graduating, and I can't see what comes next. I was feeling sort of... untethered? I can't plan, except fill out a bunch of job applications and cross my fingers, but you can't know which one will pan out. I don't know what city I'll be living in a few months from now. I hate all the uncertainty. It feels like I'm jumping off a cliff and don't know where I'll land."

"Come on, that's a terrible analogy. You have a safety net. Mom and Sarah and I are always here for you. You can move back in with Mom if you need to. It's not like jumping off a cliff at all. Maybe it's more like a hot air balloon ride. They don't know where they'll land, right?"

"You're right. I know I'm so lucky to have a support system. I guess I just feel like I've been running at breakneck speed toward something my whole life. I thought it was high school graduation, then that was done, so I started chasing a bachelor's degree, and then I still felt unfinished and like I needed to keep going so I started working on my masters. But now that's almost done, too, and it's disconcerting. I feel like I'll always be chasing something. Is this what life is? Reaching goals but not feeling satisfied? Always searching for the next carrot?"

"So, you came here alone to distract yourself, because the emotional trauma of dealing with our dead uncle's estate is a sure way to lessen the stress of unknowns in your life?"

I give a half-hearted laugh. "I missed him, Ben. I missed him so bad, and I felt so terrible about not spending more time with him that I could hardly bear it. I always felt so at peace here, so I came searching for that feeling again."

"But you're punishing yourself, too, for not spending enough time with him while he was alive."

I shrug, tears welling in my eyes. "I guess so."

"Well, the phone works both ways and Rowan could have tried a little harder to connect with us, too. It's not all on you, OK? But I understand what you're saying, and I feel that same regret, too. Everyone feels that with the death of a loved one. But regardless, he wouldn't want you moping around his house. He would tell you to get off your ass and chase your joy."

I laugh. "I'm not moping around! Well, not today, anyway." Despite everything, I can't control the smile that starts to spread across my face.

"Ethan is a great guy. I'm happy that you are happy, Millie. You deserve to be."

"He is a great guy. What am I going to do? This is such a mess."

"How is it a mess?"

"He's so tied to this place in so many ways. Did you know he moved here to help Rowan?" Ben shakes his head, so I fill him in on the details of Ethan's story that he doesn't know.

"He built a house, revived the orchard, and started a woodworking business. It's so beautiful, you have to come see it tomorrow, it's like something from a storybook. But he is giving it up—he's off at a job interview right now at a career that he hated and abandoned. He's built a new life here, rebuilding some of his family legacy, and I feel like we are taking it out from under him by selling. I feel terrible about it." I pause before saying, "He told me he wanted me to come with him, that we could start over in a new place."

"Really? Wow. Sudden."

"I know. It's a beautiful thought, but it's too soon. And I'd be the reason why his world is upended. He told me to do whatever I needed to do, but I feel like you can't start a relationship with that—he'd resent me someday. Deep down."

"I've thought a lot about keeping the inn, telling Ethan to stay put, and trying to get a job for myself in town. But there aren't any in my field here so it would be like I put myself through school for nothing. I guess I could wait tables or something? But I would be giving up on my career. And what if we break up?"

I rub my face.

"I'm not throwing away my future for a guy, no matter how much I like him. Plus, if we don't sell, or if we delay selling, that would mean you and Sarah wouldn't get startup money from the sale to start your business, because I can't afford to buy out your portion—not right away, anyway. So, even if I somehow managed to talk you into not selling, I would feel like I was choosing him and his happiness over you and Sarah."

"This is a pickle, as Dad used to say," Ben says, eyes soft on mine.

"Yeah. I'm not sure what to do."

"I'll tell you what you're going to do," he says, starting to play the piano again. "You're going to be a little more like Ben and a little less like Millie. Let yourself get swept up in it. We don't need to decide anything today. Give yourself more time. See how the cards fall. I've been doing my best to keep Mom off your back and have stopped her from listing the property before you've finished working on it."

"You have?" I inhale sharply.

Ben nods. "I've been pushing on her guilt button. She feels bad about marrying a pig and making us put up with him. You especially."

"Thank you, Ben."

He nods again. "I'll hold her off as long as I can. And if it's supposed to work out with you and Ethan, you two will figure it out. We all will."

I wrap my arms around his waist. He smells like Axe body spray. So gross and so comforting all at the same time.

"You're my whole heart, you know that, right?" he says, hugging me back. "Or at least half of it, and I'm finally admitting to everyone that Sarah has the rest. She has for a long time."

"Yeah, she's got half of my heart, too." I agree. We sit in silence awhile.

"Ben, I have an idea," I sit up suddenly. "A solution to this pickle that might make all of us happy. But I need your help figuring out the details."

"Anything. We're in this together."

I hear a *scritch, scritch, scratching* pulling at my ear. I detangle myself from Ben's embrace.

"Do you hear that?" I ask, turning my head in the direction of the sound.

"Yeah, Sarah, what are you doing?" he calls out.

She steps in from the sunroom, which is in the opposite direction of the source of the noise. She's holding a watering can, Frank trailing behind her. "Frank and I were watering the plants—what's that sound?"

We all stare at each other, then our heads turn in unison to the dining room, and the *scritch, scritch, scratching* beckoning us.

The lights buzz and flicker.

Ben stands and grabs an iron poker from the fireplace, hoisting it on his shoulder like a bat ready to swing.

"Get behind me," he orders, his voice a deep whisper.

Sarah and I line up behind Ben and we tiptoe in a row through the vaulted doorway into the dining room.

Sarah gasps. My hands fly to my mouth.

"No way," Ben murmurs, and drops the poker. It drops to the floor with a shuddering clang.

One by one, we surround the enormous table, where the Ouija board lies.

The planchette is scraping across the board, and the lights above flicker erratically.

Sarah and I look at the board, back at each other, then back at the board. Ben reaches his hand out toward it.

"Don't touch it!" Sarah whispers, panicked.

"How is this happening?" Ben looks under the table for some sort of trick. But there's nothing—there's no explanation.

I lean over the board. The planchette is swinging from letter to letter, scraping across the board. "Sarah, pull out your phone, get ready to type. I'm going to read the letters aloud. It's trying to tell us something."

She nods and whips her phone out of her pocket.

I watch as the planchette swings from letter to letter, purposefully pausing on one letter at a time.

"O-L-I-N-A-?" I read out.

The planchette stops.

"Olina? What does that mean?" Ben asks.

The planchette swings back to the letters. "I don't know, it's still moving, like it's starting again. C-A-R-O-L-I-N-A-?"

The flickering lights stop, returning to their normal glow.

"Carolina? Like the states?" Sarah asks, eyes daring nervously from me to the board. The planchette doesn't move. "What does that mean? Are you trying to tell us you're from North or South Carolina?"

But the planchette doesn't move. "I guess it said what it wants to say?" I step back, wrapping my arms around myself to hold in my shivering.

"Why is there a question mark at the end?" Ben asks.

"It's not telling us something, it's asking us something," Sarah finishes for him.

"But what?" The furrow between my brows deepens.

CHAPTER TWENTY-THREE

After a shower, I make myself presentable with jittery hands. Fix my hair. Swipe on some mascara. All while obsessively checking the clock on my phone. He'll be home in three hours. Then two hours.

With a half hour to spare, I set off to his house. On the way out, I tuck Stephen under my arm.

I walk—no, jog—through the woods with Max as my shadow. Frank has decided to stay home, since he's taken a liking to Sarah. When I left, she was draped on a chaise like a queen with Frank purring loudly in her lap.

My heart sinks when I don't see his truck in the driveway, even though I'm here a little early. I check my phone again, hoping for a message from him. Nothing.

I unlock the door and Max pushes past me into Ethan's house. The trees are swaying outside, shadows dappling across the room. I take a deep contented breath in, like I can't help but do every time I'm here. Fresh cut wood. Coffee. Spicy warmth. Peace.

The paranormal encounter feels a million miles away.

Max leads me over to his food bowl and I fill it for him. I watch his tail slowly wag while he eats. I sit down and watch out the windows, my leg starting to bounce with impatience. I haven't worked all my shivers out after seeing the Ouija board move. I've never seen anything like that before.

What does Carolina mean?

The place?

Or maybe a name?

I stand up and start tidying the kitchen, washing our coffee cups from the other morning. I hide Stephen in the towel closet—he's ready to scare Ethan with his leering smile.

I straighten the sheets still rumpled from us. As I fluff the pillows, my cheeks heat at the replay of images of everything he did to me in this bed.

Headlights swing into the apartment, casting their beams across the space. I jump up from the chair and run downstairs, outside.

"What took you so long?" I holler from the porch, struggling to keep myself composed as I start walking toward his truck. I purposefully keep my pace slow, casual. As if I haven't been silently counting down the minutes for him to get home. He eases out of the truck and drops down on one knee to get covered in kisses from Max, who is hopping around with a wagging tail.

"Your turn! What are you doing over there? Get over here!"

"How did it go?" I ask as I step off his porch.

"I think I have a good chance of getting hired. They said they were finishing other interviews and would touch base in a few weeks."

Wow, congratulations, Ethan, I should say. But the words stick in my throat.

"When would you start?"

How many days do we have left?

"If they offer it to me, I'll have to think it over."

"Why?"

"*Why?*" he asks, slamming his truck door. He's loosening his tie as he closes the distance between us. "You know why. I've got this girl stuck in my head and I can't think about anything else."

Then his eyes are searching my face.

"What do you want? Do you *want* me to leave?"

Oh, we're doing this right now. In the driveway.

I shake my head.

"Then what *do* you want? Say it." He steps closer, toe to toe with me, and I can see how tired and lost he looks.

"I want you, Ethan. I can see a future for us. Is that crazy?"

He shakes his head and reaches for me. I hear the sound of his duffel bag hitting the gravel a moment before his hands cup my face.

"I meant what I said the other night. I had days away from you with a clear head to think about it. And I still mean it. All of it. I also know that if we quit this right now, I will regret it. I need to be with you. Everything else is inconvenient minor details."

I let out a shaky breath. "I feel the same way."

I can see some of the tension leave his shoulders at my answer. "Good," he says, wrapping me into a fierce hug.

"But *minor* details?" I echo. "It's more than minor details. How could we possibly make this work? I've been tearing myself apart trying to figure it out."

"Do you want to live in the city? I'll take this job and you can come with me. You could take your time finding a job. Or there's a university downtown—we can visit campus this week to see if you want to take classes there. Or if you don't want to live in the city, I'll apply somewhere else—"

I stand up on my tiptoes and kiss him softly and it feels like coming home. Like sliding into a warm bath on a cold night. Like taking off an uncomfortable bra at the end of the day. Like a towel fresh out of the dryer. He makes my soul sigh in relief every time I touch him. He makes me feel like everything is going to be OK.

I picture the life he's envisioning for us. Me studying, him coming home in the evenings after working at a firm all day.

Max and Frank in an apartment.

But it doesn't quite fit, does it?

Could he be happy?

He wasn't before. He was so desperately unhappy that putting on his work clothes again sent him into a nonverbal, no laughing stress spiral.

Would he resent me? How could he not?

We would start off with good intentions, but the cracks would show.

He'd miss this place. I would, too.

"Ethan I'm crazy about you."

"I'm crazy about you, too. My leg was bouncing the whole way here. I bit my fingernails." He holds up a hand, nails nibbled down to the quick.

"Gross."

"Disgusting," he agrees. "I was crawling out of my skin wanting to get back to you."

"Me too. I couldn't sit still. I was running circles around Sarah and Ben. We finished staging the inn for the realtor photos! But I don't know how I feel about that anymore. Does it make you happy?"

"It makes me feel like you and I are coming up to a finish line so, no, that does not make me happy."

"I don't know how I feel about it either. Would you stay if you could?" I'd asked him as much before, but I don't know how truthful he was. I need to hear it again.

He blows out a sigh. "I don't know. I love it here, of course I do, it's my home. But it's crazy... sometimes I have the urge to burn it all down. Or leave so I never have to be reminded of my mom and Rowan."

"It's not crazy. I know how you feel. And I also feel like I would be disappointing them if we left. Which is also crazy because they're dead."

"Not crazy—I feel that, too."

"Well, there's one more big thing on Rowan's list," I say.

"The kitchen."

"The kitchen. Are you up for stalling a few weeks longer? Ripping out some old cabinets while we figure out what to do about us next?" I ask.

"I am if you are."

"Deal."

He kisses the top of my head and wraps his arms around me in a hug.

"And besides," I say to his chest. "I can't leave yet because there's another mystery to solve."

He holds me back at arm's length.

"What are you talking about?"

"Does *Carolina* mean anything to you?" I ask him.

He shakes his head. I tell him about what Ben, Sarah and I saw with the Ouija board. Even if I know it's real, even if I saw it with my own eyes, I can feel the skepticism, the fear in myself as I describe it. As I finish my story I wonder if Ethan will even believe me.

"I don't know what it means." There isn't a trace of doubt in his eyes. He trusts me completely. He does look uneasy, his eyes lingering on the forest, in the direction of the inn. "But whatever it is, Millie, we'll figure it out together."

I sink back into his embrace. No matter what I throw at this man, he's always in my corner.

"You truly meant all the sweet things you said the other night, didn't you?"

He takes my face in his hands and locks eyes with me.

"I meant every word, Millie. I want a future that suits us both." Then he kisses me and it's the sweetest kiss yet, full of promises and hope.

"You would leave your home?"

"I told you already. It's just a place. Meaningless without love."

"Come on, let's go inside," I say. "I hate your shirt. You're going to have to take it off."

"Are white button downs offensive to your gothic sensibilities?" he asks with a smirk.

"You look so hot and busy and important, but you don't look like you, and my favorite Ethan is naked Ethan anyway."

"I think I can make that happen," he replies, his voice full of promise.

CHAPTER TWENTY-FOUR

"There's this baker you have to meet. He makes the best croissants," I hear Ethan say, and Sarah's smiling up at him, their cheerful energies lighting up the whole room.

I've loved watching them connect over baking. They both have that knack, that desire to figure out the basics of how things work, of how to do it yourself with your own hands. Their mediums are different—his is wood and hers is food—but their respect for the process and ingredients is the same. That insatiable curiosity to get to the root of how something is made and master it. He asks her about the details of what she's making, in ways that I would have never thought of. One maker's soul recognizing another.

We eat breakfast that they prepared for us in the sunroom on the wicker furniture, which looks fresh and welcoming with the deep cleaning and the new cushions Sarah picked out.

"So, for the memorial? I thought we could have it here," I say. "It's big enough to host dozens of people inside. Hundreds outside—the grounds are sprawling. It might be a little cold in November for an outdoor gathering, but we can set up bonfires."

"Rowan would have loved to see the place full of people," Ethan says.

"Out-of-towners can stay overnight. First full house at the inn in sixty years," Ben says.

"Would you help with planning the food?" I ask Sarah.

"Of course I will. I may need a few extra pairs of hands. Depending on how many people are coming."

"Well, you have unlimited free apples, so definitely plan for that," Ethan adds.

"Pies. Got it," she says with a dimpled smile.

"I'll ask Maria. She knows her way around a kitchen, and she would be happy to help," Ethan suggests.

"That would be amazing," Sarah says.

"Do we want to have a whole ceremony? Or an open house?" I ask. "Not that he doesn't deserve a whole ceremony. I just...I'm not sure if I'm up to public speaking on the best of days, and I'm going to be a mess that day."

"I have something I want to say. Others will, too. Maybe we can have an open mic? People can walk up and speak if they feel like it," Ethan suggests.

"I like that idea," Ben says.

"Was Rowan religious? Should we invite a priest or something?" Sarah asks.

"No. He told me once that oblivion was good enough for him," Ethan says.

"Ah, that's dark," Ben says. "But I suppose he is finally able to rest now. There's some solace in that, right?"

We finish our breakfast in mostly silence.

"I'll take care of setting up speakers and stuff. I can make a playlist of music to play while people are mingling. I'll make sure to include his favorite songs," Ben says finally.

"I think this will work. We need somewhere for everyone to sit all at once," Sarah continues.

"What about out back, by the old gardens? You could stand up on the porch stairs to speak," I suggest. Ethan nods in agreement.

"Let's do it. Sarah is figuring out food. Ethan, can you take care of seating? Figure out where to rent chairs?"

"Sure thing."

"I will start working on invitations. Maybe we can put an announcement in the paper," I add.

Sarah and Ben leave after breakfast, and I feel that familiar oppressive melancholy sinking in as we send them off.

"You're magical. You're the fairy decorator godmother of the Starling Inn," I say, squeezing Sarah tight.

"I'm going to miss this place. Honestly," she admits. "It's beautiful here. I love it. And I'm going to miss you."

"You'll be back for the memorial?"

"Of course I will."

Then she turns to Ethan, who is loading her bag into the trunk of the car. "Keep taking care of our girl."

"You know I will."

"See you soon, Millipede. We'll be back for the memorial." Ben plants a kiss on top of my head, and then they're gone.

CHAPTER
TWENTY-FIVE

"LUCY! I FOUND HIM!"

"You did?!" She slides off her stool and rushes over to my microfilm station. The librarian is wearing berry lipstick today and a dress covered in bright spring flowers, a rebellion against the gray weather outside.

I'd stopped by the local history department this morning to donate the inn's ledgers to their collection and stayed to gather information on Louis Starling. My back is sore from sitting in the uncomfortable wood chair, paging through the articles for hours.

I started with the archival collection she ordered on site for me—a small gray box, filled with folders. Most folders had articles and information about the construction of the inn. There was a short biographical piece about John Starling who built the inn in 1890. An assortment of newspaper clippings, many of them advertisements for the inn throughout the years. So far, I haven't learned anything new.

But then, in one of the last folders, I pulled out a black-and-white photograph of a soldier. His wool uniform coat is buttoned up to his chin. A 32nd Division patch is emblazoned on his shoulder and a cap sits on top of short, cropped hair. He's staring proudly, defiantly at the camera. He is posed on a stool in front of a mottled studio backdrop. His eyes are in sharp focus, looking right at me. It's a colorless photo, but I can tell he is fair-haired. His irises are so light colored they look translucent.

"Hey, Lou," I say to the portrait. Goosebumps erupt all over my arms as I study his profile. He looks unmistakably similar to Ethan—something about the shape of his nose.

He's so young.

With a steadying breath, I take a picture with my phone and carefully returned the photograph to the box before heading over to the microfilm to start looking for his obituary again.

I don't mind how long it's taking. I love research—it's so satisfying to sate my curiosity this way. And I like this place. This beautiful, solid building. The soft rustle of pages, laughter of kids drifting in from the children's section. The smell of paper and old books, the smell of coffee and chocolate drifting up from the little cafe in the basement. Plus, I showed Lou's letter to Lucy earlier and she's almost as invested in solving the mystery as I am.

"Louis Starling, age twenty, son of John Starling Sr. and Eleanor Starling, died in France on the first of November, 1918. He is survived by his parents and brother, George Starling," I read the obituary aloud to Lucy when I finally find it.

"November first? Unlucky fellow."

"What do you mean?

"The war ended ten days later."

"Oh, that's right. His poor girlfriend. I hope she heard the death announcement before the end of the war announcement. How tragic would it be if she was celebrating, feeling relief, thinking he might be coming home?"

"Do you know anything about her yet? She pulls up a chair beside me, her notebook in hand.

"No. I don't have many clues to her identity. His military record said he was unmarried. So, she got pregnant out of wedlock. That makes identifying her harder because there isn't a paper trail."

"Did you look at birth records?" Lucy pushes up her round, gold-rimmed glasses.

"Yeah, birth records for 1918 to 1919 and there weren't any new Starlings born in the county. So, if the baby was born, it didn't take Louis' surname."

She drums her pencil on her notepad in concentration. "They were keeping their relationship a secret, right? Did you get that impression from the letter, too?"

"I did, yeah."

"Why would they need to? Maybe our answer lies there." She stands up and starts pacing, her heeled boots making *clip clops* on the glossy stone floor.

"Louis was an heir to the Starling family. Quite wealthy. Especially as a returning war hero. He would have been prime bachelor material. His family would have had some expectations about who he would marry. Because with dynastic money like that, a wedding is a business arrangement, cementing your place in the upper social class."

"So, she was someone his family wouldn't approve of," I say with a conspiratorial smile. "We need to think outside of records. We need to think about context. What sort of person would his family have shunned?"

"Maybe she was someone of a lower class. Like a domestic worker, or a non-white person. She probably worked at, or lived near, the inn," Lucy explains.

"Why do you say that?"

"Because if they moved in different social circles, they would have gone to different schools. How else would they have met?"

"Worked at the inn," I repeat slowly, a thought blooming in my head. "Like... a housemaid?"

She nods, eyes wide. "You just solved something, didn't you?"

"Oh my gosh, Lucy. I think you helped me rid a family of a curse. I have to go!" I say, running over to my locker to grab my coat. "Thank you!"

"Anytime!" she waves me off with a laugh.

***

Ethan's hands are curled around my phone, looking down at the picture of Louis—his project, an end table, is abandoned on the workbench beside him.

"This is so strange to say, but I feel like I know him."

"I understand what you mean. I felt the same when I saw it. Ethan, he didn't make it home to his girl from the letter. He died in France in 1918. He's buried in a French cemetery."

"Poor Lou. We suspected as much already, right? But what happened to his girlfriend and the baby?"

"Ethan, tell me the story again. The story of why the Russo's hate the inn."

He looks at me quizzically for a moment. Hands my phone back to me.

"Joe's great-grandmother, Nonna's mother, was a maid here. She got pregnant, and the father never came forward to marry her. She died of heartbreak not too long after the baby was born. Nonna was brought up by her grandparents. Nonna and Maria stay away from the inn because they think it's cursed."

"What if the baby in the letter is Nonna Russo? She just turned 100 so she was born in 1918."

The furrow between his brow deepens.

"How can we be sure?"

"It will be impossible to prove without a DNA test. We won't find our answer in any records. If a father wasn't present at birth, his name is likely not listed on the birth certificate. But here's my hunch. Louis Starling—Lou—was in love with Nonna's mother. She would have grown up with Louis as a next-door neighbor. Her parents were recent immigrants from Italy, right? So, getting a job at the inn would have made a lot of sense for her."

"Do you think they used the passageway to meet each other in secret?"

"The passageway. The woods. Because of her class and ethnicity, Louis' parents would not have supported or maybe even acknowledged their relationship. And then he died without ever coming home. She died not long after the child was born. Then the child, Nonna, was raised by her maternal grandparents, the Russo's next door. The Russo family curses the inn for the next few generations."

"It all makes sense."

"Call Joe, ask him what his great-grandmother's name was."

"Joe and I might be cousins?" Ethan asks, pulling out his phone and dialing.

"We can do a DNA test to check but... I think it's possible that you are third cousins, yeah."

"The obituary says that the family built a memorial on their land. Does that sound familiar to you at all?"

"Hey, Joe, what's your great-grandmother's name?" Ethan asks into his phone.

"Carolina Russo," Ethan repeats at me after a moment.

All the breath leaves my body.

When I'm able to talk again, I say, "The disturbances at the house, your mom's imaginary friend—it's been Louis, looking for the love he lost, Carolina."

"Joe, change of plans. Meet us at the headless man in the woods."

***

High on a bluff, overlooking the lake and surrounded by wind-stirred evergreens, the statue of a man stands proudly. The head had fallen off ages ago and is now propped up haphazardly at the base. There's no trail to the man, or if there once was, it's now overgrown. He's rising up out of the forest, speckled with moss. Joe sits on near its base, waiting for us.

I stand beside Ethan as he drops to his haunches, reaches out to touch the featureless face, sunken in the leaves, worn away by time.

"So, the bastard great-grandfather that left my great-grandmother to die alone in childbirth—" Joe starts.

"Didn't leave her at all. He didn't make it home from the war."

Ethan and I recount the story for him, what we've discovered.

Joe sits, running his hands through his hair. Stands, paces. Sits again. Stands up and rounds on me.

"We never knew what this statue was," he finally says, his voice full of emotion.

"We used to dare each other to touch it," Ethan adds.

"I can't believe this could be a monument to our ancestor," Joe says. "One that we share."

"A war hero," Ethan says.

"A sweet one, romantic. Based on his letter," I say.

"We thought this statue was a cop. Or a scout or something. Because of the hat." Joe's voice is husky with emotion.

"It's a doughboy statue. There are hundreds of them around the country to honor the soldiers who died during the first World War. The Starlings unfortunately chose to make this one out of marble," I explain, searching the base carefully. "There probably used to be an inscription here. But it's gone now. Marble is acid-sensitive, so it melts in the rain. How'd he lose his head?"

"He's been headless for as long as I can remember. My dad told me he used to play out here when he was a kid, too. How did you find all this out?" Joe asks.

"Millie did. She put together some clues in an old letter we found at the inn, one Louis sent home during the war."

"This is... I can't tell you how much this will mean to my family, Millie. This lifts a burden. Thank you." He wraps me in a hug, and I squeeze him back.

"You're welcome. We can get a DNA test to confirm if you want."

Their eyes meet.

"Don't need to. We're cousins," Ethan shrugs.

"Always knew it. Somehow," Joe adds. "Let's go tell Nonna."

***

Maria pulls Ethan into a hug, her eyes laden with tears. The pot of water on the stove is boiling over, forgotten. "You're my family. I always suspected, knew in my bones, in my heart, that you were. I'd have loved you even if you weren't. But I knew."

I sit with Nonna and Ethan and Maria at the kitchen table and we listen as Joe reads Louis' letter aloud to his grandmother. Nonna listens with hands gripping her rosary, hears for the first time in her life that her parents cared about each other, and that they wanted her. They had imagined a future with her. Her father didn't abandon her mother at all.

I slide my phone across the table to show her his picture.

"He was a hero, Nonna. All this time we thought he was a good for nothing, got her pregnant, and left her to die alone, but he didn't. He loved her; he just couldn't get home to her. He died away at war," Joe says, his voice incredulous.

"Those Starlings. Those awful Starlings." Nonna bites her thumb. Then she turns to Ethan. "Not you; you don't count as a Starling, you're a Russo through and through. Why didn't they tell us? They must have known. I was growing up next door, my grandparents raising me without a penny in their pockets and they had all that money, but they never even glanced my way."

"Elitism. Racism. Evangelical Christianity," I answer. "And they didn't want to tarnish the memory of their dead son. They'd rather pretend his love affair didn't happen and build a shining marble statue to him as a war hero, instead of acknowledging that he was someone who'd sinned and conceived a child out of wedlock, with the daughter of immigrants, a servant in their household no less. They were ashamed. They wanted to uphold their untarnished name in the community."

Maria tuts in anger, her cheeks flaming red. She finally gets up from the table to turn off the boiling pot.

"We were so poor," Nonna continues, "we didn't even have indoor plumbing. I was hungry sometimes. Cold in the winters. My *nonno* was a tradesman, a bricklayer, but he was old, and work came and went, you know. And those Starlings saw it, they knew I was their son's daughter. But they didn't help. How could they? Their own grandchild. Those monsters."

"It's in the past now. Focus on the good news, Mama," Maria says, squeezing her hand. "Your father loved you. Your mother loved you. They loved each other. And Ethan! Ethan is our good news. Our family."

Nonna pinches his cheek, and I watch his shoulders rise and fall with a shaking breath. "Always knew it," she says.

CHAPTER TWENTY-SIX

"Isn't it strange, the way history repeats itself?" Ethan asks, his eyes fixed on the horizon. We're sitting on his porch, sipping on hot cider in mugs and watching the sun set over the orchard, our breath frosting out in front of us. My nose is pink with cold, but I don't mind—it's too beautiful out here to go inside, the sunset a blazing orange and pink.

I can't remember the last time I sat and quietly watched a sunset. Driving home and noticing it, sure. But intentionally sitting there, watching the sun dip below the horizon? Painting the sky in warm, vivid hues. Filling my chest with peace and wonder and admiration for this beautiful world we live in. I can't remember the last time.

"What do you mean? How is history repeating itself?"

His gaze flicks toward me. "Do you know anything about starlings? The birds?"

I shake my head.

"They are a menace, an invasive species. They sometimes lay their eggs in the nests of native birds, expelling the occupants."

"Ethan..." I put my hand on his arm to start telling him how *not* like an invasive bird he is, but he cuts me off.

"My grandparents didn't want anything to do with me. They were ashamed of their daughter and me by extension, so they washed their hands of me. And the good Russos picked up the pieces of their neglect. The same thing happened to Nonna. It seems people don't learn from the past. Prejudices will always exist. Starlings, the birds and the people, are assholes and we're destined to make the same mistakes over and over."

"I don't believe that at all," I say, snuggling into the blanket he had so carefully tucked around me. "You're the change, Ethan. You're the bright light in all of this. You're the Starling that's different."

"I guess so," he says, like he doesn't believe me, and his eyes drift back out to the orchard, the sun setting over it, turning the leaves pink and gold. He's uncharacteristically unsettled, lost in thought. I can sense the storm inside him. It's terrible and I can't stand it. I want to see him smiling again.

"You are the absolute opposite of that," I say with conviction. "The most extreme opposite. You are one of the most selfless people I've ever met."

His arms are crossed tightly across his chest. I sit up to grab his chin and make him look at me before continuing.

"It's true. You're so steady. Thoughtful. Patient." His stony gaze starts to soften. "You know how to show up—do you get how rare that is? I know you will always take care of me, no matter what, because that's just who you are in your soul. You take care of others, always. I'm so lucky that I found you and get to be an apple tree in your orchard, blooming because I'm around you, basking in your kindness. Even if it's only for a little while." I need him to understand. It's so important that he understands.

He kisses my palm, my words heavy between us; the faintest smile spreads across his face and quickly fades.

"Hey. I have an idea," I say. He turns to look at me, his face cast in shadows, and I am determined to chase the sadness out of his eyes and hear his laugh tonight.

"Do you want to watch a '90s sitcom with me?"

"What?"

I shrug off the blanket, stand up, and set my mug of cider down on the porch. Then I stand in front of him, catch my fingers on the hem of my shirt, and slowly pull it over my head. I shake my hair back into place and look him in the eye. Goosebumps erupt at the cold air hitting my skin and I know he can see my nipples through my bra.

"What are you doing?" he asks, voice low.

"We're going to go inside and have our shirtless '90s sitcom watch party. It's your turn. Take your top off. Go on."

He considers me for a moment, in my lacy black bra, hands on my hips, the sunset casting a warm golden glow on my skin.

"You better hurry up, I'm getting cold."

I let out a sigh of relief when he takes the bait, deciding to play along, and I see a bit of that sparkle come back into his eyes. He sighs, stands up, and pulls his shirt off, and butterflies stir low in my belly as I take in the sight of him. I wonder if I'll ever get used to this or if he'll always make me feel this way.

He leans down to kiss me, a sweet cider kiss, and the butterflies take flight.

***

"Ethan!" I shout. "Ethan, I finished it!"

41,257 words. Weeks of research and writing. I submit my completed thesis to Professor Smith with a thudding victorious heart before shutting my laptop and stretching my arms over my head.

It's done.

Finally.

I have everything I need for the National Register of Historic Places application, too. I've got a first draft done and sent it to Lucy for her thoughts before I submit it to the state office that issues the permits.

The past few weeks have been a daze.

Nearly every day I work in the kitchen with Ethan. We pause around lunchtime. Some days he keeps working at the inn, other days goes back to his woodshop. My afternoons are spent solo, typing away at my thesis at Rowan's desk. We are reunited in the evenings, when Frank and I make our way to his house for dinner.

We tore out the ugly kitchen cabinets. I got to use a sledgehammer to smash one to bits and it was so cathartic. Contractors came by to help with rerouting the electric and plumbing to suit Rowan's designs. Ethan taught me how to repair the drywall and lay floor tile. We painted the walls soft white, and he installed new windows and light fixtures.

Somewhere along the way, it got easier to stop sleeping at the inn. I can't stay somewhere that doesn't have a kitchen, after all. My toothbrush and most of my clothes are at his place now. I spend nights tangled up with him in his sheets, and I wake up in his arms each morning.

We go for walks with Frank and Max every morning. Sometimes we go to his mother's grave, but more often we wander. Sometimes it's silent; other times we trip over each other's words because we can't stop talking.

I crack my knuckles and look around.

It's strange that he hasn't answered me.

That old familiar uneasiness slips in. It's so uncharacteristic of him to not be making noise. He's always making some sort of noise. And I know he's not outside because he always tells me when he leaves, plus the security system would have alerted me.

I peek around corners and look behind every closed door, thinking, *Why is this so place so big?* Does there really need to be a living room, a drawing room, *and* a parlor? Why isn't he in any of them?

I finally spy his legs hanging over the end of the green couch in the living room.

"There you are." I put my hand to my chest in relief.

He doesn't answer, and as I step closer, I realize he's asleep, Frank curled up on his chest.

"Ethan?"

He blinks awake, then he catches sight of my face. "What's wrong?"

"Nothing. I just couldn't find you, that's all. I guess I get spooked by this place still." Then I remember why I went searching for him in the first place. "I just submitted my thesis!"

He sits up and I can immediately tell something is off. He looks different than when I saw him a few hours ago. His eyes look glassy, and his cheeks are red.

"Hey, that's great, I'm proud of you." Then he sets Frank gently aside and tries to stand up. I watch him sway on his feet, and he reaches out to me to help steady him. "Are you going to let me read it now?"

"You have a fever. Why didn't you tell me you didn't feel good? What are you even still doing here? Go home."

"Nah, I'll be fine. I knew you were working—and I didn't want to interrupt you—so I just tried to take a nap to shake this headache. Our cabinets were delivered, they're in the shed. I need to move them down to the kitchen so they can acclimate for a few days before install. I'm just having a little sit down with Frank before I start."

"Oh really? You're up for hauling around cabinets?" I ask, my hands on my hips.

"It's only a headache." He squints at me, clearly miserable.

"Stubborn man. Let's get you home."

For once, we have to drive to his house instead of trekking through the woods. I lead him to the passenger side of my car and open the door for him.

"Millie." His hands clutch the door frame and he's refusing to go in.

I shove him but he doesn't budge.

"Millie," he says again, sounding pained. "This car is older than the inn. I won't even fit in it."

I roll my eyes as I climb into my own seat. "It is not older than the inn. Just get in."

"Why are you driving this death trap? Are there even airbags? I'd be so worked up if I didn't feel so bad right now."

I watch as he gives up, folds into the front seat and buckles himself in. He fits. Kind of. His legs hit the dashboard and his arm is hogging all the armrest, putting us shoulder to shoulder.

"Please don't take this on a road trip again. Remind me to nag you later to upgrade your car to something safer."

"It was my dad's car." I will drive this car until it literally rusts out from under me. It's just this one thing I haven't been able to let go of.

"Oh, yeah, I'm sure your dad would want you to die in a car crash without all that newfangled safety equipment."

I start the car and back out onto the country road. "I'll consider it."

Ethan drops his head back to the headrest and I get an unobstructed view of his Adam's apple and thick neck disappearing into his V-neck t-shirt.

It's... absurdly hot. All the times I have worshipped that neck flash in my mind unbidden. Heat overtakes my body, and a blush climbs up my cheeks.

I turn my attention back to the road.

"What are you thinking about?" I can hear the knowing smile in his voice. "*Obviously* not car crashes, like I am."

"You're just showing a lot of skin, that's all," I say, refusing to take my eyes off the gravel road in front of me.

Out of the corner of my eye, I see him look down at himself. "I think I'm fully clothed?" His voice raises in question.

"It's your neck. You have a very distracting collarbone to jaw situation," I admit begrudgingly.

He bursts out laughing.

"I forgot for a second that you were a vampire, my mistress of the dark."

"Don't make fun of me." I grip the steering wheel.

"I am absolutely not making fun of you. *Every* part of your body is sexy to me."

My eyes dart over to him. "*Every* part? I don't believe you."

"I'll prove it."

"Fine. My... ears." I say the first non-erogenous zone that pops into my head.

"Millie, you're so bad at this game. Don't you remember you make those little noises when I nibble your ears?" His voice drops an octave.

"OK, OK." He's not wrong. I squirm in my seat and try again. "Toes."

"Put them in my mouth and I will give us both a new foot fetish. Thank you for giving me ideas for the next time we—"

"Elbows!" I interrupt.

My gaze stays intently fixed on the road as he wordlessly takes my right hand in his. With a punishingly slow pace, he starts at my fingertips, caresses my hand, my forearm, my inner elbow, teasing and light. With the next pass, the teasing caresses turn into a gentle steady, massage. Every inch of my skin from my fingertips to my elbow is explored, worshipped.

My left-handed grip on the steering wheel tightens.

He follows the same path again but with his feverish lips. I feel my pulse quicken at the sensations of his warm breath and scratchy stubble against the sensitive skin of my forearm.

I press my lips together and will myself not to look away from the road as he swirls his tongue over the tip of each of my fingers.

My heart stops when he drags his mouth from the tip of my pinky finger, across my wrist, all the way up my forearm to my elbow, where he pauses to make circles with his tongue. When his teeth sink playfully into the tender spot on my inner elbow, my whole body shivers.

I slam on the brakes.

"You win," I concede, my voice all breathy and ridiculous.

He chuckles victoriously and closes his eyes again.

***

"Please go. You don't have to stay. I don't want you to get sick, too," he says, leaning in the doorway of his bathroom, eyes closed, while I fill a glass of water and rummage around for ibuprofen and a washcloth.

"I'm staying."

I watch him swallow the pills and empty the cup of water.

"Off to bed now." I pull his shirt over his head with minimal help from him and he kicks off his jeans before crawling under his covers in just his undershirt and briefs, his eyes closing instantly.

I run the washcloth under cold water, wring it out carefully, then sit at the head of the bed and pull his head into my lap. I gently place the folded, cold washcloth on his forehead, then start to massage his temples, his brow line, his cheeks, in sweeping motions and little circles.

"That feels so good," he says with a groan, and I can see some tension leaving his face, replaced with peaceful relief.

I unfold my legs to get more comfortable and Ethan rolls onto his side, then grabs my thigh, using it as a pillow.

I shift my massage to the back of his neck, fingertips sinking into tense muscles there.

"Thank you," he says without opening his eyes, and plants a reverent kiss on my cellulite.

My fingertips skid over the stubble on his cheeks, the start of a beard.

In that quiet moment, I know that I love him.

I suspected it before, but I know it now, with a certainty that is staggering. When I look at his face, I see my past. I see my present. I dream about the future.

My dreams of the future have changed since I met him.

There's an idea I have, so secret I haven't looked at it too closely yet. It's precious and fleeting, and I'm afraid if I think about it too much, if I come too close, it will burst.

So, it's tucked away for now.

***

"Hey, you're my temperature. I think you're sick now, too."

"Ugh, you're right." I squint at the sun pouring into the windows. My head hurts and I feel sweaty and cold all over. "Is it morning? Coffee doesn't even sound good."

"Call an ambulance," Ethan chuckles and I kick him under the sheets, my foot connecting with his shin.

"Go back to sleep," he says, pulling me closer.

"*You* go back to sleep."

We spend days in luxurious laziness. Sharing blankets. Deliriously giggling while we watch Hank and his ghost hunter nephew stomp through old houses with whirring sensors on the Afterlife Investigations ghost hunting YouTube channel.

Ethan reads my thesis meticulously, page by page, and writes thoughtful questions and comments in neat handwriting in the margins. We take flagrantly long showers, make an impressive mountain of booger tissues and nap anytime we want.

"I thought you couldn't cook?" I ask, sliding my arms around him from behind and resting my head against the gray cotton shirt spanning his back. I just got out of the shower, and I'm wearing an oversized sweatshirt I pilfered from his closet. I find him in front of the stove, stirring a saucepan full of tiny star-shaped noodles.

"Before I moved out, Maria made sure I knew how to cook this one thing. This is what she always made me when I wasn't feeling good."

"It smells amazing."

"Pastina. Star pasta with chicken broth, butter, and cream."

"My dad used to make me those instant chicken noodle packets when I was sick. After he died, I would make it for Ben. Then, I made it for myself in my apartment last year when I wasn't feeling well, and it tasted awful. It was so gross. I don't know what's different. He probably doctored it up to taste better somehow."

"Maybe. Or maybe it's because someone didn't make it for you," he says, setting the bowl down in front of me. "It's all about the love, right? Nothing says *I love you* like taking care of someone when they are sick," he finishes as he grates a wedge of parmesan cheese over my bowl.

I blow on the steaming spoon before taking a bite. The pasta is decadent and creamy, enveloped in a sauce rich with buttery notes, a hint of chicken broth, and the salty tang of parmesan cheese. Each indulgent bite chases away the last of my sickness, warming me from the inside out.

"It's delicious." Delicious isn't a big enough word. If there's one thing that could rival my dad's soup, it's this.

Ethan winks at me over his bowl.

***

After lunch, I return to my blanket fort on the couch. Ethan must be feeling better because I am watching him bustle around, cleaning his apartment, washing the dishes, and stripping the sheets off the bed. I've started feeling better over the last few hours, too, but I've been having so much fun being a sloth with him that I haven't admitted it.

He opens the linen cabinet, and I know what's coming next. I suddenly regret everything, so I hide, pulling a blanket over my head.

I hear a terrified shout, then the sound of something heavy landing on the floor.

Uncontrollable cackling bursts out of me, then the blankets are ripped away with a jerk, and I stop mid-laugh. I blink up at Ethan, who is standing in front of me holding Stephen in one hand.

"Millie." His voice is measured, icy, his face dead serious. "Did you hide the mannequin head in my closet? To prank me?"

I press my lips together and shake my head. Shrug my shoulders. It's so very obvious I'm lying.

He sets Stephen down on his kitchen table, facing away from us. Then sits down at the opposite end of the couch.

With another swift jerk, he rips all my blankets off and tosses them on the floor.

"Hey!"

"I'm going to get you back for this."

Goosebumps erupt all over me at his declaration and the flirtatious glint in his eye. Unlike most of my time spent here and at the inn, it is the good kind of goosebumps, not the kind that come from being scared. I set a new personal goal for myself: find all the ways to get the good kind of goosebumps.

His hands wrap around my ankles, and he pulls me so I'm lying flat on my back in the center of the couch. Then he flips me over, so I'm face down and I lose all my breath in a huff. I'm stunned for a moment as he gathers up all my hair in his right fist and pulls my head back, so my neck is arched toward him.

"How should I pay you back, Millie? Hm?" He starts kissing my neck, then playfully biting.

I feel the fingertips of his left hand at the waistband of my sweatpants.

"Maybe a spanking," he decides, meeting my gaze. He's asking for permission.

"Spanking seems fair," I swallow. I've never done this before, and I'm flooded with nervous anticipation.

He jerks my sweatpants down.

"You have the perfect ass, you naughty little—"

His words are cut off by my yelp and the sound of his hand connecting with my skin.

To my surprise, I'm immediately overwhelmed with lust, my pulse quickening, heat flooding to all the right places. It didn't hurt. It just stung a little and obliterated every thought in my head except for one.

"Do it again."

CHAPTER TWENTY-SEVEN

"Look at him. Just look at Joe. We started dating in high school and he has gotten hotter every day. Well, except for that one week when he tried to do the mustache look. But look at that body. Me? Look at me," Liz gestures to herself. "I look like an ice cream cone that got left outside too long."

My gaze shifts away from Liz and back to the guys. They have been wrecking trees and brush all afternoon, making it really hard to focus. Ethan started with a thermal top but has removed layers as the afternoon went on and now, he's in a tight fitting athletic tee.

"Liz, that's not true at all, you're beautiful," I say, and hand her a toothbrush. She's helping me carefully scrub the lichen off the statue of Louis in the woods. The boys are clearing a path so Nonna can visit. Maria wants to have a memorial plaque installed about Louis. I started writing the script for her a few days ago.

"That's kind, thank you. It's easy for you to say, you're so willowy! I wish I had a long waist like that. When I tuck in my shirt, I look like a grandpa with his shorts pulled up too high. You probably look so cool."

"Well, I've always been jealous of the curves. We want what we can't have, I think."

"There's truth in that for sure." She sighs and sets down her brush and leans back on her hands. "What's the one thing you want most, that you can't have?"

My eyes dart back to Ethan, but I don't answer, I just shrug instead.

"Well, I know what I want. Time."

"What do you mean?"

"This time you have with Ethan right now, enjoy it. It's so precious. I was in a rush to get married and have the girls. Don't get me wrong! I love my daughters more than I ever thought was possible. They are each so remarkable, each one so different and beautiful. And when you have someone hand you their boogers, literally put their boogers in the palm of your hand and you laugh about it, instead of being nauseated, that's motherhood. That's love. I am truly, deeply, obsessed with my children, not even grossed out by their boogers."

She looks over at Joe. I follow her gaze. He's bent over laughing at something Ethan said.

"But I miss taking my time with Joe. You and Ethan can have a full, uninterrupted conversation with each other. Romantic dinners. Watch an entire movie in the middle of a Saturday. Make out on the couch. Make out everywhere. Don't put pants on all day long. Go out on dates any time you want," she sighs. "We try to make time for each other, but it's so hard. Because the girls come first. And that's the way it should be. I know Joe and I will have our time again when they are older. But this moment you are in with Ethan, don't take it for granted."

They step in front of us, sweaty, dirt-smudged chests heaving with heavy breaths, smiling big smiles. It can't be more than 50 degrees outside, but they are dripping sweat.

"Well, how does it look?" Joe asks, turning to look at the path they started.

"Looks... good," Liz manages to say, biting her lip.

"*Mrs. Russo*," Joe says accusingly, his hands on his hips and a grin from ear to ear. "Have you been checking me out?"

"I'm *always* checking you out. But yes, the trail looks good. Nice start, guys. I think you can clear out the rest with a brush hog. Maria and Nonna will appreciate it. We'll try to bring Nonna out next week."

"Wait, one more thing before we go." Ethan pulls a worn, wood carving, the little starling toy, out of his jeans pocket. A cold draft of air tickles my neck and I shiver.

"I've been thinking—what if this belonged to Lou? What if he was the one who gave it to my mother? She said she just found it at the inn one day and her imaginary friend Lou would play with her. What if Lou isn't imaginary?"

I watch as Ethan turns the figurine over and over in his hands. It's rough-hewn, like it was whittled.

"Lou is not imaginary," I say with certainty. "And we know from his letter that Lou knew about his child before he died. If our guess is correct—that Lou is haunting the inn looking for Carolina—do you think he might have made this for his child, and mailed it home before he died?"

"That's exactly what I think," Ethan says as he places the starling toy gently at the statue's feet.

***

When we get back to the inn, there's an unfamiliar car parked out front. I peer inside as we walk past it. It's empty, save for a paper coffee cup. We find its driver as soon as we peek behind the house. He has a camera on a tripod, pointed out over the water.

"Hey man. How can we help you?" Ethan calls out.

"You must be the owners!" he says. He's wearing dark-framed glasses and a cardigan over narrow shoulders, and he reminds me of my high school English teacher. "I'm with Vanessa Brighton Realty. I'm here to take your listing photos. I knocked on the door and didn't get an answer. I hope you don't mind me getting started on exterior shots."

"Oh, we weren't expecting you so soon…" I falter. I haven't talked to Vanessa in a few weeks, I've just realized. I told her I would touch base when we were ready for the next step.

The man takes his final shot of the rear exterior then detaches the camera and hangs it around his neck. "Vanessa said you were chomping at the bit to get this done. She's paying me double. But I can come back another time if you want me to."

"No. No, that's alright. Come on in, I'll show you around." Ethan eyes me as I say, "We have to do it eventually I suppose."

The man picks up his tripod and follows us back into the house.

Ethan and I lead him from room to room. I look at the house with new eyes. The eyes of a stranger, the eyes of potential buyers.

And it's beautiful today. The way the afternoon sun is streaming in, highlighting the details. The fresh paint and gleaming floors. The living room with its impressive fireplace. Each room is so carefully updated and decorated by Ethan, Sarah, Ben, and me. He snaps pictures of the stained-glass window with a starling in it. A gleaming clawfoot tub. The hotel lobby counter with its little brass bell. The original historic photos I've framed and hung around the place. The Adirondack chairs on the porch repaired by Ethan, overlooking the cold lake.

He is uncharacteristically silent, his arms crossed as he watches the man take several pictures in each room.

But when he steps into Room 3, Ethan leaves, wordless.

It doesn't have any of Catherine's things left in it.

He asked me to do it for him because he couldn't bring himself to do it. With careful reverence, I packed every memento he might want to look at someday—her photos, her jewelry, her music, her journal, and a few shirts that showcased her favorite bands. I donated anything usable and threw out the rest. Now, all that's left is the furniture, wiped clean, sitting on mauve carpet with fresh vacuum lines.

I think the sterile room is equally as hard for Ethan to see as a room full of her stuff.

"Take your time," I tell the photographer, and follow Ethan downstairs to the lobby.

We watch as a truck pulls up outside. I can barely make out the sign on the door—Lakeview Appraisal Services, LLC.

"What are you in such a rush for all of a sudden?" he asks me. His words are soft, and I can hear the conflicting emotions in them. He looks tired.

"Vanessa mentioned outbuildings. Could you lead me to them?" the photographer asks, coming down the stairs behind us.

"I'll take you," Ethan tells the photographer, and leads him out of the inn, past the inspector stepping up on the porch, out to the trail in the woods.

"Ethan, I didn't do this!" I call after him.

I whip out my phone and call Vanessa.

"Hi, sugar! I've got some people on the way over today to look at the house."

"They're here already."

"Oh, sorry, hope they didn't surprise you. I just got off the phone with your mom. She's ready to get the ball rolling and post the listing."

"My mom did this?"

"She insisted that she wants the property listed for sale by the end of the day. I just sent you the listing details to proof."

"Thanks for all your hard work, Vanessa. I guess I need to have a chat with my mom. I'll talk to you later."

"Sure thing, sugar."

I disconnect and dial my mom, pacing on the porch.

"What the hell, Mom?" I say with vitriol as soon as she answers.

"Don't talk to me that way."

"You blindsided me. I thought we agreed to wait awhile. I'm mid-project. The kitchen isn't done."

She sighs into the phone.

"How much longer could it possibly take? I know why you're stalling for time. Ben told me you're dating Ethan."

"I don't know how much longer it will take! Why do you suddenly care so much? You told me to finish Rowan's list."

There's a long pause before she continues, and the sadness in her voice surprises me.

"Roger and I separated. The property needs to sell before I can move out. I'll need my third of the money to get on my feet. I might get alimony eventually, but not until after the divorce—which could take months and months to finalize."

Silence falls between us, and I pace, my footsteps echoing on the scrubbed-clean floorboards.

"You're leaving Roger?" I ask with disbelief.

"Yes, Millie. And it's long overdue."

"Mom," my voice is gentle. "You don't need money for a new place or a new start. You have a place. You have this place. Stop trying to sell it. Come and stay here with me. The memorial is at the end of next week. You were planning to visit for that anyway. Bring all your stuff and plan to stay as long as you need. We have room."

There's a long silence on the other end.

"I'll think about it."

Click.

CHAPTER TWENTY-EIGHT

"I THOUGHT YOU'D BE sleeping." It's the night before the memorial and I find Ethan in his shop. I left Ben and Sarah back at the inn, where we'd stayed up late prepping food for the service tomorrow. The kitchen renovation was completed just in time. Well, not completely done—there are some finishing touches we need to add. But it's functional. And *gorgeous*. Sarah had palpitations when she saw it and I think her eyes turned into actual heart emojis.

"I don't have time to sleep. Some girl has been pestering me to finish the kitchen at the inn and I've got a backlog of projects, so I started to work at night."

"Sorry."

"Don't be sorry. There's nowhere else I'd rather be. And I wouldn't be able to sleep tonight anyway."

"Me either. What are you listening to?" I ask. He has an earbud in his ear.

"Just something to take my mind off tomorrow."

I pick up his phone and look at the title of the audiobook. "Stephen King?"

"Yeah, it's very distracting. You seem surprised?"

"I thought you were going to say Wendell Berry," I say, recalling a book on his shelf.

"No, he's not for taking my mind off things. He makes me think *more* about things. Wendell Berry is for contemplation. Reading under a blanket by the fire. Or on a picnic surrounded by nature."

"He's your hot chocolate book."

"Yeah, I guess so."

"Why Stephen King?"

"When my mom died, Rowan gave me a stack of his paperbacks."

"What? Weren't you a little young?"

"No, it was perfect. I was reading a lot of *Goosebumps* books at the time—he knew I liked horror—but they weren't holding my attention anymore. So, he slipped me those books, and I literally couldn't do anything but read them. And for the blissful hours I was lost in that dark, horrifying world I completely forgot that my mom was dead."

"Oh, I get it. Same reason I listen to the murder podcasts, I guess. It's like no matter how bad my day is, it's not as bad as the people in those stories. And Stephen King just tortures his characters. Poor Roland on the beach with the lobstrosities," I say, tapping his phone. "Poor guy. Definitely worse than going to a memorial."

"Dad-a-chum," Ethan says, making crab hands.

"Dum-a-chum. Ded-a-chek," I say back.

Ethan pinches me on the ass with crab claw hands. I swat him away.

"So what food would you compare Stephen King books to?" he asks.

I ponder for a minute. "One time, Ben showed me this horrifying video of diners trying to spear a live octopus with a fork, and it was crawling all around the table, and they are all screaming."

"Do you want to listen too?" I nod and he puts an earbud in my ear, and we listen to poor Roland and try to forget about tomorrow.

***

It's today.

Today's the day I lay my uncle to rest. The day I acknowledge with finality that it happened, that he's gone. The day I say goodbye. Nerves are thrumming through me with every heartbeat since the moment I opened my eyes.

Everything's ready. Invitations sent; announcement posted. The chairs are on the porch, ready to be set up this morning. Ben has a list of songs he wants to play. The food is prepped.

When I wake up, Ethan isn't in bed beside me. The aroma of coffee fills the air, but I don't see him anywhere in the apartment. I pour myself a mug and slip on a sweater.

I slide on a pair of shoes and tiptoe down to his workshop. He isn't there either—the lights are off.

Peeking out the window, I see him sitting outside. I grab a blanket and head out.

I find him sitting in the grass, his back against a tree, looking out over the orchard. He hasn't gotten dressed yet, and his coffee is growing cold, untouched on the frosty ground beside him. He is absentmindedly scratching Max's head. There are dark circles under his eyes and his hair is messed up from sleep. He looks like a lost little boy.

Max lifts his head from under Ethan's arm and wags his tail at me as I step closer. Ethan opens his arms in invitation. I slide into his lap, careful not to spill my coffee. He tosses the blanket around us both, wrapping his arms around me.

"What are you doing out here?" I ask.

"Thinking."

"About your speech today."

"And other things."

"Are you OK? It's cold out here."

"No, I'm not OK," he answers, squeezing me tight. "Better now, with you. Are you OK?"

"No," I say softly, and close my eyes. "Why do people always ask that at funerals? I'm terrible. You're terrible. Everyone is terrible."

"You're right. When my mom died, everyone kept asking me how I was. I didn't know how to answer. I didn't want to make people uncomfortable, so I lied."

"What would you say?"

"Oh, something noncommittal, like 'I'm hanging in there.' And I would thank them for coming to the service. But I hated it, I hated everyone staring at me and whispering, feeling sorry for me. What did you say at your dad's funeral?"

"I didn't talk to anyone. I tried, but I just wasn't... capable. I felt like I was drowning, you know?" Ethan squeezes me tight because he *does* know.

"Rowan noticed. So, he pulled me out of the receiving line and sat with me on a fancy upholstered couch at the funeral parlor. He held my hand the entire time and would shoo people away. He was always watching out for me." My voice cracks with the last few words and Ethan squeezes me tighter.

For a moment, I let myself feel it all. I let today sink in. I let the tears come as they might. Maybe if I get them all out now, they won't bother me so much later.

We sit in silence for a while, holding each other. I can't see his face, but I can tell by his breathing that he's crying.

"Look at this sunrise, Millie," he says against my hair. "Fill your heart with it. Take a moment to rest in the grace of the world."

So, I do. I listen to Ethan's heartbeat and the cooing of a mourning dove. We watch a squirrel flit around, hiding nuts before winter comes, rustling in golden brown leaves fallen from the apple trees. I feel his arms around me, holding me close. The rise and fall of his chest.

"I wonder if it's like a cup I can fill. Fill me with sunrise and coffee and moments of quiet peace and your arms around me. In the worst moments today, maybe if I just close my eyes and imagine this, I'll get through," I say.

"That's been my secret all along," he admits. His eyes are distant, though—he's gone someplace I can't reach.

"So, no matter how hard today is, remember that tonight, you and I will be sitting right here. Looking at the stars," I promise.

CHAPTER TWENTY-NINE

BEN, SARAH, AND I form a somber receiving line in the lobby. One by one, people from the community fill the inn, fill the chairs on the lawn. The Russo family takes up the front row—I'm so glad to have the little girl's laughter brightening our day. I see Hank the sandwich shop guy. Oscar the pastry maker - next great American novelist. Lucy the librarian. One by one, they share their stories of Rowan with us.

A Mercedes rolls to a stop in the driveway, and we watch as my mother steps out, one high black heel at a time like a spider. She looks regal in a pantsuit, not a hair out of place. When I get out of a car after a road trip, I look like a pile of dirty laundry.

Ben embraces her first, then gives me a look of reassuring support. It's a crystal clear *I've got your back* look.

"Hi, Mom." I reach out and hug her. Her returning embrace is fierce for such a slight woman. As she squeezes me tight against her, I inhale her familiar perfume.

"I missed you, darling," she whispers, and the hoarseness in her voice makes the knot in my throat flare.

I haven't talked to her since we invited her to come stay with us. I'm still not sure what her answer is.

"Your dress is amazing, but you should have straightened your hair," she says, smoothing her palms over my waves.

"Thank you?" I laugh. I'm wearing the black dress from Sarah, and because I'm tragic, earrings that Rowan gave me for my thirteenth birthday.

"Rein it in, Mom," Ben says.

Mom's eyes flit to Ben and smile approvingly as he defends me.

I search for that familiar bit of anger that I've held onto for so long. The bitterness, ready to snap at her.

It's gone, and I suddenly feel weightless with the revelation that I've forgiven her. Somehow, at some point during this journey, my anger has faded.

"I missed you, too, Mom." I smile at her. I know she's not perfect. She never will be. But I can see who she is and choose to love her anyway, despite our past, despite her not being who I wished her to be, despite everything.

"You look good, though," she continues, holding me at arm's length and surveying my face. "Even though your hair is a mess. There's pink in your cheeks. Does that blue-eyed burly caveman have something to do with this?"

Her gaze focuses over my shoulder. I turn to see Ethan sitting at one of the tables we dragged out on the lawn. Rosa is standing beside him, feeding him crackers and apples off her plate. He's pretending to eat them like a Cookie Monster, resulting in her loud gleeful giggles and cracker crumbs everywhere.

"That's Ethan. How did you know?"

"Well, he couldn't take his eyes off you until that little girl distracted him with snacks," she says flippantly.

"Sounds about right."

"So, he's Catherine's son?"

"Yeah, Catherine's son."

"He is blonde and pretty, like she was," my mother admits, appraising him.

"And kind like she was. Funny, like she was. Or so I hear."

She nods in acceptance. In understanding. "I am so happy for you Millie, that you found someone who looks at you like that. I understand why you don't want to leave."

"So, did you think about the offer? About staying here for a while?"

I can see the flex in Ben's jaw as he asks her. He's nervous. She has to say yes. If she doesn't, our plan won't work.

She nods. "I have been thinking about it, yes."

"*And?*" Ben's ready to burst with aggravated anticipation.

"I'm going to take you up on it." She nervously fixes her perfectly coiffed hair that does not need to be fixed. "I think it would be good for us all, too, to spend some time together. Reconnect. Losing Rowan has made me reevaluate my priorities. And you two are it." Her eyes flit between us and her careful facade slips, I see the intense emotion underneath. "You're the only priorities for me. I'm sorry that I've lost sight of that so many times. I'm here now, and I want to support you. I'm so proud of you both."

The breath I was holding comes out in a sob as I hug her again. "I think it would be good for us all, too, Mom."

I thought I would be the one set adrift, trying to find my place. But instead, with the help of the inn, I've become the tether holding us all together.

***

Eventually, Ethan steps up to the podium and clears his throat. A hush settles over the crowd.

"Rowan died at age 48, leaving behind a sister, a niece, a nephew. Frank the cat. This inscrutable inn, which was quite a character in his life. And me."

"For those who don't know me—Rowan was almost my stepfather. He and my mom were engaged when I was young. And then, tragically, she died before our family was officially joined by marriage. But Rowan never let my mom go. He loved her unconditionally until the end of his story. And Rowan never let me go, either." Ethan's voice cracks, and he pauses. I watch his shoulders rise and fall before he continues.

"He taught me which designs were the good ones, and which books were the best ones. Through his devotion to my mother, he showed me what it meant to love someone so passionately and completely that it consumes you." Ethan's gaze briefly meets mine and the tears I've been holding spill over.

"He changed my life irrevocably through his acceptance of me, his kindness. Kindness is a powerful thing, you know. It takes so little to make such a big difference. It can be a domino, with a single act toppling into another, knocking down isolation, sadness, and suffering as it grows. You never know what demons people are fighting, or how big your small act of kindness can be to them. I know that I would not be standing here today without the kindness of Rowan and the people in this community."

"Rowan was there, always in my corner, so I followed in his footsteps. I went to architecture school, just like him. He was immensely talented at it, and his enthusiasm for it was so contagious. And he stood by my side the day I graduated college. I'll never forget how proud he was of me that day. But I was never as good at architecture as he was." There's a smattering of chuckles from the crowd.

"It's true. I was homesick. And that's when he taught me another lesson. He told me it was OK to start over. He told me to come home. Because *family* is the most important thing." Ethan's voice cracks again when his gaze lands on the Russo family.

My mom reaches out to Ben and me, entwining our arms.

"*Love* is the most important thing. And if you have it, hold on tight."

I squeeze my mom's hand.

"Rowan wasn't perfect," Ethan continues. "He had his demons. But I will be forever grateful to him, I'll forever miss him, I'll forever remember and repay the kindness that he showed me. So let's raise our glasses. Go forth today with Rowan in your heart and try to spread a little kindness. And hold on tight to the people you love."

Ethan raises his glass in the air.

Joe shouts, "To Rowan!"

The crowd echoes, "To Rowan!" and we tip back our drinks, mostly poured from the drink cabinet, Rowan's final bottles. My throat burns with the oaky sting.

I watch my mom catch a tear with her freshly manicured nails.

I want to run to Ethan but there's a line.

Ben goes inside, sits down at the piano in the drawing room, and starts to play, gentle music drifting out through the open windows and doors. Sarah sits beside him, her head on his shoulder, like she isn't letting him go for a single second tonight.

I'm halfway across the lawn when Ethan notices me coming and begins stealing frequent glances my way.

"Oh, darling, what a heart you have," my mother says to Ethan when we finally reach him. "Thank you for such a beautiful speech. Millie loves Rowan just as much, but she would have never said something like that," she continues. "She's always been so shy."

"Mom, I'm standing right here." I glower. She and I have so much work to do on our relationship. But I'm grateful for the chance to be able to do it.

"I'm confident Millie can do anything she puts her mind to. She surprises me all the time." Ethan looks down at me and I melt a little.

"Is that so?" she asks with an upraised eyebrow and a smile.

But her attention is lost as Maria and Nonna greet her.

"Thank you for defending my honor," I say, squeezing his hand.

"Anytime." He smiles, but it doesn't quite reach his eyes.

"She's right, that was a beautiful speech," Maria interjects as she pulls Ethan into a hug. I get choked up at the tender look on his face when she squeezes him. I get a Maria hug, too, then she pulls back and holds me at arm's length. She and Nonna were the first to arrive today, and they both hesitated before coming inside the inn. It took a lot of courage for them to step over the threshold. But I'm so glad they did.

Ethan escorted them around the inn like queens, and their superstitions dulled, replaced by curious wide-eyed wonder. I wonder if they were imagining Carolina and Louis falling in love here a hundred years ago in the secret corners of this place, just like I have been.

"Millie, I thought this house was cursed and would ruin you." Maria said. "But you've transformed it. You and Ethan have filled it with joy and people."

Nonna turns to me. "You've solved my mother's story. It isn't a sad one, not really. She was loved. I was loved. We put flowers on her grave this week and told her so. You've brought us so much peace. Thank you. Thank you."

"You chase away ghosts by surrounding yourself with the living," I repeat Ethan's words. It's not a haunted scary place. It's a sanctuary. A sanctuary for my brother and me. A sanctuary for Catherine. "Please come any time."

"I'd like that," Nonna says, patting my hand.

***

When the last of the guests are leaving, I sit down on the patio in my Adirondack chair and wish with all my heart that the chair next to me wasn't empty, that my uncle was sitting next to me, and we were staring out at the pine trees and the lake together.

"I hope you are proud of what we did here. I hope you feel the love. Because I love you so much, Uncle Rowan. And I know you loved me. I feel it every day. I carry it with me. Thank you for that. And I'm sorry. I'm so sorry for not being there in the end."

I wipe my eyes, take a shaky breath, and continue.

"I know you aren't here anymore, and I can't fix what's happened, but I promise to be better in the future. I promise not to make the same mistakes."

The wind brushes my hair. I close my eyes.

"Hey, Millipede, how are you holding up?" Ben sits down in Rowan's spot, like he's been summoned as I thought about him.

I just reach out and hold his hand.

We sit side by side and get lost in the weight of quiet memories.

"Mom said she'd move in. We don't have to sell the place," I finally say.

I've been making excuses, wavering in indecisiveness, puzzling out possibilities. No more. Not with my mom on board now, too.

"We're staying." Ben smiles at me, the first of the day.

"We're staying," I echo resolutely. "When should we tell them?"

"Not today. I have a few more details to work out," he says, turning his eyes back out to the horizon. "Keep our secret for a few more days, Millipede."

CHAPTER THIRTY

I push my chair back and stand at the head of the table, ready to get everyone's attention. My mom, Ben, Sarah, Ethan, and I have just finished our third dysfunctional family dinner together. We're far from perfect, but there is so much love I know we'll figure it all out in the end.

I tap my glass with my fork, and they all turn to look at me.

"Ben, Mom, and I have been working on a secret plan."

Ethan's eyes lock onto mine, searching for clues to what I'm about to reveal.

"We had the land parceled out. My third of the inheritance—I'm gifting it to you, Ethan." I pause, letting the words sink in, then reach for a legal-sized envelope that has been sitting on the drink cart throughout our meal. "Here is the title to your workshop, the orchard and the cemetery, along with an additional ten acres."

I pause for a moment, then add softly, "Plenty of room for all the bees you want."

Everyone looks at the envelope I set on the table in front of Ethan.

He doesn't open it; his gaze is steadily fixed on me. His arms are crossed over his chest tightly, like he's holding himself together. He hasn't said anything yet, but I can see all the emotions flitting across his face. Starting with denial.

He clears his throat. "You can't—" he starts to say, roughly.

"We did it already. It's done. We're paying kindness forward. Just like you said." I've thought this through, I'm ready to counter any argument.

"We had to do right by you, man," Ben says. "And there's one more thing. Millie?"

"Ben and I have been talking about ways we can afford to keep the inn. After we all spent some time together here, we decided that's what we want to do—reopen it. Not for Rowan and Catherine. For us," I say.

Ben opens his laptop to the draft of a website we've been working on together. The listing photos taken by the realtor flash before us in a slideshow, with *The Starling Inn* emblazoned across the top in elegant cursive script. There's also a page on the website featuring a condensed version of my thesis, detailing the history of the inn and its pending status on the National Register of Historic Places.

"In order to facilitate reopening the inn, I registered an LLC with four equal owners—myself, Millie, my mom, and you, Ethan," Ben continues.

Ethan begins to shake his head, but my mom cuts him off before he starts speaking.

"You've invested so much into this place already. It only makes sense that you should see that hard work pay off. As Catherine's son, you must accept. It's what Rowan would have wanted. There wasn't a will, but if there was, you would have been in it."

"Show them," I say to Ben.

There are multiple tabs on Ben's laptop open. For the past week, he's been working so hard on business plans and budgets and pieces of this project that I would never have been able to do on my own. He takes a moment to go through some of the details with us all.

"Mom is going to be the general manager," Ben explains.

"I'll help with bookings and greeting guests and event planning and that sort of thing," she says proudly.

"And we'll need a chef," Ben adds. "Sarah, would you do me the honor of being executive chef for the reopened Starling Inn?"

"What?! Yes! Yes!" Sarah bursts out of her chair and hugs him. She's not trying to hold in her tears like Ethan. She's all blubbery and laughing and crying and her joy is making my chest hurt. "I'd love to!"

"We need your talent in the kitchen, Sarah," my mom adds. "Ben's going to hire a few other staff members, and I'll be managing them. Your salary won't be very high until we start making a profit off the bookings, but you'll have free lodging. It will be a worthwhile investment in your future. After some time here, I'm confident you'll have all the experience necessary to open your own bakery, if you wish."

"Yes. Yes. Yes. I'm so excited," Sarah says through her tears.

"I thought we'd wait for the lease to be up on our apartment in Chicago, after the semester is over. Then we can move here in May. Plan for a soft opening in the spring?" Ben asks.

"The first big event should definitely be a wedding," I chime in, smiling secretly at Ben. He's jittery, his leg bouncing under the table. "The first of many."

"A spring wedding! Yes! All those lilac bushes outside blooming, and the view over the lake, oh my, that would be *gorgeous.*" Sarah's eyes are all misty as she imagines the event.

"Ethan, do you think you could make us an arbor for this spring wedding?" I ask carefully, looking over at him. I think he's in shock.

"That's a great idea!" Sarah exclaims. "Something dramatic and lovely and we can wrap flowers all over it. We'll build it up in the side garden, overlooking the lake." She pulls out her phone and shows him inspiration photos.

Ethan clears his throat and makes a valiant effort to say, "Of course, anything you want, Sarah."

"Oh, or the conservatory! Can you imagine that repaired? It would be an amazing venue for weddings!"

"Joe's wife, Liz, used to work in marketing," I say. "I talked to her about our ideas, and she's going to help us draft a marketing plan. She wants to help us get the word out in the community about the inn re-opening."

"Maybe we can get Hank's nephew to do a paranormal investigation YouTube video for us. That will definitely get the word out," Ethan says with a cough.

"Well, I don't know about that last one but…" My mom looks around the table at each of us. "It takes a village. Look at all you've done here! Your village is rising to the occasion. I must admit, I am impressed with my kids."

"For our first wedding, we will have to make it *extra* extravagant. It will be the wedding to set the tone for all future weddings," I continue.

"Yes, we'll have to get a professional photographer here and use those photos to advertise the inn as a wedding destination on the website," Sarah adds, her eyes misty. "Can you imagine the wedding photos people will take, with all that scenery in the background? Bridal parties lined up on the porch of the inn. Lacy white bridal trains spilling down the staircase inside? All that architecture. The drama! The gardens. It'll be *so* beautiful."

Ben stands up out of his chair and pulls a small box out of his pocket as he walks over to her side of the table.

He looks more nervous than I've ever seen him in my life.

My secret smile widens, and I stop breathing as Ben drops to his knee beside her chair.

"Sarah?"

She looks down at him.

"What are you—" she starts, but her hands fly to her mouth when she realizes what he's doing.

"These past few months have been the best of my life. Would you do me the honor of being my wife? Will you be my bride in the springtime?"

"Yes! Yes!" She kisses him, and we all cheer and bang on the table, making as much jubilant noise as we can.

"That'll be our wedding?" she whispers, tears spilling onto her cheeks.

"Yeah, babe. We will have to live at the inn until we can afford to build something on the property."

"I love you, Ben."

"I love you, too, Sarah."

I'm so filled with joy for them my chest hurts.

"And I love *you*," she says, then wraps her arms around me. I squeeze her back as tight as I can. "We'll be sisters now."

"And I love you!" she says, circling around the table and hugging a surprised Ethan, who can't hold back his tears anymore. They are running down his cheeks.

My mom stands up to hug Sarah.

"And you, too!" Sarah says. "Thank you for all of this."

"Congratulations, darling."

"Louis, did you hear all that? We're moving in!" Sarah declares to the inn. "You'll have to make room for guests, hope you don't mind."

"Who is Louis?" Mom asks.

"The ghost, of course!" Sarah explains.

"Ghosts aren't real," she scoffs.

"I'm not sure if he's here anymore," I say. "Since we solved who Carolina was. Since we brought his daughter to his statue. I think he was looking for her. Looking for them both. I hope he's at peace now."

"Wait, are you saying that you believe ghosts are real?" my mom asks.

"You'd better sit back down, it's a long story." I fill up her wine glass.

***

"Can I talk to you outside?" Ethan asks me later, after Ben and Sarah have slipped upstairs with effervescent smiles, and my mom has retired to her room with a glass of wine and one of Rowan's photo albums.

He holds the door open for me as we step out onto the porch. It's softly snowing, white flakes spinning past us, dizzy and magical.

"Millie, giving me your part of the inheritance is too much. I don't deserve this, you can't—" he catches my hand. He's having a hard time meeting my eyes.

"I can. I did. It's the right thing for me to do."

He shakes his head and starts to say something, but I cut him off.

"Ethan, this place is a part of you, and you're a part of it. Your family is here—your business, your home. The thought that you'd leave all that behind to do what you believe is right is staggering to me. But I don't want you to."

I take a deep breath, look him in the eyes, and say all the things I've been holding in for the past few weeks.

"And I'm in love with you. I'm in love with you, Ethan. I'm in awe of you, of who you are as a person. You've lost so much, you've been through so much, and instead of letting it eat away at you and make you bitter like I did, you did the opposite. You spread joy constantly, even when you feel terrible inside."

I pause before continuing as he pushes my hair out of my face. "You told me once that I see people. Well, I see you. I see your hands that work so hard. I see the beautiful things that you build, of everything you've done to the inn and your home and the orchard and your community. I see your smile. You don't ever keep it to yourself. If you're in the room, you make sure everyone else is smiling, too. I see your beating heart. I see that it's a little bit broken because of what you've lost. I see how wise you are because of those losses, too. You don't take people for granted, and you love unconditionally. I've learned from you and your heart. You don't hold hate the way I do. I see how much you've been hurt by your mom, yet you still hold so much love for her. I want to be more like that. I've been repairing my relationship with my own family because of it. And I see your patient eyes. I see the same patient eyes today that I saw ten years ago. I flit away when people get close, but you never gave up on me."

I trail off awkwardly, my gaze dropping to my feet. I can't believe I said all of that out loud. I opened the flood gates, all my infatuation with him spilled forth in a string of clumsy sincerity. "So yes. You do deserve it," I finish lamely.

He tilts my chin up. "I love you, too. You're my favorite person."

"You're *my* favorite person."

He laughs. "You made that clear. I should ask you to list your favorite things about me more often—please tell me more."

I giggle, and it sounds thick with tears.

His hands are cupping my face, the rest of the world is falling away.

"Thank you, Millie. You've changed my life. I accept your offer, on one condition."

"What?"

"Move in with me."

"You know I can't. What am I going to do here? There aren't any jobs for history majors."

"Me. You're going to do me here. Every day. Many times a day—we'll be exhausted all the time."

"I owe it to myself to finish what I've started with my education—start a career."

"Do it. I'll wait for you. As long as you come home to me sometimes. Now, is it my turn to say all the things that I love about you?" He starts listing all the places that his lips are touching me. "These lips, these cheeks, this neck," he says in a silky whisper as the snowflakes cascade around us.

CHAPTER THIRTY-ONE

"The inn looks so beautiful. Truly," my mom says. The pale gray sky stretches above her, interrupted by vines and the skeleton of the conservatory. "We'll have so many bookings in no time, I'm sure of it. Rowan would be so proud of you all. You honor him."

"It's not finished yet," I say, using a push broom to move broken glass on the ground into piles. "There's this place to repair. I'm not even sure it *can* be repaired. And we still need to paint the exterior. And a million other little things to do."

She sets a pot upright, turning to look at me. Like me, she's bundled up in a big coat to keep warm, with Ethan's borrowed work gloves on to protect our hands.

"I'm not sure what color."

"Well, emerald, of course," she says without hesitation.

"His favorite. I like it. Good idea, Mom."

"I do have those sometimes," she says, dragging a heavy planter into a new spot. "But Millie," she pushes her hair out of her face and settles her gaze on mine, "it won't ever be finished. Old buildings are like people. We're all constant works in progress."

"Constant works in progress?"

My mom grabs a dustpan and holds it on the ground while I push glass into it. She dumps it into a metal trash can before continuing.

We've been out here for a cold, busy twenty minutes. It will take ages to clean it up entirely. But it's a start.

"When your dad died, I..." she trails off. Then she sets a bench upright and sits down, gesturing for me to follow. "I dream about it constantly. Torturous dreams, imagining if your childhood was different, imagining that I was a better mother."

I meet her eyes.

"And you have no idea how much I regret the way I handled things when you told me Roger touched you. He fooled me in so many ways. I should have trusted you, stood up for you."

I reach out and pull her gloved hands into mine.

"Now with Rowan's passing, I am reminded once again how fragile life is. How fleeting these ties with our loved ones are. I thought I learned from your father's death, but I didn't. My brother died—" her face crumples. "My brother died, and I can't remember the last time I hugged him."

My eyes fall on the spot where Ethan found me, falling to pieces in the rain.

"I felt the same way when I got here. Awful about myself, overwhelmed with the mistakes I'd made. I was in agony over not spending more time with him," I admit.

"We can't go back. But we can go forward and choose to live differently. We must forgive ourselves. We must look to the future. So, I *choose you*, Millie. I'm here for you this time and I'm not going anywhere, and I hope that someday you might find it in your heart to forgive me."

"I do forgive you," I say, and my voice cracks.

"I better learn how to garden, too," she says with a laugh, wiping away a tear while looking around at all the empty pots.

"You? Gardening?" I just can't imagine her manicured nails sinking her hands into a pot of dirt.

"Works in progress," she says, smiling at me.

"I forgive you, Mom," I say, again, pulling her into a hug.

"What about yourself? Do you forgive her, too?"

"I do."

"Good. I love you, darling." She kisses my hair.

***

Professor Smith's office is stacked floor to ceiling with books. Spilling out of the shelves, topping her desk. It's pleasantly claustrophobic, and I must tell myself not to tidy them while I listen to her talk.

"You've constructed a compelling and unique narrative. Argued your points well. Your research is varied and solid. You've got a good paper here, well done."

"Thank you. You have no idea how much that means to me."

"I do. I've been in your seat before. And my thesis wasn't as good as yours."

"I worked so hard on this. Put my heart into it."

"It shows. Do you know what you want to do next? Have you thought about continuing your work and pursuing a Ph.D.?"

"I have. I wasn't sure if I would be a good candidate."

"Well, you have all my confidence that you will succeed if you go this route. We have an excellent program if you want to continue here. We would be happy to have you. You'd have to apply first. But unofficially, I'm on the committee, and I'm confident that you would get in if you wanted to."

What do I want? I twirl the brown paper sleeve on my coffee cup while I piece together my thoughts.

I want this. I want to be in her seat, reading and researching and teaching and breathing history for myself and the next generation. It's all I could think about today as I walked across campus to her office, crossing paths with my peers, peeking out behind scarves and dark-rimmed glasses. Campus coffee thermoses in their hands. Cold air outside, dry leaves skittering along brick sidewalks in front of white stone collegiate Gothic buildings. This all feels so exactly right to me.

What else do I want?

I think about quiet things.

The sound of thunderstorms in the wind stirred trees and creaking wood floors. The way fresh air smells coming in through the open transom windows. That eerie feeling of never being alone. The beauty of my purple room, my favorite book cracked open on the nightstand, waiting for me. Rowan's hand in mine, walking me down to the beach when I was a little girl, making sure I didn't slip. His auburn hair was so much darker then.

The feel of my head on Sarah's shoulder as we danced and talked about love and eternity. The set of Ben's jaw as he worked so hard on this dream I had for us all.

The taste of buttery croissants melting in my mouth. The smell of woodsmoke and coffee. Those blue eyes I loved when I was young, meeting me again, more confident now. Watching Ethan work in his shop, biting his lip in concentration. Sunset painting the apple orchard, spilling into his apartment, onto his sheets. Firelight on his skin, the taste of cider on his lips. The feel of his stubble beneath my fingertips. The way he says my name.

I remember revealing my heart to him, after he saved me, after he pulled my hands into his lap and so carefully mended me. He mended me in so many ways.

And I think about the sound of my boots on the wildflower lined gravel road as I walk with Frank. The smell of the inn filled with Sarah's baking. Playing piano with Ben beside me. Sitting with my mom on a cold bench and breathing forgiveness.

The sound of Ethan's laughter. I'll never get it out of my head as long as I live.

I remember how full my heart was when the inn was filled with people for the memorial, the way it is supposed to be, the way it should always be.

Before, when I would think about what's next, I would be filled with uncertainty. Restlessness. Dread. Anxiety so thick I'd feel it tangibly.

But now?

Hope.

Wonder.

I decide something in that moment.

"Is there a grad school in Michigan that you recommend?" I ask Professor Smith.

"U of M has an excellent Ph.D. program. I can get you in touch with one of my colleagues there if you'd like. Is Michigan where your home is? Your family?"

"Yeah. It is."

***

When I arrive, it's late. I expected Ethan to be asleep. But the lights are on in the woodshop. I can hear him whistling while he works. We've hardly talked the last few days, while I was away. I've been wrapping up my semester and he has been trying to catch up on orders. I listen for a moment, trying to puzzle out why the song he's whistling sounds so familiar. Then it hits me, and I laugh as I step up to his wood shop. It's the theme song of my murder podcast.

He stops working as soon as I close the door behind me, shutting out the blustery December air.

I watch as he removes his gloves and apron while not allowing his gaze to move from mine.

"Get over here." He doesn't have to put any volume in his voice.

Like in a movie, I run at him and jump into his arms. He lets out a contented breathy groan when my lips sink to his. He leans against a table, and I devour him. Our kiss is slow, sweet and decadent.

"You were gone so long," he says, finally pulling away.

"It was only four days."

"Eternity." He kisses my eyes, my cheeks, the tip of my nose. "What did your professor say about your thesis?"

"She loved it."

"Of course she did."

"I think you're just saying that because you like my butt." His hands are resting comfortably on my backside.

"I do love your butt." He gives it an appreciative squeeze. His hands start roving, exploring, hungry.

"She gave me the contact information of her colleague, at the University of Michigan's History Department," I say against his neck. His hands still, where they are sunk deep under my shirt, warming up my skin. "I am going to apply to their Ph.D. program."

"But that's only an hour away." He stares down at me, hopeful, unspoken questions lingering between us.

"It wasn't on my radar before. But doing the research for my thesis made me realize that I want to do it, I want to get the Ph.D. I want to build on the research I started. And if I'm writing about Michigan, it makes sense to be in a program in Michigan so I can conduct local history research more easily. This program could be a good fit. I've been thinking about your invitation to let me move in. I think I can commute from here. I don't know what will happen when I graduate. We'll figure that out when the time comes. But if I get into the program, I'll be around for another four years or so, maybe longer if I get a post-doc position."

The smile that spreads across his face is so brilliant it's difficult to look at.

He doesn't say anything for a while, and we stare at each other, both imagining this glimmering future unfolding. I never had wild imaginings about this coming true. It was too painful to think too closely about. I didn't let myself dream. I never thought this would be possible to have it all, without sacrificing anything.

"Millicent, my dearest," he finally says, his joy barely contained under the surface of his voice.

"You can't do the Civil War general thing when you don't have a ridiculous beard. It doesn't work," I interrupt whatever he's about to say.

"Starting today, I vow to never shave again so I can torture you anytime I want."

"I wouldn't have you any other way."

"You really want to move in with me?" His eyes are suddenly serious. He tucks my hair behind my ears after it falls in my face. "You're not giving up on your goals? You'll be happy here?"

"I'm not giving up on my goals. I think I found my home here, in this corner of the world. I'm suddenly less tempted to explore the rest of it."

"I have conditions."

"Of course you do."

"Performative yoga at least three times a week."

"Naturally."

"Maria will also require your presence at family dinner once a week."

"I can't wait."

He drops his face to mine, so our noses and forehead are touching, his voice soft. "Walk with me every day."

"Even if it's raining?"

"I'll buy you a raincoat. A black one."

"OK. What other conditions?"

"Talk to me every day. Even if you're feeling sad. Especially if you're feeling sad."

"Deal."

CHAPTER THIRTY-TWO

One-and-a-Half Years Later

Turquoise water and vibrant green trees line the road as my companions. The shade from their towering heights casts dappling shadows across the dashboard of my new car as I drive up, up, up the twisting road to home. Wildflowers dot the forest in vibrant purples, whites, and yellows. My windows are rolled down and I can't stop the smile on my face as I breathe in the warm air, my hair whipping in the wind, my heart soaring.

It's May, the end of the semester. The Intro to American History class I was teaching had just wrapped up a few days ago and I submitted the last of my coursework for the classes that I am enrolled in.

I pull to a stop in the freshly paved parking lot of the inn. I open my car door and Frank hops out. He doesn't like the hustle and bustle of the inn now that it's full of guests all the time. He prefers the quiet days in my apartment near campus. I appreciate his companionship even more now. He kept me company on lonely weeknights that I had to spend away from home.

It didn't take long for me to figure out that driving back and forth every day from campus was too hard for me. After a few weeks of trying to live in two different places and losing my mind, I got a small studio apartment on campus, where I stay most weekdays, or when I'm crunched for time under an assignment. I come home for all weekends and holidays, and some slow midweek stretches.

It was nice to give our relationship a chance to unfold and breathe after the grief-laced connections, the forced proximity, and the heavy strangeness that surrounded our early days together.

We were able to take our time. We were able to date, like a normal couple.

We got to miss each other and be joyously reunited over and over.

And now that the semester is over, I'm looking forward to a whole, uninterrupted summer with him.

A new plaque—*The Starling Inn, National Register of Historic Places*—catches my attention as I step up onto the bright white painted porch, bracketed by lively green bushes. Nearly all thoughts of ghosts have been chased out of this place, overpowered by fresh paint, bright memories, and pride.

It hasn't stopped me from hosting the occasional walk-through or ghost tour of the inn.

The scrubbed clean doorknob opens easily. It's rarely locked these days—with all the guests coming and going—and a cheerful bell jingles overhead.

I'm greeted by the sight of my mother sitting at the lobby counter. She looks up from her laptop at the sound of the bell. Next to her, on proud display, is a published copy of my thesis. *The Starling Inn: A History.*

She is thriving in her new role as manager. She's precise and exacting and throws herself into event planning. Because of her talent for it, the bookings haven't stopped. At our last family dinner—which we have nearly every week—she told us the inn is booked for weddings for the next two years.

"Hello darling," my mother says, and her eyes are sparkling. "Your room is ready, and I have a letter for you."

She hands me the key to the purple room, a conspiratorial glint in her eye.

"My room is ready?" I repeat. *I haven't stayed at the inn in years.* "And where's Ethan? He was supposed to meet me here for breakfast."

"Just read the letter. It will all make sense."

I look down at the thick creamy paper, my name scrawled across it in familiar handwriting. Quizzically, I pull it open.

My dark and dreary queen,

I have prepared a remarkable day for you. If you desire your reward, you must discover it. May fortune favor you in your pursuit. However, I am aware that you have not yet had coffee. Thus, the first clue lies where we partook in many coffees together, and our first meal together, and you displayed your fiercest scowls. Our first meal is best consumed cold and directly from the pan.

Very truly yours,

Ethan

I run downstairs to the brightly remodeled, bustling kitchen. The crooked old cabinet doors have been replaced with timeless white ones. They look amazing with the glossy stone countertops and vintage copper finishes.

Inside the industrial-sized fridge I find a lasagna with an envelope on top. Waitstaff carry plates of breakfast past me as I snatch up the envelope and shut the door again.

"Oof!" I jump. "You scared me."

Sarah is suddenly standing on the other side of the refrigerator door, smiling at me ear to ear, and holding a thermos of coffee.

"Sorry!" she laughs and squeezes me in a fierce hug. I try to wrap my arms around her, but it's getting harder with her big pregnant belly in the way—she's due in just a few weeks. I can't wait to meet the little soul that's half her and half Ben. Being part of their wedding, officially welcoming her into the family, watching Ben dote on her every need throughout her pregnancy and the two of them glow and blossom under each other's love—the past year has been one of the happiest of my life.

"I'm just so excited for you," she says, her voice brimming with emotion. "I'm supposed to give you this." She passes me the thermos of coffee, and a single red rose wrapped in black tissue paper.

"What are you so excited for? Did you help him with these shenanigans?" I ask, looking down at the envelope.

She nods. "Don't ask me anything else. You know I can't lie to you."

"So, you know what my reward is at the end?"

She nods again, her eyes wide. Then she pantomimes zipping her mouth shut like a zipper, waving at me to open the letter.

Beloved,

Huzzah on discovering the first clue. Today, I present you with roses, not as a symbol of romantic love alone, but as a tribute to the unique qualities that have endeared you to my heart. It was in this very room that I witnessed your unfathomable ferocity for the first time, and it is among the many reasons why my admiration and affection for you have flourished these past years. Just as the rose's thorns protect its delicate beauty, your sass safeguards your heart. Considering your discerning taste, I am well aware that you refrained from partaking in the lasagna. Therefore, to continue your quest, you shall require a croissant.

Devotedly yours,

Ethan

***

"Thanks, Oscar." I sink my teeth into divine buttery pastry smothered in tart berry jam as he hands me the next clue with a wink.

"Sure thing. Hey Millie, what's another word for *happy?*" Oscar is always thinking about writing. I've gotten used to him using me as a thesaurus and for questions about the psychology of women.

"Blissful? Ecstatic? Contented?" I grin at him.

"Blissful, that's a good one." He keeps a notepad in his apron to scribble my answers on. This time, he doesn't pull it out. I don't think he's talking about his novel.

As I open the letter, and my smile quickly fades. "Wait, I can't read this one, do you know what it says?" I show the paper to Oscar. It's encoded, the letters are spelling gibberish.

"I'm supposed to tell you to go to the caretaker of old and secret things... and uh..." He glances down at a note on the counter next to his cash register and continues. "With a hieroglyph forever etched upon her skin. She, with her... astute abilities, shall aid you in deciphering this encoded message."

He grins at me. "I hope you know what that means? This is for you, too." He passes me a rose.

"I do. Thank you, Oscar."

"Anything for you guys."

The shop bell dings closed behind me as I step across the street to the library.

***

"Millie!" Lucy calls out my name in a singsong voice as soon as I step through the doors.

I've spent so much time here doing research that we started taking lunch breaks together and we have become fast friends.

"I have something for you." She holds out an unmistakable envelope in front of her with two hands.

It's a cipher key.

I sit down at a library table, and spend a few moments decoding the words, letter by letter, on a piece of notebook paper.

The subsequent clue lies nestled within the pages of a book, authored by you, my beloved. Seek the wisdom inked upon those printed words, for they shall guide you closer to your objective.

I know my book is on the shelf here, a signed copy in fact, because Lucy hosted a book release / author meet and greet for me when I first published it.

I wander up and down the rows, searching for it, until I see Atwater, M. on the spine, a single rose protruding from its pages.

I pull the book off the shelf, and it falls open to a letter tucked inside with the rose.

My love,

I offer you this rose as a symbol of my deep appreciation for your curiosity and thirst for discovery. You remind us all of the importance of seeking answers. I find myself in constant awe of your remarkable ability to unveil hidden truths and unravel complex mysteries. Your dedication in writing this book has left me immensely proud. Not only has it been instrumental in reuniting my family and I, but it has also bestowed upon us all a sense of wholeness and belonging. As I reflect upon your achievements, I am filled with anticipation for the future. I eagerly await the unveiling of your next research projects, curious to witness the depths you will delve into and the discoveries that lie ahead. Make your way to the neighboring establishment, my dear one, where an array of exquisite attire awaits your perusal. Within the walls of that shop, you shall find the means to acquire a truly enchanting dress, befitting this evening's occasion.

With all my love and admiration,

Ethan

***

As soon as I step inside the little boutique clothing store, the shopkeeper, a sweet-faced old woman who smells like magnolias, says, "You must be Millie! Oh, this is *so romantic,* I called my friend Marge and told her all about how that sweet, handsome man stopped by this week and told me you'd be in to pick a dress. Pick anything you'd like, he said—there's a tab open for you."

I try on dress after dress, texting pictures to Sarah, until I settle on the right one. Roses and butterflies and bees frame the open back and tumble across the crinkled black silk. It's a flirty fit-and-flare shape, with box pleats at the skirt for volume and movement. It's a celebration of springtime, new life in harmony with darkness. It feels like the perfect dress for today, the most beautiful of days.

As I checkout, the shopkeeper slides the dress across the counter to me, carefully folded in a paper bag, the next letter from Ethan on top alongside and my fourth rose.

I rip it open and the shopkeeper glances eagerly over my shoulder. "What's your next clue, honey? Oh, I can't wait to tell Marge! He was so tall. So handsome, did I say that already?"

I laugh as I pull the next envelope open.

My Dearest,

This rose serves as a symbol of my deep appreciation for the elegance and beauty that emanates from you. When first we met, your beauty shined like a beacon of hope, a respite from the darkness that surrounded us. I dream of a future where we stand hand in hand, witnessing the passage of time. I long to see the lines etch upon your beautiful face, a testament to the many joys and challenges we have conquered side by side. I yearn to witness the graying of your raven black hair, a silver crown on your ethereal head that signifies the wisdom and experiences we have gathered throughout the years together. After all this sleuthing and shopping it will be almost lunchtime. You'll need a sandwich with a side of ghost hunting stories.

With all the affection in my heart,

Ethan

***

"Not sure what that rascal Ethan is up to, but here ya go, Millie!" Hank hands me the next envelope and rose wrapped in black tissue with a joyous guffaw before taking my sandwich order. "You know my nephew visited the old county jail last month, did you see the episode?"

"I watch every single one," I say with a laugh. The show is definitely ridiculous, but also amazing, and a balm for homesickness when I'm away on campus.

"Ah, you do? That's great to hear. That's great to hear. I'll get that sandwich started for you so you can be on your way."

I slide the rose next to the others where they stand upright in my paper bag, next to my new dress, and all of Ethan's letters so far. I can't wait to take it home and pull the dress on again. I'm hoping the next clue points me back toward home.

And him.

His words are fizzling around me like magic, buzzing and joyful and full of romance and dreams of the future and I'm simply overwhelmed with the sweet sincerity of it all.

I'm aching to see him and thank him for all of this. I'll remember this day as long as I live. I've never felt so loved. So at peace. So absolutely certain that I am on the correct path for myself.

I open the next letter.

Milady,

Your quick wit and playful banter have brought moments of joy and levity to even the darkest of times. In this rose, I encapsulate the mirthful essence that you bring to my life, for it is your sense of humor that serves as a constant reminder of the beauty that exists amidst the trials we face. As we continue on this journey through life, let us never lose sight of the power of laughter and the ability to find joy in the simplest of moments. With this rose, I offer you a piece of my heart, infused with gratitude for the light that we bring to each other. For your next clue, you shall find it at the spot we kissed for the second time.

Eternally yours,

Ethan

***

The next clue is tacked to a tree, on the trail between Ethan's house and the inn.

This is the spot where I chose him, entanglements be damned. Our second kiss, but the more important one. I've chosen him again every day since then.

I pull the letter and rose from the tree and turn around, leaning against it as I read, twirling the rose in my other hand. The spring sun filters through the breaks in the trees, casting light onto the dirt path.

My fire-hearted vixen,

It was here that I first witnessed your passion, to which I offer up the next rose. Each time I see you I am overcome by the allure of your presence, the fire that sets your soul ablaze. My love, you transcend all my wildest desires and imaginings, and it is in your arms and in your bed that I find solace, a sanctuary where the world outside fades into insignificance. You are the flame that warms my spirit, the elixir that rejuvenates my soul. My thoughts are forever consumed by the memory of your sensual touch, the intoxicating scent of your presence, and the promise of the passion that awaits us. Our love shall be the flame that guides us through the darkness.

Your next clue lies next to a freshly drawn bath.

With unquenchable desire,

Ethan

***

As I pull the door of the back porch open, I am reminded of the time he carried me in. How careful he was with the broken pieces of me. I know that no matter what I face, no matter how badly I fall apart, he'll be there to help pull me back together.

I take the steps two at a time up to the purple room, nodding at guests and dragging my fingertips along the new gorgeous wallpaper lining the stairway.

Along the way I pop my head into Rowan's office, where Ben sits behind his laptop at the big oak desk. He stands as I walk in, his eyes soft.

"Hey, Millipede."

I wrap my arms around his waist. "Did you have something to do with all of this?"

"Of course, I helped him. No, I'm not giving you any hints, so don't even ask."

"I don't need any hints. I know what it's all about. I just want to tell you that I love you."

"Love you, too. I'm so happy for you both."

"Me too. I'm so happy. I've been so happy this past year."

He holds me at arm's length. "Happiness looks good on you."

"Happiness looks good on you, too."

***

I drop my bag and dress on the bed of this gorgeous little room that I'll always think of as mine, and take a deep contented breath in.

My eyes fall to the pink tufted sofa where I'd climbed in his lap, planted kisses up his neck.

And when I open the door to the bathroom...

Roses.

Roses everywhere, covering nearly every surface. By the dozens in crystal vases, and petals strewn on every inch of the floor, except for a clear path to the bathtub. The clawfoot bath is full of bubbly hot water, petals floating on the surface. Beside the tub is a stack of my favorite books, topped with the next letter.

Millie,

I offer up every rose my arms could carry to express the depth of my admiration for your strength. You fell apart before my eyes in this room, and through strength you overcame it. Your resilience shone like a beacon, illuminating my own path, and I was forever changed. Your unyielding spirit emboldens me to be a better man. I know that you have the strength to face things on your own. But for each other, we are steadfast pillars that support each other through the tempestuous storms that surround us. If you let me, I'll never leave your side. I promise to always hold your hand, and lay down beside you in the rain. Rest here awhile, my love, think about all I've said, and when you're ready, put on your dress and meet me in the conservatory, for there is something I wish to ask.

With unending love,

Ethan

***

Before I even open the door to the glimmering glass and metal structure my heart is thundering, because I know what he's going to ask.

He's in a suit, standing with his hands in his pockets at the far end of the structure and I can't control my breathing as I meet his eyes and see all the emotion in them as he spots me in my new dress.

I walk down the stone path, framed by blooming roses and glossy green botanicals, tropical and lush thanks to the hard work of my mother.

Halfway to him I freeze, tears overtaking me. He's just so...*everything*. So thoughtful, joyful, smart, sexy and I can't shake the feeling that I don't deserve him or that this isn't real.

He meets me on the path, and I feel steadied when he takes my hands in his. My shoulders lift and fall as I take a shuddering, tear filled breath and meet his blue eyes.

"Thank you for today. Thank for the letters and the roses. It was all so beautiful." My voice is choked with emotion. "I don't know what to say. Except I love you. I love you so much, Ethan. And I hope that I make you feel as loved as you make me feel."

He kisses the tip of my nose. "Every day."

All the air leaves my body and tears start streaming down my face when he pulls a smooth wood box out of his pocket and gets down on one knee.

"Millie, will you marry me?" I look at his hopeful, upturned face.

"Yes!" My answer felt inevitable in the most profound and comforting way. I barely glance at the diamond surrounded ruby as he slides it onto my finger.

I gather his face in both my hands and kiss him with all my heart.

"What do you have planned for us next?" I ask.

"A celebration." He kisses my forehead, and I feel it all the way down to my toes.

"Oh, I wondered why the family wasn't here."

"They are all waiting for us back at the inn. Your mom and Sarah planned a big dinner celebration and invited most of the town. Guests should be arriving soon. But this moment was about you and me—I didn't want you to feel pressured to say yes. Or maybe I didn't want to get rejected with an audience? I don't know." He plays with the few hairs at the nape of my neck that have escaped my bun and gotten curly from the bathwater. "I just didn't think a proposal with an audience was what you would want."

He's right. Everything about this proposal showed how deeply he understands me. He laid all these clues for me to puzzle it out, with all the reasons why he wanted to marry me and then gave me space to consider my answer on my own.

"When we get married, and you have your Ph.D., will that make me Mr. Dr. Millie Atwater?"

"No."

"I'm pretty sure that's how it works."

"Agree to disagree."

"Always."

Hand-in-hand, Ethan and I walk out of the conservatory, up the stony path to the Starling Inn.

AFTERWORD

If you or someone you love is struggling with substance abuse, there are so many resources to help.

Emergency substance abuse hotline

For substance abuse treatment and mental health referrals, contact the Substance Abuse and Mental Health Services Administration's (SAMHSA) National Helpline at **1-800-662-HELP (4357)**.

The Substance Abuse and Mental Health Services Administration offers these additional services to help with drug and alcohol abuse:

- Search for a treatment facility near you.(www.findtreatment.gov) Get help with problems related to substance abuse and addiction. Choose filters when you search for a facility to find various types of care, including inpatient, outpatient, and telehealth therapy options.

- The Alcohol Treatment Navigator (www.alcoholtreatment.niaaa.nih.gov) explains how to choose among different treatment programs. And it offers advice on getting support for yourself or a loved one through the recovery process.

- Find medication-assisted treatment (MAT).(www.samhs a.gov/medications-substance-use-disorders) This combines medications with counseling and behavioral therapies to treat substance use disorders.

Find local support groups for substance abuse

Get help from local support groups and other services in your community.

Alcoholics Anonymous (A.A.) Helps people who have had a drinking problem. Find a local meeting center or an online support group.(aa.org/find-aa)

Al-Anon Supports family members or friends of people with drinking problems. Find an Al-Anon meeting in your area.(www.al-anon.org/al-anon-meetings/)

Alateen Part of Al-Anon and offers help for teens affected by someone else's alcoholism. (www.al-anon.org/newcomers/teen-corner-alateen/)

Narcotics Anonymous (NA)Assists people who want to stop abusing prescription or illegal drugs. Find an NA meeting center, helpline, or online support group.(www.na.org/meetingsearch/)

NAR-AnonSupports people affected by someone using and abusing drugs. Search for a Nar-Anon meeting in your area. (www.nar-anon.org/find-a-meeting)

SMART RecoveryAssists young people and adults with alcohol or other addictions through group therapy. Find SMART Recovery meetings in person or online.(www.meetings.smartrecovery.org/meetings/)

ACKNOWLEDGEMENTS

To my readers! Thank you for taking a chance on an indie author. I hope you love Millie & Ethan as much as I do. Take care of yourselves, and surround yourself with people who take care of you.

To my husband, my other half. You asked me to be your girl-friend sixteen years ago under the stars, and I'm still finding new reasons to fall in love with you every day. We are so intertwined I couldn't get through life without you. Thank you for making me laugh and for believing in me and calling me a special kind of witch who can put words on a page and make people feel things. Thank you for chatting about literature with me and dissecting books with me. Thank you letting me run all my ideas by you and thank you for reading every one of my pages over and over again. Thank you for being hot and charging all my electronic devices and bringing me snacks and electrolytes and caffeine while I write this thing. Thank you for taking care of me in a million tiny ways and all of the big ways. Thank you for our two amazing babies and thank you for being such an amazing dad. I can write about true love and healthy supportive relationships because you show me what it looks like every day.

To my parents for giving me a stable foundation, for always being so supportive and being there for me any time I needed it. Thank you for taking me to the library all the time when I was a kid so I caught this big imagination and book addiction. Thank you for watching my little ones so often while I worked on this secret project.

To my brothers for being so fucking cool. I had to write a book just so I could keep up with your accomplishments. I'm so proud of you both. Thank you to J. for lighting the match that made me love literature and for always stoking that fire. Thank you to G. for inspiring me with your creative artistry and telling me to get back on my bike all the times that I fell off. I wouldn't be me without both of your profound impacts on my childhood.

To my best friend, I'm so glad we were paired up for that group assignment in 7th grade and that you loved Linkin Park and Harry Potter as much as I did so that we both immediately knew we were soul mates. Thank you for reading all the shitty first drafts I ever wrote and cheering me on every step of the way regardless. Thank you for pointing out that wine is actually a fruit, and for every other integral suggestion you made. You're so smart and so funny and I'm so grateful to have you in my life.

To my writer friend Josh B., with the passionate and creative soul, for writing and publishing first and showing me that it was an attainable dream if I worked my ass off like you did. You inspired and encouraged me every step of the way and I wouldn't be publishing this book without your guiding light. Thank you for all of the constructive criticism on my drafts and for chatting with me about writing every time we were together. You're brilliant in every sense of the word, and I can't wait to read what you write next.

To Sean for calling me milady in high school! Be still my heart. Clearly I never got over it.

To my editor Sierra Campbell for her thoughtful, essential editing.

My beta readers Katie B. Jordan D., Kaycee R., Whitney T. for your helpful critiques and for lighting a fire under me to polish this manuscript and publish it already.

For the ARC readers, there are too many of you lovelies to name. Every one of your reviews is a gift of time, thoughtfulness, creativity and energy and no one would have bought the book without you.

To the Moms Who Write Facebook group for being such a helpful, supportive community. I see all you moms frantically writing in the carpool pick up lines. I believe in you. I did it and you can too.

Thank you to Brandon Sanderson, Mary Robinette Kowal, Howard Tayler, and Dan Wells and all of the guest hosts of the *Writing Excuses* podcast. Your episodes were critical in helping me turn the intimidating, nebulous task of writing a book into actually getting my hands on the keyboard and words on the page. Extra special thanks to Brandon for inspiring a whole new crop of authors because of your absolutely contagious passion for writing and devotion to teaching the craft to everyone you can reach for free.

Thank you to Sarah Maclean and Jen Prokop - the hosts of the *Fated Mates* podcast - for so passionately articulating what I love about romance novels. I've learned so much about writing, and my to-read list is so blessedly long, because of you two queens.

To all of the musical artists whose beautiful soulful melancholy is woven into this manuscript, thank you for helping me close my eyes and slip into a creative space. There are too many to thank here, but links to my Spotify list are on my author socials.

ABOUT THE AUTHOR

Claire Therese has worked behind the scenes of many museums and archives, and these experiences had a profound impact on her imagination. Every artifact has a story. Sometimes, the story isn't apparent despite all her research, so she invent one in her head for herself. *The Starling Inn* was born from the picture of an unidentified World War I soldier, and a forgotten statue of him she found in the woods. She hopes you love this story she dreamed up about him.

When she isn't reading or writing, Claire is chasing her children, teaching, librarian-ing, watching period dramas and spending as much time outside as she can. She lives in the Midwest with her family. You can follow her updates at www.clairetheresewrites.com or on Instagram at @ claire.therese.writes

9 789899 123690 4